'It's all right,' Polly said. She looked down at their hands. Hers, small and slim, was almost lost in his big hand. She saw that, like herself, he wore a plain gold wedding ring. That was unusual, she thought. Not many men did that. She drew in a shaky breath and said, 'I think I'm getting over it a bit now. I mean, so many things have happened and so many people have been killed. You just have to get on with life, don't you?'

'Yes,' he said. 'You do.' There was a moment's silence and then he tucked her hand into the crook of his arm and they walked on. Polly took a deep breath, and then another. Mentioning Johnny always brought an ache to her throat, but she could feel a comfort in the warmth of this big man, with her hand tucked so securely against his body. She had a sudden longing to be held close, to be hugged. No more than that – just to be hugged. To feel the closeness of another human being. To feel the warmth of a living body close to hers.

Oh Johnny, she thought, where are you? What happened to you? And did you think of me, during your last few moments? Did you know how much I loved you – and did it help at all? Or did you forget everything and everyone in those last desperate efforts to stay alive?

The tears came to her eyes and, without knowing it, she tightened her grip on Joe Turner's arm. He glanced down at her but said nothing, and if she had looked up at him then she would have seen that his eyes were wet too.

Lilian Harry grew up close to Portsmouth Harbour, where her earliest memories are of nights spent in an air-raid shelter listening to the drone of enemy aircraft and the thunder of exploding bombs. But her memories are also those of a warm family life shared with two brothers and a sister in a tiny backstreet house where hard work, love and laughter went hand in hand. Lilian Harry now lives on the edge of Dartmoor where she has two ginger cats to love and laugh at. She has a son and daughter and two grandchildren and, as well as gardening, country dancing, amateur dramatics and church bellringing, she loves to walk on the moors and – whenever possible – to go skiing in the mountains of Europe. She has written a number of books under other names, including historical novels and contemporary romances. Visit her website at www.lilianharry.co.uk

By Lilian Harry

Under the Apple Tree

LILIAN HARRY

ORION

An Orion paperback

First published in Great Britain in 2004
by Orion
This paperback edition published in 2004
by Orion Books Ltd,
Orion House, 5 Upper Saint Martin's Lane,
London WC2H 9EA

Third impression 2005

A CIP catalogue record for this book is available
from the British Library.

Printed and bound in Great Britain by
Clays Ltd, St Ives plc

www.orionbooks.co.uk

For my dear grandson, Peter

My grateful thanks are due to Rosie Farrant, who suggested the WVS as a subject for this book, and to all members of the WVS (now the WRVS) past and present; to Maurice Flack, who spent his war years watching for aircraft from the rooftop of the Royal Beach Hotel, Southsea (and once got stuck in a lift with one of the staff); to Julie Anderson, who took the time to show us over the hotel, taking Maurice back to the roof for the first time since the war ended; and to all those whose memories, research and chance remarks, have helped me along the way.

Credit is theirs; errors are mine

The words of the song 'Friend O'Mine' were written by Frederick Weatherley, who died in 1929. The song was one which I remember my father singing to my mother at family parties, and never fails to bring tears to my eyes.

Chapter One

The Taylor family already knew what they would find when they crept out of their Anderson air-raid shelter on that bitter morning of 11 January, 1941. Huddling together on the two camp beds that Dick Taylor and his son Terry had set up before Terry had gone away to sea, they had listened in fear to the tumult outside and, when the ground beneath them swelled and shook, when the very air seemed to collapse in the roar of that almost unbelievable explosion, when they knew that their own house must have been hit, they had clutched each other in terror that they were about to be blasted from their hiding-place.

The sheets of corrugated iron that formed a shelter over the hole Dick and Terry had dug, had rattled and shaken about them, and earth had crumbled through the cracks between them. But they had held firm, and when the crash of falling masonry and the smashing of glass had ceased, Dick and Cissie and the others were still alive. Alive – but not yet safe. It was another six hours before the All Clear sounded and they dared to creep out and see, in the cold, grey light, what had been done to their home.

'It's gone,' Cissie whispered, covering her face with both hands. 'Oh Dick, it's all gone. Our home, all our furniture – everything. *Everything*.'

'The bastards,' he said slowly, staring at the huge pile of debris. 'The bloody, bloody *bastards* . . .' He broke into a fit of coughing and bent over, his thin shoulders shaking with the effort, while Cissie steadied him with her arm.

'We might be able to salvage a few things.' Judy took a

1

step up the garden path. Her fair hair, cut to a short bob, was tousled from the night in the shelter and her eyes were gritty and sore. 'We might be able to get a few bits and pieces out.'

'Bits and pieces!' Cissie shook her head. 'That's all they'll be – bits and pieces. There won't be a thing left whole. It's not even any good searching.'

Judy went forward just the same, with her Aunt Polly close beside her. Polly had been living with the Taylors ever since her husband Johnny had been lost at sea in the early days of the war. At thirty-five she was twelve years younger than Cissie, and the same number of years older than her niece, thus she was more like a sister to twenty-two-year-old Judy and they had long ago dispensed with the title of 'Aunt'. Now, as they crept up the garden path towards the mound of broken beams, shattered glass and tossed bricks, they reached out to each other and touched hands.

'It's awful,' Judy said shakily. 'Everything smashed to bits, just like that. And what for? Why us? The man who dropped that bomb doesn't even know us. Why are they doing it, Poll?'

'It's not just us,' Polly said quietly. 'You know that. Look at what's been happening in London and all those other places. We're all getting it. And I reckon Pompey got it as bad as any last night. Look – you can still see the flames. It looks as if the whole city's on fire. There must be thousands like us, bombed out of their homes. And thousands killed too, I expect. At least we're all alive.' She bit her lip and Judy knew that she must be thinking of Johnny. 'Thank God we were down in the shelter.'

Judy nodded. There had already been over thirty raids on Portsmouth. The people had grown used to the eerie wail of the siren and the frantic dash for shelter. They had heard the thunder of the explosions and felt the earth quake as craters were blasted into roads, and houses demolished. They had emerged into devastated streets, picked their way through the rubble and seen dead and injured lying like broken dolls where they had been flung. They knew what had happened in London and Coventry. Yet they were still not prepared for this terrible Blitz. Perhaps you never can imagine the worst, she thought. Perhaps you always do think it'll never happen to you.

She had almost refused to go down to the shelter the night before. She hated the confinement of the small space half underground, with the corrugated iron curving low over their heads. But the family's insistence had forced her to conquer her fears and now, seeing the ruin of her home, she was thankful. If they'd let me stay indoors, she thought, I'd be dead now, buried in all this rubble.

They paused and lifted their heads. A pall of dust and filth hung about them like a fog, filling their mouths and noses with its grit and stench. The sky was blackened by smoke, shot through with searing flashes of red and orange flame. Judy stared at it and felt her heart gripped by dread.

'And how long are we going to stay alive?' she burst out. 'We were lucky not to get a direct hit on the shelter. They'll come again, Polly, they'll keep on coming till we're all dead.' Tears were pouring down her cheeks. 'Look at that. Our house. Our *home*. Nothing left. All Dad's books and Mum's sewing things, and our Terry's gramophone and all our records, and your Sylvie's dolly that she left to keep you company while she's away, and – and . . .' Sobbing, she ran forward and began to tear at the rubble.

Polly gripped her arm tightly and drew her back.

'Leave it, Judy. Cissie's right – we won't find anything here, and it's dangerous to try. We'd better—' She stopped abruptly and her voice rose with a touch of panic. 'What *do* we do now? What *do* people do when they've got nowhere to go?'

They stared at each other and at the jagged ruins of their entire street, then turned their heads and saw their neighbours, also homeless, coming out of their own shelters,

3

and they heard the wail of fear and grief and anguish that must surely be echoing around the entire city – perhaps in every city in the land.

'It's hopeless,' Judy said, her voice trembling. 'We can't win against this, Polly. They're going to invade. They must be. They might be here already, for all we know. They're going to do the same to us as they've done to all those other countries, and we haven't got a chance.'

Polly stared at her. Her grey eyes, so like Judy's and Cissie's too, hardened, and her mouth drew tight. She shook Judy's arm and her voice was low and fierce.

'Don't say that, Judy! Don't *ever* say that. We're not going to let them win. We're not going to give them the chance. Remember Dunkirk! They didn't beat us then and they won't now. They'll *never* beat us. Never!'

Gradually, the people who had been bombed out of their homes that night began to sort themselves out.

'There was an ARP man round just now with a loud hailer. He says we've all got to go to the church hall,' Mrs Green of number three told Cissie as the Taylors straggled out of the back alley at the end of the street. Everyone was out now, standing and staring in dumb stupefaction at the destruction. Of the houses left standing, none had a single window with glass in it, most had lost their chimneys and several had their fronts torn away, so that the rooms inside were exposed for all to see, like those of a dolls' house. Mrs Green's bedroom wallpaper, that she'd been so proud of when she'd had the room done up just before the war started, was ripped and dirty, and there was a mass of laths and plaster all over the bed. The bath was full of broken slates and the lavatory hung half off the wall, with water pouring out of the cistern above it. The floors had broken away and there were boards, ceiling joists and all manner of rubble piled in the downstairs rooms.

'Look at that,' she said bitterly. 'We put all we had into

that house. Our hearts and souls. And look what they done to it. All smashed to bits.' She turned away, her face working. 'We'll never get it back to how it was, never.'

Cissie shook her head. 'How many d'you think have been bombed out like this? What's it like in the rest of Pompey?'

'Gawd knows. That ARP bloke says the whole city's been blasted away. All the big shops out Southsea way have gone – Handley's, Knight & Lee's, all them – and the big Co-op down Fratton has burned to a cinder, *and* the Landport Drapery Bazaar, *and* Woolworth's, *and* C&A.'

'And the Guildhall too,' someone else chimed in. 'He said the Guildhall's still burning. So are the hospitals – the Eye and Ear, and part of the Royal – and the Sailor's Rest, and the Hippodrome and—'

'Blimey, ain't there nothing left?' Dick asked, his chest wheezing.

Judy stepped forward quickly. 'The Guildhall's gone?' She turned to her mother. 'I ought to go there.'

'But we don't know where we'll be. If we've got to go to the church hall . . .' Cissie stared at her, white-faced and frightened. 'What can you do anyway, if it's all burned down? You can't go off now, Judy.' Her voice rose. 'And there's your gran too, all by herself up in April Grove – what about her? Someone ought to go round to see if she's all right.' She shook her head worriedly. 'I just don't know what to do first. I don't know what to do for the best. Oh dear.'

'I'll go to Gran's first, but I really ought to try to get to work. There must be all kinds of stuff to sort out.' Judy gazed back helplessly, and Polly came to her rescue.

'People have got to try to carry on just the same, Cis, you know that. It's the same for me. I ought to go round the salon to make sure things are all right, though I can't think there'll be anyone wanting their hair done today.' Automatically, she put a hand to her own hair, dark like her sister's and still tousled from the night spent in the shelter. It felt

5

gritty from the dust that still hung in the air, and she grimaced. 'Well, maybe there'll be a few. I reckon mine could do with a good wash, for a start . . . But Judy's right, the Guildhall's important, it's where the city's run from. If you can go into Mum's first, Judy, it would set our minds at rest. I'm sure she'll be all right, mind, she's got a good shelter.' She turned back to Cissie and took her arm. 'You and me and Dick'll go to the church hall and see what's what, and Judy can come over once she's found out what's going on. Come on – Dick's getting shrammed with cold, stood out here with all this dust getting down into his lungs and all.'

Cissie stood undecided for a moment, then Dick coughed again and she nodded. 'You're right, it's not doing him no good at all being out in this cold air with all this smoke about.' She glanced up at the blackened sky. 'There's still places on fire, you can see the flames.' A fresh thought struck her and her voice began to rise again. 'And look at us, got nothing but what we're standing up in – my best coat gone, and that nice red frock you made yourself, Poll, and that warm jumper I knitted Dick for Christmas. I don't know what we're going to do, I don't really.'

'Don't worry about that now,' Polly said gently. 'Come on, let's get down the hall into the warm, they'll sort us out. I dare say they've got clothes and other stuff. Come on, Cis.'

Cissie nodded. 'All right. We can't do nothing here, that's for certain.' She took a deep breath and straightened her shoulders. 'Now then, Judy, you make sure you come back the minute you can, and you will look in on your Gran, won't you? She ought to have come up to us like I wanted, not stopped down there by herself where we don't know what's happening to her . . . Dick, are you all right?'

He nodded, though he was holding his chest as if it pained him. 'This blasted dust, it's everywhere. It's plaster dust, you know – it's that fine it gets right down inside.' He coughed again and Cissie clicked her tongue. 'Lot of use I'm going to be,' he said bitterly. 'Useless article.'

'Now you're not to talk like that,' his wife said sharply. 'You did your bit in the last lot, that's why you're like this now. Come on, we're going down the church hall; they'll have somewhere to sit down there and a nice hot cup of tea. That's what we all need.' She started to move away, her hand hooked firmly through her husband's arm, and then turned back to Judy. 'You do whatever you can for your gran, Judy, and come back once you've found out what's happening. If we get sent on anywhere else we'll make sure the people at the hall know the address.'

Judy watched them go, torn with doubt. She wanted to support her mother and help her father and she was racked with fear for her grandmother, all alone in her own small terraced house. But as well as her concern for the family there was her loyalty to her job at the Guildhall offices and her anxiety for the people who spent the nights there – the Lord Mayor himself, who had moved in when the bombing started, and the ARP staff. What had happened to them, if the Guildhall had been destroyed?

She turned and made her way through the streets, passing groups of people scrabbling through the debris in search of possessions or – even worse – for family members or neighbours who had been buried. At every turn, she longed to stop and help, but you couldn't help everyone and her fears for her grandmother grew. Suppose she hadn't gone to the shelter – suppose her house had been bombed before she could get out – suppose the Anderson itself had had a direct hit! Everyone knew they couldn't stand up to that. Suppose her granny was even now lying under a mass of twisted metal and earth and stones, crying for someone to come and rescue her . . .

It was impossible to get through some of the streets, and although she knew the city well, Judy often found herself

7

stopping and gazing helplessly at an unrecognisable land-scape. Some streets were blocked off by fire engines and long, snaking hosepipes, with firemen and ARP wardens and police waving at people to get back from craters or suspected unexploded bombs. Time and time again she was turned back and had to find a different way through streets and alleyways she had never seen before, until she began to despair of ever finding a route out of this nightmare.

At last, when she had almost given up hope, she found herself in September Street, at the top of October Street which led down to April Grove, and she broke into a run. There had been some damage here – slates torn off, windows smashed in, and towards the bottom of the street a whole house ripped to pieces, leaving a smoking gap between its neighbours. Her heart in her mouth, Judy came to the little row of houses that ran along the end and then let out a long breath of relief when she saw that the street had been virtually undamaged.

She came to the front door, varnished and polished by her father just before the war had started, and hammered on it, calling at the top of her voice. 'Granny! Gran – it's me, Judy. Are you there? Are you all right?'

'She ain't there, love.' The voice brought her whipping round, to stare in dismay at the wrinkled face of the old woman who lived next door. Then the crumpled lips stretched into a toothless grin. 'She's gorn round the church hall, see if she can 'elp out a bit. Got all the bombed people there, they 'ave, givin' 'em soup and cupsa tea and that. I told her, I could do with a cuppa meself after the night we bin through, but she never bit. Anyway, thass where she's gorn.' She blinked her rheumy eyes at Judy. 'You don't feel like a cuppa tea, I s'pose?'

Judy shook her head. 'I'm on my way to work, Mrs Kinch, but I wanted to make sure Gran was all right first. I'd better go and see if I can find her.'

She ran back up to October Street. The church hall was

about a quarter of a mile away, across the railway line and past the shops. It was crowded with people, all looking bewildered and lost, but she caught sight of the brisk little figure standing behind a long trestle table, wielding a teapot, and pushed her way through the throng.

'Gran! I've been looking for you! Mrs Kinch said you'd be here. We were worried.'

Alice Thomas looked round and gave her granddaughter a quick nod. 'Judy. I was wondering about you, too – thought I'd come up and see once I'd finished here, but the rate we're going it don't look as if we're ever going to finish. Must be thousands bombed out, thousands . . . How d'you get on down home? Any damage round your way? I hear the Guildhall's on fire, and the Landport Drapery Bazaar, where young Jean Foster works, and God knows what else down Commercial Road.'

Judy stared at her miserably. 'Gran, the house was bombed. Everything's gone – everything. Mum and the others have gone to our church hall – we've got nowhere to go. All we've got left is the Anderson!' She began to cry, covering her face with her hands, swept by sudden desolation. 'Oh *Gran*.'

Her grandmother put down her teapot and came quickly round the end of the table. She laid her arm round Judy's shoulders and led her back behind the table, pushing her gently down on a pile of blankets. 'You sit there, love, and I'll get you a cup of tea. I don't suppose you've had a thing to eat yet, have you?'

Judy shook her head. 'There wasn't anything *to* have. And no kettle or anything. Oh Gran, what are we going to do?' She gestured helplessly round the hall. 'All these people – all of us with nowhere to go and nothing left but what we stand up in. What are we going to *do*?'

Alice handed her a thick white cup filled with dark brown tea. 'Drink that, for a start. It's nice and sweet – good for shock. And stop talking about having nowhere to go. Of course you've got somewhere to go! You'll come and stop with me, that's what. Haven't I got a house all to myself? I knew I was right to stay on there instead of giving it up and coming round to you. Fine state we'd have been in if I'd done that! Now, you drink that up and you'll feel better, and then you can give me a hand here.'

Judy shook her head. The tea was hot and warming, and she barely noticed the sweetness. She drew in a long, sobbing breath, then said, 'I can't stop, Gran, I've got to try to get to work. Goodness knows how long it'll take me – it's terrible out there – but I've got to try. And I must find Mum and Dad and Polly first, to tell them you're OK. If we can come to you for a few nights, while we get sorted out . . .'

'Few nights nothing!' Alice said smartly. 'You'll come for the duration. They won't find you nothing better, I can tell you that, not with all these other people needing a place. Now, you're not leaving here without a bit of food inside you. There's some bread and marge at the end of the table, and another cup of tea wouldn't do you any harm.'

'No thanks, Gran, but I'll take the bread to eat on the way.' Judy pulled herself to her feet and bent to give her grandmother a kiss. 'I'll see you later, back in April Grove. Don't overdo it, mind.'

'Cheek!' Alice said, poking out her tongue. 'I could give you youngsters the runaround any day. Mind you tell your mum and dad what I said, now. I'll expect you all for tea at number nine.' She filled her teapot from the steaming urn and turned back to the queue. 'Now then, love, you drink this. It's nice and sweet, good for shock. You'll feel all the better for it . . .'

Judy headed for the exit and set off back to the hall where her mother and father would have gone. After that, she'd get down to Commercial Road and try to find out what was happening at the Guildhall, and where the office staff should be going.

Back outside, it seemed like hours since they had crawled out of the Anderson shelter to find the house blown into oblivion. Yet the sky was still darkened by the pall of stinking smoke, and the streets were still crowded with people, wandering bewildered and stunned by all that had happened during that terrible night. It was as if day had decided not to break, as if the sun had taken one look at what was happening and turned away its face.

The sun would come back though, she thought. It would come back when the sky had cleared, and let light back into their lives. As Polly had said, they weren't going to let the Germans beat them. They wouldn't give them the chance.

Chapter Two

The sight that greeted her as she came down Commercial Road took her breath away.

By then, she'd seen enough damage and heard enough stories to have a fair idea of what was happening. But she still wasn't prepared for the scene of total devastation here – the great shops nothing more than smoking ruins, the road swarming with firemen and police and ARP wardens, the knots of stunned bystanders – and the few shops that hadn't been hit, open and with counter staff valiantly trying to carry on as if nothing had happened.

Worst of all was the Guildhall itself. The great, proud building on the square was still ablaze, its bell tower sending flames high into the sky, shot with flashes of brilliant green fire as the copper of the cupola melted and ran down the tall stone pillars. Judy stopped where she was, on the opposite side of the square, and stared at it. Her eyes filled with tears.

'Terrible, innit,' said a man standing nearby. 'Just terrible. They'll never be able to put it back, you know, not like it was. The whole of Pompey's bin ruined. Never be the same again, never.'

'But what happened to the people inside?' Judy whispered. 'The Lord Mayor was *sleeping* there, so that he could always be on hand if he was needed. And there were staff, and firewatchers on the roof. What happened to them all?'

The man shrugged. 'Don't ask me. Mind, I did hear as they'd all gone out to Southsea, took over a hotel or summat. Fine time to go on their holidays!' He snorted derisively.

Judy stared at him, then turned away. She started to cross the square but was held back by a large policeman. 'Sorry, love, you can't go over there, it's dangerous. We got enough to contend with here, without sightseers getting under our feet. What you doing here anyway? Ain't you got no home to go to?'

'As a matter of fact, I haven't,' Judy said, suddenly angry. 'We were bombed out last night, like a lot of other people.' She ignored his embarrassed flush and went on quickly, 'I work in there – or did till yesterday. I came down to see what I could do. Is it true the Lord Mayor's gone out to Southsea? Is he all right? Are all the staff safe?'

The policeman shook his head. 'I don't know about the staff, love, they ain't told us nothing. The Mayor's all right, I do know that, but what I heard was he'd gone up Cosham.' He lifted his head as someone gave a yell from across the square. 'Look, you can see we're busy, love, just be a good girl and get out of the way, will you? And all you others too,' he added, raising his voice to include the rest of the crowd. 'Go and give a hand to someone what needs it – there's plenty of clearing up to be done.' He turned away and the crowd began to shuffle off, muttering.

Judy stood wondering what to do next. Southsea and Cosham were at opposite ends of the city. Someone must know, she thought. And wherever the Mayor was, he'd need his staff, the secretaries and office workers who knew where everything was kept. Her heart skipped as it suddenly struck her that the offices themselves must have been destroyed, and everything in them. The papers, the files, the type-writers – everything the city depended on to keep it functioning smoothly, would all be gone. How would they ever manage to sort it all out?

'Judy!'

She turned quickly. 'Miss Marsh! Oh, I'm so glad to see you. I couldn't find out what was happening. Someone told me the Mayor was in Southsea, and then the policeman said Cosham and I just didn't know *what* to do.'

The office supervisor came forward quickly and took her arm. 'All right, Judy. Don't worry. We're getting things sorted out gradually.' She rubbed her face wearily. She was carrying a notebook and wearing her office suit and her smart hat with the little veil, and Judy felt suddenly ashamed of her own clothes – the skirt and jumper she'd worn to go to the shelter last night, with her old coat thrown over the top. She began to stammer out an apology, but the supervisor cut her short.

'Don't be silly, child. You've got here, that's the important thing. Was it very difficult, getting through the streets?'

'Well, it was a bit.' Judy thought of the ruined houses, the fires, the devastation on all sides. 'And we were bombed out ourselves.'

'*You* were bombed out? My dear girl!'

'Yes – our house was blown to bits,' Judy told her, nodding miserably. 'There's nothing left at all.' And to her dismay, she began to cry, again the tears pouring down her face as she stood at the edge of the square with the Guildhall and, it seemed, the whole of Portsmouth, in flames around her.

'Judy. Come here, love.' She felt the older woman's arms around her and leaned against the solid body, half amazed at what was happening. Miss Marsh had always been strict and unapproachable, not the sort of person you'd cry on at all – yet here she was, patting Judy's shoulder and murmuring, 'There, there,' just like a mum or an auntie would.

'I'm sorry, Miss Marsh,' Judy said shakily. 'I didn't mean to give way like that – but I was so frightened when I saw the Guildhall, and so worried about the Mayor and everyone, and then when I saw you—'

'It's all right, Judy. You don't have to go on.' Miss Marsh gave her a handkerchief. 'It's not very clean, I'm afraid – there's so much dust in the air. Now, let me get this straight. Your own home was bombed last night, is that right? Was anyone hurt?'

'No.' Judy blew her nose. 'Oh, I'm sorry, I didn't mean to use—'

'Don't be silly. Who else lives in the house? Your mother and father?'

'Yes, and Polly – she's my auntie, my mum's sister – and her little girl Sylvie, only she's evacuated, and my brother, when he's at home, but he's away at sea now. He's in the Navy.'

'So it's just you and your parents and your aunt at home at the moment?' Miss Marsh said, trying to unravel this information. 'And where are they now?'

'They went round to the church hall. They're going to my gran's up at Copnor after, but they had to stay there to register. Someone said there's clothes, and there might even be a bit of money to help get straight again. It's not that we want charity,' Judy said earnestly, 'but we've lost *everything*, and there's the electricity bill to pay, and—'

'Well, all that will be sorted out. And will you be staying with your grandmother in Copnor?'

'Yes. She lives in April Grove, off September Street.'

'I know where you mean. So at least you've got somewhere to go tonight?'

'Yes. That's why I thought I ought to come down and see what's happening here.' Judy sniffed and blew her nose again. 'Only it took such a long time getting through the streets, and I know I'm ever so late . . .'

'For heaven's sake, girl, don't apologise for being *late*! I'm amazed you came at all. Now listen, the Lord Mayor's arranging to take over part of the Royal Beach Hotel at Southsea to use as offices – it was closed when the war started and is already being used as a casualty clearing station – so that's where you'll be reporting for work. It's the ARP who have relocated to Cosham. As you've seen, there's been a tremendous amount of damage all over the city, and there's a great deal of work to do. The Lord

Mayor's made arrangements already for people like yourselves who have lost everything – he's managed to find a bank that's open for business and they've released a substantial sum of money for the Air-Raid Distress Fund, so that people can be given some ready cash. The War Emergency Committee will divide it between all their members so that it can be distributed. They'll also be evacuating any homeless women or children who want to leave the city and, as you know, Emergency Centres have been set up in schools and church halls.'

'Yes, that's where Mum and Dad went,' Judy nodded.

'And you remember the Lady Mayoress set up her own Clothing Fund at the beginning of the war, so there will, we hope, be enough clothes to give everyone at least one warm outfit.' Her glance took in Judy's own shabby attire. 'I suppose that's all you have yourself now?'

Judy said glumly, 'I'm afraid it is, Miss Marsh. They're my oldest things, I always change into them, to keep my work clothes nice, and when the siren went—'

'Well, I wouldn't expect you to be dressed in your best for an air raid!' The supervisor's face broke into a rare smile. 'Now, you're not to worry about that. Come to work in whatever you can find. But today, I think you ought to go back and help your family.'

'Oh no! I mean, I ought to be at work – there must be so much to do. And there isn't really anything I can do at home – at Gran's, I mean –' To her horror, she felt the tears gather in her eyes again and blinked them away furiously. 'I'd much rather be doing something useful, Miss Marsh.'

The supervisor looked at her consideringly. 'Very well, then. But you don't have to come all the way out to Southsea, not today. What you can do is stay here and look out for any other Guildhall or Municipal staff like yourself, who come down to find out what's happening. Tell them to report to the Royal Beach.' She sighed. 'We still don't know who is likely to turn up and who isn't. There may be others who've been bombed out, or even hurt in the raids. But those who can, will surely do as you did and come here. Now, do you think you can do that? You know everyone, don't you?' She held out her notebook. 'Write down the names of all the people you see.'

Judy nodded. 'I can do that, Miss Marsh.'

'Good. That enables me to go out to the hotel and get on with the work there. We're having to start completely from scratch. Now, Judy, when you're sure you've seen everyone – everyone who comes here, that is – you're to go back to your grandmother's and be with your family. You've had a dreadful time and you must be exhausted.'

'We didn't get much sleep last night, but I don't really feel tired, Miss Marsh – just sort of light, if you know what I mean.' Judy put her hand to her forehead and swayed slightly. 'I expect I'm just a bit hungry.'

Miss Marsh gave her a sharp glance. 'A cup of tea and something to eat for you, my girl. Come on – there's a stall over there, they'll see to you.' She led Judy over to a makeshift stall where an urn was boiling on a large stove which appeared to have been built out of bricks salvaged from the piles of rubble. A woman in a green uniform was dealing out mugs of tea and sticky buns to the firemen and soldiers who were still desperately trying to put out the fire.

Gratefully, Judy ate a bun, surprised to find just how hungry she was, and swallowed the tea. She smiled a trifle shakily at the supervisor. 'I feel a bit better now. Sorry about that.'

'That's all right. You've got more colour in your cheeks, anyway. Now, I'm off back to Southsea. Don't forget – it's the Royal Beach Hotel – and once you're sure you've seen everyone, you're to go straight home. Don't stay here too long, anyway. If they haven't arrived by mid-afternoon, they won't be coming.' Her face twisted a little and she turned away. 'I'll look for you at the hotel tomorrow morning.'

'Yes, Miss Marsh.' Judy watched her walk briskly away.

She knew well enough what the supervisor had meant. There might be casualties, even deaths, amongst the staff. In the chaos that the raid had caused, nobody knew what might have happened.

How did other places manage when this happened to them? she wondered. Places like London, Bristol, Liverpool, Coventry. They'd been through this as well, yet somehow they still managed to carry on.

Perhaps that was the answer. Perhaps that was all you *could* do. Just carry on.

It was growing dark again as Judy walked wearily down October Street and turned into April Grove. The pall of smoke was still drifting above the rooftops, and with no street-lights and every house blacked out there was no glimmer of cheer in the devastated streets, no hint of warmth in the bitter cold. What will we do if they come again? she wondered. How could we stand another night like last night?

She came to her grandmother's door and knocked. It opened, and her aunt drew back the blackout curtain for Judy to push past. They felt their way down the short, dark passage to the back room, where she found the family sitting round by the glow of a small fire with a kettle resting on the coals, and the light of a single candle. Her mother and grandmother sat in armchairs on each side of the fire, and Dick and Polly were on kitchen chairs in front of it. Dick got up and moved his chair aside, pulling another into the space for Judy.

'That's better,' she said. 'It's horrible outside.' She shrugged off her coat and hung it on the inside of the door to the staircase.

'Oh Judy, thank goodness,' her mother said. 'We were starting to get worried about you.'

'I've been down the Guildhall Square, looking out for the other people at work. They've moved the offices out to Southsea.' Judy sank down on the chair and stretched her hands out to the fire. 'It's awful, Mum. The whole place has gone. The Guildhall's still burning, and they say everything inside's been destroyed. All those lovely pictures, and the wooden panelling, and the carpets – everything. And there's street after street just ruined. You can't get through some of them at all. Someone told me there'd been nearly three thousand fires. Three thousand! How could they hope to put them all out?'

'It's wicked,' Cissie said, her voice trembling. 'Wicked.'

'It's war, Cis,' Dick said. 'There's worse happening than a few pictures and carpets getting burned. People are being killed. Like that young woman just up the road here.'

'What young woman?' Judy looked at him. She'd visited her grandmother often enough to know most of the neighbours in April Grove by sight and from Alice's talk. 'Who's been killed, Dad?'

'I'm not sure if you knew her,' Alice said. She looked down at the black and white cat on her knee, stroking his head. 'She'd only been here a few months – bombed out in the first big raid she was, and came to live in March Street. Kathy Simmons – had two little girls and a baby boy.'

'I remember you talking about her.' Judy stared at her grandmother. 'Wasn't the baby born in the shelter? Don't say she's been killed? Was that her house I saw this morning, bombed flat?'

'That's the one. Olive Chapman as was – you know, she married Derek Harker from the builder's – had just gone over to fetch her to their shelter but Kathy went back indoors to boil some water for her Thermos flask, apparently, just as the bomb fell.' Alice shook her head. Her face creased with sadness. 'They said she couldn't have known anything about it – but still, it's cruel, a young mother like that killed for no reason.'

'Oh, how awful.' Judy put both hands to her face. 'What about the children? Those little girls – and the baby?'

Cissie took out a handkerchief and wiped her eyes. 'Olive

had the girls with her, out in the street. They were blown halfway up the road by the blast, but they weren't hurt, not as such. But the baby – he was with his mummy, poor little scrap.' She stopped, her mouth working. 'Only six months old. It don't bear thinking of.'

Polly put her hand on her sister's arm. 'Don't upset yourself all over again, Cis. It's terrible, I know, but like Mum says, they couldn't have known anything about it.'

'But it's their lives gone, isn't it!' Cissie cried. 'That little baby, with his whole life ahead of him – he never even had the chance to learn to crawl! As for those two girls, they've lost their mother. And they're not the only ones, are they? There's you, Polly, with your Johnny gone, and poor Olive Chapman lost her baby that she was expecting, and others, hundreds and hundreds of others. What was Mrs Shaw along the road telling you about her Gladys, driving that ambulance last night? Went down a cellar she did, and found a whole family dead down there, all except one little girl. How's that poor little soul ever going to get over it? How are *any* of them ever going to get over it? And this is just the beginning!' She pulled her apron up over her face and began to cry. 'I don't think I can stand it any more!' she said in a muffled voice. 'I just don't think I can *stand* it!'

The others gazed at her and then looked at each other miserably in the glow of the fire. There didn't seem to be anything anyone could say, Judy thought. They all felt pretty much the same. But you couldn't give in. You just couldn't.

'Come on, Mum,' she said gently. 'We all depend on you, you know. You're the one that keeps us all going.'

'Well, I'm not much use to you now,' Cissie said bitterly. 'I'm not much use to no one. I've just had enough, that's all. We've been having raids for months, and there's been all those terrible things happening in London and Coventry and the rest, and now it's our turn, and they're just bashing us to pieces, to *pieces* – and what can we do about it, eh? Tell me that. Oh, I know we can bomb them too, but what good's that going to do? It just means a whole lot more people get killed in their own homes, people like us who never wanted a war in the first place. How's it ever going to end?'

'We can't just let them ride roughshod over us,' Judy said. 'You know what they've done in Poland and all those other countries. We can't let that happen here.'

'So it's better to be bombed to bits, is it? It's better to have everything smashed to pieces around us and have little babies killed?' Cissie took the apron from her face and stared at them. 'Oh, I know what they say, I know what they tell us, and I'm just an ordinary person who doesn't know anything about these things – but I just can't see the *sense* of it all.' She took a deep breath. 'I'm sorry, I know we're not supposed to talk like this, but I've just had enough of it all today, that's all.'

'You need a cup of tea.' Judy got up, but her grand-mother put out a hand.

'There's no gas, love. The mains got fractured, see, and they turned it off because of the danger. That's why we've got the kettle on the fire.'

Judy sank back. 'No gas and no electricity. It's the same all over the city, I suppose. It's a good thing we've got some coal.' A thought struck her. 'Here, what about *our* coal? From – from home? Hadn't we better get that over here?'

'We've done it, love,' her father said. 'Been going backwards and forwards all day with my old barrow. Had to leave one of us on guard, too. There's people swarming all over the place, looking for anything they can pick up. Not that there was much to find in our place,' he added ruefully.

Judy stared at him. 'You mean they were stealing things?'

'Well, they wasn't offering to pay for them! There's always people out for easy pickings, no matter what's happened.'

She nodded. 'I know. The shops have all got soldiers standing outside them because of looters, but I never

21

thought they'd take stuff from people who'd been bombed out. That's awful.'

'It's all awful,' Polly said, 'but sitting here telling each other about it won't make it any better. Now look, I know we'd all like something hot but we can't, and that's all there is to it – but we can make a few sandwiches. There's plenty of marge and fish paste and some of that blackberry and apple jam Mum made in the autumn, and you'll never guess what else I found in a tin in the cupboard.'

'What?' Judy asked obediently, and her aunt gave a little crow of triumph.

'Christmas cake, that's what! Keeping it for Easter, your Gran was, but I reckon we need it more now. We can all have a really good slice, and thumb our noses at Hitler while we eat it!'

Judy laughed and after a moment or two the others joined in. Their laughter was a little shaky, and sounded dangerously close to crying, but somehow they all felt better for it, and as Dick stoked up the fire and the kettle boiled and Polly began to cut bread, and the Christmas cake was sliced up and handed round, the little gathering began to seem almost like a party.

'I reckon we ought to play a few games,' Judy said. 'Or sing some songs. Cheer ourselves up a bit. Just in case there's any Fifth Columnists listening down the chimney. We don't want them reporting back to Hitler that we're downhearted, do we?'

They ate their sandwiches and cake, then did as she had suggested. But as their voices rose in a wavering rendition of 'Roll Out the Barrel' and 'It's a Long Way to Tipperary', they were each still thinking of the devastation outside, and of the people who were homeless tonight, or who had been killed or injured. They were each thinking of Kathy Simmons and her baby boy, of the two little girls who had lost their mother, and of all those others up and down the country who had had their lives shattered.

Later on, when everyone else had gone to bed – Cissie

and Dick upstairs to the front bedroom, Polly to the back room she would share with Judy, and her grandmother Alice to the front room downstairs – Judy sat by the dying fire and tried to write a letter to her fiancé, Sean.

It seemed so long since she had seen him, so long since the night last May when they'd got engaged, only three weeks after they'd met at a dance on South Parade Pier. Dick and Cissie hadn't been at all keen on such a hasty courtship, but Judy was twenty-two, so they couldn't very well say no. And there was no question of a wedding yet, with Sean going back to sea the very next day.

For most of the past eight months, Sean had been in the Northern Atlantic, off Norway and Iceland. During that time, he had sent letters – none for weeks, and then a dozen all arriving at once. Letters that were now buried beneath a heap of rubble in Friday night's blast.

How did you tell your fiancé the sort of things that had happened during the past twenty-four hours? Judy sighed and sucked the end of her grandmother's fountain pen, and started to write.

> *Dear Sean,*
> *We had a bit of trouble in Pompey last night. There were a lot of aircraft and we got badly bombed. We're all OK but Mum and Dad and Polly and I are staying with Gran up in April Grove. I hope things are OK with you, as they find me here. I'm too tired to write any more now and will close for tonight.*
> *From your loving Judy.*

It didn't seem much, but she felt that if she started to tell him what it had really been like, she would still be there come morning.

Chapter Three

Polly got up early next morning and found Judy already downstairs, lighting the fire.

'I know Gran wouldn't usually have a fire in the morning, but there's no other way of making any tea. I wanted to get everyone a hot drink before I go off to work.'

'You're going to work?' Polly looked at her niece in surprise. 'But it's Sunday.'

'Doesn't matter. We've got to get the new offices sorted out. People will be flooding in wanting help, and we can't just tell 'em to go away and come back on Monday. There's all the Emergency Centres to be seen to, and people evacuated or found new homes – any amount of things to be done.' Judy held a sheet of newspaper in front of the fire to make it blaze up. 'It's a good thing you went and got our coal. I don't know how long it'll be before we get the gas and electricity back.'

'It's not just that, either. They were going round telling people to boil water for ten minutes before drinking it in case of typhoid.' Polly put some plates on the table and began to slice the rest of yesterday's loaf. 'Well, at least Jerry gave us a quiet night; we'll all feel better for a few hours' sleep. Me and your mother have got to go round the Emergency Centre again this morning, get new ration books sorted out and see what money they'll give us. They were too busy yesterday, so once we'd registered we just came on here. And there's people we ought to let know – your Auntie May and Uncle Fred, and your mum's friend Mrs Walker. One of us ought to go round and see Jean Foster too, let her know where we are. She's Terry's girlfriend after all, almost one of the family.' She stopped and stared at the loaf in her hand. 'I wish I could go out and see Sylvie.'

'Oh, Polly! She must be wondering if you're all right. They won't know what's been going on, out there in the country.' Judy lowered the newspaper just as it was beginning to scorch in the middle. 'Why don't you go on the train?'

'I don't suppose they're running, do you? Anyway, I don't feel I can leave your mum and dad, not with the way Cis is, and your dad was wheezing all day long yesterday. There's such a lot to see to here. I did send a telegram yesterday, just to say we were all well, but she don't know nothing about the house, of course. There's not much point in telling her, is there – not straight away. She's only seven and I don't want to frighten her.'

'She'll have to know, though, because of addressing her letters.' Judy stood up, irresolute. 'Perhaps I shouldn't go into work, after all . . .'

'No, no, you go, you can't let the office down. We can manage here, and what Sylvie doesn't know won't hurt her. I'll try and go out sometime next week if the trains are running again, and I'll write her a letter. Now, is that fire hot enough for the kettle yet?'

The two of them got together a scrappy breakfast of bread and margarine, just coloured with jam, and by the time the kettle boiled Alice had emerged from the front room where she had slept on the sofa and Cissie had come down from upstairs. 'I told Dick to stay in bed; he's had a terrible night, hacking away. That dust and smoke really got into his chest. How were you on that settee, Mum? I felt proper bad, turning you out of your own bed.'

'Don't be daft, girl, I was snug as a bug in a rug. Stood to reason you two would have to have the double bed. I might be able to get a camp bed or put-u-up for later, but the settee'll do for now.' She bustled through to the lean-to scullery. 'I suppose there's no gas on yet?'

'Nothing's on yet. And we haven't got all that many candles left, neither. I don't know what we're going to do if they don't get things straight soon. There's going to be people desperate.' Polly poured out five cups of tea. 'There, are you going to take Dick's up to him, Cis? There's not much sense in him coming down till the room's warmed up a bit. And look, I'll toast a slice of bread, he needs something hot inside him. Spread some Marmite on it.'

Cissie took her husband's breakfast up the stairs and the others sat round the table, drinking their tea. Polly looked at her mother.

'Cis and me are going down the Centre this morning, see what's what. Are you going to stop here with Dick?'

'I am not!' The old woman looked at her indignantly, her bright eyes snapping. 'Stop here when there's work to be done? No, I'll be helping on the tea-stall, same as yesterday. There'll be plenty glad of a cuppa while they're clearing up.'

'Yes, but I don't want you to overdo it.'

'I'll be the judge of when I've overdone it!' Alice retorted. 'Just because you've moved in here, our Poll, it doesn't mean to say you can start ordering me about. I'd have done as I pleased if you hadn't been here and I'll do as I please now you are, and don't you forget it.'

Judy grinned and Polly shook her head. 'I'm not likely to forget it, you independent old besom! You'll be ordering us all about from your deathbed – that's if you don't outlive us all. All right, you go and pour tea for firemen while me and Cis go and see about our ration books and try to put together a few clothes and things. How about you, Judy, do you want us to try to get you anything?'

Judy shook her head. 'Miss Marsh said there were going to be some things out at the new offices – the Lady Mayoress was going to see to it. After all, if she can't get us a few things from her own Clothing Store, nobody can!' She

26

put down her cup and stood up. 'I'd better be going. Goodness knows how long it'll take me to get all the way out to Southsea. I don't suppose there's any buses running. Better expect me when you see me.' She shrugged into her coat and called up the stairs to her mother. ''Bye, Mum – I'm off now. 'Bye, Dad.'

Polly watched her go. 'I hope she'll be all right. She was tossing and turning all night long. It really upset her, seeing our house bombed to bits and then going down and seeing the Guildhall in flames – not to mention all the other damage. We'll have to keep an eye on her, Mum.'

'She'll be all right. She's made of the right stuff – like you and me. And she knows that the best way to take your mind off things is to get on with your work. No, it's Cis that I worry about, she takes everything so hard. And Dick, too. He was grey when he got round here yesterday, proper grey.'

'Well, with all that smoke and dust about . . .'

'It's not just his chest. It's what it's doing to his mind. It's bringing it all back, you can see that. What he went through before . . . you know what I mean.' The old lady nodded significantly. 'He'll be getting those nightmares again, you see if he don't.'

Polly opened her mouth to reply, then closed it again quickly as they heard the sound of footsteps descending the stairs. By the time Dick appeared at the staircase door in the scullery, Polly was already at the sink, pouring water from the kettle into the enamel bowl. She added a small lump of washing soda and gave him a bright smile.

'Hello, Dick, how're you then? Sleep all right, did you? I must say it was a treat to be allowed to stop in bed all night instead of having to get up and go down the shelter . . . D'you want another cup of tea?'

He shook his head. 'No, thanks. Just going out to the lav.' He opened the back door and a bitter wind scoured into the scullery. 'Strewth, it's like an icebox out here.' The door slammed behind him and he passed the scullery window on his way to the lavatory, tacked on to the back of the lean-to. Polly sighed. It was going to come hard to them all, not having an indoor lavatory any more. And no bathroom either. None of the little two-up, two-down houses in April Grove had a bathroom. They all had a tin bath hanging on a nail outside, which had to be dragged in every Friday or Saturday night and filled with kettles of hot water, or from an Ascot if you were lucky enough to have one. It would be hard on them all, having to go back to that.

'Have you still got that old bath, Mum?' she called. 'Only I was just thinking, you won't be able to come up to us any more of a Friday afternoon for your bath, will you? I wondered if you'd got rid of it.'

'Not got rid of it, as such,' Alice said, coming through and taking a tea-towel from the back door. 'It's still out there – but don't you remember, I got Terry to fill it up with earth and plant potatoes in it. Won't be much cop for bathing in now!'

Polly stared at her and began to laugh. 'Potatoes! Well, we'd better get 'em out. I don't suppose you can buy tin baths for love nor money now.'

'Get 'em out? They're me earlies! I've been looking forward to them for Easter. We'll have to use the small one – stand up and wash ourselves down. You know they're on at us to save water anyway.'

Dick came back indoors, shuddering with cold. 'I could do with that tea now, if there's any left. Did I hear someone talking about a bath?'

'I was just saying, we're going to miss having the lavvy and everything indoors.' Polly dried her hands and poured him a cup of tea. 'There you are, Dick, and don't laugh at it, you'll be old and weak yourself one day . . . Here, guess what, Mum's gone and planted spuds in her old tin bath, and says we'll have to wait till Easter before we can have a good soak. What's it like outside, apart from cold?'

'I never hung about to look. You can still smell the smoke and that. I saw that woman next door, what's her name, the thin scraggy one that hangs round the dockyard gates, but I never said nothing. Wouldn't want her to get the wrong idea.'

Alice laughed. 'Nancy Baxter's all right! She wouldn't bother with you, Dick, she's got her own customers. And you won't get past her old ma without speaking, I can tell you that. Granny Kinch has a word for everyone that goes along the street.'

'I know that, nosy old faggot. What about those nippers? They been evacuated?'

'No such luck,' Alice said. 'Young Micky's as full of mischief as a barrel-load of monkeys; got into trouble with young Gordon Hodges after Christmas last year, but it was only Gordon got sent away though everyone knows it was as much Micky as him. The other one's just a baby – Vera, she's called, and she's as scrawny as her mother.'

Cissie had come downstairs again and was sitting in the back room making more toast over the fire. She called to her husband to come and have some more, and he took his cup of tea through and sat down at the table. They sat in silence, each wrapped in thought.

'It don't seem possible we've lost everything, does it, Dick?' Cissie said at last. 'Our home, and all our furniture and clothes, and the wireless you and Terry built, and all Terry's Meccano and model aeroplanes . . . I can't sort of take it in. I keep remembering things – our photos too, and your Brownie camera . . .' Her voice trembled.

'I know, love. And they'll never be able to give it all back. All we'll get is a few clothes and some cash to tide us over. We'll have to start all over again.'

'But we'll get something from the insurance, won't we? I mean, we've got all the papers – we've got the tin box with everything in, that we always take down the shelter with us. We'll have to look it out, Dick, see what it says, and we'll have to let the collector know where we are too.' She rubbed her face. 'There's so much to *do* – so much to think about. I don't know how we're going to get through it all.'

He was silent for a moment, then he said, 'Nor do I, Cis. It's all too much for me. I keep remembering the last lot – what it was like out in the trenches. Blokes screaming and crying and going off their heads, and then the gas . . .' He coughed, his thin body racked, and gazed at her with red-rimmed eyes. 'I've been dreaming about it all night. I thought I was back there. I don't know how I'm going to face up to it all over again, Cis, I really don't . . .' His voice trailed away to a whisper and he began to shudder.

His wife got up quickly and came round the table to put her arm around his shoulders and draw his head down against her breast. 'Oh Dick,' she said, her voice trembling. 'It's not fair, not when you've been through so much already. But we'll get through it together. We will, really. Look, we're not hurt, any of us, we're all right, and we've got somewhere to live too – we're better off than a lot of people. And our Judy's still home, and we've got Polly too, and Mum as bright as a button still. We've got a lot to be thankful for. We'll face it together, you and me, all of us. And if we've got to start all over again, then that's what we'll do. We're not going to let Hitler get the better of us. We beat the Germans before, didn't we? And we'll beat 'em again!'

Dick stayed still, his head resting heavily against her, for a long time. Then he drew in a deep breath, lifted his head and gave her a shaky grin.

'You're right, love,' he said. 'We didn't give in last time and we won't now. *We'll* give 'em something to remember us by!'

She smiled down at him and he reached for her hand and squeezed it. They looked into each other's eyes with a mixture of pride and defiance. But behind their eyes, each had the same thought.

What would happen if they were wrong? What would happen to them all if the Germans really did invade?

Despite his protests that he ought to go to the Centre with them and do his bit, Cissie insisted that Dick should stay at home in the warm. 'I don't want you in bed with your chest again,' she said, winding a long scarf round her neck. 'And you can put the kettle on a bit later so there's a nice cup of cocoa for us when we get back, we'll be shrammed. Tibby'll keep you company.'

Dick looked at the cat, curled up in Alice's chair. 'I'm not sure he doesn't make me cough even more. All right, Cis, I'll stop here, but I'll make meself useful just the same. You can sort out some veg for dinner and I'll set about peeling them. I suppose we can put the saucepans on the fire?'

'It'll make them sooty,' Polly said, 'but we can scrub that off. We've got to have something hot inside us.' She pulled on the woollen mittens Alice had knitted from an old unpicked jumper. 'Come on, Cis. The sooner we get there the sooner we'll be back.'

The two sisters went out into the street. A bitter wind was slicing across the allotments which ran along the back of the houses and came down to the wide part at the end of April Grove. A pleasant-faced woman with beech-brown hair tucked under a dark red hat was pushing a pram up the street, and she nodded and smiled as she came up to them. 'Hello, you're Mrs Thomas's daughters, aren't you? Popped in to see if she's all right, have you?'

Polly shook her head. 'Come to stay, more like. We were bombed out, Friday night. We're going round to the Emergency Centre now to see what they can do for us, but we won't get another house, not when Mum's got this place. It's going to be a bit of a squeeze, though.'

'No! You never were!' The woman looked at them in dismay. 'You poor things. None of you hurt though?'

'No, thank goodness. I hear there was a bit of a tragedy here though. You're Mrs Budd, aren't you?'

The woman nodded. 'That's right, I live in number fourteen. Poor young Kathy Simmons. Such a nice little body, too, and those two little girls. They're in with me now, I've left my Rose looking after them. This little madam's my youngest, Maureen.' They all peered into the pram at the little girl sitting inside, and she beamed back at them. She looked about eighteen months old, Polly thought. Jess Budd went on, 'I'm just going up to my sister's at the end of March Street. Her girl Olive's not very well.' She stopped, folding her lips as if she didn't want to talk about what was wrong with Olive.

'Mum told us,' Polly said gently. 'That's a shame. I know, I've been through it myself – lost two after our Sylvie was born. Well, we'd better not keep you, Mrs Budd. I dare say we'll be seeing you again.'

They walked on up the street, each thinking how lucky they had been to lose no more than their home and possessions. There was no doubt about it, they agreed, you could always find someone worse off than you were yourself. Olive Harker, losing her baby, Kathy Simmons and her baby killed, the two girls left motherless . . . And that was in just one street, with no other damage. What terrible tragedies were happening in all those other streets, where house after house had been destroyed?

'I feel I ought to be doing something to help,' Polly said after a moment or two. 'Ever since Sylvie went off to the country, I've felt I should be doing more than just cutting people's hair. I mean, it's not exactly vital war work, is it?'

'Well, no, but it's good for morale, isn't it? That's what they say. Anyway, what else could you do? You're not thinking of joining one of the women's services, are you?'

'I don't think they'd have me, not at my age. Thirty-five's too old. No, I was thinking of doing something voluntary. I mean, I've got Johnny's pension and if I could work part-time at the salon I'd have enough to live on, and then I could give a bit of time to something else. There must be plenty of things to do. Look at Mum, she's always on the go, doing her bit, and she's getting on for seventy. It makes me feel ashamed.'

Cissie was silent for a minute or two, then she said, 'I suppose I ought to be doing a bit more, too. I mean, there's nothing to stop me.'

'You've got Dick to look after. You know he needs you with him if he gets one of his chests. And there's got to be someone at home to keep the place going, if all the rest of us are out.'

'I suppose so. And I could do knitting and needlework and things.' They were almost at the church hall. 'Look at that, Poll, there's still a crowd of people inside. Looks as if they've been there all night, some of them, poor souls. And those women taking their names, they look worn out, don't they. What a job.'

'Yes,' Polly said, gazing at them. 'What a job.'

Chapter Four

With soldiers, sailors and marines throwing themselves into the work of helping to clear the streets, there were a few buses able to get through and Judy managed to get to Southsea without too much trouble. It took her over an hour all the same, and she thought ruefully of the extra time it would add to her working days while the Council offices were there.

The Royal Beach was a large hotel, directly opposite South Parade Pier. It was eight storeys high and probably one of the grandest hotels in the city, its rooms lavishly decorated and lit with chandeliers. At least, that was what it had been like before the war, Judy thought when she arrived. The chandeliers had all been removed for safety – partly their own and partly because of the danger of flying glass to people if the hotel were bombed – and some of the furniture had been taken away to make room for the makeshift beds and trolleys for the casualties who were brought here after a raid.

Most of these had gone now, for the hotel was being used as a clearing station rather than a hospital, but the big ground-floor lounge, bar and restaurant where they had been brought were littered with blankets and sheets, piled ready for washing, and there was a smell of blood and vomit and disinfectant. First-Aid workers were busy cleaning up and sorting fresh bandages and bedclothes ready for the next raid. They looked exhausted, as if they'd been there ever since the bombs began to fall, and Judy thought they probably had.

'Do you know where the Council offices are going to be?' she asked a woman who was near the door, scrubbing at a patch of what looked like blood on the floor. 'I was told to report here for work.'

The woman, her sleeves rolled up and a scarf wound like a turban round her head, looked up, and to her surprise Judy recognised the face of one of the WVS volunteers who had come to the Guildhall for meetings with the Lady Mayoress. They looked at each other and the woman smiled.

'You didn't expect to see me here, did you! Well, we all have to do our bit. I think the offices are going to be upstairs, though I did hear that the Mayor will have the meeting room on the ground floor as well.' She sat back on her heels and pushed a few straggling hairs out of her eyes. 'I expect you'll get a guided tour, but just in case you don't, the basement's being used as a shelter – the stairs are over there, behind that door – and there's a lookout post on the roof. The Fire Brigade are manning that at the moment, but I did hear they're going to put Observers up there, to see when planes are coming. Anyway, you should find your people on the next floor.'

Judy thanked her and went up the gracious stairs that wound their way from the big foyer all the way to the top of the building. The balustrade was of elegant wrought iron and the well was lit by a single thick flex that hung from the very top, bearing glittering chandeliers at each floor. I suppose it was too difficult to take these away, she thought, looking at the shimmering crystal drops. The touch of luxury sent a little thrill through her body. It was almost like working in a palace.

There wasn't much luxury in the new offices, however. Once comfortable, spacious bedrooms with balconies on which the guests could sit and look out over the sea only yards away, across the road, the rooms were now stark and empty. Beds, dressing-tables and wardrobes had all been removed to make space for utilitarian desks and tables, and plain wooden chairs that looked as if they'd come from the cheapest furniture shop in the city. There were no cabinets, shelves or drawers and people were standing looking a little helplessly about them. Presumably office furniture would be brought in as soon as it could be obtained, but for now they had to make do with what there was.

'How long d'you think we'll be out here?' Judy asked when she found the former bedroom that had been assigned to her department. 'It's taken me ages to get here this morning.'

'It'll be for the duration, I'm afraid,' Miss Marsh said. 'It's the same for us all, Judy.'

'I know.' Judy rubbed her cold hands together. There was no fire in the grate and a bitter wind was scouring in from the sea and finding its way through the windows. 'Well, what is there to do? I suppose none of the office papers were saved?'

'Nothing at all. The Lord Mayor only just managed to get out of the Guildhall before the roof caught fire and fell in, and the ARP were too busy trying to save the building. There were people firewatching up on the roof too, but they got down just in time, thank goodness.' Miss Marsh sat down at a desk that had been brought in from the hotel's reception area, and massaged her forehead with her finger-tips. 'We've just got to start from scratch. Organise ourselves as best we can, and try to get things in order again – but it's not going to be easy. Think of all the forms we used to use, all gone; we'll have to get them printed all over again, and I haven't even heard from the printers yet. Most of the phones are out of action, and for all we know they could have been bombed too and all the plates destroyed . . . It's a nightmare, Judy.'

Judy looked at her helplessly. 'But there are people

downstairs already, wanting help – what are we going to tell them?'

'Tell them we'll do our best but it may take time. They can't expect miracles.'

They would though, Judy thought as she went to face the huddle of men and women who were down in the reception area. 'We can't get no information,' one man complained. 'We've had to trek all the way out to Southsea, and you know what the streets is like – and then when we do get here we can't find nothing out. What are we supposed to do? There's no gas, no electricity, not even any water laid on down our way, and nobody seems to know nothing. It's a flipping disaster.'

'Well, so it is,' Judy said. 'You know how much damage there's been. It's bound to take time to sort things out, I'm afraid.'

'And what're we supposed to do in the meantime?' the man demanded again. He had a pugnacious face, with small eyes and a flattened nose, and his ears looked as if they'd been chewed. He glowered at Judy and she took a step back. 'I got a wife an' three nippers to look after. They ain't had a decent meal for two days, only what that WVS stall or whatever it's called has been able to dish out. My missus can't even boil up a kettle to make a cup of tea.'

'I'm really sorry,' Judy said. 'We're doing all we can.'

There was a mutter of discontent from the crowd, and a woman in a brown herringbone coat with a scarf wrapped round her head said, 'Well, what about the Public Assistance, then? Can't they do nothing?'

'They're not here,' Judy said. 'They've been sent somewhere else – I'm not sure where.' She escaped back into the makeshift office. 'They're really upset,' she told Miss Marsh. 'I feel sorry for them but it's not our fault.'

'They won't understand that. They're worried and frightened and a lot of them have lost their homes. Well, you know yourself how they must feel. Look, here are the addresses of the Public Assistance, the Police Headquarters and the Medical Offices. They're spread all over the place, I'm afraid. You'd better put a notice on the wall.'

Judy went back and tacked up the notice, listening to the aggrieved remarks as she did so. She couldn't blame the people for feeling upset – as Miss Marsh had said, they were all under strain – but she did think they ought to make some allowances. After all, nobody had known the Guildhall was going to be destroyed, and all these arrangements had had to be made at a moment's notice. 'I've had to come a long way, too,' she pointed out as one young woman with a baby in her arms started to complain about having to go miles away for Public Assistance. '*And* I was bombed out on Friday night. It's the same for us as for everyone else.'

'Yes, but you're paid to come here,' the woman snapped. 'We've got to find our own shoe-leather.' She hoisted the baby higher on to her hip and glared at Judy before turning to push her way out of the building. Judy looked after her and sighed.

'Never mind, my dear,' said a voice in her ear. 'I don't suppose she means to be nasty. She's just tired and frightened, like the rest of us. Come inside and have a cup of tea. There's something I want to ask you.'

Judy turned and saw to her surprise that it was the Lady Mayoress herself who was speaking to her. She was a familiar figure in the Council offices and had often smiled at Judy as she went by, but had never spoken to her before. Puzzled, Judy followed her back to the office, where the tables were being taken over as desks by various members of staff. The Mayoress walked across to a corner of the room and motioned to Judy to sit down. She gave her a friendly smile. 'I've seen you in the offices quite a lot, haven't I? Your name's Judith Taylor, and you've been working for the Council for some time, haven't you?'

'Yes, madam. Ever since I was sixteen. I worked in a shop when I first left school and did shorthand and typing at night school, and then I saw a job advertised in the Council office and I applied for it.'

'Well done. You're obviously a girl with some initiative.' The Lady Mayoress paused. 'Now, I know just how busy we're all going to be here, and I know how difficult it's going to be for Miss Marsh to get her office organised, but I have a very special request to make. As you probably already know, I'm the local President of the WVS – the Women's Voluntary Service. You may have seen our Head, Lady Reading, when she visited us last July.'

'Yes, madam, I remember her. She came to the Guildhall with another lady.'

'That's right. That was Lady Northampton. Now, the WVS does a lot more work than many people realise – I expect you've seen the stalls giving out tea and buns and soup that have been set up in all the bombed areas. We were there when the men came back from Dunkirk, and we've been helping out at Emergency Centres and First-Aid Posts. But we do a lot of other things, too: we've cooked Christmas dinners for folk who wouldn't otherwise have had anything, we've sorted out coal rations for old people, and we've even enrolled people into the Blood Transfusion Service. In fact, wherever people need help, you're likely to find a WVS volunteer offering it.'

She paused again and Judy gazed at her, wondering where all this was leading. Feeling that she was expected to make some response, she ventured, 'My granny helps on tea-stalls and things, but I don't think she's in the WVS. They have a uniform, don't they?'

'Yes, we wear dark green with a dark red blouse or jumper, and a green beret. But we're not like the women's Services – we don't call people up. We just ask for volunteers. And we pay for our own uniforms,' she added.

Judy began to guess what this was about. 'And you'd like me to be a volunteer? Well, I will, of course, but I can only help out in the evenings. I couldn't do anything in the daytime because of my job.'

The Mayoress shook her head. 'No, my dear, I'm not asking that, although I hope that you will be able to help, in whatever way you can. What I'm asking you to do is work for me – for the WVS – full-time.'

'Full-time?' Judy stared at her. 'I don't understand. I thought it was all volunteers?'

'I'm sorry, I haven't explained properly. Look, my dear, it's obvious that with Portsmouth now under severe attack – we're sure to get more bombing raids like the one on Friday, we're in the front line here – there are going to be a lot of people needing help. Immediate, practical help with things like clothes, rations, food, accommodation – the sort of things the Council would do, certainly *will* do – but the WVS can do so much more quickly, leaving the Local Authority to get on with the job of permanent rehousing, putting the city back to rights and so on. That means we're going to need more volunteers and more office staff to help them. I'd like you, Miss Taylor, to join my staff.'

'Me? But . . .' Judy glanced round the room, looking more like a bustling office now with men and women sitting at tables which were already covered in sheets of paper. Typewriters were being carried in, packets of envelopes being opened. Where had they all come from? she wondered, and felt guilty at not helping. 'But I've already *got* a job, madam, and I ought to be doing it now. I don't want to be rude – I'd really like to be able to help you, and I promise I will, in the evenings and at weekends, but there's going to be so much to do here—'

The Mayoress held up her hand. 'Just wait a minute, Miss Taylor, while I finish explaining. I've already spoken to Miss Marsh and she understands the position. She's agreed to let me have two of her girls to help for as long as I need them. I'm afraid I asked for her best girls,' the Lady Mayoress smiled, 'and she said that in that case one must be you. But of course, this will only be with your agreement – nobody's going to force you. That's not the WVS way at all!'

Judy gazed at her, unable to think of anything to say. She glanced across the room to where Miss Marsh was busy at her own desk, deep in discussion with two of the senior male clerks.

'And Miss Marsh doesn't mind?' she asked at last.

'I wouldn't say that – she doesn't want to lose you at all, and I don't blame her. But she understands the need.' The Mayoress leaned across the little table. 'You see, the kind of person I need will be someone who can respond to an emergency – who can work on her own initiative, and who is practical and won't mind going out of the office and giving a hand wherever it's needed. Someone who can organise anything from the evacuation of small children to collecting scrap metal. It takes a very special kind of person to do all that's going to be required in these coming days and months, Judith – not the sort of girl who just wants to sit at a desk in a nice warm office all day.'

'And you really think I could do all that?' Judy asked, with a little twinge of excitement.

The Lady Mayoress gave her a steady look. 'You were bombed out on Friday night, weren't you? You and your family lost everything. Yet you still made your way to the Guildhall – your place of duty – having first made sure that your family would be cared for at an Emergency Centre. You even stopped on the way to help others who needed it, and you then stayed at your post all day, despite the dangers – there could have been fallen masonry or unexploded bombs anywhere in the Guildhall Square – to make sure that everyone from the offices knew the situation here. Today is Sunday morning, and you're here again, ready to start work. That's how I know that you're the sort of person I need.'

41

Judy glanced round the room once more. 'But I'm not the only one, madam. All these others . . .'

The Mayoress smiled again. 'I also like the look of you, Judith. I think we can get along – and that's important too. Now, what do you say? You don't have to agree, and if you do say yes and then find you're not happy with the work – I warn you, it'll be hard, with long hours, and not always as clean and pleasant as you've been accustomed to – then I won't hold you to it. You'll be able to return to normal staff duties. But will you at least give it a try?' She tilted her head a little and lifted her fine eyebrows.

Judy bit her lip, longing to say yes, yet still held back by a sense of loyalty to her workmates. She looked over at Miss Marsh again and the supervisor caught her eye, said something to her companions and came swiftly across the room.

'Well, Judy? Has the Lady Mayoress explained what she wants?'

'Yes, Miss Marsh. I don't know what to say. There's all the work of getting the office together again, and—'

'Say yes,' the older woman advised her. 'It's an opportunity for you, Judy, and I believe you'll be good at it. I can manage with the rest of the girls, and the male clerks, and we may be able to take on extra staff as well. But the Mayoress needs someone with Council experience as well as initiative, and in you she'll have both.'

Judy felt her skin colour. 'Well, if you really think so . . .'

'I do. I'll be sorry to lose you, Judy, but we all have to use our abilities where they're most needed, and the WVS does an excellent job. They'll be needed even more as this war goes on. Now, you'll have to excuse me, I must get back.' She bobbed her head at the Lady Mayoress. 'Let me know if there's anything else you need, madam.'

Left together, the Lady Mayoress and Judy looked at each other. Judy smiled awkwardly and said, 'Well, it looks as if that's settled then, madam. And – and thank you for asking me.'

The Mayoress held out her hand. 'I'm very pleased to have you on my team. Now, I told you that I was stealing two girls from Miss Marsh, but I haven't told you who the other one is. It's Laura Godsall – I think you know her, don't you? She's rather senior to you and will be my secretary, but to all intents and purposes you'll share the work between you. We don't have "hierarchies" in the WVS – we like women to be able to use their own individual skills – so if you have any ideas of your own, or think things could be done differently, you must say so. Now, I've been given the office next door for my own use, so come through and we'll get started.'

'Yes, madam.' Still feeling rather bewildered, Judy followed the Mayoress through to a smaller room where she found another desk and two of the dining tables. Laura Godsall, a tall girl a year or two older than Judy, with long blonde hair rolled up in a thick pleat over her forehead, Betty Grable style, was sitting at one with a pad of notepaper in front of her.

'Here's Miss Taylor come to help us,' the Mayoress said briskly. 'You know each other already, and I'm sure we're all going to get along famously. Now, what's been going on while I've been out of the room, Laura?'

'I'm trying to make lists of all the things we need to do,' Laura said. She had a low, rather musical voice, and Judy remembered that she sang in one of the church choirs in the city. Her father was a vicar. 'If we appeal for more volunteers, we need to be able to give them jobs to do straight away. The tea- and soup-stalls all have a rota, but we need more people for the Emergency Centres, and more Evacuation Helpers. Mrs Daysh was in here just now from the Clothing Fund; she says they're desperate for more clothes—'

'You see why I need help!' the Mayoress said to Judy.

'There's an enormous amount to be done. Now, as Laura says, the first thing we must do is find more volunteers. That means plenty of notices to be put up, and we can't get them printed – the printers have got far too much to cope with – so I think you'd better spend some time making them by hand. Big, bold and simple, there's no time for anything fancy. We'll get them into all the Emergency Centres and First-Aid Posts, and everywhere else we can think of. I've managed to get hold of some large sheets of paper – here, spread them out on the table. Now, I must get down to the Clothing Store. We had a new consignment in last week that I don't think has even been unpacked yet. I'll take Mrs Daysh with me and we can sort them out at once.'

She was gone, leaving the two girls with a pile of paper and a box of crayons between them. They looked at each other and Judy grinned a little ruefully.

'Well, I suppose it's important work.'

'It is,' Laura assured her briskly. 'Even if it does feel a bit like being back at school. Let's see how many we can get done by lunchtime – and what's the betting that by then she'll have thought of something else for us to do!'

As it turned out, by lunchtime the Mayoress had thought of quite a few things for them to do. Most of the women who were already volunteers had gone straight to the Emergency Centres, but some had come to the hotel with its new offices to ask for orders. Laura and Judy, by now inundated with requests for help, were kept busy matching them up, and Judy soon lost any sense of embarrassment at asking a well-dressed woman to take a frail old lady to the lavatory, or sending a young mother with three small children of her own to look after a crowd of bedraggled urchins who didn't seem to have any parents at all.

'They wouldn't volunteer if they didn't mean it,' Laura remarked as she helped an efficient old lady to unload a pile of woollen jumpers that someone had sent in. 'It's like the Mayoress says – if you're in the WVS you've got to be flexible. Ready for anything. I can't see anyone offering if they're not prepared to do whatever they're asked to do.'

'Well, I hope we get lots more offers from these notices,' Judy said, printing WANTED – VOLUNTEERS FOR THE WVS out for the hundredth time. 'It's been busy enough before, it'll be even worse now, especially if we get more raids like Friday's.'

'D'you think we will?' Laura paused in her sorting. 'D'you think they'll bomb us that badly again? I don't know how much more people will be able to stand.'

'We'll stand as much as we've got to,' Judy said grimly. 'We don't have any choice, do we? And the Germans aren't going to stop because they feel sorry for us. They'll hammer and hammer and hammer till they think we'll give in.' She drew a thick black line under the words and looked up. 'We'll get more raids all right, Laura. They haven't finished with Pompey yet – but what they don't know, is that Pompey hasn't finished with *them*.'

Chapter Five

Back at home at last, Judy stretched her toes out to the fire and took a cup of tea from her mother. 'Thanks, Mum. I really need this. It was a horrible journey back. There's any amount of streets still blocked, the bus kept having to go a different way. Some people said they were further away from home when they got off than when they got on!'

'It's a shame you've got to go all the way out to Southsea,' Cissie said, offering her a tin of broken biscuits before settling a saucepan on the coals. 'I hope they manage to get the offices back into town before long.'

Judy shook her head. 'They won't go back now. You haven't seen the damage, Mum. We'll be out at Southsea for the duration, that's what Miss Marsh says.' She nibbled a piece of Rich Tea. 'Anyway, what sort of a day did you have? Did you manage to get the rations sorted out?'

Polly nodded. 'We've got temporary books, and we've registered at the Co-op where Mum gets her rations. They've opened up a grocery store not too far away, being as the big one's been bombed. Had to queue half the day but at least we've got a bit of food in the place now. And we got a bit more coal too, since we couldn't manage to get all ours out, but the woman was a bit funny about that, said it didn't take any more to warm five of us than one. I told her, we've got to have something to cook on while there's no gas, and we've got an invalid in the house too, and she gave way in the end but she didn't like it.'

'She only give us enough for a couple of hours a day

46

anyway,' Alice observed. 'I could have practically carried it home in my pockets.'

Judy smiled. She was tired and cold after the long journey from Southsea, and it was good to be back with the family again. 'I feel as though I've been working forever,' she said. 'It doesn't seem like Sunday at all today. Did you manage to get to church?'

'Yes, we did, and so did just about everyone else in Pompey,' Polly told her. 'Our church was full and I reckon all the others must have been as well – the ones that are still standing, anyway. The vicar told us there was – how many churches did he say got bombed, Mum?'

'Well, there was the Wesley down Arundel Street, and the one in Elm Grove, and Kent Street and Lane Road – oh yes, and Immanuel too, all Baptist places they were. And the old Unitarian in the High Street, that's nothing but a pile of rubble now, they say.'

'What, old John Pound's church?' Dick said, glancing up from his armchair. He was looking a bit better now, although still with a slight greyish tinge to his face. 'I never heard that. Well, that's a proper shame – bit of history, that church was. It was where old John Pound the cobbler started up his Ragged Schools. Many a time I've looked at the old wall tablet that said about how he used to take kiddies in off the street and teach 'em their letters while he mended shoes. Used his own money to feed 'em too, he did, and put shoes on their feet and clothes on their backs. I call that a real shame.'

'I don't think he actually mended shoes in the church,' Judy began, but was silenced by a glance from her mother. She bit her lip. It hardly mattered anyway. The tragedy was that so many buildings had been bombed, whether they were fine old churches or tiny terraced houses. The city was having its heart torn out.

'Tell you what,' she said. 'I've got a new job!'

The others stared at her. 'A new job? Why? Have you been promoted? You never told us about this, Judy.'

Judy laughed. 'I didn't know, that's why! And it is a kind of promotion, I suppose, in a way. The Lady Mayoress has asked me to work for her, helping with the WVS. You know she's high up in it, and she says they're going to be even busier now, helping in all sorts of ways. She needed some more staff, so she asked Miss Marsh if she could have me and Laura Godsall.'

'But surely they're all volunteers?' Cissie said. 'Does that mean you won't get paid?'

'No, I'll get the same wage as before. She's allowed some paid staff, you see, so that she's always got people who know what's what. And we're stopping out at the Royal Beach because the WVS works with the Local Authority – it's something like the way the Wrens help the Navy and the ATS help the Army, that sort of thing – but we might find ourselves doing all sorts of jobs. I think it sounds interesting,' she said and finished her tea while the others gazed at her.

'Well, fancy the Lady Mayoress herself asking for you, our Judy,' Alice said at last. 'They must think a lot of you.'

Judy shrugged, feeling pleased all the same. 'I don't know about that. I reckon I just came in the door at the right moment.'

Polly's face was bright with excitement. 'So you're going to help with the WVS. Well, what a coincidence. Because I am, too!'

'*You* are?' Judy turned to her. 'How d'you mean, Polly? Are you volunteering?'

'I already have. Put my name down at the Centre this morning.' Polly beamed at her niece. 'I've got to come out to Southsea tomorrow to sign on. I'll come with you on the bus, first thing.'

A huge smile broke out over Judy's face. 'That's smashing! We need lots and lots of volunteers, and it's going to be really interesting work, Poll – you've no idea all the jobs they do. It's not just serving out tea and sorting old clothes. Though those things do have to be done as well, of course,' she added fairly.

'Well, I don't care what I do so long as it's helping the war effort,' Polly declared. 'I've been thinking ever since I let Sylvie go out to the country that I ought to be doing something, but what with having a job and not being able to go in the Services, I didn't really know what to do. But this will suit me – I can put in all the hours I want to and still do a bit of hairdressing as well. I went round to Mrs Mason's this morning to make sure it was all right with her if I just did part-time. We decided afternoons would be best; seems to me it's mornings that volunteers'll be needed most, when there's been a raid overnight.'

'They'll be needed morning, noon and night,' Judy said. 'But whenever you work, you'll be welcome, Polly. You're just the sort they need. I'm really pleased.'

'And I'll still be giving a hand where I can,' Alice chimed in. 'I'm going to go round the Centre regular. Annie Chapman works there – you know, Jess Budd's sister from over the end of March Street, it was her Olive that was with Kathy Simmons – and she says I'll be welcome any time. There's always something to do there. And Peggy Shaw, from down the street, she works in the First-Aid Post and her Gladys drives an ambulance, so we'll all be doing our bit round this way. Well, most of us,' she added as an afterthought. 'I don't suppose that Ethel Glaister will lift a finger to help – wouldn't want to chip her nail varnish – and Nancy Baxter has her own ways of helping, as we all know.'

'Mum!' Cissie protested, amidst laughter from the others. She got up from her chair and bent to lift the lid from the saucepan simmering on the fire. 'I reckon this stew's just about ready now. There's only enough meat in it to cover a half-starved mouse, but plenty of veg, so let's get round the table and tuck in.' She brought the pan to the table and began to spoon stew into the bowls. 'And just in case you think I'm not pulling my weight, I'm going to be doing needlework for the Marine barracks, helping make uniforms, and Dick's going to be making rag rugs for people who are being rehoused and got no furniture.'

'That's right,' Dick said, drawing up a chair. 'It'll be a hive of industry round here. She'll have me knitting next.'

'Well, that wouldn't be anything to be ashamed of,' his mother-in-law told him. 'Plenty of sailors used to do knitting when they were at sea. I don't know where they'd have got new socks from otherwise, when they were away for years at a time.'

They sat round the table, eating their meal. As Cissie had said, there wasn't much meat in it but what there was had given it some flavour, and the vegetables were good. Afterwards they had boiled rice with golden syrup, and while they were eating that Cissie put the kettle on the fire for another cup of tea.

'Wonderful how you can manage when you've got to,' she remarked. 'But I'll be thankful when we've got the gas and power back on. Have you heard anything about that, Judy?'

'I know they're hoping to get the Dockyard generators linked into the city electricity supply,' Judy said, gathering up the dishes. 'If they can do that, everyone will have some power in the next day or two. I don't know about the gas, though.' She hesitated. 'There's going to be a big funeral on Friday – some of the people that were killed. They say there were over a hundred and fifty. They're going to be buried all together at Kingston Cemetery, and the Mayor and all the Corporation are going. I don't know how many of their robes they'll be able to wear; a lot of them were burned in the Guildhall.'

There was a moment of sadness, then Polly said, 'Talking of uniforms, I'll be getting the WVS one. It's quite nice – green with a sort of grey thread running through it. We've got to pay for them ourselves, though.'

'I'm having one too,' Judy told her. 'I don't mind paying for it – I'd have to get some more clothes for work anyway. Did you manage to get much at the Centre, Mum?'

They went on talking as they cleared the table, made tea and put the kettle on the fire yet again for washing up, and then settled down with their knitting. All the women were making something. Judy and Polly had started balaclavas for the Navy, Cissie was unravelling one of Dick's old cardigans to make gloves, and Alice was making squares from scraps of leftover wool, to be sewn together to make blankets. Polly lit an extra candle, to give them more light.

'I'm getting a bit worried about this coal supply,' Cissie said, rolling wool into a ball. 'With all this cooking, and needing water for washing and scrubbing the floors, you've got to keep the fire going but what we've got in the shed's going down really quick, even with those few loads we managed to bring here from home.'

'Well, once the gas is back on we can sit in our coats during the day and just keep the fire for evenings,' Dick said. 'One thing about making rag rugs, they do keep your knees warm while you're working on them!' He glanced at the clock on the mantelpiece. 'Let's put the wireless on – it's nearly time for the nine o'clock news.'

'Good thing I had the accumulator charged last week,' Alice remarked, doing as he asked. 'At least we can still find out what's going on.'

The news, read by Alvar Liddell, was as gloomy and frightening as usual. There had been more Luftwaffe attacks on British warships in the Mediterranean; a destroyer had been damaged, the aircraft-carrier *Illustrious* crippled and another ship, unnamed so far, sunk. In the Netherlands, all Jews had been ordered to register with the authorities. Mr Churchill had insisted to Parliament that assistance to Greece must be given top priority.

'The trouble is, everywhere needs to be top priority,' Dick said, switching it off again. 'We can't be in all those

51

places at once. It's like a disease, breaking out everywhere, and as fast as you try to stop the bleeding in one place it starts somewhere else.'

Cissie shuddered. 'That's horrible, Dick.'

'Well,' he said quietly, 'war *is* horrible.' He looked down at the fire and then pulled his cardigan close around his thin chest. 'I don't know about you, but I'm for bed. I dunno, ever since Friday night I seem to feel so tired I can hardly keep my eyes open. I reckon I'll be a bit warmer there, too. Did you put the bottle in, Cis?'

His wife nodded. 'Half an hour ago. You go up, Dick, and get comfortable. I won't be long.' She waited as he went outside to pay a last visit to the lavatory and then had a quick wash at the scullery sink before climbing slowly upstairs. 'It's the shock,' she said to the others. 'It's knocked him sideways, and I'm not surprised. It's not right, men like him having to go through this all over again.'

'What happened to him in the Great War, Mum?' Judy asked. 'I know he was gassed, but there was more to it than that, wasn't there?'

Cissie looked at her and sighed. 'Well, I suppose it's only right you should know. Not that I know all the ins and outs of it myself, mind – a lot of it, I just had to pick up from what Dick said and what other people have told me. And Dick's never told me the full story, never will. I don't think he can bear to remember it.'

'Bad as it was, I don't think the gas was the worst of it,' Alice said. 'I think it was what else happened to him that upsets him most.'

There was a brief silence, then Cissie said, 'I reckon you might be right, Mum.' She turned back to Judy. 'See – your dad and me were childhood sweethearts – always knew each other, and we always knew we'd get married one day. But there didn't seem to be no hurry till the war broke out, and then when he joined up we thought it'd all be over by Christmas, so we decided to get married then, when he came back. And so we did, only it wasn't all over, and he'd had a taste of the trenches by then and he didn't want to go back.'

'Didn't have no choice, though, did he,' Alice said. 'You either got shot as a deserter or went back and probably got shot by the Germans.'

'That's right. He had an awful time – I only know about it from the nightmares he used to have. Still has, sometimes, specially since this lot started . . . He didn't come home again till the next Christmas – our Terry was three months old then. I tell you, when he walked through that door over there, I didn't even recognise him. He looked like a ghost. No – more like a skeleton, he was so thin and drawn. And he couldn't even talk for three days – just sat and cried in the chair. Wanted me with him all the time, couldn't bear to let the baby out of his sight . . . It was pitiful. Pitiful.'

Judy stared at her, shocked. 'But what was the matter with him?'

'What do you think? He'd had just about all he could take. A lot of them had. They'd been living like rats in holes, being shot at day and night – it wasn't human, what they had to go through. Why, we couldn't even bang a door shut without him jumping out of his skin. Shell-shock, they called it,' Cissie said bitterly. 'Gave him a few weeks' leave to get over it and then dragged him back. He wasn't over it, not by a long way. He isn't over it now – he never will be. It's why he flares up sometimes, all over nothing. Something happens that touches him on the raw and he loses his temper. He never used to be like that. It's all through what happened in the war.'

'And was it after that when he was gassed?' Judy asked quietly.

'That's right. Saved his life, that did.'

'*Saved his life?* But it's left him more or less crippled!'

'And if it hadn't, he'd be dead,' Cissie said bluntly. Judy, accustomed to gentleness from her mother, caught her breath at the harshness of her voice. 'They called it shell-shock when he was home and they wanted him back again, but out there they had a different name for it. Cowardice. And you know what they did to cowards, don't you?' She gave Judy a bitter look. 'They shot them.'

Judy caught her breath. 'You mean they were going to *shoot Dad*?'

'I'm not saying they were going to, but I think that's what he expected. And then they got this gas attack. He only got a whiff, mind – he said there were boys that got a full whack, and they died screaming. It turns your lungs to a sort of mush . . . But your father wasn't too close. It was enough to make him poorly for a bit, mind, and leave his lungs damaged for life, but it got him invalided home and there was no more talk about cowardice. He was all right to work too, for a few years, till it started to get worse, but at least he's still alive. I thank God on my knees every day that he's still alive.'

Judy was silent. She had always known that her father's illness stemmed from the Great War, but had never heard the details before. She glanced at her Aunt Polly.

'I suppose you didn't realise – you were only little then.'

'Nine, when he first came home,' Polly said. 'I was a bridesmaid at the wedding. I was only twelve when the war ended, and Dick went back to his job in the Dockyard – and then our dad died and I don't think I really noticed much. Cis didn't tell me till I was a lot older, when Dick started to get worse.'

'Poor Dad,' Judy said softly. 'Poor, poor Dad.'

'Well, he's got plenty to be thankful for, all the same,' Alice said briskly. 'He's not had such a bad life. The gas didn't kill him, he's got a good wife and two children to be proud of, and there's plenty of others went through the same as he did, and worse. I'm not playing it down, mind, just saying it could have been worse.'

'You're right, Mum,' Cissie said. 'It could have been a lot worse. That's what I thank God for.' She rolled up another ball of crinkly, unravelled wool and got up. 'Well, I'm going up now, too. Don't you be too long, Judy, you look tired. So do you, Poll.'

Fifteen minutes later, Judy and Polly were left alone by the dying fire. Alice had gone into the front room, where a mattress had been put on the floor for her, and a few minutes later they heard her snoring. They looked at each other.

'That's awful, what Mum said about Dad,' Judy said. 'But Gran's right, isn't she? At least he's alive. You must wish you could have your Johnny back, even if he'd been injured.'

'I do,' Polly said quietly. 'But I'm not sure it's what he would have wanted. He was always so proud of being fit and strong – I don't think he could have put up with being an invalid. And I was thinking about you, too. You haven't said anything about Sean, but you must be worried stiff. I saw your face when the newsreader said about the ship that's been sunk in the Med. You were thinking about him then, weren't you?'

Judy bit her lip. 'I don't even know exactly where the *Southampton* is, but she could be out there, Polly. And they wouldn't let me know, would they – not straight away. They'd notify his mum, over in Ireland. I'd have to wait for her to write to me.' She sighed. 'I try not to worry, but sometimes it feels like a great lump of jagged metal inside me. I don't know what I'd do if I lost him, Polly. We knew each other such a short time.'

'I know,' her aunt said softly. 'I know just what it's like. All you can do is wait. That's all any of us can do – wait, and do something useful in the meantime. At least we can do that.'

'Yes,' Judy said. 'At least we can do that.'

Chapter Six

Several of the April Grove residents attended the mass funeral at Kingston cemetery the following Friday. They were there to mourn Kathy Simmons and her baby Thomas. Alice, Cissie and Dick walked down with Freda Vickers, from the end of April Grove. Her husband Tommy was an air-raid warden and had been one of the last men to come down from the roof of the Guildhall when it had caught fire.

It had snowed during the week and the pavements were slippery with ice. They walked carefully, holding on to each other's arms.

'He was named after my hubby, the baby was,' Freda told them sadly. 'Tommy was with her in the air-raid shelter when he was born, see. Took care of Kathy right through, and she was so grateful. Hadn't lived in October Street all that long, but they were a lovely family, and the two little girls are dears.'

'It's terrible,' Cissie said. 'All those people killed, and all the families left behind to grieve. What about her hubby, then – where's he?'

'I told you, Cis,' Alice said. 'He's in the Merchant Navy. On convoys somewhere.'

Judy and Polly were at the funeral too. Judy had gone down from Southsea with Laura and the rest of the Council staff and the Mayor, Mayoress and Corporation, all in ordinary clothes because their grand robes had been lost in the Guildhall fire. The Mayor's regalia, which had been kept in a safe, had been saved, however, and he wore that over his dark suit, while the bishops of both Anglican and

Roman Catholic churches were resplendent in blue and gold, and black, gold and cherry-pink respectively.

The procession was led by the Royal Marine Band, its trombones dazzling, its drums muffled with black crêpe. It was followed by twelve Rolls-Royce and Daimler hearses, each driver wearing a top hat, and the coffins draped in Union Jacks. Beside the hearses, in a slow march, walked the servicemen who were to act as pallbearers, and behind them came a parade of all the Armed Services, including some from the French Navy, as well as members of the ARP and Home Guard. Tommy Vickers was there, his yellow hair glinting in the sunlight when he took off his hat in respect for the dead.

Polly was smart in her new green WVS uniform, standing in line with the other volunteers along the road. The icy pavements were packed with mourners, and a number of people who had just come to watch.

'Sightseers!' Judy said indignantly as they walked back to Southsea afterwards. 'Got nothing better to do. As if watching a lot of coffins being put into a grave was entertainment!'

'Well, I'm sure they were upset about it too,' Polly said. 'And you've got to admit it was a real sight, for all it was so sad. I didn't know Kathy Simmons but I couldn't help shedding a few tears. All those poor souls being put into one grave – and all those people standing there, absolutely quiet, watching. And those words the bishop said, about us being a "proud people" and calling them "Citizens in the City of God". I don't know how they think these things up.'

'Neither do I,' Judy said caustically. 'All that about them being "happy dead" and "winning a victory"! I bet Kathy Simmons isn't happy being dead, and I bet she doesn't think she's won a victory either. It's just *words*, Polly, and they don't mean a thing!' Her cheeks flushed and her eyes brightened with anger. 'Just because he's a bishop, we're meant to believe him and be *proud* that so many people were killed and injured and bombed out of their homes, and I tell you, I'm not! I'm not proud at all!'

Polly looked at her in surprise. Judy had never expressed such feelings before, but when you came to think about it, perhaps she had a point. The bishop's words *had* made her feel proud, but it was true that she hadn't felt like that beforehand. She'd been sad and upset and frightened. She thought for a moment and then said carefully, 'I suppose he's trying to make us all feel better – stronger. Being miserable isn't going to help them, or us. If we can feel better about them dying, perhaps it helps us to carry on.' She sighed. 'Pompey's not the only place hit this week. Plymouth and Bristol have had bad raids too. I suppose this sort of thing's happening there as well. What I wonder is where they get all the coffins from. They surely don't have all that many ready at the undertakers.'

'I reckon they've got places making them specially,' Laura said. She and Judy were also in their new WVS uniforms, with warm greatcoats over their jackets and skirts. 'They won't tell us about them though, because of spreading panic.'

They reached the Royal Beach and went inside. The offices were busy, with half a dozen girls clacking away at a bank of typewriters and clerks sitting at paper-strewn desks and dining tables. All the forms and official documents had to be printed and sent out to homes and businesses all over the city, and on top of that the bombed and damaged premises must be surveyed for repair or rebuilding. There were lists of people who needed rehousing, lists of places where they could be sent, lists of those who had decided to take evacuation, lists of places in the country that could accommodate them. Lists, lists, lists, Judy thought as she pulled off her coat, gloves and hat and hung them on a hook. There's no end to them, but without them we couldn't even begin to get everything done. She sat down at her own desk and gazed at the mound of paper that seemed to have grown during her absence. Each list, each entry, she knew, represented some personal problem or even tragedy – a workman needing new clothes, a family bombed out just as her own had been, two little sisters whose mother had been killed.

'That's Kathy Simmons,' she said, staring at the sheet of paper in her hands. 'She lived just across the road from my gran, where we're staying now. She was killed with her baby boy in her arms, and now the little girls have got no one. Oh, Laura.' Suddenly, she was in tears. The strain of the past week – the horror of seeing her home in ruins, the desperate struggle to get through the streets, the sight of the Guildhall that was the pride of Portsmouth, the funeral of so many people that afternoon – overwhelmed her with a rush of emotion, and she put her elbows on her desk, her face in her hands and shook with sobs.

'Judy!' Laura came and put her arms round Judy's heaving shoulders. 'Oh Judy, don't. I know it's awful.' She held the girl's head against her, stroking the bright hair. 'I've cried, too. I cried all night, thinking of it all. Perhaps it's best to cry. Let it out, Judy, let it out. It'll make you feel better.' She went on murmuring and stroking, and Judy's tears slowly began to subside, until at last she was able to look up and blow her nose and give a small, shaky smile.

'Sorry, I didn't mean to break down like that. It was just seeing their names. It's different when it's someone you know.'

'I know. It makes it so real. Not that we're in any doubt about that,' Laura said with a sigh, glancing round the office. 'I just wish we could wake up and find it was all a dream – a nightmare. But it's not.'

'No. It just seems like one. A nightmare we can't wake up from.' Judy blew her nose again. 'And being sorry for ourselves isn't helping anyone. We've got so much to do – there's so many people needing things.' She drew the sheet of paper towards her again. 'Stella and Muriel Simmons.

They're staying with Mrs Budd, down at the other end of April Grove from Gran, but I suppose they'll have to be evacuated. Poor little scraps. They'd already been bombed out once, you know.'

'Would you like me to see to that?' Laura asked gently, but Judy shook her head.

'No, I'll do it. I can't give up over everything that upsets me, or I'll never get a thing done. It's the same for all of us, after all. We're all going to come across people we know, sometime or other.' She looked at the paper again. 'What do we do, though? Send someone to go and see Mrs Budd, or get their evacuation organised first and then just tell her?'

'Haven't they got any other relatives? A granny or aunties? What about their father?'

'I think he's in the Merchant Navy.' Judy sighed. 'I suppose someone had better go and find out.' She glanced round the room and saw her aunt standing by the window, talking to another WVS volunteer. 'I know – I'll get Polly to do it. We're staying in April Grove after all, and Gran knows Mrs Budd. Polly and Mum grew up there themselves, though I don't think the Budds moved in till after they'd got married and moved out. It's better than sending a stranger though, and we can find out about the girls' family before we do anything else.'

She made a note in the ledger she had been given to keep a record of what action had been taken in each case, and went on to the next, two boys whose mother was in hospital with a broken leg. They ought to have been evacuated too, she thought. She was surprised how many children there still were in the city – children who had been evacuated right at the beginning of the war and then come home when nothing much seemed to be happening, children who had refused to go or whose parents refused to send them, children who were under five and too young to go without their mothers, whose mothers wanted to stay at home with their husbands . . . Surely some of them would go now, she thought. Surely, after this, their parents will see the danger they're in.

But not everyone wanted to be parted from their children. There was Jess Budd, whose boys were at Bridge End. She and her elder daughter Rose, together with the baby Maureen, had all gone out there to begin with, but Jess had come back to look after her husband Frank, who worked in the Dockyard, and naturally the baby had had to come too. And then Rose had wanted to come back with her mother, and after some argument Frank had agreed to her return. He wouldn't hear of the boys coming back though, and they didn't really want to. They were enjoying their stay in the country and, apart from being disgruntled at missing the air raids, they were content to stay there, especially now that there was some snow.

'I thought perhaps Stella and Muriel could go to the vicarage there,' Jess said when Polly went to see her. 'That's where my boys are now, and they're well looked after. The vicar's got a housekeeper who's like a mother to them, and the vicar's like an overgrown boy himself, by all accounts. There's plenty of room there and I'm sure they'd be welcome, and they met Tim and Keith at Christmas.' She took a photograph from the mantelpiece and looked at it fondly. It was a studio portrait and showed the whole family in their best clothes, with baby Maureen seated on Jess's knee and Frank and Rose behind her while the two boys stood straight and proud beside them. 'My Frank had this taken specially, before they went back. He wanted us all together, just in case . . .' She bit her lip, then added brightly, 'You've seen my boys in the street, I expect, before they went away?'

'The whole school went to Bridge End, did they?' Polly asked, trying to get the picture straight in her head.

'That's right. The teachers are there, too – Miss Langrish and the others. They're happy enough there. Well, mostly,' she added, remembering the children like Martin Baker and the little Atkinsons who had not been at all happy. 'They didn't all get good billets, I'm afraid. But the girls would be all right at the vicarage.'

'What about the father? Do they have any other relatives?'

Jess frowned, trying to remember. 'Well, Mr Simmons is in the Merchant Navy, he doesn't get home very often, of course. As for other relatives – well, I got the impression there weren't many. They're not Pompey people anyway. Kathy told me once they both came from Basingstoke. Her parents died when she was a kiddy and she was brought up by her gran, but the old lady's over ninety now. And I think she said her hubby's mother was in a home – doesn't really know what's going on.'

'It doesn't look as if they're going to be much help,' Polly said. She looked down at her notebook. 'They're staying with you at the moment, is that right? But I expect you'd rather they were evacuated.'

'I don't mind having them at all, but I think they ought to be somewhere safe. The poor little mites have been bombed out twice and they're terrified every time we hear a plane go over. We've had to go down the shelter quite a few times already since the big raid, and you can see they're almost out of their minds with fear, especially Muriel, the younger one. And Stella's like a little old woman – you'd think she was carrying the weight of the world on her shoulders. They need to be somewhere they can feel safe and start to be children again.'

Polly nodded. 'We can certainly contact the vicar and see if he'd be willing to take them. What's his name?'

'Mr Beckett. But I think I ought to talk to their father first – he's hoping to be able to get back and see them soon. His ship comes back to Pompey, you see, for supplies. I wouldn't like him to come and find them not here, not when he's lost his wife and baby boy as well.'

'Well, we'll wait a little while,' Polly agreed, 'but we can't leave it too long. As you say, they ought to be somewhere safe.' She put her notebook away and stood up. 'Thanks, Mrs Budd. It's been nice to talk to you.' She glanced around the small room. 'You've got a lovely place here.'

'We do our best to keep it nice,' Jess said modestly. 'Frank does a lot of work on it – woodwork and decorating, and that – at least, he did when you could still get the materials. It's not rented, you see, like most of the houses round here. Frank wanted his own place – likes his independence, and likes to be able to do what he wants with his home. A lot of his mates said he was daft, taking on a mortgage, said it'd be a millstone round his neck, but we've never regretted it. He always says he'd sooner put the money into his own bricks and mortar than pay rent for the rest of his life.' She looked round proudly. 'It's been a real struggle at times, but this house will be ours one day, with no more to pay – well, that's if the Germans let it!'

Polly nodded. Before Johnny was killed, they'd rented two rooms, and even Dick and Cissie's house had been rented. Her mother Alice had been lucky to be able to stay in the house at the other end of the street, where Polly and Cissie had grown up, after her husband had died in the 'flu epidemic after the Great War, but she was still paying rent. Frank and Jess Budd had been sensible, she thought, as well as brave to take on such a commitment.

'Well, let's hope they do,' she said, referring to the Germans. 'It's no picnic, being bombed out, I can tell you.'

Jess's face softened in sympathy. 'Yes, I heard about your trouble. It must have been a terrible shock, coming out of the shelter to find everything gone. Thank goodness you were all down there, though. I've heard of people who just popped indoors to make a cup of cocoa . . . well, look at Kathy, killed in just those few minutes. It doesn't bear thinking of.'

Polly walked back up the icy street towards her mother's house. No it didn't bear thinking of, but you had to think about it when it happened to you. There were a lot of things these days that didn't bear thinking of, but you had to do so all the same. Things like her Johnny, drowning or blown up at sea – she would never know just what had happened to him. And their little daughter Sylvie, out in the country near Romsey, living with strangers. They were kind enough to her, Polly knew that, but it wasn't right, a kiddy of seven living with people she didn't know. And how long was it going to be before she could come home and be with her mummy again? Nobody knew.

'You're Mrs Thomas's girl, Polly!' a cracked voice exclaimed, making her jump. 'I knowed you when you was a little 'un. Come back to stop with your ma then, I hear.'

'Mrs Kinch!' Polly said, stopping. 'Yes, we were bombed out of our house, so me and Cissie and her husband, and their Judy, have all come back to April Grove. It seems funny, being back where I was born,' she added, glancing along the street where she had played so often as a child.

'Ah, I remember you two, skipping and playing two-ball up against the walls.' The old woman looked just the same as always, Polly thought, her thin grey hair wound tightly into metal curlers and covered with a brown net. 'My Nancy often talks about you – she'll be pleased you're back. You can come in and have a cuppa tea with us one of these days, have a bit of a chinwag about old times.' She peered at Polly's green uniform. 'You joined up then, have you? Which Service is that?'

'It's not one of the Armed Services. It's the WVS – the Women's Voluntary Service. Anyone can volunteer,' Polly said proudly. 'We do all sorts of things – help people who've been bombed out, run tea-stalls down by the docks, take children to be evacuated, collect scrap – anything that needs doing. Nancy could join if she wanted to,' she added a little doubtfully.

Granny Kinch cackled. 'My Nancy's already doing her bit towards the war effort,' she said, confirming Alice's remarks about Nancy Baxter. 'But you carry on, young

Polly, there's plenty of other comforts our boys need these days. Anyway, I can't stand here nattering all day, I got our Micky's dinner to get. He does a bit of work down Charlotte Street market; brought home a nice string of pork sausages last night, he did, and he'll expect 'em on the table when he comes in.' She grinned toothlessly at Polly and went indoors.

Polly opened the door of number nine and went inside, smiling. Her brother-in-law was in his armchair, a piece of canvas spread over his knees as he hooked bits of coloured material into it. 'Hello,' he said, 'what's tickled you?'

'Granny Kinch. Just said she couldn't stand nattering at the front door all day. I thought that was all she ever did! You know, she doesn't look a scrap different from how she looked when I was a little girl – I think she must have been born toothless and with curlers in her hair.'

Dick grinned. 'I don't know about the curlers but I expect she was born toothless. Look, what d'you think of my rug? Bit of all right, isn't it? I'm getting proper nifty with this hook.'

'You are,' Polly said, admiring it. 'Some family's going to be pleased with that to put in front of their fire.' She sighed and sat down in the other armchair. 'It's awful, though, Dick, when you think of it. I've just been down to see Mrs Budd about those two little Simmons girls. There must be hundreds of kiddies like them, lost their homes and parents. It's so tragic.'

'You weren't much older when you lost your own dad,' Dick said, 'so you can understand what it's like for them. And it's the same for your Sylvie. D'you reckon you'll be able to get out to see her soon?'

'I hope so. It's just that with everything so upside down all over the city, and now we've got all this snow, there's hardly any trains or buses running and they're needed for getting people evacuated.' She looked into the fire, thinking of her daughter. 'I'm glad I had her home for Christmas. At

65

least we all had a few days together then for Terry's bit of leave, but I'm even more glad I made her go back. I felt awful when she begged me to let her stay, but it was the right thing to do.'

Dick rolled up his work and got up. He went out to the scullery and filled the kettle. The gas was back on now, as well as the electricity, and soon the kettle was whistling and he made the tea and brought in two cups.

'Here. You look a bit done up. It's upset you, talking to Jess Budd.'

'I think it has, a bit.' Polly stirred a saccharin tablet into her tea and sipped it. 'I want to help, Dick, and I'm glad I joined the WVS, but it does bring it home to you what terrible things are happening. Not that we *need* it bringing home to us – I think we've had our share already. But it seems worse, somehow, when it's other people. You can see that some of them just can't cope with it. It's in their eyes – they look sort of lost and bewildered. They're like little children.'

'It's shock,' Dick said. 'I've seen plenty of it, Polly. They'll be all right after a bit – at least, they would be if they had a chance of some peace and quiet. But that's just what we don't get, isn't it?'

She shook her head. 'It's as if the Germans are just banging away at us all the time. They knock us down and then hit us again, just as we're getting up. Nobody gets a chance to recover from one blow before the next one knocks them for six. You just don't know what's going to happen next.' She glanced up at the mantelpiece. 'Is that a letter for our Judy?'

Dick nodded. 'Came by second post. Got an Irish stamp on it. I dare say it's young Sean's mother – she writes now and then, doesn't she?'

'Yes, she does. Perhaps she's got some news from Sean. I know Judy's been a bit worried, not hearing from him just lately.' Polly looked round as the front door opened and closed again. 'I expect that's her now. There's a letter here for you, Judy,' she called.

Judy burst into the room, her face alight. 'A letter? From Sean?' She held out her hand for the envelope Polly was taking down from the mantelpiece, and as she caught sight of the stamp, the colour drained from her face. In the same instant, Polly remembered her remark a few days earlier.

'They wouldn't let me know, would they – not straight away. They'd send any telegram to his mum, over in Ireland. I'd have to wait for her to write to me.'

'Oh Judy,' she said, getting up quickly. 'Oh, *Judy* . . .'

Chapter Seven

Only Polly could give Judy any comfort during the dark days that followed.

The *Southampton*, a cruiser, had been sunk on 11 January – the day after the Blitz on Portsmouth. Perhaps, Judy thought, Sean had been dying at the very moment she and the family had crawled out of their Anderson and stared in horror at the wreckage of their home. Or, if not then, it must have been at some other moment during that dreadful day – as they walked into the Emergency Centre, perhaps, or while she was struggling to reach the Guildhall, or when she came into the square and saw the great building going up in flames, the copper melting in green streaks of fire down its scorching walls . . . At some time during that day, Sean, the merry Irish sailor she'd met and fallen in love with at a South Parade Pier dance – the laughing young seaman who had swept her off her feet, begged her to marry him and given her the tiny diamond she was wearing on her finger now – had died in the sea he had loved and which had become his killer. Had he been thinking of her as he died? Had he called her name, regretted that he would never see her again? Or had he forgotten everything else in his desperate struggle to stay alive?

'It's no good torturing yourself over it,' Polly told her as they huddled together on the single bed in Alice's back bedroom. 'You've just got to do your grieving and then come to terms with it. It's hard – no one knows that better than me – but you've got to do it.'

'I can't,' Judy sobbed. 'I can't stop thinking about him,

Poll. What was it *like*? If only I knew, if only I could *imagine* it, I could feel I was sharing it with him then. I could feel that perhaps it wasn't so lonely. I know that's stupid, it can't make any difference to him now – it couldn't ever make any difference to him. But it might help me to *understand*.'

'I know. I know just what you mean.' Polly stroked her niece's bright, fair hair. 'I went through it all when I lost Johnny. I felt cheated, somehow. Not just of his life, though that's bad enough, losing the life we were going to have together, but of his death, too.' She looked at Judy, whose sobs had lessened a little. Her face was still buried in her hands but Polly sensed that she was listening. She hesitated, hoping she wouldn't increase the girl's pain, and then went on. 'It's like it says in that old song – you remember, the one your dad used to sing to your mum sometimes, when we were round the piano. My dad used to sing it too. All about sharing the good things in life, and the bad ones too. "Am I not yours for weal or woe? How else can friends prove true? Tell me what breaks and brings you low, And let me stand with you."'

She paused again. Judy lifted her head. Her eyes were red and swollen, her skin puffy, but she looked at Polly and nodded. 'I remember it. The last verse always made me cry.'

'It makes me cry too,' Polly said, her own eyes filling with tears as she thought of the two men who had meant so much to them – both sailors, both lost at sea. I shouldn't go on with this, she thought, it's too heartbreaking – yet that last verse, sad though it was, had expressed so well the loss she had felt, and it had helped her to think that someone else knew and understood that loss. 'Do you remember how it goes?' She sang the words, very softly. ' "So when the night falls tremulous, When the last lamp burns low, And one of us, or both of us, The long, lone road must go . . . Look with your dear old eyes in mine, Give me a handshake true. Whatever fate our souls await, Let me be there – let me be there. There, with you." '

69

They were both crying now, their tears falling like rain, yet Polly felt that for Judy the tears were healing ones, no less bitter, but the tears of a grief shared and understood. She held her niece's shoulders firmly, feeling the slim body shake against hers, and felt her own grief as fresh and sharp as on the day when she too had received that terrible news. And we're not the only ones, she thought. There are thousands of us, all over the country. All over Europe. And perhaps, before this awful war is finished, all over the world.

Lives torn apart too soon; wives and husbands robbed of a lifetime together. Robbed even of that last goodbye.

Judy felt for a handkerchief. There was scarcely a dry one left in the house, and the one she used now was already sodden. But there was an air of finality as she rubbed her eyes and turned to look at her aunt.

'It'll always make me cry, that song,' she said 'but I'm going to try to stop now. I'm going to do all I can to help people who're worse off than me – and there's plenty of them. I'm going to do it for the war effort, and to beat Hitler, same as before – but I'm going to do it now for Sean as well. So that he won't have died for nothing.'

Polly gave her a shaky smile. 'That's right, Judy. That's what I'm doing. Working for Johnny and my Sylvie – so that he won't have died for nothing, and so that she's got a life to look forward to. A *better* life.'

'There'll never be anyone else for me,' Judy said sadly. 'I don't suppose I'll ever get married and have children now.'

'I thought that, too,' Polly agreed. 'But I don't know, Judy – no one ever knows what life will bring.' She sighed. 'It'll have to bring someone pretty special to take Johnny's place, all the same. And I don't even know that I want it to. Johnny's got his place in my heart – I don't think there's room for anyone else.'

'We'll be old maids together,' Judy said with an attempt at a smile. 'Well, *you* won't be an old maid, because of

Sylvie. But when she's grown up and got her own family, we'll stay together, won't we? You and me?'

Polly hugged her. 'We will. As long as we've got each other, we'll never be really alone, Judy. Never. You will be happy again, Judy – I promise. And we'll always share things. All right?'

'All right,' Judy said, and then her eyes filled again and she cried out in a voice sharp with anguish, 'But I'm going to miss him so much, Polly! I'm going to miss him *so* much . . .'

The end of January 1941 and beginning of February brought several important visitors to Portsmouth.

Winston Churchill was the first. Accompanied by Franklin Roosevelt's Envoy, Mr Harry Hopkins, he went on a tour of the city's bombed areas before arriving at the Royal Beach to meet the City Council members. Judy, lining up with the rest of the staff to greet him, gazed in awe at his stumpy figure and the famous cigar wedged in his mouth. He really does look like a bulldog, she thought – absolutely determined, as if nothing can stop him. If anyone can make us win the war, he can.

He made a speech too, as good as any on the wireless. 'I thought about you a good deal a few weeks ago when we knew how heavily you were being attacked,' he told them, 'and I am very glad to find an afternoon to come to see you here and wish you "Good Luck". Our buildings, our dwellings, may be destroyed, but the spirit of Britain glows warmer and brighter for the tribulations through which we pass. We *shall* come through. We cannot tell when. We cannot tell how. But we *shall come through*.' He paused and seemed to look at every person present, as if calling on each one to live up to his expectations. 'We have – *none of us* – any doubt whatever. And when we have done so, we shall have the right to say,' his voice swelled and deepened, 'that we live in an age that, in all the long history of Britain, was most filled with glorious achievement and most graced by duties done.'

There was a pause as he finished speaking, and then a spontaneous outburst of applause. All the women and many of the men had tears in their eyes. Mr Churchill stood for a moment, smiling broadly, then he nodded his big head and waved his hand, giving them the famous Victory salute, and turned to go out of the room.

'Isn't he wonderful!' Judy said, going back to her desk. 'You can't help but follow a man like that. I mean, even on the wireless he makes you feel you could do anything, but when you see him in person – well, he's like a tidal wave, rushing you along.'

'And the way he puts things,' Laura agreed. 'I used to be good at English at school, but I could never put things the way he does. And it wasn't even a big speech, not to go on the wireless or in Parliament, I mean. It was just to us, here in Pompey.'

'It'll be in the newspapers though,' Judy said. 'The *Evening News* will print it – there was a reporter here taking down every word – and some of the others will too, I expect. Plenty of people will get to know what he said to us.'

They went back to work, heartened by the Prime Minister's words. Judy thought about them, wondering just why they seemed so different from the bishop's during the mass funeral. He, too, had been trying to give them hope, but somehow it hadn't been the same. It was as if he were trying to brush aside and glorify the horrible deaths that so many people had suffered, whereas Mr Churchill seemed to suffer with them. He'd seen deaths like that himself, he knew what they were like and didn't pretend they were glorious or 'happy', but at the same time he seemed to draw strength from them, and hand it on to others. What was it he'd said in that other speech? *'I have nothing to offer you but blood, toil, tears and sweat.'* And, *'We shall fight them in the streets and the hills and on the beaches. We shall never surrender.'* He didn't pretend, but at the same time he gave you hope and some of his own stubborn determination. And he made you feel that, however small a part you played yourself, it was important. It was all a part of the great national effort.

Just at the moment, Judy's part in that effort was trying to set up a system for salvage collections – there had been appeals for binoculars for the Navy, for saucepans and other aluminium goods for making aeroplanes, for clothes, for rags and bones. Nothing, it seemed, was to be thrown away; everything could be put to some use.

'There are going to be special bins for food scraps,' she said. 'They'll be collected for pig swill – pigs will eat anything. There'll be one on the corner of every street to start with.'

'One pig?' Laura was sorting through a pile of temporary ration books to be issued to people who had lost theirs in the bombing.

'One *bin*, twerp!' Judy threw a screwed-up scrap of paper at her and Laura caught it and threw it back.

'I hope you weren't going to waste that – it'll do for one of your collections.' They made faces at each other, grinned and went back to their tasks, feeling more light-hearted.

The next special visitors were the King and Queen themselves. Judy, in a flurry of nerves, made Polly help her drag in the small tin bath the night before, muttering to each other that it would be a good thing when the potatoes could be harvested and the big bath returned to its proper use. They poured in hot water from kettles and added some bath salts Polly had been given for Christmas. Judy got in first, luxuriating in the pleasure of having a bath on a Wednesday instead of the usual Friday or Saturday. Then she got out again and Polly got in, followed by Alice, Cissie and finally Dick. 'We might as well all have a treat,' Alice said. 'No sense wasting the hot water.'

With their hair newly washed and set with Amami lotion,

Judy and Polly joined the rest of the staff and volunteers at the hotel early next morning to receive the Royal visitors. The King, looking serious but ready with a shy, friendly smile, was wearing Naval uniform – he'd actually served during the Great War, Polly whispered to Judy, and been in the Battle of Jutland. The Queen was in a dark costume, with a hat that was swept up away from her face, four rows of pearls around her neck and a fur stole draped over her arms.

All the bigwigs were there too – the Lord Mayor and Lady Mayoress, of course, Admiral Sir William James the Commander-in-Chief of Portsmouth, Brigadier Harter, Major-General Hunton, Colonel Walker and the Town Clerk. The men bowed deeply and the Mayoress dropped a graceful curtsey. As they passed the staff, the latter all bowed or curtseyed as well, most of them terrified that they would fall over or get their hair caught in someone's buttons. As the door of the Mayor's office closed behind the visitors, the staff heaved a general sigh of relief.

'She looks just like a film star!' Judy exclaimed. 'Did you see those pearls? And that fur – it must have been real mink!'

'I can't see why she needs to dress up like that,' remarked Eileen Hall, who didn't really like royalty. 'Especially when she's going to see people who've been bombed out and got nothing. It's just flaunting herself and all her money.'

'No, it's not.' Polly was an avid follower of the Royal Family. 'They can't help being rich, and if they've got nice clothes they might as well wear them. Anyway, she says that if people go to see her they dress up in their best, so why shouldn't she do the same?'

'Oh, know her personally, do you?' Eileen sneered, and Polly flushed angrily.

'No, I read it in the paper, and so could you have done if you didn't have your head buried in penny romances all the time. Anyway, I've got work to do and we'd better not start

74

yelling at each other or they'll hear us in there and a fine impression of Pompey that'll give them!'

They went back to their desks, the excitement of the morning slightly dimmed by the squabble. Polly felt angry with herself for letting Eileen get under her skin. I ought to learn to ignore her, she thought as she tried to sort out lists for the salvage collections, a job she had taken over from Judy who was now busy helping the Mayoress with the Clothing Depot. All the WVS staff and volunteers were extra busy that morning, as they were all going to St Mary's Hospital in the afternoon to meet the Queen again as part of her tour.

'It was lovely,' Judy told her mother that evening as they sat round the supper-table eating bubble and squeak. 'There must have been a couple of hundred of us there, all WVS, and there were some Red Cross nurses too. The Queen's ever so pretty – smaller than you'd think from her pictures, with gorgeous blue eyes – and she was so *interested*. D'you know what I heard her say? "Sunshine will come again," she said. Don't you think that's lovely? She couldn't talk to everyone, of course, but she managed to have a few words with quite a lot. And they did so much during the day. They went and looked at some of the bombed areas down Commercial Road, and the Guildhall, and some of the ordinary streets as well, and she saw our Clothing Depot, and the billeting people, and the welfare offices, and then they went and had lunch on the *Victory*.'

'Oh, that must have been lovely,' Alice broke in. 'And nice for the King, too, him having been in the Navy.'

'Well, I don't think he was ever on a ship like the *Victory*,' Polly said with a grin. 'And after that, he went to see the Gunnery School and she came on to the hospital and some of the First-Aid Posts. They were on the go all day.' She was silent for a moment, then she said, 'I think she's right about dressing up, you know. It wouldn't have been so special if they'd come in old clothes – even if they've got

75

any! And it does make you feel better, knowing someone like that's taken the trouble to look nice for you. It makes you feel as though you matter to them.'

'Yes,' Judy agreed. She was still grieving for Sean, still thought about him all the time, still felt cheated of all they might have known and had together. But Polly was right, she thought. 'It does make you feel better.'

'That bit about sunshine coming again,' Alice said after a moment. She looked at the two faces, showing the same sorrow, and her own face softened in sympathy. 'It's true, you know. You can't go on without letting in a bit of sunshine now and again. You've got to start living again. You've got to.'

Chapter Eight

The raids continued, although all through January and February the concentration was on other cities. Bristol, Plymouth and Swansea all came under heavy attack, and all along the south coast the sirens went night after night, sending people to the shelters to sit listening to the snarl of German bombers overhead, and wonder where they were making for.

The firewatcher's post on the hotel roof had been taken over by the Royal Observers' Corps. Judy had noticed the young men in their RAF uniforms coming in and out several times before she found herself in the lift with one, on her way to the fifth floor with a message. He was tall, with fair hair and blue eyes and a nice smile, and she smiled back and asked, 'What is it you're doing up there? Looking out for enemy aircraft?'

'That's right,' he said. He touched the badge on his arm. It showed a Spitfire in flight. 'The RAF advertised for chaps like me who are keen on spotting aircraft, so I applied and here I am.' He grinned. 'It's like a dream come true, sitting up there in the best place in Southsea, looking for aeroplanes. I used to do it for a pastime and now I'm helping the war effort as well!'

Judy looked at him, so clean and smart in his uniform, obviously enjoying himself on the roof of a nice building, with nothing uncomfortable or difficult to do, and thought of the pilots who risked their lives every day in the air, and the sailors like Sean and Johnny, who died horrible deaths at sea. 'Nice work if you can get it,' she said tartly.

'Well, someone's got to do it!' he said jocularly, and then caught the note in her voice. 'Look, I know it must seem a cushy number – and maybe it is, compared with what some poor blighters have to do – but it's essential work just the same. We're the ones who spot the aircraft first and identify them so that others can shoot them down and stop them bombing Pompey. I know a lot still get through, but that doesn't mean we've just got to sit back and let them all come in. It'd be even worse if we did that.'

'Yes, but why does it have to be people like you? Why not people who can't go on active service? People who've been injured or can't serve for one reason or another?'

'Like poor eyesight?' he asked quizzically. 'Well, don't ask me. I suppose because we're the ones who volunteered. Blokes like me who've always been keen on aeroplane spotting. We're the ones who're good at it. And it does take a bit of skill, you know, to be able to spot an aircraft coming in at twenty thousand feet and be able to recognise what it is. It's not all that safe sometimes either,' he added as if as an afterthought, 'sitting up on top of an eight-storey building right on the beach. We're an easy target.'

'I suppose so,' Judy said a little grudgingly. The lift had arrived at the fifth floor and she got out. The young Observer went on to the top; here he would climb the steel ladder to the roof, originally installed as a fire escape. On her way to one of the offices with her message, Judy passed a room that the Observer Corps was using as a classroom and glanced in through the open door. A row of young men and two or three girls were sitting at desks while an instructor fixed large sheets of paper covered with the silhouettes of aircraft on a board.

I suppose it *is* skilled work, she thought, and I suppose it's a bit dangerous being up there like sitting ducks – but all the same, it doesn't compare with what other people are doing. It doesn't compare in the least with what Sean and Johnny and all those others in action are doing.

Even without the raids, the war news was bad. Malta, its position in the Mediterranean making it a vital possession, was bombarded day and night while the islanders, with only three Spitfires to protect them, dug themselves into caves and catacombs and sat out the raids which all but destroyed their island and capital city.

Meanwhile, the war had spread. Italy had taken over the vital supply ports of Tobruk, Somaliland and Libya, as well as Greece and Albania. Most people in Britain had never even heard of these places and had to search out old school atlases to find where they were, and daily newspapers published large maps of the world which could be pinned on walls. Even then, it was difficult to make sense of what was happening.

'I don't see why it's spread so much,' Cissie said, staring at the coloured pins Dick had put in to mark the progress of the different armies – red for Britain, black for Germany, blue for Italy. 'It was just Poland and Austria, and places like that, to begin with. Why does Africa have to get mixed up in it?'

'It's because of Italy coming in on Hitler's side,' Dick explained. 'They've got all these places in Africa, you see, and so have we, so we've got to defend ours against them.' He paused doubtfully, his chest wheezing a little. It still didn't seem to make much sense. 'Frank Budd was saying the other day that they're getting worried about the Japanese now. They think they might come in.'

'The *Japanese*!' Cissie stared at him. 'Why? Whatever's it got to do with them?'

'Well, nothing, but apparently they don't like America being in the South Pacific. They've got places in Hawaii – naval bases – so they're quite close to Japan really.' He looked at the map again. 'You can see it better on a globe. They look far apart on a map, but if you imagine it sort of bent round the back, then you can see how close they are.'

'But America's not even *in* the war,' Cissie said. 'What's the point of Japan butting in?'

'They think the Americans want their oil. And they'd like to take over China as well, and maybe even go up into Russia, and this would be a good chance, while we're all busy defending everywhere else.' Dick began to cough. His chest was getting worse again and he'd had two mild asthma attacks in the past week or so. 'I don't understand it any more than you do, Cis, but that's what I've heard.'

Cissie shook her head. 'I can't make it out at all. Seems to me they've all gone mad. The whole world's going to be fighting each other at this rate, and what's the good of that? What's going to be left when they finish? What's the point of it all?'

Judy, who had been sitting quietly mending her stockings, looked up and said, 'Freedom, Mum. That's what it's all about. We couldn't let Hitler march all over Europe and take away everyone's freedom like he did to the Jews and all those other poor people. We had to stop him.'

'Yes, but all these others – Africa and Japan and Russia – he wasn't marching into *their* countries. It's like boys fighting in the street. One or two start scrapping and then the rest all pile in just for the sake of it, and in the end no one knows what it was all about. It was the same in the Fourteen-Eighteen War – someone shot that man in Yugoslavia and before we knew where we were, all our men were being marched off to fight. Millions were killed, and thousands like your dad, messed up for the rest of their lives. It's like a disease.' She stopped and stared at them all. 'Like a horrible, mad disease.'

Mike Simmons turned up on Jess Budd's doorstep one day and, after some discussion, agreed that the two little girls should go out to Bridge End and be billeted at the vicarage. 'I wanted them to be evacuated right at the beginning,' he said sadly, 'but Kathy wouldn't hear of them going without her, and she wouldn't go herself because she wanted to stay in Pompey for when I got home. We went over it again and again, but all she would say was that the Queen wouldn't let her girls go to Canada without her, and she wouldn't go because she wanted to be with the King, and it was the same for her. I stopped trying to talk her round in the end. I didn't want to spend all my time arguing.' He shook his head. 'Perhaps I ought to have put my foot down – said she'd *got* to go. But how could I make her, Mrs Budd?' He lifted his head and looked at Jess. 'How could I?'

'Well, it's the same with me,' Jess said a little uncomfortably. 'I feel the same about leaving my Frank, and so of course the baby has to be here, too. And Rose went to start with, but she wanted to come home . . . But I do think your little ones'd be better off out there now, Mr Simmons.'

Polly was given the task of taking Stella and Muriel out to Bridge End on the train. So far, she'd not had any specific job to do in the WVS but had just helped wherever she was needed, but since the Blitz, more and more children who had returned to Portsmouth for Christmas and stayed there – or perhaps not been evacuated at all – were going back, and they all needed escorts. Polly had accompanied several already, and enjoyed the task, though the children varied greatly.

'You should have seen the boys I took last week,' she told Laura when she was in the office collecting the documents that would have to go with the two girls. 'I thought I knew Pompey pretty well, but I've never seen anything like the home they came from. It was no better than a hovel. And their clothes! Well, I've seen better on a scarecrow – toes poking out of their boots, hardly any backside to their trousers – I felt ashamed, I did really, to be taking them to strangers in that state.'

'Weren't there any clothes in the Store they could have had?' Laura asked, shuffling the papers together.

'Yes, there were as it happens, and I got them fitted out

with nice flannel shorts and a jacket and shirt each, and a pair of wellington boots – there weren't any other shoes that would fit them. But that was only one outfit. I just hope they can put something together in the country.' Polly shook her head. 'But it's not just that, Laura. It's the boys themselves. They were sick on the train, all three of them – I don't know why it is that boys are always sick, the girls don't seem to suffer like it – and they'd obviously never seen a hanky before in their lives, their noses never stopped running. And their language! I tell you, I didn't know half the swear words they came out with!'

'How did you know they were swear words then?' Laura asked with a grin and Judy, who was putting some papers away in a filing cabinet in the corner, chuckled.

Polly smiled too, pleased to hear her niece laugh. 'It was the way they said them. And the way they looked at me, too, as if they wanted to see what I'd say – I knew they were swearing all right. I don't suppose they knew what they really meant, though, any more than I did. And I'm not going to repeat them now,' she added firmly as Laura's mouth opened. 'Goodness knows what I might be saying!'

She collected the railway tickets and other papers and went out. She was to deliver the children next day, and went down to Jess Budd's early in the morning to find the two girls waiting for her, neatly dressed in clothes that Jess had found for them amongst her own daughter's old things, with their faces shining and hair brushed.

'Well, you do look smart,' Polly said, gazing at them. 'I should think anyone would be pleased to have two nice little girls like you billeted with them.' The little one, Muriel, was nearly eight, just the same age as her Sylvie, and Stella was ten and old enough to be sensible. They looked back at her and then turned to Mrs Budd.

'Do we have to go, Auntie?' Muriel asked, her bottom lip trembling. 'We like it here with you.'

Jess Budd looked down at them tenderly. 'I like having

you, Muriel, but you'll be safer out in the country. And you'll be with Tim and Keith and the other children.'

'Tim and Keith are *boys*. I'd rather stay here with you and Maureen and Rose. *They're* not going out to the country.'

'I know.' Jess looked helpless. 'But your daddy wants you to go, doesn't he? Don't you remember, he had a talk with you both when he came to see you? He told you then he wanted you to go, so that he wouldn't have to worry about you in the bombing.'

'Well, *I* want to go,' Stella said suddenly. 'I'm fed up with being bombed. And Tim and Keith don't matter, Mu. We don't have to take any notice of them – there'll be plenty of girls to play with.'

Jess and Polly glanced at each other, trying not to smile. Polly picked up one of the little cardboard suitcases. 'Come on, then. We'll catch the train at Hilsea station. Have you been on a train before?'

'I'll come with you,' Jess said, putting Maureen into her pram. 'We'll wave goodbye.' To Polly she said quietly, 'I'll miss the little dears, but it'll be better for them to be away from Pompey. Every time they walk up the street they see the house they lived in – well, the space where it used to be. It's not good for them, being reminded what happened that night.'

Once on the train, the girls perked up and looked out of the window eagerly. Neither had ever seen the countryside before, and they cried out with excitement at seeing cows and sheep in the snowy fields. There were even one or two early lambs skipping about and Muriel turned to Polly, her face alight, and asked if she would be allowed to have one of her own.

'Maureen Budd's got one. The butcher gave it to her.'

'The butcher gave her a *lamb*?' Polly asked in surprise. 'Are you sure?'

'It's not a real one,' Stella said. 'It's the one he used to have standing on his counter. He gave it to her at Christmas.'

'Well, what a lovely present. There can't be many little girls who've got a lamb like that.'

'Yes, but I want a real one,' Muriel persisted. 'Like Bo-Peep.'

'No, that was Mary,' Stella corrected her. 'Bo-Peep *lost* her sheep.'

They started to recite nursery rhymes and then went on to songs. They were on their third rendition of 'Run, Rabbit, Run' when the train arrived at Bridge End station. Polly gathered together their few pieces of luggage and helped them down on to the platform.

'We're supposed to meet Mrs Tupper,' she said, consulting her instructions and glancing around. 'I don't see anyone here, though.' An elderly porter was shovelling snow into piles on the platform and she approached him. 'Do you know if there's been a lady called Mrs Tupper here? She was supposed to meet us.'

He straightened up and pushed back his cap to scratch his forehead. 'Mrs Tupper? Big lady, is she, in charge of the evacuees?'

'I don't know what she looks like,' Polly said, 'but these are evacuees so I expect that's the one. Have we missed her?'

He shook his head. 'Ent coming. Gone down with 'flu, that's what I heard. Message come through on the telephone half an hour ago.' He started to shovel again.

Polly looked at him in exasperation. 'Well, what was the message? Didn't she say what I should do with the girls? I was supposed to hand them over to her.'

He shook his head. 'Wasn't her that telephoned. Told you, she's got the 'flu. Too poorly to come to the telephone, I dare say, so she got someone else to do it for her.'

'Yes, but what did they say? Wasn't there any instruction for me?'

'You?' he repeated blankly.

Polly took a deep breath. I shall laugh about this later, she told herself, but she didn't feel much like laughing now. 'Yes, me. Presumably that's why she – or whoever it was,' she added hastily as his mouth began to open, 'telephoned the station, to let me know that she wouldn't be here. And I expect they left a message to say what I should do. Didn't they?'

'Well, so they might've done,' he muttered resentfully, 'only I don't know who you are, do I? I ent going to give messages to people I don't know. Might be someone else's message, mightn't it? I got a responsible position here,' he told her severely, 'and there's a lot of funny people about. Spies and Fifth Columnists and that. You know what the posters say: *Walls Have Ears*. Well, I ent going to give no messages to nobody, not unless I knows who they are, and that's flat.' He sniffed and made to start shovelling again.

Polly reached out and grasped the handle of his spade. 'All right. Perhaps I should have told you who I was. My name's Mrs Dunn, and I'm escorting these two little girls from Portsmouth to their billet at the vicarage here. We were supposed to be met by Mrs Tupper. Now she's not here and I'd like to know if she left any message for me, or whether I should just take Stella and Muriel straight to the vicarage. And I'd like to know quickly, please, because we've been on the train all morning – goodness knows why it took that long, but it did – and I have to hand them over and then go back. *On the train*,' she added, just to make everything clear, and looked him in the eye.

The porter shrugged and looked away. 'Well, that's all right then, because that's what you're supposed to do. Take 'em to the vicarage. It's straight down the lane, by the church. I dare say they're waiting for them there – Mrs Mudge and the vicar, and those boys they've got there already. Pair of rapscallions,' he added vengefully.

Polly looked at him with a mixture of exasperation and

curiosity. 'What do you mean, rapscallions? And why couldn't you give me the message in the first place?'

'I told you, I wasn't giving out no information till I knowed who you was. And all boys is rapscallions, stands to reason, it's their nature. I was, when I was a boy.' He stared at her, as if defying her to doubt that he'd ever been a boy. 'Anyway, you should see what those two gets up to, leading the vicar astray. Man of his age too. Oughter know better.' He shuffled off down the platform, leaning on his spade rather than shovelling with it, and muttering to himself.

What on earth can he mean? Polly wondered, but it was too cold to stand on the platform any longer. She led the two girls out of the station, each carrying a suitcase and festooned with brown paper bags containing their few possessions.

'It can't be too far to the vicarage,' she said encouragingly. 'You can see the church tower there, look, across the fields. But I'm sure we can get there by the lane,' she added as Muriel stared at the cows over the hedge and began to look alarmed.

'They're ever so big close to, aren't they? They're as big as elephants.'

'Well, not quite.' Polly herself had never been quite so close as this to a cow, and was glad they didn't have to go into the field with them. Sylvie must be quite used to them by now, she thought, and sighed. She'd hoped to get over to Ashwood today to see her. If she could have just handed the little girls over to Mrs Tupper, she could have got straight back on to the train. She sighed again.

A small hand slid into hers. 'Is it a big nuisance having to take us to the vicar's house?' Muriel asked, and Polly looked down at her and felt ashamed.

'No, of course it's not. I'll be pleased to see where you're going, and I can tell Mrs Budd I've seen Tim and Keith as well. I can give them the cake she's sent.'

The church tower, which had been over to their left, had

disappeared behind some trees and then, mysteriously, reappeared on their right. I hope it isn't too far, Polly thought. It's so cold and the girls haven't had anything to eat since breakfast. I hope the housekeeper's got something hot for them.

They began to pass a few cottages. There were one or two on their own, then a small row, then some more in pairs. Some were thatched, some had slate roofs, and with the snow covering them like quilts and their gardens a mysterious jumble of white bumps, they looked like a Christmas card. Polly even spotted a robin sitting on a holly bush and pointed it out to the girls. They nodded glumly, too cold, tired and apprehensive to be excited by Christmas cards.

The lane turned again and the tower appeared directly ahead, at the end of the village street. There were cottages on both sides of the road, which widened to a village green with a small pond in the middle. Beside the pond stood a large snowman, and some boys were sliding on a long strip of ice along the edge of the road.

'Well,' Polly said, 'doesn't this look lovely?'

The two girls regarded the scene without enthusiasm. Poor little scraps, they've had enough, Polly thought. But it did look a happy place, with all these cosy-looking cottages and the snow-covered green and the children playing. They'd be better off here, away from the war and all the terrible things that had happened to them. Polly rather wished she could stay herself.

The vicarage was easy to find – a large house, set back from the road in a big garden with lots of trees, close to the church. Polly opened the iron gates and they went up the path. They climbed a few steps to the front door and Polly lifted the knocker.

'I don't like this place,' Muriel said, putting her thumb in her mouth. 'It's too big.'

Before Polly could reply, the door opened and they saw a

woman standing there. She was as tall as Polly but a good deal rounder, with curly grey hair and very bright eyes. She wore a cherry-red jumper and skirt, covered by a flowery apron, and her sleeves were rolled up as if she'd just been mixing cakes or scrubbing a floor. She beamed at them.

'You're here!' She sounded as though this was the moment she'd been looking forward to all day. 'Come in out of the cold. Come through to the kitchen, it's nice and warm and I've got some good stew simmering ready, and a loaf of bread just out of the oven. Here, let me take your coats. My, what pretty little girls. Mr Beckett's going to be so pleased!'

She swept them along the passage and into the kitchen. It was a big room, almost as big as the rooms at the Royal Beach, and its warmth equalled the warmth of the housekeeper's welcome. Polly, finding herself pressed into a large rocking chair by the stove, felt as if she had been wrapped in a comforting eiderdown. She looked at the girls, who had been ensconced on small stools and were now having their wellington boots removed, and hoped they felt the same.

'The boys are out playing in the snow,' the housekeeper continued, warming Muriel's feet between her hands. 'And the vicar's probably with them if I know anything about it! Nothing more than a boy himself, and that's the truth. My name's Mrs Mudge, by the way. I've looked after the vicar for years – me and my hubby both, before he passed away. Anyway, they'll be in soon clamouring for their dinner. You'll have something before you go back, won't you, Mrs . . . ?'

'Dunn,' Polly said. 'Well, if it's not too much trouble. I don't want to take your rations.'

'Rations!' the housekeeper exclaimed, as if she'd never heard the word before. 'You don't want to worry about rations! My stew's all vegetables from the garden – Mr Beckett and me dug over a big patch as soon as all this started. There's a bit of rabbit in it too, that Mr Knight brought round. There's not a single *ration* been near it!'

'Well, it smells delicious,' Polly said, eyeing the pan simmering on the stove. 'And it will be nice to see the boys – I can go back and tell their mother how they are. They're not being too much trouble, I hope?' she added, remembering her official position.

'Trouble? Tim and Keith?' Mrs Mudge laughed. 'Well, they're boys, aren't they – bound to get into a few scrapes. But no, they're no real trouble, no trouble at all, though young Tim's a bit of a live wire. If there's anyone who's trouble in this house, it's not *them*, I can tell you.' She folded her lips and nodded darkly.

Polly looked at her doubtfully, but before she could ask what the housekeeper meant the back door burst open and they could hear excited voices in the scullery beyond the kitchen. Polly recognised the voices of Tim and Keith Budd, whom she'd often seen playing in April Grove when she'd visited her mother, and decided that the deeper tones must belong to Mr Beckett himself. Aware of a sudden nervous tension in the two little girls, she drew them close and stood up as the vicar entered.

'Why, they're arrived!' he exclaimed, rubbing long thin hands together. He came forward hastily, draping a pair of navy-blue woollen gloves over the rail on the front of the stove before holding one of his hands out to Polly and smiling at the girls. 'I was expecting Mrs Tupper.'

'She couldn't come. She's got 'flu. My name's Polly Dunn, I brought the girls from Portsmouth.'

'How kind of you. How very kind.' The vicar beamed at her, then turned to the girls and dropped to one knee so as to be able to look into their faces. He was like a spider, Polly thought, or one of those stick insects they'd once had in the classroom at school – all long, thin arms and legs that looked as if they ought to have at least two elbows or knees each. But his smile was as wide, as joyous and as unforced as a baby's, as if – like Mrs Mudge – he was really pleased and happy to see them.

'How very good to see you both,' he said, taking one of the girls' hands in each of his. 'How very, *very* good to have you here with us. I hope you'll be very happy here.'

They stared back at him without expression. Then Stella said bluntly, 'Our mummy's dead. She was killed by a bomb. And our baby, too.'

There was a brief, appalled silence. Polly put a hand to her burning face. It was a clear reproach, as if to say *'How do you expect us to be happy, here or anywhere else?'* But Mr Beckett didn't seem at all put out by it. He nodded gravely, his smile put away for the moment, and drew them a little closer.

'I know, my dears, and I'm very, very sorry. You must miss her so much. I lost my own mother when I was just the same age as you.'

They looked at him uncertainly. 'Did you?' Stella asked at last.

'Yes, I did. She was riding a horse and it jumped a fence that was too high. She fell off and her back was broken. She never woke up again.' There was a moment of quiet, then he said, 'I was very unhappy about it for a long time. I'm *still* unhappy about it. But do you know what happened? After a while, I found I could still be happy about *other* things. And that will happen to you too, as time goes on. So I hope you'll be very happy here with us – even though I know you'll never stop being unhappy about your mother, and you'll always miss her.'

There was another moment of quiet. Polly was aware of Tim and Keith standing in the doorway, their eyes fixed on the vicar's thin, stooping back. She was struck by the expression in their eyes. It's the sort of look boys only give to someone they really think a lot of, she thought – an older boy or a teacher, or a father – and a sense of warmth stole across her heart.

Muriel took a deep breath. She nodded matter-of-factly

at the vicar, then let go of his hand and looked up at Mrs Mudge.

'I'm hungry,' she said in her small, clear voice. 'Can we have our dinner now?'

The rabbit stew was, Polly thought, the best meal she had eaten for months. It was followed by a rice pudding and then Mrs Mudge made a large pot of tea and set it on the middle of the table.

'You children can go and play now,' she said. 'Put your wellingtons on, and your coats and scarves. Have both you girls got gloves?'

'Mittens,' Stella said, holding them up. 'Auntie Jess knitted them. She was teaching me,' she added proudly.

'Well, that's good. I'll go on teaching you, then. We can do with some more knitters around here to make things for soldiers and sailors.' Mrs Mudge buttoned Muriel into her coat. 'Tim and Keith will take you out and show you their snowman, won't you, boys? And you can go for a walk round the village. The boys know most of the people here now, so you don't need to worry about anything. You look after them, now, boys.'

Tim, who had been talking about a snowball fight that had been arranged between the evacuees and the village children, looked somewhat disgruntled by this instruction, but the vicar gave him a firm look and he went without argument. In any case, Stella, who had recovered her normal assertiveness, was already taking charge. 'We'll look at the snowman first,' she was saying as they went out through the back door, 'and then you can take us to look at that pond. There were some boys sliding near it . . .'

The door closed behind them and Mr Beckett smiled. 'I foresee a few battles there. Tim won't like being bossed about by a girl, and that's the boys' slide.'

Polly grinned back. 'Not now Stella's here. I haven't known her long, but I can tell you this – anything a boy can do, Stella can do better! I don't think you'll have any problems getting her to settle, Mr Beckett. I'm not so sure about Muriel, though. Stella mothers her a lot, but she's a sensitive little girl and she's been through so much in this past year. She may need some extra care.'

'Well, she's come to the right place for that,' Mr Beckett said, warming his long, thin hands round his cup of tea. 'Mrs Mudge and I have had quite a lot of experience in looking after children now, haven't we, Mrs Mudge? I think both those little girls will settle in very well. They can be safe and happy, and forget about war now. They can be children again, as God intended them to be.'

Polly glanced at the housekeeper and was surprised to catch the expression on her face. She was looking at the vicar in just the same way as Tim and Keith had looked at him when he was talking to the little girls. As if she thought the world of him. And there was an added tenderness in her face that reminded Polly of Jess Budd, when she looked at the photograph of her two sons.

Tenderness, and indulgence for boys and their ways. But Mr Beckett wasn't a boy. He was an elderly man.

Polly finished her tea and thanked them both before gathering together her coat and gloves and getting ready to walk back to the station for the return journey to Portsmouth. As they went outside, she saw the four children careering madly round the big garden, hurling snowballs at each other. One caught Mr Beckett on the shoulder and as Polly gasped in dismay he chuckled and bent to gather up a handful of snow.

'I'll show you!' he yelled, flinging a huge snowball that caught Tim full in the chest. 'I'll show the lot of you!'

Polly and Mrs Mudge looked at each other, and the housekeeper raised her eyes to heaven and spread out her hands.

'Boys!' she said. 'They never grow up . . .'

Chapter Nine

When Polly reached the station the aged porter told her that there wouldn't be a Portsmouth train for another two hours.

'That's if it comes at all,' he added, with some satisfaction. 'Never know where you are with the times these days.'

'Two hours!' Polly looked at the station clock and wondered what to do. She didn't like to go back to the vicarage, even though she was sure Mrs Mudge would be kindness itself, and it was too cold to stand on the icy platform all that time. I suppose I'll just have to go for a walk, she thought. But it'll be getting dark in an hour or so . . .

As she stood there, gazing at the unhelpful face of the porter, she heard the whistle of an approaching train and turned quickly. To her disappointment, it was heading away from Portsmouth, towards Salisbury. A sudden idea struck her.

'Does that train stop at Ashwood? The little halt just before Romsey?'

'It do,' he admitted unwillingly.

'Then I'll get on that and catch the Portsmouth train back from there,' she said. 'I can go and see my daughter.'

'You'll need a ticket.'

'Well, you can sell me one, can't you? A return ticket? Then I can come back here and use my Portsmouth return for the rest of the journey. Hurry *up*,' she urged him as the train drew up at the platform. The guard got out and she waved to him. 'Don't go yet, please! I'm just buying a ticket!' The porter, evidently unable to think of any reason why not, was shuffling reluctantly towards his little office and she ran after him. 'Oh, *please* hurry!'

Begrudgingly, he made out the ticket and Polly handed him the money and ran out on to the platform again. The guard was holding a door open and she leaped aboard and threw herself down into a seat. For once, the train wasn't crowded and there was only one other person in the compartment – a man with wavy, iron-grey hair brushed back from a broad forehead, wearing a shabby greatcoat and khaki woollen gloves. He grinned at her as she flung herself down, and said, 'You only just made it, love.'

Polly looked at him. His voice was deep and warm, with a London accent, and he had a good-natured face, with three corrugated lines on his forehead that somehow added to the twinkle in his dark brown eyes. She smiled back.

'I didn't think the man was going to let me have a ticket. He doesn't seem to like passengers.'

'I 'spect he thinks they make the station look untidy,' the man said. 'You can't see what it's like now, with all the snow and ice, but in spring and summer it's a real picture. He wins prizes for the Best Station Garden – I reckon he thinks trains and passengers are a bit of a nuisance. They get in the way of his garden!'

Polly laughed. 'Well, you'd think he'd have been glad to get rid of me, then. I just think he wanted to be awkward.'

There was a slight pause and then the man said, 'You don't live at Bridge End, then?'

Polly shook her head. 'No, I'm from Portsmouth. I've just been taking two little girls to an evacuation billet.'

He looked concerned. 'But this train ain't going to Portsmouth – it's just come from there. You're going the wrong way, love.'

'No, I'm going on to Ashwood to see my own little girl. There isn't a train back to Portsmouth for two hours, so I thought I'd take the chance. It's only a short journey – I'll just have time to see her before I have to go back. I haven't seen her since Christmas,' she added wistfully, 'and a lot's happened since then.'

'You're telling me.' The corrugated lines on his forehead deepened a little. 'Had a big raid in Pompey last month, didn't you? Were you there through that?'

Polly nodded. 'We were bombed out.' She stopped suddenly, wondering if she had said too much, then decided that even if spies or Fifth Columnists were listening there wasn't much worth reporting back to Hitler about the fact that the Taylors and Polly Dunn had been bombed out, or that little Stella and Muriel Simmons had been sent to Bridge End. All the same, you never knew who you might be talking to and she resolved to watch her words. Portsmouth was an important city and almost any snippet of information might be of use to the enemy.

'Bombed out?' he echoed. 'Here, that's rough. Were you inside the house, or did you manage to get to a shelter?'

'Oh yes, we always went down there. We lost everything, but at least we were all right. We're lucky too, because we could go and stay with my mother. And Sylvie – my little girl – was already out in the country so she wasn't there.'

He shook his head. 'Bloody awful, all the same, if you'll pardon my French.' He glanced at her uniform. 'I see you're in the WVS.'

'Yes, I am,' Polly said, pleased that he had recognised it. 'You know about the WVS, then?'

The man laughed. 'I ought to! My sister works at the Headquarters in London – 41 Tothill Street. She never stops telling me about all the good work they do – if I wasn't a man she'd have recruited me long ago. Mind you, she's right – they do wonderful work. All the things nobody else will do.'

'Well, we're not dogsbodies,' Polly said, 'but I suppose it's true that there just doesn't seem to be anyone else to do a lot of the jobs we take on. But that's because in wartime there are a lot of new jobs to do, like taking children out to the country – it just doesn't happen in peacetime.'

''S right. And we're lucky there are women like you ready to do them.' He grinned at her. 'Tell you what, I reckon this war'll be won by you women. Not by fighting, I don't mean that, but 'cause you're always there on the spot, ready to do whatever's needed to keep the country running. Look at all the young girls who're joining up now, so that the men can go and fight – and all the others like the WVS and that, doing all sorts of work, driving buses and ambulances, farming, you name it – and still managing to keep homes going for their menfolk and kiddies.' He nodded. 'Without them, I reckon the war would've been lost from the very start.'

Polly gazed at him. 'You really mean that?'

'I do. I really do.' Their eyes met and Polly felt a thrill of warmth touch her heart. The man looked out of the window. 'Here, look, we're just coming into Ashwood now. Well, it's been a real pleasure to meet you, love.' He smiled at her again and, as the train slowed down, leaned out to open the door. 'I hope you find your kiddy OK,' he said, 'and good luck. Don't get bombed out again, will you!'

Polly laughed and stepped down on to the platform. 'I'll try not to. Goodbye, and thank you for the things you've said. It's nice to be appreciated.'

'Oh, you are, love,' he said, and his eyes met hers again. 'You don't have to worry about that. You really are.'

The train set off again with a loud snort from the engine, and Polly stood on the platform waving as it steamed off along the track. It rounded a bend and disappeared from sight and she let her arm drop with a sigh. A nice man, she thought. The sort of man you could feel comfortable with. A pity she would never see him again.

All the same, he'd more than made up for the old porter's cantankerousness, and the station clock told her that she had an hour and a half before the Portsmouth train was due.

Sylvie's billet was in a farmhouse only ten minutes' walk away. She would be just coming back from school now, and certain to be there. With a leap of excitement in her heart, Polly turned to walk briskly out of the station, and forgot about the man in the fawn greatcoat, with the warm dark eyes and the corrugated forehead.

'So I had over an hour with her,' Polly told the family later when she finally arrived back at April Grove. 'It was lovely – she was *so* excited to see me. And the people she's billeted with, Mr and Mrs Sutton, they couldn't be nicer. They've got two other evacuees there too, a brother and sister; the boy's Sylvie's age and the girl's a bit older. Jenny and Brian, they're called. They were all playing Ludo when I got there.'

'I didn't know there were other children there,' Cissie said. 'Sylvie's never mentioned them in her letters.'

'Well, you know Sylvie's letters, they're not much more than *Dear Mummy, I hope you're well, I'm well, I hope Granny's well . . .*' Polly said, laughing. 'After all, she can't write all that much. But these two haven't been there long. They were sent out after the Blitz, apparently, like Stella and Muriel.'

'And d'you think they'll settle in all right?' Judy asked. She'd spent most of the day trying to sort out other hasty evacuations. 'We've had complaints from a few people. Some of the parents think their children aren't being looked after properly and some of the country hosts say the children are so badly behaved they can't put up with them. Mostly ones from Rudmore and areas like that,' she added.

'Everyone knows what a slum Rudmore is,' Alice remarked. 'Though they're the salt of the earth just the same. And I dare say there's a few from Old Portsmouth too, with backsides hanging out of their trousers and no shoes. Look at the Hodges family who came here just before the war started. They lived in a pub in Old Portsmouth, so

Tommy Vickers told me, and didn't have a penny to bless themselves with. Mr Hodges works down the Camber dock, steady enough work but you know what the pay's like. And that boy of theirs, the older one – Gordon – you could see from the start he'd be a troublemaker. Got mixed up straight away with Micky Baxter, and now he's in an approved school for pinching stuff from an antique shop. You remember that, don't you? Caused a real rumpus in April Grove.'

'Don't understand why they didn't send Micky away too,' Dick said. 'He was in it just as much as the older one. Wasn't there a younger boy, too?'

Alice nodded. 'Sammy. He's not a bad little chap, helped his mum a lot before she died. Mr Hodges couldn't manage at all after that, left the kiddy on his own for two or three days at a time. If it hadn't been for Freda Vickers giving him his dinners I don't know what would have happened. Anyway, Tommy went down the billeting offices in the end and they took Sammy out to Bridge End, where the other youngsters went.'

'It looks a nice village,' Polly said. 'The vicar's a real gentleman, a bit odd but you expect that of a vicar, don't you, and his housekeeper Mrs Mudge is a proper motherly soul. Stella and Muriel'll be all right there.'

They were just finishing up the tea left in the pot when the familiar wail of the siren rose in the air. It had sounded almost every night since the Blitz, but the raids hadn't been as bad as on that terrible night. All the same, you couldn't take chances and there was a hasty gathering up of coats, blankets and the tin box that contained all the important household papers – insurances, birth certificates and so on – and within five minutes they were all in the Anderson shelter at the bottom of the garden, huddling on the bunks Dick and Terry had fitted there. Dick lit the hurricane lamp and they all looked at each other and shrugged.

'Might as well have a game of cards,' Cissie said, but Polly shook her head.

'I'm going down to the Emergency Centre. I said I would, if there was a raid. What about you, Judy?'

Judy nodded. Like Polly, she was still wearing her WVS uniform. 'You'll be all right here, won't you, Mum? You've got Dad and Gran with you.'

'I'm not worried about us,' Cissie said anxiously. 'It's you, going through the streets in the blackout, in the middle of a raid. Surely they can't expect you to do that?'

'Someone's got to, Mum,' Judy said. 'We were glad enough of the Centre when we got bombed out. Anyway, if we go quickly we'll be there before the planes come – and they might not even be coming here, this time.'

There had been alarms almost every night since the big raid, and a few bombs dropped on the city and its outskirts, but there had never been as much damage again, and nobody had been hurt. More often, the planes went over on their way to London or some other city. You still had to take shelter, just in case, but Portsmouth people were beginning to hope they'd had their share.

'I feel sorry, leaving Cissie like that,' Polly remarked as they groped their way through the pitch-black streets. 'She's always been a bit nervous, but we've got to do our bit.' She grabbed Judy's arm as they heard the first drone of enemy aircraft approaching. 'Oh Lord – here they come!'

They flattened themselves against a wall, staring up at the sky. It was criss-crossed with the long swords of the searchlights, and now and then the dark shape of a plane, high above, was caught in the shining white beam. Immediately, a rattle of ack-ack fire would break out from one or more of the gun emplacements around the city – on Southsea Common, or the slopes of Portsdown Hill – and once the two women saw a burst of orange as a plane was hit, and the streak of flame like a ribbon as it fell to earth.

'Suppose it fell on buildings?' Judy whispered, but she

knew that the gun crews couldn't think of that. It was too important to destroy the plane and its deadly cargo, for if it were allowed to go on its way, many more buildings might be demolished and people killed.

'Come on,' Polly murmured, giving her arm a little tug. 'We're not far away from the Centre now. Let's get there as quickly as we can.'

The Centre was an old church, and its crypt was being used as a shelter. Polly and Judy reached it safely and scrambled down the steps. The basement was already crowded with people, and there were a few hurricane lamps set about, lighting their faces eerily. At the far end someone had set up a long trestle table, and a WVS volunteer was busy with a large steaming urn.

'You can spread this bread with margarine and fish paste,' she directed the two newcomers. 'We're not expecting too much trouble tonight, but you never know. Here, aren't you Alice Thomas's girls? You know me – Mrs Chapman, from the bottom of October Street.'

'Yes, of course.' Polly started to slice the bread. 'The house with the turret. How's your Olive now?'

'Oh, not so bad, considering. She's still cut up about losing the baby, of course, but she's not letting it get her down. Gone back to work at Derek's dad's place, just like before.'

They worked busily, making cocoa and sandwiches. A lot of the people there had no shelters – in some streets, because of the way the water mains and sewers were laid, it was impossible to dig the hole needed for an Anderson, so those who lived there had to go to street shelters or Centres like this. Mostly, they brought their own food and drink with them, but there had to be plenty on tap for anyone who was bombed out, or brought in as casualties. There were First-Aid workers too, and ARP wardens popping in and out to bring news, glad of a hot drink and a 'wad', so one way and another they were kept busy enough even if there were no bombs.

Peggy Shaw, who lived next door to Jess Budd, joined them and began talking about her daughter Gladys, who drove an ambulance. 'Well, a bread-van, to be honest, converted. She's on standby all the time in air raids. And it's not just driving, neither. She got a kiddy out of a ruined cellar in the Blitz, saved her life, she did. Dug some poor boy out of a pile of rubble, took I don't know how many to hospital, and then came home for a wash, changed her clothes and went straight off to work.'

Peggy shook her head. 'I had to hand it to her, I did really.'

'But you must have been worried to death,' Annie said 'knowing she was out in all that bombing.'

Peggy laughed. 'Worried? I was out there with her! And I can tell you this, there was no time for worrying – no more than you had when you were sorting out all the people who got bombed out.' She picked up a fresh loaf and held it against her chest as she sliced it. 'Anyway, there's no use worrying, is there? If a bomb's got your name on it, it'll find you, wherever you are. That's what I think. Doesn't matter whether you're down the air-raid shelter or standing on top of the Guildhall like Tommy Vickers was that night. If it's got your name on it, it'll find you.'

Polly glanced up as a plane snarled overhead. There had been several explosions already, and the roar of aircraft had been increasing. The rattle of ack-ack fire came from Portsdown Hill. 'I don't know about you,' she said, 'but it seems to me it's getting worse.'

They all lifted their heads and listened for a moment. There were obviously a lot of planes overhead, their nasal snarl unmistakable as German craft. At that moment, a tremendous explosion rocked the hall, and Judy put out a hand involuntarily to Polly's arm. They looked at each other.

'You're right,' Annie Chapman said grimly. 'This is going to be a bad one. It'll be more than cocoa and hot soup we'll be needing before it's over. Here come the first ones now, look.'

People had begun to straggle into the hall. There were already plenty who had come in for shelter when the siren had first sounded, but these were men and women, and children too, who looked frightened and bewildered. Some were covered with dust and others were injured, limping or holding their arms, or with blood running down their faces and staining their clothes. Polly, who had just finished a First-Aid course, went over at once to take charge.

'She's as good as my Gladys,' Peggy said, watching her. 'Hey-up, what's happening now?'

The door burst open and one of the Rover Scouts, the older members of the Boy Scouts who ran messages between the Centres, came panting in.

'They want someone to go and open an Incident Centre in Portsea,' he told them. 'It's bad down there – any amount of places bombed. People all over the place, don't know what to do. A copper sent me on my bike to fetch someone to take charge.' He looked from Annie to Judy. 'Come *on*!'

'All right, young man, no need to get so aeriated,' Annie said severely. She started to take off her apron. 'I'd better go.'

'No, I will. I can run faster.' Judy was pulling on her coat and hat as she spoke. She looked at the boy. 'Or I'll ride your bike, and you can do the running.'

'But it's got a crossbar!'

'So what? Think I can't manage it? I've been riding my brother's bike since I was ten years old.' She hustled him out of the church and grabbed the handlebars of his bike, hoisting up her skirt to cock her leg over the bar. 'Which way?'

Portsea was, as the Scout had said, badly bombed. The streets presented the now familiar sight of ruined houses, rubble-blocked roads, fire engines and ambulances – and pathetic knots of people huddled together in shocked bewilderment, or wandering in a daze, calling out for family members or friends.

'Joanie! Where's our Joanie?'

'My Fred – has anyone seen my Fred?'

Others were scrabbling desperately at piles of rubble. 'Our Brenda's down there somewhere; she was under the stairs and it's all fell in on top of her. Oh my *God*, my *God*, she'll be killed. We've got to get her out! *Help* me, for God's sake, *help* me. Our Brenda's in there, our *Brenda*!'

The Scout pushed Judy past them and through a doorway. The building had been a small church with a meeting-room at the back. The windows had been shattered but the glass had been safely caught by the criss-crossing of brown paper and the thick blackout curtains, and it was otherwise intact. Judy cast a nervous glance at the remaining walls, wondering what damage had been done to them unseen, and if another blast was all that was needed to bring them tumbling down. But there was nowhere else fit to use, and already a short, chubby man in an overcoat and dog-collar was setting up trestle tables and brushing dust off them with his sleeve.

'I'm WVS,' Judy said, joining him. 'Judy Taylor. I've come to set up an Incident Enquiry Centre.'

'Oh, bless you, it's so good to see you.' He grasped her hand briefly in his. 'Look, we've started to take information – the wardens are bringing in news all the time. They tell us which Emergency Centre people have gone to, or which hospital. Then, as people come in to enquire about their family and friends, we know where to direct them.' He shook his head. 'All too often, it's the mortuary, I'm afraid. Let's see if we can get an urn of tea on the go; there's nothing like a cup of hot sweet tea for shock. Where have you come from, my dear?'

'Copnor.' Judy felt a pang of anxiety, wondering how her

parents and grandmother were faring amongst all the bombing. The noise now was almost unbearable, each explosion sending shock waves through the ground and up through your whole body. Even bombs falling a mile or more away could be felt – and Portsmouth was a small area, the island of Portsea on which it was situated only five miles long and half as wide. Every now and then there was a duller thud which meant a bomb had landed in one of the two harbours, sending mud and sea water flying into the air. Portsdown Hill, to the north, was alight with incendiary bombs.

However, there was no time for thinking about the family, or bombs, or anything but the people who were straggling into the meeting-room, their faces lost and confused. Another woman had arrived, who seemed to know the clergyman and to be familiar with the battered tea urn, so Judy left her to it and sat down at one of the tables, drawing a sheet of paper towards her.

'You'll need to go to the Emergency Centre – there's one about half a mile away. If you're not hurt, you'd best get into a shelter until the raid's over, and then go. Give me your name first, in case anyone comes looking for you . . . There's a First-Aid Post at the infants' school round the corner – take him there and they'll bandage him up and see if he needs to go to hospital. Give me your name and address first.'

An air-raid warden pushed past the queue and bent to speak in her ear. He gave her a scrap of paper, covered with dirty fingerprints, and Judy read it quickly. She looked at him in consternation.

'You think his parents will come in here?'

'More'n likely, ducks. They'll be looking for him, see? Stands to reason, dunnit. You'll have to tell 'em.'

Judy bit her lip and looked down again at the scrap of paper. It bore the details of a child found dead in the street – a boy of no more than three years old, horribly injured, who must have run from a bombed house and then been caught by a second explosion. There was a brief description – chubby, with fair, curly hair, wearing blue pyjamas and still clutching a teddy-bear. The body had been taken to the local morgue.

Tears came to Judy's eyes but the warden had already gone, called by a shout from the doorway. The next minute, someone was standing before her holding out a length of thick string. The other end was attached to a wire-haired terrier of some indeterminate breed, leaping and barking hysterically.

'Found 'im wandering about outside, miss. The ARP man said to bring 'im in 'ere.'

Judy glanced helplessly at the clergyman, who nodded briskly. 'Put him in the church, my dear. We've already got quite a menagerie in there.' He turned away to attend to someone else and Judy took the makeshift lead and dragged the frantic dog through the door leading into the main church where, as the minister had said, there were already several animals including two black cats who leaped up on to the altar and began spit and hiss furiously.

'I hope to goodness you don't all get free and start fighting,' Judy muttered, tying the dog to the leg of a pew. The church was very plain, with little ornamentation, and she hadn't even known it was here until this evening. She found two large cardboard boxes and having – with some difficulty – caught the two terrified cats, she crammed them in and then hurried back to the meeting-room where a queue of people was building up, some wanting to know where they should go, some desperate to find family or friends they had lost.

Judy recorded all the new arrivals and checked her list to see if the missing had already been sent on.

'Yes, he had a head injury, they took him to the Royal. No, it didn't look too bad, really . . . A black cat? Yes, we've had two brought in. They're in boxes in the church through that door, but please be careful not to let any of the other animals out ... The whole family were sent to the Emergency Centre – yes, they're all quite safe, not hurt at all ... A little boy?' She looked up, her heart sinking, and saw the fear in the face of the woman standing before her.

'He's called Bobbie,' the woman said. Her voice was rough, her eyes huge and dark, her cheeks drawn with fear. 'We were in the shelter – next door was hit. I looked out to see what was going on, and he just slipped past me. He hated being in the shelter. I couldn't find him nowhere, and then another bomb ...' She stopped, the tears running down her face, and stared at Judy piteously. 'Has he been brought in here, miss? Have you seen him?'

Judy swallowed, not knowing how to find the words to tell her. 'Was – was he wearing blue pyjamas?' she asked, praying that the woman would say no. But she nodded her head and with a sick sense of doom, Judy went on. 'And – and did – does he have fair, curly hair? And – and a teddy-bear?'

'Yes! Yes, he never goes anywhere without it, screams the place down if we take it away! Oh, where is he, where's my Bobbie?' the woman cried eagerly, and then her voice faded to a whisper and she stared at Judy with terror in her eyes. *Where is he?*

'I'm dreadfully sorry,' Judy said wretchedly. 'It might not be your little boy – I didn't see him myself – but the warden told me there was a little boy like that found a few streets away ...'

'Where is he? Tell me!' The woman leaned forward. 'For God's sake! *Tell me where my Bobbie is!*'

'It might not be him,' Judy repeated. 'But the – the little boy the warden told me about – they had to take him to the – the mortuary.' She bit her lips, angry with herself for breaking the news so badly, for not being able to find the right words. 'I – I'm so sorry. He couldn't have known anything about it.'

'The *mortuary*? You mean he's *dead*?'

Judy nodded miserably, tears filling her eyes. The woman stared at her. Then she banged her fist on the table. 'My Bobbie? *Dead*?' She stared wildly at Judy. 'But he was only *three.* It was his birthday last week – I made him a cake. He *can't* be dead. He can't, he can't, he *can't*. I won't let him be dead!' Her voice rose to a shriek and she turned and began to scream at the queue. 'I won't *let* him be dead! I won't, I *won't*!'

'I'm very sorry,' Judy said, crying almost as much as the woman herself. 'It's terrible. I'm very, very sorry.'

The clergyman came round the table and laid a hand gently on the woman's shoulder. 'Come along, my dear. Come and sit over here for a few minutes. I'll bring you a cup of tea. Then I'll go with you to see if it is your little boy. Come along . . .'

She stared at him, and for a moment Judy was afraid she was going to hit him. Then her face crumpled, and she covered it with her hands and began to weep. She allowed him to lead her into a corner, where she sank on to a chair, sobbing as if her heart were broken. Which, Judy thought, it probably was.

She watched them ruefully. Well, a fine job I made of *that*, I don't think! she told herself. She groped for a hanky and rubbed her face fiercely, then looked up to see who was next in the queue.

The raid became known as Portsmouth's Second Blitz. Thousands of incendiaries and nearly three hundred high-explosive bombs were dropped on the city. Fourteen hundred people were made homeless, just under a hundred killed and over two hundred injured. Had it not been for the shelters, there would have been many, many more.

Polly and Judy met as they both made their way wearily along September Street. They stopped for a moment, tears of thankfulness filling their eyes as they hugged. 'I've been so worried,' Polly said, and Judy gave a shaky laugh. 'I was just going to say the same thing!' Their eyes met, and each knew what the other was thinking. What had been happening in April Grove?

Stumbling with fatigue, they continued along the street. The shops were already beginning to open. Mrs Marsh was polishing the dairy windows, and Alice Brunner was opening the door of the newsagent's to take in a pile of newspapers. She looked tired and unhappy, and Judy remembered that her husband Heinrich had been interned as an alien. They said good morning to her and she nodded, a wavery smile briefly lighting her pale face.

'It doesn't look as if there's been any damage round here,' Polly said as they turned down October Street. Near the bottom, the ruin of Kathy Simmons's house made an ugly gap between the houses, but apart from a few slates in the road and a broken window or two, there seemed to be nothing worse. With a sigh of relief, they turned the corner at the bottom and saw that number nine was still intact.

'Oh, thank goodness,' Judy said, and nearly ran the last few steps, eager to be indoors with her family again. With Polly close behind her, she unlocked the door and went inside.

Cissie was hurrying along the passage to meet them, her face drawn.

'Don't look like that, Mum,' Judy said. 'We're back safe and sound.'

'It's not that,' Cissie said, her voice shaking. 'It's your dad. He's having an asthma attack – a bad one. I think he needs to go to the hospital.'

Chapter Ten

Polly took one look at Dick, who was sitting hunched over the dining table, gasping desperately for breath, then turned round and went straight down to Peggy Shaw's house, where she and Gladys were just crawling into bed. Gladys put on her clothes and came out again, dashing off through the streets to fetch the converted baker's van. Alice had been out in the scullery making tea, and they all had a quick cup while they waited. By the time Gladys came back, Judy and her mother were bending over Dick, trying to get him to breathe out by pressing on the sides of his chest.

'Can't – breathe,' he wheezed, his eyes filled with panic. 'Got to – get me – *breath*. Ahh – ahh – ahh . . .'

'You've got to breathe *out*, lovey,' Cissie urged him, pressing harder as he tried ineffectually to shake her off. 'You know that's what the doctor said. You can't get any more breath in, you've got to let it out first. Now calm down, Dick, and try – please, just for me.'

'Can't – *breathe*,' he wheezed again. '*Cis*.' He stared at her with pleading, terrified eyes and beat feebly on the table with his hands. 'Cis!'

'It's all right, Dick.' She spoke calmly, trying to still her own panic. Dick had had enough attacks over the years for the family to become accustomed to them, but they were always frightening. You could see that Dick was afraid he was never going to be able to breathe again, and when he was as bad as this Cissie feared that he might be right. She pressed his chest again, signalling to Judy to do the same and suddenly Dick began to cough, his thin body torn with the violence of his retching. A gobbet of dark yellow phlegm spat out of his mouth and landed on the tablecloth, and they stared at it in horror. It was tinged with black dust, like soot, and there were streaks of blood in it as well.

'Dad!' Judy gasped, and looked wildly round for Polly. 'Is Gladys coming? He's got to go to hospital!'

'She's here.' Polly came in swiftly, followed by Gladys Shaw. 'Come on, Dick – let's get you out to the ambulance.' She helped Judy and Cissie lift him to his feet.

Dick, still wrenched with coughing, was trying frantically to breathe. He leaned on the table, his face almost blue.

'Hot,' he gasped. 'Too hot.' He tried to throw off the blankets, but Cissie firmly wrapped them round him again.

'You've got a temperature,' she said anxiously. 'If you take all those off you'll catch a chill. Come on, now, let's get you outside.'

'Keep him wrapped up,' Polly said, 'it's bitter out here.' They half carried him along the passage to the front door and lifted him into the van. 'That's it, Dick. You'll be all right now. Shall I come with you, Cis?'

'No, you stop here, you need your rest.' But it was clear that Cissie needed company. Polly and Judy glanced at each other, and Judy said quickly, 'I'll go, you've been up all night and you were travelling all day yesterday. Look, I'll get to work as soon as I can, but you can explain if I'm late. I can't leave Mum by herself.'

'No, she's got to have one of us.' Polly chewed her lips. Gladys had started the engine and was in the driver's seat now, impatient to be off, and Polly leaned in through the window. 'I just hope to God they'll take him in at the hospital. They must be crowded out with casualties as it is. Knock on the door when you get back, Gladys, would you? And thanks for turning out again.'

Gladys nodded and Judy jumped up beside her. Cissie was already in the back, kneeling beside the makeshift bed.

The van jolted off down the road and Polly and her mother went back indoors.

'I dunno,' Alice said, sitting down and picking up the cup of tea she'd poured before Gladys had arrived. 'It's just one thing after another. I've never seen Dick as bad as that, never. This tea's gone cold.'

'I'll make you some more,' Polly said. 'It's all these nights down the shelter. It's so cold and damp, it's bound to set him off. And then the worry of it all. He's never got over what happened to him in the Great War, you know. It brings it all back, hearing the planes go over and bombs falling. It was a bad raid tonight, too – as bad as that big one in January, I wouldn't wonder.'

Alice nodded. 'Don't trouble about the tea, Poll. I can't be bothered. I just want to go to bed, though whether I'll be able to sleep is another matter.'

She went into the front room. They'd got a bed-settee in there now, bought with the money Cissie and Dick had been given for being bombed out. It was more comfortable than the old sofa and could be folded away during the day. Polly heard it creak a bit as Alice got into it, and then silence.

She sat gazing at the ashes in the grate, her coat pulled round her shoulders for warmth, thinking over the long day. It seemed a lifetime since she'd collected young Stella and Muriel from Jess Budd and taken them on the train. Then there'd been the surly porter and the walk to the vicarage through the snowy lanes, and the warm welcome given them by Mrs Mudge and the vicar. That rabbit stew had been the best Polly had tasted for a long time – and not a 'ration' in it, she thought, smiling. And then there'd been the sudden decision to go on to Romsey to see Sylvie, the pleasant man on the train, and the joy of seeing her daughter again, even though it meant the pain of parting only an hour later.

'I wish you could come out and stay here too,' Sylvie had whispered, burying her face against Polly's coat. 'I miss you ever so much.'

'I miss you too,' Polly had said, brushing away the tears before they fell on to Sylvie's blonde curls. 'But I've got work to do in Portsmouth, and it's safer for you to be out here. And you're having a nice time, aren't you? Mr and Mrs Sutton are looking after you well, and you've got Jenny and Brian to play with.'

'They're all right,' Sylvie said dismissively, for all the world as if she hadn't been engrossed in a game of Ludo with them when Polly had arrived. 'But I'd rather be home with you.'

'Well, I expect all the children feel like that. And let's hope it won't be long before you can come back.' Gently, Polly unwound the child's fingers from her coat. 'Now, give me a big kiss and say you'll be a good girl for Mummy, and I'll come back and see you as soon as I possibly can. And tell Mrs Sutton I'll write again soon.'

Sylvie nodded and sniffed hard. A large tear rolled out of her eye and down her cheek. Polly bit her lips fiercely, hugged her and then turned away. She closed the kitchen door behind her and walked swiftly down the garden path.

It must be the hardest thing anyone has to do in this war, she thought, feeling the ache of tears in her throat again as she stared at the cold ashes. Saying goodbye to your children. It must be just as bad when they're grown up too, and going off to fight like Terry, serving on one of Britain's biggest battle cruisers, and Annie Chapman's boy Colin. Just as bad as saying goodbye to your husband, not knowing whether you'll ever see him again. And knowing, when that telegram comes, that you've said goodbye for the last time ever.

The sorrow of it all – of leaving her little girl with strangers, however kind, of losing her husband at sea, of knowing that this anguish was multiplied a thousand times up and down the country, and now, on top of it all, the worry over Dick – surged over her like a tidal wave and, worn out by her day and by a hopeless, overwhelming misery, Polly put down her head and wept.

'It's pneumonia,' Cissie said later to Freda Vickers, who had called to ask how Dick was. 'Well, what can you expect, with his lungs being so bad anyway. They were ever so kind – stretchers and injured people everywhere, but they still took him in straight away and put him in an oxygen tent. Wouldn't let me and Judy stop, of course. Said I could go in and see him at visiting time – that's three this afternoon.' She blinked away tears. 'I don't know as they can do much for him, though. I mean, there's not much you *can* do for pneumonia, is there? Only keep him warm and look after him till the crisis happens, and even then it can go either way.'

'I think they can drain the fluid off from his lungs, can't they?' Freda said doubtfully. 'Stop it building up, like. And if he's on oxygen, that'll help the breathing. Anyway, he's in the best place, Cis. At least he won't have to spend any more nights in a hole in the ground for a while.'

Cissie sighed. 'That's true, but I shall worry all the time, not knowing what's happening to him. I hope we don't get any raids while he's in there.' She turned as they heard the tapping of high heels coming along the pavement behind them, and nodded at the woman in a powder-blue suit and feathery hat. 'Morning, Mrs Glaister.'

Ethel Glaister gave them both a cool look. 'Good morning,' she said in her rather sharp voice. 'I'm surprised you've got time to stand gossiping after a night like last night. I'm going up to the butcher's shop – he had some fresh stewing steak brought in yesterday, I've heard, and I mean to get some.'

'Mum's gone up there already,' Cissie said. 'And Mrs Vickers just called to enquire after my hubby. He was taken into hospital with pneumonia this morning.'

'Oh.' Ethel Glaister looked slightly taken aback. 'Well, I

hope he'll soon be better. Of course, he doesn't work, does he?' She stepped past them, leaving the two women open-mouthed.

'Well!' Cissie said at last. 'And just what do you suppose she meant by that? That he's some sort of parasite? No loss if he doesn't get better? I've a good mind to go after her and give her a piece of my mind!'

'She's not worth it,' Freda said, although she looked equally indignant. 'And I don't suppose she meant anything by it, not really. She's just got to say something and she can't help saying it in a nasty way. That's Ethel Glaister all over.'

'Well, you won't catch me giving her the time of day again,' Cissie said, turning away. 'Anyway, I'm going in now – I thought I might have a bit of a lay-down. If I'm going to see Dick this afternoon I want to look a bit brighter for him. I caught sight of myself in the mirror just now and I look like death warmed up.'

She went indoors and stood for a moment looking around the room where she had grown up. It still felt funny to be back, with so many of the neighbours she had known as a child. Ethel Glaister, who had always thought herself a cut above the rest of April Grove – Granny Kinch and her daughter Nancy, who most people thought were a cut below – and good, friendly people like Freda and her husband Tommy, and Peggy Shaw and her daughters, and Jess and Frank Budd. It was a good place to be, she thought. And there were so many streets like this in Pompey – streets of small terraced houses, where families lived all their lives and got to know each other, always ready to help out, with just the odd one or two like the Glaisters and the Kinches and Baxters, who didn't quite fit in with the rest yet were still part of the pattern. So many streets like this, in every city in the land.

We may not have much, Cissie thought, going upstairs to lie down on the bed she and Dick shared, but we've got a lot more than some. We've got ourselves – family, friends and neighbours. That's what you need most in times like these.

Judy had gone to work straight from the hospital. There was so much to do that she felt that even if she did go to bed she wouldn't rest. Getting there through the newly bombed streets was the usual problem and she wondered if Polly would like the idea of looking for a couple of second-hand bikes so that they could cycle to Southsea. It would be better than having to rely on the uncertain bus service.

As usual after a raid, the casualty station on the ground floor was frantically busy and there was plenty to be done for those who had come looking for help, grumbling as always about having to trek all the way out to Southsea where the nobs were living in luxury in one of the best hotels. The staff were used to these complaints by now and tried to ignore them and get on with the business as cheerfully as possible, understanding that most of the grumblers were shocked and bewildered by what had happened to them.

As she came through the front door, Judy had encountered the young Observer she had met in the lift a few weeks earlier. The staff were accustomed to seeing the RAF uniforms about the building now, and knew most of them by sight, if not by name. Judy had discovered that most of them – the night staff in particular – were volunteers, with other jobs during the day, and her antagonism had faded. She looked at the tired young face with sympathy.

'Have you been up there all night?' she asked, looking up at the roof of the big building. 'It must have been pretty scary.'

He nodded. His eyes were bloodshot with fatigue and rimmed with red. 'I suppose it is. You don't think about it at the time, though. You just have to get on with the job. I hope we managed to get a few of the blighters.'

'It was a bad raid. I've been at an Incident Enquiry

Centre. There was this little boy . . .' She swayed and put out a hand to steady herself against the wall. 'I don't know how they can do it – bomb people like this. I just don't know how they can *do* it.'

'It's the same for us,' he said quietly. 'We're doing the same to them.' He ran his fingers through his fair hair. It was straight and thick, and looked as if it could do with cutting. If he'd been in the Army, Judy thought irrelevantly, he'd have been marched off to the barber's, but the RAF didn't seem to bother so much about that sort of thing, and what did it matter anyway?

'You look all in,' she said, and he gave her a wry grin.

'So do you. Pity really, or I'd have asked you for a date.'

'A *date*?'

'Yes – you know, when a bloke takes a girl out. To the pictures or for a drink, that sort of thing.' He grinned again, and the grin reached his eyes. They were nice eyes, she thought, very blue and a bit shy despite the cheekiness of his grin. 'I've been thinking about it for a while now but I never seem to catch you. And now I have, we're both too whacked even to think about it.'

'I can't think about it anyway,' Judy said, her tone more brusque than she had intended. She turned quickly away. 'I've got to go now. Sorry.' She went through to the office and shut the door behind her. Laura glanced up in surprise.

'Hullo, what's been eating you? Didn't I see you talking to Chris Barrett in the corridor? He surely hasn't upset you, has he?'

'Is that his name?' Judy said off-handedly. 'I've never bothered to ask. I don't like him much.'

'Don't like him?' Laura asked in astonishment. 'Why, half the girls in the building are head over heels about him. He's gorgeous!'

Judy shrugged. 'He's all right, I suppose. Thinks a bit too much of himself, that's all. Anyway, I've got more important things to think about. My dad was taken into hospital this morning – he's had a really bad asthma attack. I've got to find Polly and tell her what's happened, and then I've got a load of work to do.'

Laura looked concerned. 'Oh Judy, that's awful. I am sorry. Look, Polly's in the small office – you go and see her first. And don't take any notice of Chris, it's just his way. He's a nice chap, and if he asked you for a date he meant it. He wouldn't fool about. I tell you what, he wouldn't have to ask me twice!'

Judy shrugged again. She found Polly and gave her a brief account of what had happened at the hospital, then went to her desk and started to deal with the pile of papers that seemed to have appeared overnight. The Lady Mayoress was there this morning, interviewing some new recruits and Judy was in charge of sending them in. After a time, Polly came over and asked if she could have a few minutes, too.

'Why, you're not thinking of resigning, are you?' Judy looked at her aunt in alarm. She knew that seeing Sylvie yesterday had upset her and she wondered if Polly was thinking of going out to the country to be with her daughter. 'I suppose you could get a transfer,' she added doubtfully. 'The WVS does a lot of work in country places as well.'

Polly shook her head. 'I'm not thinking of that. But there's a notice up about a driving course and I thought I'd go in for it. It was seeing Gladys Shaw with that ambulance last night – I'd like to do something like that, something really active. I mean, I know helping at the Centres and taking kiddies out to the country is valuable work too, and I expect I could still do that as well. But I'd like to do something *more*.'

She went in to see the Mayoress and asked if there was any chance of her becoming a driver. 'I don't really mind what I do, madam. I'll do anything to help. But I did do a bit of driving before the war – my hubby was a mechanic and he used to get a car and take me out in the country sometimes of a Sunday and give me a lesson round the lanes – and I think I'd pick it up quite quick. And when I saw the notice . . .'

'Yes.' The Lady Mayoress regarded her thoughtfully. 'Yes, I think you could do well as a driver. You'd have to learn to drive in the blackout as well, you know.'

'Yes, I understand that. Not that it's very dark when the raids are on,' Polly added, thinking of the red glow that had lit Portsmouth during the night of the Blitz. But the Mayoress shook her head.

'Not just during raids. At other times too. You see, we have a car pool and we get called upon to use it for all kinds of things, at any time of the day or night. Last week, for instance, one of our volunteers had to meet a visiting Minister at the railway station and bring him here for a meeting. Before the meeting was over she was asked to take a bundle of clothes to the Clothing Depot at the warehouse then on the way back she was flagged down by a man whose wife was in labour and had to be taken urgently to St Mary's Hospital to have her baby. She still managed to get back in time to return the Minister to the station – where she found herself collecting a load of sandbags to go to the canteen in Commercial Road! All that was during the day, of course,' she added, 'but she could equally well have been asked to do similar journeys during the night, without lights to guide her.'

'I think I could do that,' Polly said. 'I know Portsmouth like the back of my hand.' She looked at the Mayoress. 'I want to do something that – that sort of asks a lot of me,' she said quietly. 'You see, I lost my hubby over a year ago – his ship was one of the first to go down – and I feel I want to make it up to him, somehow. I can't explain it any better than that, but I want something more *difficult* to do.'

The Mayoress looked at her steadily, then nodded her head. 'Yes, I understand completely, my dear. I'll put you

118

down for the driving course, and I'm sure you'll be a credit to us. And to your husband,' she added. 'I know that wherever he is now, he's proud of you.'

Polly went out of the room and stood for a moment taking deep breaths and blinking away her tears. She was still there when Judy emerged from the main office and looked at her enquiringly.

'Well? Did she say yes?'

Polly grinned a little shakily at first, then her smile broadened. 'Yes! She did. She's putting me in straight away. I'm going to learn to drive, Judy! I'm going to learn to drive a car!'

Polly's lessons began almost at once. Determined to learn quickly, she begged to go out as often as possible and soon passed the test and gained her licence. But before she was allowed to join the WVS pool or drive an ambulance, she had to master the art of driving in pitch darkness with only two narrow slits of light to guide her.

'Honestly, it's like driving with a blindfold on!' she reported, coming home after her first lesson. 'You don't know what you're going to bump into! I was frightened to go more than five miles an hour – the instructor said it would be faster on a push-bike! It's not so bad when there's something light-coloured to pick out, but some streets are so black you could be out in the middle of the countryside for all you know.'

'Is that why all the trees along Copnor Road have got white bands painted round their trunks?' Cissie asked, and Polly nodded.

'People were forever driving into them before they did that. Still, I'll get used to it – and, as I said to Mrs Parker, there's plenty of light to see by during the raids, what with searchlights and fires and everything!'

Alice went out to the scullery and returned with a steaming casserole. She'd managed to get some oxtail from the butcher yesterday and it had been simmering all day with vegetables from the garden. She'd skimmed off most of the fat and put it aside for dripping, and it was a rich, gleaming brown.

'My, that looks good,' Polly said, drawing up her chair. 'I've been looking forward to this all day.'

Alice nodded. 'It's so tasty, oxtail – makes a lovely gravy. I just wish Dick could have some, it would build him up. Say what you like, hospital food doesn't have the nourishment you get at home.'

'How is he today?' Polly asked her sister. 'You said he was a bit better yesterday afternoon.'

Cissie lifted her shoulders a little. 'Well, they had him out of the oxygen tent then for a while, but he's back in it again today. He's still poorly. They think the crisis will come any time now.' She laid down her fork and stared at the tablecloth. 'I wish they'd let me stop with him. I can't bear to think of him so ill, and me not there. And – and when the crisis comes – he could *die*. He could die, and me not there . . .'

Polly and Judy gave each other a swift glance, remembering their own shared grief, and the words of the song Dick used to sing to Cissie. 'Let me be there with you . . .' Simultaneously, they reached across the table and laid their hands on Cissie's. Alice too laid a hand on her daughter's arm.

'Dad's not going to die, Mum,' Judy said in a shaking voice. 'He's *not*. By the time you go back tomorrow, he'll have passed the worst and be on the mend. I know he will. I can *feel* it.'

'I can too,' Polly said. 'We'll have him back here before you know it. All the same, it's a shame you can't stop with him. He must want you there.'

'Well, that's the way hospitals are,' Cissie said, wiping her eyes. 'They have their visiting hours and you've got to stick to them. But I'll be there on the dot tomorrow, you see if I'm not.'

'And I'll go with you,' Judy said. 'I know they probably won't let me in to see him but you need someone with you, Mum. Just—' She bit her lip and stopped, but they all knew she'd been going to add, '*Just in case.*' They knew that however strongly they hoped for Dick to get better, however strongly they believed that he would, he really was dangerously ill.

'We'll say our prayers for him tonight,' Polly said soberly. 'We all will.'

Once Polly had satisfied her instructor that she was competent to drive at night as well as by day, she was assigned a number of duties. Mostly she undertook these in an old van that had been converted to act as an ambulance, but could also transport various bulky items or people, but sometimes she found herself driving one of the cars that had been donated to the pool 'for the duration' as the expression was. On these occasions she usually had a passenger of some importance – the Lord Mayor himself, going to meet some visiting dignitary at the railway station, or a high-ranking official arriving from London. Once, she found herself holding a baby while its mother, the wife of a Naval Captain, struggled to get twin toddlers off the train. 'It may be the last chance for them to see their daddy for a long time,' she explained to Polly, lifting them down to the platform. 'There you are, darlings, now just stand still while this nice lady helps us with all our bags. It's just not possible to travel light with three little ones,' she said, brushing her ash-blonde hair back from her forehead while she tried to count the pieces of luggage strewn around them. 'I don't know how I'd have managed if all these kind people hadn't been so helpful.' She indicated the two blushing sailors and a middle-aged man who had formed a chain to get the suitcases and naval holdalls off the train and were now apparently awaiting further orders. 'But people always are, don't you find?'

Polly smiled and nodded, but she wondered privately if the Captain's wife would have been offered so much help if she'd been elderly and rather less glamorous. Her pearl-grey suit was probably at least three years old, yet the quality of its cut and fabric ensured that it still looked smart, and the stole draped carelessly round her shoulders looked like ocelot. Her hair was styled with the latest rolled-up pleat at the front, and her fingers glittered with diamonds. But her face was friendly and the smile she bestowed upon her helpers so dazzling that they almost reeled.

'You've got a *car*?' she said to Polly, as if she'd expected to be guided to a truck. 'Oh, how kind. If you wouldn't mind carrying Benjamin for a little bit longer . . . He's been most dreadfully spoilt on the train,' she continued, wafting down the platform in a cloud of scent. '*Everyone* wanted to hold him. And the twins have been treated like princesses. We couldn't have had a nicer journey. Oh, just *look* at that!' She stopped at the entrance to the station and gazed rapturously across the harbour.

Polly followed her gaze. I suppose it does look quite interesting, she thought, although having lived all her life with this view on her doorstep she had never taken much notice of it. Now she looked more attentively at the wide expanse of shimmering water, its green, broken surface speckled with white foam, and at the craft tossing about on its waves. Tugs, Isle of Wight paddle-steamers, Gosport ferry-boats, naval pinnaces and, towering over them all, the ships of the Royal Navy, sleek and grey, anchored in the middle of the harbour or tied to the dockyard jetties with the Semaphore Tower and the masts of HMS *Victory* behind them.

'It's splendid,' the Captain's wife said. 'Quite splendid. You're so lucky to live here. We've always been based at Chatham, so we've made our home there, but I should just *love* to live in Portsmouth. The harbour is *so* much a part of the town, don't you agree?'

By the time Polly dropped her at the hotel where she was to spend a few days with her husband, she felt that she was seeing her home town with new eyes. The Captain's wife, who seemed no older than Polly herself, was so interested, so enthusiastic and so sympathetic over the raids they had suffered that Polly felt as if they'd been friends for years. She helped her into the hotel, and said goodbye with regret.

'Now, you must come to see us,' the Captain's wife said, pressing her hand. 'Milly and Mandy have obviously taken you to their hearts and I don't think Benjamin would mind at all if you took him home with you! I know your name, and I know where you work, so I'll be in touch. Thank you *so* much, Mrs Dunn.'

'It's quite all right. It's been a pleasure.' Polly looked at her and hesitated. She didn't really believe that the other woman would contact her again. It was just the way people like her talked. But she really did seem very nice. 'I hope everything goes well with you and your husband,' she said with a rush. 'I hope it isn't too long before – well, you know, before he comes home again.'

The dazzling smile faltered a little and Polly caught a glimpse of the fear that lay behind it. She's as scared as the rest of us, she thought. She knows he could die at sea, just like my Johnny, just like Judy's Sean, but she's doing her best to hide it; she's doing her best to make things nice for other people, even if all she can do is smile at them. I bet everyone who's met her today feels better for it.

'It won't be any time at all,' the Captain's wife said firmly. 'And meanwhile, we can find plenty to do to keep ourselves busy, can't we?' She cast a humorous glance at her little brood, the twin girls standing on either side of her, clutching her pearl-grey skirt, and the baby cradled in her arms. 'Even if it's only wiping noses and changing nappies.

Speaking of which . . .' She wrinkled her nose and laughed, and Polly smiled back, then turned and hurried out.

It was time to go back to the Royal Beach and take on her next assignment. Within half an hour the Captain's wife would be almost forgotten. But her smile, and the warmth with which she bestowed it on all who came within her orbit, would not be forgotten. They would remain in every heart.

We can all do that, Polly thought. We can all do our bit, just by putting a smile on our faces and helping each other. That's what Mr Churchill means when he says we'll come through. That's what he means by the spirit of Britain.

Chapter Eleven

Dick had, at last, passed the crisis of his illness. Cissie and Judy had gone to the Royal Hospital, dreading what they might find, and had been overwhelmed with relief to see him out of his tent and sleeping more peacefully than he had done since the night of the asthma attack. Cissie, looking at his white face, had broken down in tears and the nurse had come to lead her to a chair and even brought them both a cup of tea.

'It's been a hard time,' she said sympathetically. 'He was seriously ill – Doctor was worried about him – but he's turned the corner now. He'll still need a lot of nursing before he's back to strength again, mind.'

'So long as he's on the mend,' Cissie said through her tears. 'Oh, I'm so thankful. We've got used to the asthma attacks over the years, but this one was so bad, and then when we found he'd got pneumonia as well . . .'

'Well, his chest condition makes him very vulnerable,' the nurse said. 'And I dare say he's been spending nights in an Anderson, too; the damp and cold are bound to have an effect. And then there's all the worry of the raids.'

'We were bombed out in January,' Cissie said. 'And he was gassed in 1917 – and shell-shocked too. He's not been a well man since.'

'You'll have him home again soon,' the nurse told her cheerfully. 'And let's hope we don't have any more raids like that one. That was terrible.'

Judy stayed with her mother until she was sure Cissie was fit to go home alone, then she made her way out to the Royal

Beach. She had sent a message via Polly to say she would be late, knowing that the Mayoress would understand, but she was anxious not to waste a minute. She arrived to find the place in uproar.

'We've lost an important document,' Laura explained breathlessly as Judy came into the main office. 'It was supposed to go to the top office and nobody can find it. You don't happen to know where it is, do you?'

'Which one was it?' Judy asked, and turned pale as Laura told her. 'Oh my goodness! I had it yesterday – I slipped it into my drawer for safety. It must still be there.' She ran to her desk and pulled open the drawer. 'Is – is this it?'

'Yes!' Laura snatched it away from her and raced over to the Lady Mayoress, who was sitting at her desk searching through a huge box file. 'Here it is, madam. Judy had it all the time.'

'*Judy* did?' The Lady Mayoress stared at her. 'But what on earth? Why? No, don't bother to explain. Just take it up to Mr Williams at once – you know where he is, don't you – on the eighth floor. And then come straight to me when you get back.' She shook her head as if in despair and Judy, scarlet-faced, took the file back from Laura and scurried out of the room.

She was almost in tears as she stepped into the lift. It was the first serious mistake she had made, and she had never seen the Mayoress look so annoyed. I didn't know it was so important, she thought as she waited for the door to close, and I didn't know I was going to be late this morning. Oh, please don't let her be really angry with me. Please don't let her say I'm no use to her and I've got to go back to my old job. What if Miss Marsh doesn't want me any more? What if she says I'm no use either? Oh, *why* won't this wretched door *close*?

Judy hated the lift. It was small and creaky and you could see the walls through the cage-like structure. When you were inside it, moving slowly up or down, it was like being in a long vertical tube with no windows. She always felt as if the sides were closing in on her and, if she could, used the stairs. But now, with a document to be delivered urgently to the eighth floor, she had no choice.

She wrenched at the iron door but nothing happened; she was just about to step out and face the long climb up eight flights of stairs when a cheery voice said, 'Hey, don't take it out on the door! What harm did it ever do you?' and she looked up and saw Chris Barrett, the fair-haired Observer, grinning at her from the corridor.

'It won't shut, that's what harm it's doing!' she retorted savagely. 'I've got to get an important file up to Mr Williams and I'm going to have to climb up all those stairs, and – and if you want to know the truth, I've just about had enough!' Then, to her fury, she burst into tears.

'Hey.' He came a little closer. 'Hey, come on. Don't cry. It can't be that bad. Let me have a go.' He stepped into the lift beside her, pressed the button and the door slid across immediately. 'There you are! Chocks away and ready for take-off. You just need to press the button, that's all, it won't know otherwise. Where d'you want to go? Floor eight?'

'Yes.' Judy scowled at the buttons. 'I did press it. It took no notice.'

'Well, it is a bit temperamental. It's refused to start a couple of times lately. I think they're sending out a maintenance crew from somewhere, but what with every-thing else . . .' He smiled down at her. 'Your name's Judy, isn't it? Judy Taylor?'

Judy admitted that it was. 'And you're Chris Barrett. Someone in the office told me. I didn't *ask* her,' she added quickly, just in case he might think she was interested in him. 'She just saw us talking and told me.'

The lift creaked slowly upwards. It might have been quicker to walk anyway, Judy thought, and then she wouldn't have had to stand in this tiny space with this cheeky airman. She stood gazing fixedly at the floor, determined not to glance up and catch Chris Barrett's eye. She was sure he was staring at her. There was a silence.

'So how are you getting on, up there on the roof?' she asked eventually, unable to stand it any longer. 'I suppose you've been pretty busy lately.'

'Pretty well,' he agreed. 'There are planes about all the time, even when there's no raid. We have to spot our own as well as theirs, you see. And we have to be able to recognise them straight away. It's not much good to HQ if you can't tell a Spit from a Messerschmitt.'

Judy nodded. They were passing the fourth floor now. She could see the corridor through the iron gates, its carpet taken up to leave bare boards, the doors that had once led to luxurious bedrooms open to show glimpses of the offices within. She wondered what sort of people used to come and stay here. Entertainers who were appearing in the theatre at the end of the long pier over the road, probably. People like Joe Loss, Ambrose, Max Miller. It was funny to think that she might be standing in a lift that had once carried a famous comedian or band leader . . . She tried to imagine he was here now, instead of this tall, fair-haired young Observer and, just as she was drifting off into a dream of being recognised by a famous band leader and becoming a singer like Anne Shelton or Vera Lynn, the lift gave a loud creak and shuddered to a halt. They were between floors and all they could see through the gates was the wall of the lift-shaft.

Judy and the Observer stared at each other. A worm of panic stirred deep in her stomach.

'It's stopped.' She put out her hand and pressed the button hard. 'What's happened? Why's it stopped?' The worm twisted a little. She began to shake the gates.

'Don't do that. It might be dangerous.' He gripped her wrist and pulled back her arm sharply. 'I'm not surprised. This thing's been on its last legs for years.'

'But what shall we do?' Her voice was rising. 'I've got an important document to deliver. I was late in this morning anyway. The Mayoress will be furious!'

'No, she won't. It's not your fault the lift's broken down. Don't get in a flap, Judy.' He laid his hand on her arm again, more gently this time. 'Look, there's nothing we can do. Someone will notice pretty soon and they'll send for that maintenance crew I was talking about. They'll get us out.'

'And what are we supposed to do in the meantime?' Judy demanded, her voice shaking. 'Tell each other stories? Sing songs?'

'Well, we could do worse.' He grinned. 'Come on, Judy, it's not the end of the world. A lot worse things than this have happened.'

Judy flung him a look of fear. 'I know. It's just that I – I hate being shut in tiny spaces. I've never liked using this lift – I always use the stairs if I can. And – and so many awful things have happened, and this is the last straw. I know it's a small thing really, but that's what straws are, aren't they?' She covered her face with her hands. 'I was late in this morning because I went to the Royal Hospital to see my dad. He's had pneumonia. He's getting better now but we – we thought he was going to die.' Her voice shook and she began to cry.

There was a moment's pause and then Chris put his arm across her shoulder. 'Hey, hey, come on. He's getting *better*. That's what you've got to think of. He's *not* going to die. And you're not going to have to spend the rest of your life stuck in this lift with me.' He peered upwards through the gates, trying to see to the next floor. 'At least, I hope not!'

Judy looked around. The walls of the shaft could be seen on each side. They were roughly built, not finished with plaster, and were dingy and draped with cobwebs. She shuddered.

'It's horrible. Nobody ever cleans these walls. I feel as if I'm shut in a zoo, or going down a mine.'

'It's just the lift-shaft,' he said soothingly. 'I expect they used to clean it when it was a hotel but we don't have time for those things now. Tell you what, soon as we get out of here I'll fetch a bucket and mop and clean the whole thing myself, from top to bottom. How's that?' He grinned at her.

Judy looked at his open, friendly face, his twinkling eyes and smiling mouth, and drew in a deep breath. I'm being an idiot, she thought. Letting it all get on top of me. He's right – it's just a lift-shaft and soon someone will come and get us out. There's nothing to be frightened of. She repeated the words firmly in her mind. *There's nothing to be frightened of.* And the thought of Chris with a bucket and mop, cleaning the entire eight floors of it, brought an unexpected bubble of laughter to her lips.

'Sorry, it just sort of came over me for a minute.' She managed a smile and felt a little better. 'Well, you wanted a date. Looks like you've got your way!'

'So it does.' He grinned. 'Though I had thought of taking you somewhere a bit more glamorous than this – a British Restaurant, perhaps!'

'Or a WVS Emergency Centre,' Judy said, and he laughed. He had a nice laugh, she thought, his blue eyes crinkling at the corners and his smile widening to show very white teeth. Polly's right, she thought, he *is* good-looking. It was easy to imagine other girls finding him attractive.

'We might as well sit down, I suppose,' he said, indicating the dusty floor. 'Sorry I can't offer you anything more comfortable. But if we're going to be here a while . . .'

'Why, how long d'you think it could be?' She glanced upwards, her anxiety returning. 'I don't think anyone's even noticed yet!'

A yell sounded from above and they heard the distant rattle of gates. Chris grinned at her. 'I think they have now! But they'll just think some twerp's left the gates open on another floor. It'll be a while before they realise it's stuck.'

He moved closer to the gate and shouted up the shaft. 'Hey! We're stuck – the lift's stuck! Get some help, will you?'

There was a brief silence. The yells from above sounded again, together with an even more impatient rattling. Chris renewed his own shouting and eventually a voice sounded from somewhere closer. 'Where are you?'

'Where d'you think we are?' Chris bellowed. 'We're stuck in the flipping lift!'

'Yes, but what floor? We can't tell.'

'I don't know.' He glanced at Judy.

'I know we went past the fourth floor,' she said doubtfully. 'I'm not sure about the fifth.'

'Well, we're pretty high anyway. It's no use rattling the gates like that,' he shouted. 'Get the maintenance crew, they'll know what to do.'

There was some muted conversation from above, as if several more people had joined the first. Then a new voice shouted, echoing hollowly in the shaft.

'We're sending for the maintenance people. Soon have you out.'

'What a good idea,' Chris said sardonically, and Judy giggled. 'I'd never have thought of that.'

'Who's in there?' the new voice called.

'Chris Barrett, ROC, and Judy Taylor, WVS. You'd better let our people know.'

'We'll let your people know,' the voice shouted, overriding Chris's last words. He rolled his eyes and Judy giggled again. Her panic seemed to have vanished and the humour of their situation was beginning to strike her. She followed his advice and sat down in a corner, wrapping her arms about her knees. Chris looked down at her, then sat down in another corner.

'I think we're going to be here quite a while. I don't know where the maintenance chaps are coming from, but I don't think they're on permanent duty here. Hope you're not hungry.' He gave her a wry look.

'Not really.' It was some time since her breakfast of Shredded Wheat and toast, and thank goodness she had been to the lavatory when she'd arrived at the hotel. Judy pushed her fingers through her hair and sighed. 'Oh, this *would* happen. Just when we're so busy. And Mr Williams wanted this file urgently.' She touched the brown folder.

'Well, he'll have to manage without it a bit longer. I don't suppose it was that important, anyway. People make a lot of fuss about things like that, and then it turns out they don't matter at all.' He cocked his head to one side. 'Cheer up, Judy. The worst that can happen is that you've got to spend a couple of hours alone with me. And even that's not too bad. I'm quite a gentleman really, you know. I won't take advantage of you.' He grinned wickedly. 'Not unless you want me to!'

Judy gave him a cold look. 'Well, I *don't* want you to.' Then she relented and smiled reluctantly. 'All right, I won't keep moaning. We're here and we might as well make the best of it. Tell me some more about what you do up there on the roof. It sounds quite interesting.'

'It is.' His face lit up with enthusiasm. 'We're all mad keen about spotting aircraft, you see. That's why we answered the adverts.'

'I'd have thought you'd have been called up anyway,' she said, with a touch of tartness in her voice as she thought again of Sean and Johnny. 'Why aren't you in one of the Services? Active, I mean.'

'Because most of us are in reserved occupations. I'm in the Dockyard. I filled in my papers,' he said, looking at her earnestly. 'I took them in and everything, but the foreman told me I could forget it – none of us Yardies'll be called up. And he was right, I haven't heard a thing, so when this came up – well, I wanted to do my bit so I slapped in my application straight away.'

Judy looked at him and felt ashamed. She said, 'What sort of qualifications did you have to have, then?'

'Just good sight and being able to recognise aircraft. That's all that's needed. You've got to be able to think pretty quickly too,' he added. 'But really, they just wanted blokes who already knew their stuff.'

'But there's a classroom – I've seen it. They're training people now.'

'Yes, we still have to train. We're training all the time. We've got to keep the skills up, and we've got to be able to recognise new aircraft. We have competitions too,' he added. 'Master tests, they're called. We do them once a quarter and we compete with spotters from all over the country.'

'Competitions? How do they run them? I mean, you can't actually use aircraft, can you?'

'No, they use a flashtrainer – a screen and epidiascope. You sit in a room looking at a screen, and then the bloke says, "Blink" and you blink, and they flash a silhouette up on the screen. It's only there for a hundredth of a second, and you have to be able to identify the plane in that time. If you get ninety per cent right, you get this Spitfire badge, and if you do that three times in a row you get a red badge, and then you're a Master Spotter.' He paused and then added modestly, 'I've done it twice so far.'

'A hundredth of a second?' Judy stared at him. 'I didn't think they could measure time as small as that. I can't even imagine what it is.'

'It's just a flash,' he said. 'You can barely see it. But if you're good, you can recognise a shape in that time.'

'But aeroplanes – they're not that different, surely? I mean, they've all got two wings and a tail – how can you possibly tell what they are in that time?'

'Oh, there are lots of differences. Tails, rudders, wing shapes – they're all a little bit different. That's why we've got to be able to recognise them instantly, you see. If we see a plane coming in over the coast we've got to know what it is straight away so that we can phone through to the Ops room at Winchester. We've got to know what direction it's coming from, where it's heading, and we've got to plot its position. Then they can match that up with reports from other observation posts and see what's happening in the sky. There might be just one, you see, or there might be hundreds. That's how they know where to send our own aircraft to intercept them, and whether to sound the air-raid sirens or not.'

Judy gazed at him, fascinated. She had almost forgotten that they were stuck in a lift and that Mr Williams was waiting for his important document. 'How many of you are there doing this? At one time, I mean.'

'Two. One to look at the sky and one to write the log. We write down what's happening every minute, and then our logbook can be compared with all the others so that Ops know that all aircraft in the vicinity are being observed.' He glanced at his watch. 'They'll be getting in a flap over me pretty soon, but I dare say they'll pull someone out of the classroom to stand in for me.'

There were sounds from above. Someone was rattling the lift gates. A voice yelled down, 'You OK in there?'

'Oh, we're fine,' Chris called back. 'Having a wonderful time. Always wanted to be stuck in a lift with a pretty girl!'

'You behave yourself,' the voice commanded. 'If he gives you any trouble, miss, you just scream. Anyway, you'd better make up your minds for a bit of a wait. We've got to get someone out from naval barracks to see to the mechanism. Nobody here seems to know how the bl— blooming thing works.'

'Well, don't hurry on my account,' Chris returned, winking at Judy. He settled himself more comfortably in his corner and said, 'What about you? What d'you do?' He glanced at her green uniform. 'I know you're WVS but I'm not sure what that is.'

'Women's Voluntary Service,' Judy said. 'It's run by the Lady Mayoress here in Portsmouth, but there are branches everywhere. It started in 1938 to help women get involved in air-raid precautions and then it just expanded. Now, we do whatever we're asked to do. We never say no,' she finished proudly, and then caught the glint in his eye and wished she hadn't.

'I won't take you up on that!' he said with a grin. 'But I wouldn't go around saying that to some of the other oiks we've got – they're not all as gentlemanly as me. So what sort of things have you done so far?'

Judy shrugged. 'Anything and everything. We set up Enquiry Centres when a raid starts, for people to come to if they're worried about members of their family, and we open Emergency Centres for people who've been bombed out. We take hot drinks and sandwiches round to the air-raid shelters. We go into bombed areas and do whatever we can – we build fireplaces with bricks from the rubble and brew up tea, or we take warm clothes out to people who've been bombed out in their nightclothes. All sorts of things. And we have a car pool, to drive people wherever they need to go. My auntie's learned to drive 'specially – she's driven all sorts of important people – and she drives an ambulance in the raids too.'

'That's pretty good,' he said admiringly. 'And all this without getting paid?'

'Yes, everyone's a volunteer. Well, *I* get paid,' she added honestly, 'because I'm "borrowed" from the Council. But I do a lot of voluntary work as well. I don't just work office hours.'

'Well, I think that's smashing,' Chris said. He hesitated and then said, 'I think you're pretty smashing, too, Judy.'

There was an awkward pause. Judy looked down at the ring on her finger, wondering if Chris had noticed it. For the first time since Sean had died, she wished that she had not been wearing it, and guilt immediately washed over her at the thought. She could feel Chris's eyes on her and she wanted to say something about Sean, to tell him what had happened, but before she could speak they heard another rattling from above. A voice shouted down, a voice they hadn't heard before. This one was firm and positive, as if it belonged to someone who knew what he was doing.

'The cavalry's arrived,' Chris said ironically.

'You OK?' the voice shouted. Judy imagined a naval mechanic, big and brawny, with a 'full set' of beard and moustache. 'Hold on, we'll have you out soon. Have to go up on the roof to sort out the motor. Don't worry if the whole caboodle shakes about a bit. We won't let you drop.'

'You'd better not, mate,' Chris called back. 'We're just getting to know each other in here.' He winked at Judy and settled back. 'Won't be long now.' There was a short pause, then he asked, 'Whereabouts do you live?'

The moment for telling him about Sean had passed. 'I used to live in Portchester Road but we were bombed out. We're with my gran now, in April Grove.'

'April Grove? Is that up Copnor Road?'

Judy nodded. 'That's right, just off September Street. Well, at the end of March Street and October Street, really. It runs along the bottom, by the allotments.' She was gabbling, she knew, thankful to be relieved of the necessity of talking about Sean. 'They're just two-up, two-down houses so it's a bit of a squash, but we were lucky to have somewhere to go. And since Sylvie's out in the country—'

'Sylvie?'

'My niece. Her mum's my Aunt Polly, but I never call her that because she's only twelve years older than me. She – she lost her husband early in the war. At sea.' I could tell him now, she thought, but the words were hard to find and she added instead, 'So there's just the five of us – me and Polly, Mum and Dad, and Gran. It's all right.'

Chris nodded. 'Like you say, we're lucky to have somewhere to live these days. There's a hell of a lot of people been bombed out. Far more than anyone expected.'

'The Council's had a lot of complaints about that,' Judy

136

said. 'People criticising because we weren't properly prepared. But you don't know what's going to happen in a war,
do you? They thought there'd be thousands killed, and
instead of that they've been made homeless. It must mean
that the shelters are working, yet people don't think how
lucky they are to survive, they just moan because they've got
nowhere to live. Well, it *is* awful, I know,' she added. 'It's
horrible, not having a home. But we're doing our best —
people *are* being rehoused, somehow or other. And they are
still alive. That's the main thing.'

The lift shook and rattled, and Judy put her hand on the
floor to steady herself. It trembled beneath her and she felt
suddenly scared. Suppose something went wrong. Suppose
the lift suddenly plunged to the bottom of the shaft —
somewhere down in the basement. That was at least five
floors . . . She looked at Chris in alarm.

'It's all right,' he said, moving a little closer. 'They're just
working on the motor.'

'But if it gives way . . .' She could hear the shake in her
voice. 'It'll be like being dropped off the roof in a box. We
wouldn't have a chance.'

'It won't give way. Here, let me put my arm round you.'
He slid his arm round her shoulders and held her firmly.
Judy pressed her face against his shoulder. He smelt of blue
serge and coal-tar soap and sweat. She breathed in the scent
of him, feeling a sudden quickening of her pulse. Sean had
smelt a little like this, but there was a difference . . . the lift
shook again and she gasped and pressed closer.

'It's all right.' Chris's voice was soft and soothing. His
fingers gripped her shoulder and he put his other arm
around her and stroked her back. 'It's all right, Judy. You're
safe. We're not going to fall. It's all right.'

They sat very still, pressed close together. Judy could feel
her heart beating. Her cheek was against his neck and she
could feel his pulse beneath the warm skin. His fair hair
tickled her face. She gripped his shoulders tightly.

I *will* tell him about Sean, she decided. After we've got out of here, when everything's all right again, I'll tell him about Sean. It won't make any difference. I don't want another sweetheart, not yet, not for a long time, maybe not ever. But I would like to be friends, and I want him to know about Sean. I want him to know the important things . . .

The lift gave a huge shudder. For a moment, it hung trembling, as if undecided as to what to do next. Judy held her breath and pressed her face hard against Chris's shoulder. She felt his arms tighten about her. The cables creaked, the lift groaned and there was a shiver of movement. Then, slowly and complainingly, it began to rise.

'It's all right,' Chris whispered. 'Judy, it's all right.'

She lifted her head to look at him. 'We're going up! Oh, *Chris.*'

'Thank God for that,' he said, and grinned a little shakily. 'I don't mind admitting, even I was a bit worried there for a minute!'

They laughed with relief. Their eyes met and as she saw his pupils darken Judy felt a quick surge of excitement. She lifted her face towards him and, when he bent closer and his lips met hers, she closed her eyes and relaxed against his body. For a brief, whirling moment, she forgot where they were, forgot the creaking lift, forgot Mr Williams's important document and the fact that there was likely to be a reception committee awaiting them when they arrived. It was only the sound of ironic cheering that brought her out of her daze and then she blinked, stared through the gates at the little cluster of people waiting at the foot of the steel stairway, and jerked herself out of his arms.

'For goodness sake!' Scarlet with embarrassment, she brushed back her hair, grabbed the brown folder and scrambled to her feet. Mr Williams was there himself, his hand held out, a frown of disapproval on his face. So was

Laura, her lips twitching with amusement. So were half a dozen other Observers, all applauding – all except one.

The one not applauding was a girl of Judy's own age. Tall and slim, with the sort of auburn hair Judy would have given her eye teeth for, and eyes as green as a cat's, she was dressed in the Air Force blue uniform and sported a Spitfire badge like the one Chris wore on his sleeve. She was leaning against the wall, her arms folded, her lips tight, and as she glanced from Judy to Chris her eyes flashed with temper.

Why, she's his girlfriend, Judy thought indignantly. And there he was kissing me, for all to see! The *rotter*!

She turned away angrily and found herself confronting the two sailors who had rescued them. They were packing away their tools into canvas bags and straightened up to grin at her. One was tall and thin, the other shorter than Judy herself, with a bald head and button nose.

'Well, that wasn't too bad, was it, love?' he said, and she recognised the voice that had shouted down to them, the one that she had envisaged as belonging to a big, brawny matelot with beard and moustache. 'You seem to have passed the time all right, anyway!'

Judy stared at him. Then, still scarlet, she turned her back and without even thanking him set off down the stairs, back to the ground floor.

It'll be a long time before I trust that lift again, she reflected grimly. And even longer before I trust one of those beastly Observers!

For the next few days, Judy did her best to avoid Chris Barrett.

It wasn't easy. She couldn't find out when his shifts were without attracting comment; the story of their incarceration in the lift, and the attitude in which they'd been caught when it arrived, had gone all round the building and Judy found herself the butt of a good deal of teasing. She did her best to take it in good part and it soon died down, but she knew that even to mention his name would be enough to start it all over again. To be seen talking to him would be even worse, so whenever she caught sight of him she darted through the nearest doorway, making some excuse if she found herself in an office she didn't normally visit. Once she had to wait for several minutes in a cluttered broom cupboard, as a series of footsteps went by, before emerging in the hope that the corridor was empty.

To make matters worse, Chris didn't seem to have the same inhibitions. Time and time again he tried to speak to her, until at last Judy was forced to face him on the hotel steps, where she'd met him as she hurried out. He stood just below her, the sun on his hair as he looked up, and his blue eyes laughing.

'Judy! I was beginning to think you were trying to avoid me.'

'Well, you were right,' she retorted waspishly. 'Look, I'm sorry, I'm in a hurry—'

'Don't rush off,' he begged. 'There's something I want to say to you.'

'I've got a bus to catch.'

'No, you haven't. You come by bike, I've seen you. Look, this won't take a minute.' He reached out and touched her arm and Judy jumped away as if she'd been stung.

'Don't do that! Haven't you caused enough trouble?' Pink with anger, she tried to push past him, but his hand tightened on her sleeve and she glared at him. 'Let me go!'

'Not until you listen to what I want to say. Judy, about the lift—'

'I don't want to talk about it,' she broke in, thrusting him away and walking across the road with tight, quick steps. He followed her and she turned at the top of the beach and began to stride along the promenade, too angry to notice the glint of sunshine on the rippling waves or the green rolling hills of the Isle of Wight. 'It's taken days to live it down, and if people see us here like this it'll start all over again. D'you realise how embarrassing it was for me? All those people watching – I thought I'd die, I did really.'

'I just want to say I'm sorry. I never meant to upset you.'

'Well, you shouldn't have done it, then. You should have behaved like a gentleman.'

'Oh, come on,' he said, beginning to sound angry in his turn. 'It was only a kiss, for Pete's sake. I wasn't asking you to marry me!'

Judy looked down at his hand. She plucked it away from her sleeve, then she met his eyes coldly.

'That's just as well,' she said in a tight, icy tone, 'because I wouldn't marry you if you were the last man on this earth. And I don't want to be stuck in a lift with you again, either. I don't even want to *talk* to you.'

'But why not?' he asked in bewilderment. 'Look, I thought we were getting on really well when we were in that lift together. And when I kissed you – well, you kissed me as well. At least, that's what it felt like. And it wasn't the end of the world when everyone saw us, was it? We weren't doing anything wrong. So why was it so terrible?'

Judy looked at him. 'And what did your girlfriend think about it? Didn't *she* think it was terrible – seeing you kissing another girl?'

'My girlfriend?' He stared at her. 'What on earth are you talking about now? I haven't got a girlfriend.' He glinted a wink at her. 'I was hoping when we were in the lift that that was about to change!'

Judy gave him a chilly look. 'So who was that redhead if she's not your girlfriend? The one who was looking so furious when we got out of the lift? If looks could kill, you'd have dropped dead on the spot.'

'You mean Joyce? Oh Judy,' his face broke into laughter, 'Joyce isn't my girlfriend! She's engaged to a bloke at HQ in Winchester. She wouldn't give me the time of day, let alone go out with me. And if you want to know why she was furious, it was because she couldn't go off duty until I was there – and she was waiting to go off on a forty-eight-hour pass for a dirty weekend! It was bad enough that I kept her waiting, but the thought that I might have *enjoyed* being stuck – well, that took the biscuit. I tell you, the way she laid into me you'd think I'd done it deliberately!'

'Oh,' Judy said blankly. 'Oh.' She stared at him for a moment, then turned away and looked out over the sea. There was a light breeze, just enough to blow the tops off the waves into a spray of glittering foam. 'Oh – well, I'm sorry. I thought . . .'

'I know what you thought,' he said, grinning. 'So now will you think again? Give me a smile now and then? Say hello – that sort of thing?'

She laughed. 'Of course I will! I'm sorry, Chris. It was just that—'

'Just that we seemed to be getting on so well together,' he said quietly. He took her left hand and raised it, looking at the ring. 'I did notice it, in case you were wondering. That's why I didn't ask to see you again – though I wanted to, right from the start. To tell you the truth, I couldn't believe my luck when that lift got stuck – and before you ask, no, I didn't arrange it!' His eyes laughed at her again. 'But then, when we kissed – well, I felt that there could be something more between us.' He looked at the ring again. 'This chap you're engaged to – is it really that serious?'

Judy bit her lip and looked down. She could walk away from Chris now. She could let him think she was still engaged, that she wasn't interested in any other man. She knew that he wouldn't pester her. He would accept it, and it really would be just a matter of a casual 'hello' now and then, a smile as they passed in the corridor.

But Sean was dead. He was never going to come back, and was she to spend the rest of her life alone? The next sixty years, perhaps, recalling a young sailor she had known and loved for just a few weeks?

Chris might not ever be more than a friend. They might fall in love for a little while and then part. But as she looked down at the ring with its tiny diamond, she remembered her grandmother's words. '*You've got to start living again sometime, Judy. You've got to.*'

Perhaps she could start with Chris.

She made up her mind and lifted her face to look him in the eye. He was watching her with a tinge of anxiety.

'I want to tell you about it,' she said, 'but not now – not here. Perhaps we could meet one evening, after your duty – go for a walk or something.'

'All right,' he said. 'What about Saturday – oh blast, I can't – we've got my uncle and aunt coming down from London and Mum'll throw a fit if I'm not there. How about Sunday? I'm on duty in the afternoon but I'm off at six – we could go and have some tea and then maybe see a film. That's if you'd like to do that,' he added with that touch of anxiety again.

Judy nodded and smiled. 'That'll be fine,' she said. 'I'll write down my address. Come and call for me at six.'

I've made a date, she thought with amazement as she cycled home. I've made a date! It might not lead to anything – I'm not sure I even want it to – but it's a date and I don't feel guilty about Sean, I don't feel guilty at all. He wouldn't have wanted me to live my life as if half of it was over. He'd have wanted me to start living again.

She glanced down at her left hand and saw his ring, winking up at her. On a sudden impulse, she stopped and took it off her finger and put it on her right hand instead. There, she thought. I'll still wear it for you, in remembrance. But I know now that it can never be more than that. It's not a promise any more.

With a heart lighter than it had been for many months, she pushed down the pedal and cycled the rest of the way home.

*

On 27 April, the Sunday when Judy had been due to meet Chris, the Luftwaffe came again.

The raid began early in the evening, just when the people of Portsmouth had finished their Sunday tea and were looking forward to an evening spent playing cards or listening to the wireless. The sirens wailed, cutting into their comfortable plans, and once more they ran down their gardens to huddle in their shelters, or went out to fight the fires that tore through their homes and workplaces. Once more, ambulances and fire engines raced through streets blocked with rubble; once more, the Emergency Centres were filled with homeless people while First-Aid Posts tended the injured.

It was going to be another bad night. They knew it from the incessant snarl of German aircraft overhead, from the open roar of Allied planes, from the silvery net of searchlights lighting up the sky, from the staccato rattle of ack-ack. And, most of all, from the thunderous explosions that shook the ground, rattling doors and windows, making the very walls tremble. By dawn, there would be more hundreds made homeless, more families bereaved, more patients crowding in the city's hospitals – and if the hospitals themselves were hit, as each one had been in previous raids, more desperation as to where they could be taken.

Gladys Shaw was out with her ambulance, racing through streets that were lit by incendiaries and fire. Peggy was at her First-Aid Post. Annie Chapman and Judy were at the Emergency Centre, making an endless supply of hot soup, cocoa and tea for the people who straggled in, lost and bewildered, often bleeding, their homes damaged or destroyed, their lives shattered.

As usual, Judy was ready to help in any capacity – manning a canteen somewhere amidst all the bombs, rushing off to set up an Enquiry Centre somewhere for people to report to, or to start the hunt for missing relatives, helping with First Aid for those who stumbled in, hurt, but not seriously enough to be sent to hospital.

She was bandaging a cut head for an old woman who had been sheltering under her stairs when she heard her name spoken and glanced up. 'Polly!'

'Judy.' Polly was looking anxious. 'I came in to see if there was anyone who could come on the van with me. The Red Cross nurse never turned up. But it looks as if you're pretty busy here.'

'I don't know – there are a few more volunteers here now.' Judy glanced around and called to one that she knew: 'Susan, could you take over here? My aunt needs someone on her ambulance – I'll go with her.' She followed Polly into the fire-raddled, bomb-torn night and they scurried out to the old van that had been converted to an ambulance. Polly had been out at night quite a lot by now, learning to see in what little glow was allowed from the narrow slits of light from her headlamps. It was almost a luxury, she thought, having all this light from the fires and the incendiaries, but not a luxury she welcomed. Every raddled glow meant someone's home or property on fire, every gleam of light a broken heart.

There was no other light to be had. With the first stick of bombs, the city's electricity system had failed and the city was plunged into darkness. Only those places, such as hospitals, which possessed their own emergency generators, still had light. For the rest, out came the hurricane lanterns, the candles, the torches with their precious, dwindling batteries. None of these things would last for ever, and nobody knew where the next candle, battery or half-pint of paraffin would come from. If you could manage without light, you did.

They were accustomed to the sirens going almost every night, accustomed to nights when just a few bombs fell, accustomed to nights when there was no bombing at all and you just listened to planes going over on their way to raid some other unfortunate city, and waited for the All Clear to sound. But tonight had a worse feeling about it. It was frighteningly similar to those other two nights when the bombing had been so severe it had been called a 'Blitz'. The aircraft filled the night sky with their roar, as if there were a huge cloud of them up there, blacking out the stars and the moon – the 'Bomber's Moon' – each one loaded with bombs and letting them fall over Portsmouth. It was as if it didn't matter any more whether they fell on the Dockyard, on the ships in the harbour, on the Naval establishments and military barracks, or on simple two-up, two-down terraced homes like those in April Grove. It was as if so long as people were injured and killed, so long as buildings were damaged and destroyed, the pilots could go home satisfied at having done their job.

Gladys Shaw was out in her ambulance as well. Polly and Judy had seen it as they set off – a battered old van in even worse condition than theirs – and Gladys had given them a murderous look as she swung the crank-handle. 'I'm fed up with this!' she'd yelled. 'Bloody *fed up*! I was going out with Graham tonight, and, now flaming Hitler's messed it all up again. I'm sick of him – bloody *sick* of him!'

She'd swung the van out into the road and Polly and Judy gave each other a grimace. 'We're all fed up,' Polly said, starting her own van. 'We've had nearly enough of this, Judy. But we've got to carry on, all the same.'

'She doesn't mean she's giving in,' Judy said, scrambling into the seat beside her. 'She just means she'd like to wring his neck.' So would I, she thought, thinking regretfully of her own date with Chris and wondering if he had been the first to spot and identify the new wave of attacking aircraft. 'Who's Graham, anyway?'

Polly put her foot cautiously on the accelerator. The van was liable to pretend it wasn't going to move, then suddenly leap forward, to the danger of anyone who happened to be standing near. 'I think it's Graham Philpotts, that young matelot Betty Chapman knocked about with for a while. His family used to live round here when I was still at home, before they moved over to Gosport. Where are we supposed to be going, Judy?'

'Maddens. It's on fire.' Maddens was a big hotel on the corner of the Guildhall Square. If that had been hit, there were bound to be casualties, unless they'd all got into the shelter before the bombing started. Whether the ambulance would ever get there or not was another question: they were sure to pass other emergencies on their way to the city centre, and you couldn't just drive past people desperate to get some injured friend to a First-Aid Post or hospital. There was the added problem of finding your way through streets that had been bombed already and were blocked with fallen masonry, or full of other ambulances as well as fire engines with hoses tangled like snakes all over the road – and all this in pitch darkness lit only by jagged flames or roaring infernos that warned you to reverse swiftly out of their heat. It took hours to get anywhere, and more than once Polly stopped while Judy tried to find out exactly where they were. 'I thought I knew this place,' she said despairingly, 'but we could be in the middle of Liverpool for all I can recognise now.'

At last they reached their destination, only to find that the casualties had already been removed. A fireman, his reddened eyes staring out of a face streaked with soot, yelled at them to get out of the way, Polly slammed the van into reverse once more to get out of range of the flames, then jerked to a stop and leaped out as a man jumped out in front of the van, waving his arms. 'What is it? Someone hurt?'

'It's me mum,' he shouted. His voice was drowned by the roar of the planes and the thunder of the bombs, but she could read the message in his lips and see the terror in his eyes. 'She's got caught under something – oh my God, it's awful. Come and help, miss, please, you gotta help!' He had hold of Polly's arm, dragging her across the road. Judy snatched up the First-Aid haversack and scurried after them, her heart thumping. They ran down a narrow alley and found themselves in a huddle of old houses, hidden behind the Theatre Royal and the small shops and offices that occupied the buildings along the main road. I never even knew all this existed, Judy thought, her old fear of confined spaces returning as she stared up at the high walls that surrounded them, but there was no time for panic. The man was tugging her towards a tall building, one of several around a tiny, dank courtyard that probably never saw the light of day. The building was half-collapsed, its front wall sagging dangerously over the paving stones, and the lower floor was in ruins.

'She's in *there*?' Polly asked, stopping, and Judy, close behind her, stared in dismay at the wreckage. 'Your mother's in *there*?'

He jerked her arm impatiently. 'That's what I said, innit? She's got a coupla rooms there – there's no shelter or nothing, and she wouldn't go down the public, says there's rats. For Gawd's sake, can't you do nothing? She's trapped, there's summat over her leg, I can't get her out and she's crying and moaning something awful.' He stared at the two women, his face working with fear. 'I arst a fireman but they're all too busy with Maddens and all round there. The station's bin hit, and the Post Office and McIlroy's – it's bloody chaos – and the ARP ain't no good, too bloody busy going round telling people to put lights out. *Lights!*' He cast a bitter glance at the raddled glow of the sky. 'There ain't no bloody lights to *put* out, they done in the electric again, and my poor old mum . . .' Once again, he jerked Polly's arm. 'Can't you do nothing?'

Polly shook herself and hurried forward. The wall of the house sloped out perilously above her; she gave it one glance and decided not to look again. The man urged her through the doorway of the building and she crouched to scramble under the leaning architrave. The door was stuck half-open and she had to wriggle past it, praying all the time that the building was not about to collapse on top of her. Behind her, she could feel Judy following, and a moment later the room was lit by the thin beam of the torch.

'Oh, my God,' Polly breathed, and heard Judy draw in her breath.

The room was small and you could see that even before the bomb had fallen it had been no more than a slum. The walls had old cracks as well as new – cracks that were thick with black dirt and mould. The one wall that was left undamaged was encrusted with a huge patch of damp, riddled with fungus. Half the ceiling had come down in a muddle of laths and plaster. The fireplace was filled with soot and rubble from the chimney, and didn't look as if there had been a fire in it for months, despite the bitter weather. The only furniture was an old table, now smothered with dust and rubble, a broken armchair and a chamber pot.

In one corner was a heap of what looked like old blankets and possibly a mattress, and on this lay an old woman. She was crumpled like a broken toy, her face creased with fear and pain, and across the lower part of her body lay a large beam of wood which had fallen in from the wall. There was more rubble all around her, and it was a miracle that her upper body had not been crushed as well.

Polly and Judy scrambled across the room and knelt beside her. Polly touched the withered cheek.

'My name's Polly Dunn. I've come to help you. Tell me where it hurts.'

'Every bleedin' where,' the woman muttered. Her voice sounded like a creaking gate and every word came with difficulty. 'Bleedin' Jerries.'

Polly cast a swift glance over the woman's chest and shoulders. There was no blood and she ran gentle fingers over her. Apart from a few swear words, the woman made no response. There didn't appear to be anything broken there, and Polly heaved a sigh of relief.

The pelvis and legs were a different matter. From the waist down, the old woman was pinned beneath the beam and a mound of bricks and mortar. There were probably dreadful injuries there, and even moving the weight from her body could cause more harm. Polly stared at the sight, biting her lips and wondering what to do. She glanced uncertainly at Judy and as she did so the woman groaned and began to vomit.

'She's bleeding, look,' Judy whispered, pointing at the rubble, and Polly saw a stream of blood trickling between the bricks and soaking the dust and plaster. 'If we don't manage to stop it—'

Polly nodded sharply. The woman would bleed to death. 'We've got to get the stuff off her. But carefully. Where's the son?'

'I'm here.' The man came forward, staring fearfully at the mess. 'Is she going to be all right? Ma?'

'I don't know. We'll do our best, but it's dangerous – we don't know what the injuries are. We've got to stop the bleeding, so the first thing to do is get some of this rubble off her. It's heavy, but we've got to be very careful not to hurt her any more, or even take things off too suddenly. You stay beside her, make sure all that sick's wiped away out of her mouth.'

Polly began to lift bricks away, passing them to Judy to toss into the corner of the room. Together they worked while the man cradled his mother's head in his hands, imploring her not to go, not to leave him, not to die, for *Gawd's* sake, not to die . . .

The blood continued to seep from under the rubble, soaking their clothes. How much has she got in her, Judy wondered, and how much can she afford to lose? She tried to remember what she'd been taught in the First-Aid classes all the WVS staff and volunteers had done. Was it eight pints? A gallon? But this woman looked so tiny and withered, she surely couldn't have that much blood in her body. And how much had she lost already? She's going to die, she thought suddenly, and her heart seemed to drop. She's going to die.

The old woman was rambling now, swearing at the Germans, at the Government, at the bombers, at the ARP. She called out for people she must have known during her life – Johnny, our Moll, Fred and Rags, presumably the family dog. She went further back and cried for her father and mother, who must have been dead for years. Her son pleaded with her to come back to the present, to know that he was with her: 'It's your Jack, Mum, don't you know me, your Jack what's looked after you all these years. Don't say you don't know me, Ma, I can't bear it . . . It's your Jack, your *Jack* . . .'

Their voices went on and on, calling and shouting against each other, and the anguish of it tore at Polly's heart. It might be a slum, but this was a mother and son who'd stuck together through who knew what bad times, and now they'd come to this terrible end. Like Judy, she was sure the old woman was going to die. Too much blood was being lost, too much injury suffered. And yet she could not give up. As long as the old heart could still beat, as long as the tattered lungs could still draw breath to scream, there must be hope. While there was life, there must still be hope . . .

At last there was nothing left on the crumpled body but the beam itself. It lay across the woman's abdomen, crushing her body and one leg which was curled beneath her. Polly stared at it. She saw the mess of torn flesh and broken bone, the twisted internal organs that should never be revealed, and wondered sickly how the old woman had survived this long.

'Oh Polly,' Judy whispered in her ear. 'Whatever are we going to do?'

*

Chris had been the first to spot the approaching wave of bombers.

He had been working overtime in the Dockyard until noon, then gone home for his Sunday dinner. He'd had a wash at the sink, grabbed his tin helmet, fastened his brassard to his arm and then cycled out to the hotel, looking forward to his date with Judy later on. She was a real smasher, he thought, his heart quickening a little, but it was a shame she was engaged. Still, she'd agreed to go for a walk with him so maybe it wasn't really that serious. If it was, Chris wouldn't push things, but he couldn't help hoping . . .

He arrived at the hotel and went straight up in the lift, thinking of the hour or so he and Judy had spent trapped inside. Good old lift, he thought affectionately, watching the walls as it creaked its way up. At least *you* were on my side. The lift shuddered to a stop and he got out and climbed the fire-escape ladder to the roof.

The roof was a large, flat area with a variety of small, square buildings planted apparently at random over it. Some were water tanks, one was the Fire Brigade lookout and one was the ROC Observation Post – little more than a shack, with a table inside on which lay a map with the pivoting plotting instrument mounted on top. The Observers also had a small wooden 'caboose' where they had a chair or two, a stove and a kettle. Spud Murphy, Chris's fellow Observer, was already inside, brewing up.

Chris took a quick look around. The view from up here must be the best in Pompey, he thought. To the north, you could see the green bulk of Portsdown Hill, pocked with chalk pits, with the whole city spread between. You could see all the bomb damage – streets of demolished houses, huge piles of rubble, the ruins of churches, shops and, worst of all, the Guildhall, a gutted shell amidst the desolation. His heart grew cold as he gazed at it.

Turning west, he could see the broad, glittering harbour, always crowded with naval ships, and the Camber, driving into the heart of Old Portsmouth, where the fishermen and small commercial ships came. The square, white tower of the cathedral looked deceptively strong and tranquil in the late afternoon light and he wondered how long it would be before that too was blasted to smithereens.

The Royal Beach faced south, over the Solent towards the Isle of Wight. On an April Sunday afternoon in peacetime this would have been thronged with yachts and sailing dinghies and the beach crowded with families bathing and having picnics on the shingle beach. Today there were just a few, probably people who lived close by. Most of the others who might have come out would be staying at home, wanting to be within reach of shelter in case of a raid, and South Parade Pier itself was almost deserted. Chris had been to a good few dances there; like most young men and women he was keen on the big bands and had never failed to be there when Joe Loss, Ambrose or Sid Phillips were performing. He wondered if Judy had been there on those nights too – maybe with that fiancé of hers – and thought wistfully of taking her himself. He hoped that nothing would happen to spoil their date tonight.

Spud poked his head out of the caboose. 'Tea up, mate. Anything in sight?'

Chris shook his head, turning to gaze eastwards across the sweep of Langstone Harbour, smaller and shallower than the main harbour and used mostly by fishermen and leisure sailors. It was from that direction, over Hayling Island, that enemy attackers usually came, or sometimes from the Isle of Wight. The two Observers who had been on duty came out of the shack. There was nothing to report, they said, and clattered off down the steel ladder, leaving Chris and Spud in charge.

The ROC had been formed in the 1920s, almost entirely of volunteers like Chris. Until only a fortnight ago, it had been simply the 'Observer Corps', the title 'Royal' having been conferred upon it in recognition of its services during the Battle of Britain, last September. There was talk of their being allowed to wear RAF uniform as well and Chris hoped this would happen. He still felt disappointed at not being able to join up, and to wear His Majesty's uniform and be seen to be a part of it all would go a long way to make up for that.

Carrying their mugs of tea, Chris and Spud went into the lookout post. As well as the table with the map and plotting instrument, there was a telephone and a large pair of binoculars. It was one Observer's job to scan the skies, keeping a constant watch for aircraft, while the other plotted their position and course. The details were then telephoned through to the Winchester Observation Centre, where the plotters worked at their large central table, using long poles to move the counters that represented the aircraft into their positions. With information coming through headphones from three posts at once, each observing the same aircraft, it was possible for the controllers on the dais overlooking the table to see exactly what was happening in the sky many miles away, and to take appropriate action.

Chris picked up his binoculars and immediately spotted a plane, heading for the Fleet Air Arm airfield at Lee-on-the-Solent. 'Friendly Fleet Air Arm,' he reported, and Spud quickly plotted its position and wrote it in the log book. *Friendly civil. Friendly coastal.* Each one was plotted and reported to Winchester. The overall picture was important, even when there were no raiders.

The afternoon wore on, the few people who were still on the beach went home and the sun began to dip towards the horizon. It looked as though his date with Judy would be safe. Spud took his turn with the binoculars and Chris made another mug of tea and began to relax.

His four-hour duty was almost over when he picked up the glasses for the last time and caught sight of the dark spots far away over Hayling Island.

'Raiders,' he said sharply, and Spud, who was writing up

the log book, snapped to attention. 'Blimey, there's bloody hundreds of them . . . Get their positions plotted, quick!'

Spud bent over the map which covered the table. It was marked with Ordnance Survey grid references and, with the pivoting mapping instrument mounted in the centre, he could estimate the attackers' present position as well as their direction. At the same time, reports began to come in from the post further along the coast, giving details of the invaders as they passed, and Spud began to set the Micklethwait in position. 'Altitude?'

'Around 10,000 feet. Junker Ju88As . . . Dornier Do17s . . . Heinkels . . . They're sending the bloody lot over – this is going to be a big one . . . Coming in fast now – get on to HQ . . .'

Spud grabbed the phone and spoke urgently. '3M.3 calling, numerous planes seen 7592, flying north, height 10,000 feet.' By the time he had finished, Chris was spitting out more information. Continuing to operate the Micklethwait, Spud relayed the details, knowing that in Winchester everyone would be agog, watching the development of what must be a big raid. But a big raid over which city? 'It's going to be Pompey,' he said, taking a quick look through the window. 'Bugger it, Chris, it's going to be us!'

Almost before he had finished speaking, the sirens began to wail. The steel ladder rattled and the Chief Observer thrust his way into the tiny shelter. 'What's going on?'

'Large formation over Hayling, sir.' Chris handed him the spare set of binoculars. 'Looks like a hell of a raid.'

'You've been on to Winchester?'

The question was unnecessary. Spud was still on the phone, reporting the progress of the invaders. 'Looks like they're coming here, sir.' He thought regretfully of his date with Judy. 'Blimey, they're like a flock of bloody starlings coming home to roost!' The sky was darkening with the mass of aircraft. In a few moments, the drone of their engines would be audible; a few moments after that and the bombs would begin to fall. 'Hey, look, ours are up now!' A flock of wings had risen into the air down the coast, somewhere near Chichester. 'That'll see them off! Atta boy!'

The three men watched tensely. Chris had forgotten about going off duty. The chances were that his relief wouldn't get here now. Like most of the Observers, the next two on duty were Portsmouth boys and able to live at home. If the raid were bad, they might well get caught or be unable to make it through the streets. Observers had been known to be stuck in their posts for hours, sometimes days, especially during the snowstorms of January, and you never left your post until relief arrived – not if you wanted to remain an Observer.

Chris continued to watch the planes, still rapping out estimates of position and altitude to Spud who swiftly checked them on the map and relayed them to the plotting rooms at Winchester. There was no time for anyone to think about being off duty. No time to think of anything else but the raiders, and the urgent need to prevent their deadly progress.

'One's down!' Chris could see the balloon of black smoke and the spurt of flame as a Dornier spiralled into the sea. 'Oh, bloody well done!' But one was not enough. Ten would not be enough, nor twenty, out of the mass of aircraft still steadily approaching. 'There's bloody hundreds of them,' he said again. 'Bloody *hundreds.*'

The siren had wailed into silence. The hotel was almost certainly deserted now, with everyone in it sheltering in the basements, just as all those in Portsmouth would now be crouching in their Andersons or pushing into the street shelters. Those who could not would be huddled under the stairs, while some who refused to shelter at all would be sitting defiantly in their own back rooms, convinced that if a bomb had their name on it, it would find them wherever they were. And some, ignoring the danger, would be preparing to go out into the streets, ready to put out incendiaries, fight fires, rescue the trapped from bombed buildings or give First Aid to the injured.

Judy would be doing that, Chris thought. Judy would be out there now, setting up an Incident Enquiry Centre or out on an ambulance somewhere. Oh God, he prayed, keep her safe. Don't let her be hurt.

The planes were almost overhead. The men jammed their tin helmets on their heads and watched tautly as one streaked low, heading straight for South Parade Pier. The roar of its engine shook the wooden turret, shook the hotel itself. Frozen, Chris stared as a stick of bombs fell away from its belly – four of them in a line, each falling into the sea and sending up a huge spray of foam and shingle. Then he saw that the plane was coming over the pier and straight for the hotel. There'll be another bomb, he thought, it'll be a direct hit. Someone grabbed his arm and he turned to see the Chief yelling at him, the words inaudible but the meaning clear. *'Get downstairs, you fool!'* He found himself pushed unceremoniously towards the steel ladder and tumbled down it, ducking into the rest-room at the bottom just as the explosion shook the building.

'Hell's teeth!' Spud muttered in his ear as the noise died slowly away. 'That was flaming close.'

Cautiously, they got to their feet. There were only the three of them there; everyone else had gone down to the base-ment, leaving mugs of tea and half-eaten buns on the tables. Two mugs had fallen to the floor, spreading their contents on the linoleum, while one had stayed miraculously upright, its surface barely rippled. The windows had shattered and when Chris removed his tin helmet a mass of broken glass showered to the floor. He found shards embedded in his jumper, and wondered briefly what would have happened if he had been in shirtsleeves.

'Right, let's get back up to the post,' the Chief said

tersely. 'Winchester will be wondering what the hell's going on.'

They scrambled up the ladder. The wooden shack was still standing. But there was a gaping hole in its roof now, and as they crowded through the doorway they realised at once what a narrow escape they had had.

The fifth bomb of the stick had landed behind the hotel. Apart from the shattered windows there was little damage. But it had dug a crater in the street below, and a paving slab had been blown high into the air and had landed on the table where, a few seconds earlier, Chris had been staring through binoculars and Spud had been plotting the positions of the enemy aircraft.

Cissie and Alice huddled in the Anderson, clutching each other's hands in the darkness. Both were worried about Polly and Judy, somewhere out there amongst all the bombs, and both were anxious about Dick, still in the Royal Hospital. It had been damaged once already in the first Blitz and patched up again, but who was to say it wouldn't be hit again? 'They don't bomb the same place twice,' Alice said, trying to be a comfort to her daughter, but Cissie shook her head and a hot tear fell on to the back of her hand.

'I can't believe that, Mum. All these thousands of bombs –' they both ducked lower at the roar and vibration of a bomb falling not far away '– they've got to land somewhere. I don't see how they can miss a big place like the Royal.'

'But aren't they more likely to aim for the Dockyard? I mean, the ships are more vital to them, aren't they, and the repair shops. I reckon anywhere else just gets hit by accident.'

'Mum, they don't care where they hit now. All that stuff about only aiming for military targets – that's all gone by the board. They just want to destroy and kill wherever they can. And if they can't kill us, they'll frighten us to death. It's what they call terror bombing.' Cissie clutched her hand even more tightly as another explosion rocked the earth and the corrugated iron roof of the Anderson shifted and screeched. 'Oh my God, my God! Oh, Dick – where are you? I want him back, Mum, I want him home!'

Alice was in tears. 'He's better off where he is, Cis. He's being looked after, he's safe.'

'He's not! He's not! The Royal's already been bombed once. He could be being bombed now, this very minute.' Cissie had lost all control. 'At least if he was home I'd know what was happening, I could look after him myself. I'm going to get him, Mum.' She half rose to her feet, crouching in the low space, and Alice groped for her and grasped her coat.

'You can't! Don't be daft, our Cis! Sit down at once and pull yourself together!' Her voice sharpened, became a reminder of the days when Cissie had been a child and her mother a strict disciplinarian. *Sit down this minute!*

Shaken out of her hysteria, Cissie sank back on to the narrow bunk, trembling with sobs. Alice put her arm around her and drew her close, and Cissie leaned her head on her mother's shoulder, feeling the comfort of her mother's embrace just as a moment ago she had felt her authority.

'Oh, Mum,' she said brokenly. 'Oh Mum, I don't know that I can stand any more of this.'

'I know, love,' Alice murmured, stroking her hair. 'I know. This is the worst we've ever known, and we've been through enough in our time, heaven knows. One world war already, the 'flu epidemic that took your dad, the hard times we went through in the thirties – and now this. But we've got to bear up, Cis. It's no use giving way to it all. We've got to keep going somehow, and keep a smile on our lips while we do. It don't do none of us no good to let it get on top of us.'

'A *smile*!' Cissie said, with an attempt at a laugh. 'I don't reckon anyone feels like smiling tonight.' The noise was still going on outside – the drone of planes, the rattle of anti-aircraft fire, the sudden shattering roar of exploding bombs. 'I don't see how anyone *can* feel like smiling.'

'Doesn't matter what we feel like,' Alice said with a return to her sharpness. 'It's putting a smile on our faces that counts, not what we feel like inside. It makes you *feel* better, smiling does, and it makes other people feel better to see you do it. So you try it now, Cis. Come on.'

'Oh Mum!' This time, the laugh was unforced. 'Who's going to see me? It's pitch dark in here. Who's going to know if I'm smiling or not?'

'*You'll* know,' Alice said firmly. 'And so will I. We'll keep each other cheerful, Cis, same as we've done all those other times. Now come on, put a smile on your face and let's play a game of something to pass the time.'

'A game?' Cissie repeated, but Alice heard the wobbly grin in her voice. 'And just what game d'you think we ought to play, Mum – *I Spy With My Little Eye?*'

'What are we going to do?' Judy repeated. She stared around at the dimly lit room, the shadowy corners heaped with rubbish, at the torn, broken walls, at the heavy beam that still lay across the crushed body. The darkness and the squalor of it pressed in on her and she felt the familiar worm of panic.

'I don't know,' Polly whispered back. 'I don't know what to do. I don't know what anyone can do.' She turned and saw the woman's son staring too. 'We need help. We need men – a doctor.'

'She's 'ad it,' he said tonelessly. 'She's 'ad it, ain't she? Nobody can't get her out of this.'

'We'll fetch help,' Polly said again, and turned to Judy. 'Go and see if you can find someone. Bring them here. Say they must come. We need at least two men, strong men, and a doctor. We've *got* to have help.'

Judy stared at her. 'But I can't leave you.'

'Go!' Polly shouted, and her voice was edged with fear. 'Go on, go! Get some help! We can't do it by ourselves. *Please*, Judy!'

Judy's face crumpled but she turned and scurried out of the building. Outside, the sky was crimson with flames and even the beams of the searchlights were dimmed. She could still hear planes overhead, and the sudden reverberation of exploding bombs. No one will come, she thought despairingly. Not for one old woman.

She ran out of the alley and looked both ways. Several shops and offices were ablaze now, surrounded by firemen. Over the road, she could see a huddle of people round something on the pavement. She ran over and caught at an arm. 'What's happening? Is there a doctor anywhere here?'

'Kiddy hurt,' a man said briefly. 'Doctor's looking after her now.'

'Oh.' Judy gazed helplessly at the scene. The child was stretched on the pavement, clearly unconscious, and a woman was kneeling beside her. She must be the doctor – Judy had heard of the young woman doctor who had been so brave in the bombing, coming out to help whatever the danger. She wanted to go to her, beg her to come and help the old woman who was dying in the slum room nearby, but she knew she could not. This was a child, in equal or perhaps worse danger. The doctor wouldn't leave her, and Judy couldn't ask it.

A van screeched to a halt and Judy looked round and saw Gladys Shaw scrambling down from the driver's seat. Her mother Peggy came round from the passenger's side. 'What's the trouble? Does anyone need taking to the hospital?' She looked down at the child on the pavement and the young woman doctor beside her, then pulled open the back doors of the van and dragged out a stretcher. 'Get her into the ambulance. I'll take her straight away.' Carefully, the doctor and two or three helpers began to lift the small body on to it.

'I'll go with her,' someone volunteered. 'I'm her auntie, I'll look after her.' There was a hasty consultation with the doctor, and then she pulled herself up into the van with the little girl. The crowd sighed thankfully and began to hurry away to find shelter.

The doctor stood up and pushed back her hair. Judy grabbed her arm. 'Don't go! Please – there's an old woman in a building over there. She's trapped by a wooden beam and she's bleeding terribly. My aunt's in there and we've been lifting stuff off her, but we can't manage any more. We need help.' She called out to some of the departing crowd: 'Can some of you come – *please*? She'll die if we can't get her out.'

A couple of men turned and came back. 'Who is it? Where is she?'

'Over there.' Judy pointed. 'Her son's in there with her, and my auntie. We're both WVS, she drives an ambulance, too – it's that van over there. The ceiling's all fallen in and the old lady's in a terrible way, crying and screaming and being sick.' They were all hurrying across the road now, leaping across the snaking hoses of the firemen, dodging past vehicles and fallen masonry. Judy ducked down the dark little alleyway and led them into the courtyard. 'She's in there.'

There was a brief pause. The two men, the doctor and Judy all stood for a moment, staring at the building, at the wall that still leaned outwards, looking as if it might topple at any moment. Then the doctor turned to Judy and began to speak.

Judy never knew what she had been going to say. At that moment, there was a tremendous explosion as a bomb fell only a few streets away. What glass there was left in the surrounding windows blew outwards, spattering them with lethal shards. One of the men screamed and clapped both hands over his eyes, and the other jerked him and Judy to the ground. The doctor dropped beside her and then cried out and dragged them all to their feet again, pointing wildly at the building above them.

The wall that had been leaning so precariously outwards seemed to shiver and bend in the flickering light of the flames that burned the sky. It buckled slowly and began to fall into the courtyard. There was a shattering roar, and Judy and the others scuttled back into the alleyway just in time.

The narrow passage was filled with dust; thick, fine, choking dust. Judy retched and struggled for breath. She could see nothing in the sudden swirling darkness; she could feel only the urgent hands of the young doctor, thrusting her towards the entrance to the alleyway, towards what fresh air there was. Her mind was filled with the compelling need to breathe, to stay alive. I've got to get out of here, she thought, I've got to get out. And then, following swiftly, another thought: *But Polly's still inside . . .*

'Polly!' She turned and tried to run back into the alley. 'Polly – my aunt – she was in there! *She was in that building!* We've got to go back in and get her out!'

Chapter Twelve

By daybreak, the city once again lay devastated. The mine that had destroyed Maddens Hotel had also damaged the town railway station and the main Post Office. Kingston Prison had been hit, and the railway line behind it blocked. There were massive fires in the Dockyard and many homes and businesses were hit. Over a hundred people had been killed and hundreds more injured. Once again, the Emergency Centres were busy finding homes for those who had been bombed out.

Cissie and her mother crept out of their Anderson soon after dawn. April Grove had escaped damage, and people all along the row of long, narrow gardens leading to the allotments were making their way up their paths, hoping the gas was on so that they could make tea. Cissie went straight through the house to the front, hoping to see Polly and Judy coming home. Alice followed her.

There were quite a few people out there already. Frank Budd, who had spent the night firewatching, was already setting off to go to work in the Dockyard and Tommy Vickers was coming down the street, stumbling a little with weariness. The two men paused for a moment and Alice and Cissie joined them.

'Bad night,' Frank said, shaking his head. 'There'll be all sorts of damage done. You could read a newspaper by the light of the flames. I suppose it was the city centre and the Yard got it worst again.'

Tommy looked at him. Usually a bright, cheery man with a quip for every occasion, he looked, as Frank put it later, 'proper done in'. His eyes were red-rimmed with smoke and fatigue, his face drawn and grey. He rubbed a hand across his face.

'I just come from Powerscourt Road. There've been more bombs there.' He shook his head slowly. 'Kids – boys – in the cellar of one of those houses that were bombed last year. Where young Kathy Simmons lived before she come to October Street.' His voice was trembling a little. 'Reckon they had some sort o' den there – you know what boys are. Collecting stuff – shrapnel, that sort of thing.' He took a deep breath while Frank stared at him. 'Seems like they had a bomb in there with them – unexploded. They must have found it and took it there.' He stopped.

'A bomb?' Frank said. 'Why, the silly young fools. Didn't they realise it could go off at any time?' He stopped and looked more closely at Tommy. 'What is it, Tom? What happened?'

'The place was hit again,' Tommy said wearily, 'and the bomb went off as well. They'd got out of the cellar, they were out in the garden when it went, but . . . ' He looked at Frank and the women as if begging them to say it wasn't true. 'They were youngsters from round here, that's the worst of it. That Micky Baxter. And young Jimmy Cross. And that little Nash boy – Cyril, is it? – the one that always looks as if butter wouldn't melt in his mouth. Not that we found much of him,' he added bitterly. 'Blown to bits, poor little tyke. And Jimmy Cross – well, he's lost a leg, blown clean off, and they reckon he'll be lucky if that's all the damage.'

Cissie stared at him. 'But youngsters like that ought to have been down in their shelters. What on earth were they doing out there? What were their mums and dads *thinking* of?'

'I don't suppose Nancy Baxter even knew Micky was out,' Alice said. 'She's not home herself at night all that much. But the other two – well, I'd have thought they'd be better looked after.'

'It'll have been that Micky Baxter who was the ring-leader,' Frank said grimly. 'There's always trouble where that boy is. What about him, Tom? Was he hurt?'

'I dunno. I don't think he was, much, just knocked out by the blast.' Tommy rubbed his face again. 'But those other two – I tell you, I don't never want to see nothing like that again. That little Cyril Nash – he used to come round here with his guy, Firework Night, asking for pennies. My Freda always used to give him something, she said he had such a sweet face. I dunno how she's going to take this.'

'And Jimmy Cross too,' Alice said sadly. 'I used to live in the same street as his grandpa when I was little – played together, we did. They were a nice family, the Crosses. What a terrible thing.'

Tommy went indoors and Frank continued on his way. Alice and Cissie looked at each other.

'I'm worried sick about our Polly and Judy,' Cissie said, her voice shaking. 'Something's happened to them, Mum, I'm sure of it. Something awful's happened to them.'

'I just don't know what we ought to do,' Alice said. She'd managed to persuade Cissie to come back indoors and boil up a kettle for some tea; just for once, the gas supply seemed to have survived the raid. That didn't mean it wouldn't be cut off later, of course, if there was danger from an unexploded bomb or some fracture further along the mains. But for now, you could at least make a hot drink. Alice put a couple of slices of bread under the grill too, but when she spread margarine and Marmite on the toast Cissie shook her head.

'I couldn't eat a thing, Mum, not till I know what's happened to them. And there's Dick as well, he's supposed to be coming out of hospital in the next day or two. What am I going to tell him when I go in at visiting time if our Judy still isn't home?'

'She'll be back by then.' Alice spoke with more conviction than she felt. 'Bound to be. But I don't know what we can do about it anyway, Cis. I suppose we could go down the Emergency Centre. They'll know what's what.'

Cissie began to get to her feet. 'I'll go now.'

'You'll eat your breakfast first.' Once again, Alice's voice was stern, reminding Cissie of her childhood. 'You don't take a step out of this house without something inside you. Eat up your toast now, there's a good girl. You don't want me to waste it, do you?'

If she'd really been the child her mother seemed to think she was, Cissie would have retorted that she hadn't wanted her to make it. But she was a grown woman, for all her nervousness, and knew that you couldn't afford to waste good food these days. Alice was right – she did need something to eat before she went out. So she picked up the toast and nibbled it, then realised that she really was hungry and ate it without further argument. She drank the tea and then got up again.

'I'll go down the Centre now, Mum. You're right, they'll know what's happened. They might even be there, our Judy and Polly, having a rest before they come home. They must have been so busy last night . . .' Her voice wavered again and then strengthened as Alice too began to make ready for going out. 'No, you stop here. You need a rest too and I'd rather there was someone here in case they come while I'm gone.'

She shrugged on her jacket and let herself out into the street again. April Grove was busy now, with women at their doors washing their steps and delivery vans already beginning to arrive with bread, milk and vegetables. It was a marvel how people just got on with their lives even after a night like they'd just been through, Cissie reflected. Mind you, the baker's van didn't seem to have many loaves to hand out, and old Mr Briggs who drove it seemed to be operating his own rationing system ('No, Mrs Kinch, you 'ad one yesterday, you can't 'ave got through that already'), while his horse seemed nervous, as if it had been frightened all night, which it probably had. But the milkman was whistling cheerfully and the burly man from the greengrocer's was weighing out potatoes as if he didn't have a care in the world. So perhaps the raid hadn't been so bad after all, she thought hopefully as she hurried along.

It was a different matter when she came out into the main road. There were no buses running, and she could see a pall of smoke further south, over Portsea. A woman walked past crying, with a handkerchief held up to her face, and there was a group of workmen standing on a corner looking stunned. Cissie began to feel anxious again, a heavy sense of dread settling over her like a cloud. She thought again of the little boy who had been killed and the one who would be 'lucky if he only lost a leg'. How many others were there like that?

Her chest and throat tight with anxiety, Cissie almost ran along the pavement. I ought to go to the hospital too, she thought, and let Dick know we're all right. Even if they don't let me in, I ought to go. But I don't *know* that we're all right, she reminded herself. Until I know where Polly and my Judy are, I don't know that at all.

Dick would be all right, anyway, tucked up in bed and well looked after. He was over the worst now, and yesterday they'd told her he'd be home in a few days. He'd be worrying about them, she was sure, and the minute she knew about Polly and Judy she'd go straight to the Royal and get a message to him, but just for now her sister and daughter came first.

She arrived at the Centre at last. It was thronged with people and as Cissie came round the corner and saw the queue her heart leaped with relief. Not for all those poor souls who'd been bombed out, of course, but just because she knew that if there were so many people needing help it was no wonder Polly and Judy hadn't been able to get home. They'd been there all night, handing out cocoa and sandwiches, and probably that's where they were still. Some of the daytime volunteers might have been bombed as well, or just couldn't get through the streets to take over. That was all it was. She'd see them the minute she went through the door, looking tired but cheerful, glad as always to be able to lend a hand.

Getting through the door wasn't so easy, however. The people waiting were reluctant to let her through. 'Oy, no queue-jumping if you don't mind! Go to the back. It's first come, first served.'

'I need to see my daughter.'

'You've got a wait, then,' said a woman with pinched lips and a deep vertical line between her eyebrows. 'Gawd knows what they're doing in there, but whatever it is they're handing out there's not going to be much left for us poor buggers. We bin here since five, and hardly moved.'

'No, she's a volunteer – a helper. She's been out all night. I just want to make sure she's all right. And my sister too, she drives an ambulance. Please let me through,' Cissie begged. 'I've got my hubby in hospital, too, in the Royal, he's had pneumonia. I've got to go and let him know we're all right.'

'In the Royal?' A man standing just in front of them turned. 'Well, you'd better go and see if *he's* all right too. Didn't you know it got hit last night?'

'The Royal?' Cissie stared at him, her heart suddenly cold. 'The Royal Hospital got hit?'

''S right. Mine fell on it. Hundreds killed, so I heard. There was ambulances backwards and forwards all night, and what I heard was, the Casualty Ward got the worst of it. Maybe that's where your girl's gone, if your sis was one of the drivers.'

Cissie felt sick. She put out one hand and leaned against

the door jamb, swept by a wave of dizziness. The woman who had been reluctant to let her through steadied her with one arm.

'Here, hold on, ducks. I dare say your girl's all right, and your sister too. They're probably in here now, dishing out tea and filling up forms. And if it was just the Casualty that got hit, your hubby'll be all right. Don't you worry. Now look, you go on in and make sure they're here and then pop off to the Royal. Let her through,' she said, raising her voice to those in front. 'Let this lady through, she's got a girl and a sister in the volunteers, and her hubby's down the Royal. Come on, move yourselves!'

The queue shifted, some of those at the front grumbling a little but, as the details were passed along the line, changing dramatically as they went, Cissie was allowed to pass. By the time she reached the head of the queue the whispers had arrived before her, and she was receiving sympathetic glances. 'Lost her hubby and daughter and sister in the raid,' someone murmured as she passed, and Cissie swayed again. Suppose it were true! Oh, let it not be true, she begged.

To her relief, the woman pouring tea was Annie Chapman. 'Cis! Whatever are you doing here? I thought you'd be at the hospital.'

Cissie stared at her. 'At the hospital? You mean the Royal?'

'Well, no. They were taking people to Queen Alexandra or St James's. The Royal was hit, you know.' Annie's hand flew to her mouth in consternation. 'Oh, my goodness. Your hubby's in there, isn't he? How is he? Have you been to see?'

'No – I didn't even know about it till a few minutes ago.' Cissie put her hand to her head. 'I was looking for Polly and Judy – they never came home. I thought I'd find them here, but . . .' Annie's words sank in and she caught her breath.

'D'you mean to say *they've* been taken to hospital, too? They've been hurt?'

Annie looked dismayed. 'Cis, I'm ever so sorry to break it to you like this. That's what I heard, anyway. They were in some building when it collapsed. They can't have been killed,' she added swiftly. 'They can't, can they, or they wouldn't have been taken to hospital. But that's all I've heard. I'm sorry.'

Cissie felt as if all her surroundings – the hall full of people, the noise, the clatter of kettles and teacups – had fallen away from her, leaving her swinging giddily over a yawning abyss. For a moment she was aware of nothing but a deadly fear, a horror of the roaring darkness that rushed in upon her. Then hands gripped her and she felt herself guided to a chair and her head pressed gently between her knees. Someone put a cup to her lips and she tasted cold water. She spluttered and swallowed, and gradually the sickness receded and she was aware once more of the clatter in the hall, the hubbub of voices. Slowly, she lifted her head. Annie was crouching beside her.

'I'm ever so sorry, Cis,' she said again. 'All we heard was that they'd gone to hospital – we don't know which one it was ourselves. They'll let us know later, but it was such a bad night, everything's just an awful muddle.'

Cissie nodded. 'What am I going to do?' she asked bleakly. 'I don't know where to go first. Someone said there was hundreds killed in the Royal. I've got to find out what's happened to Dick. But if Judy's been hurt – and our Poll – and they might be in QA or St James's . . .' A fresh thought struck her. 'St *James's*! That's the mental hospital! Does that mean—?'

'It just means they were taking casualties there,' Annie said firmly. 'It doesn't mean anything else at all. Cis, I don't know what to tell you. We can't even ring up – the telephones are mostly out of action again, and what lines there are they need for the emergency services. It's like a madhouse out there.' She bit her lip, obviously regretting that choice of phrase, and turned as someone called her. 'Look, I'm sorry, Cis, I'll have to go. You can see how we're placed here. Tell you what I think, you might as well go to the Royal first, since it's nearest, and then when you've made sure your Dick's all right, you could go on up to St James's or QA. But why not pop in home first, because they might be back by then. A lot of people who aren't hurt bad are being sent home, and I dare say that's what's happened to your two.'

Cissie nodded and stood up. She handed the cup back to one of the other volunteers and made her way out of the hall, not hearing the anxious enquiries from those who had let her through. They looked at her stricken face and shook their heads sadly. 'Shame, poor soul,' the whisper ran, but Cissie heard nothing. She ran blindly through the streets, seeing nothing of the damage, anxiety beating at her mind like a bird with broken wings. Dick – Polly – Judy – what had happened to them all? And she was gripped by a dark certainty that they were all dead.

The Royal Hospital had been hit by a mine. It had blown the Casualty Ward apart, and the entrance where patients were being brought by ambulance. Everyone in the reception area was killed. There'd been several ambulances arriving at the time but most of the drivers had been outside and blown clear. Those who had been hurt had been taken to St James's.

'But what about my hubby?' Cissie asked desperately. She didn't know where to go. The hospital forecourt was a mass of rubble and splintered wood and glass, and there were soldiers, sailors and ARP men pulling at it, trying both to clear the forecourt and to find anyone who might have been buried. Their faces were set and Cissie saw to her horror that there was already a row of objects lying on the ground nearby, humped under torn and bloody blankets. Bodies, she thought, and panic edged her voice.

One of the ARP men looked up. His face was grimed with dust and his eyes were red and sore-looking. He rubbed the back of his hand across his face and said, 'What's up, love? Who're you looking for?'

'My husband. He's in hospital here.' She glanced fearfully at the row of bodies. 'How can I find out if he's all right?'

'Brought in last night, was he?'

She shook her head. 'No, he's been here for weeks now. He had pneumonia. I don't know where to go.'

'He'll have been took down the basements,' the man said. 'He wouldn't have been up here. You'll have to go and ask.' He turned away. 'Sorry, love, but we're busy here, you can see.' Someone called out and he went across to help a small knot of men who were carefully lifting a beam away from a heap of smashed bricks. Cissie made to follow him, then stopped abruptly as she caught sight of red, bloodstained flesh, the jagged end of a bone and a fragment of the blue serge worn by sailors.

Sickened, she turned away. Picking her way through the rubble, avoiding the bodies, she eventually reached a door where a crowd of people were gathering, all seeking information about friends and relatives who were patients. Three or four nurses were sitting at makeshift desks with lists in front of them, looking harassed. Cissie joined the queue, listening anxiously.

'No, nobody in that ward was hurt. All the patients from that part of the hospital who could walk went down to the basements. There were several people in the reception area when the mine hit, and they were all killed – a doctor, some nurses, some new patients coming in and a sailor who was helping on one of the ambulances. Yes, there were some women ambulance drivers as well, they were taken to St James's.' The nurse looked up as Cissie reached the head of the queue. 'Men's Medical? If he was able to walk he'd have gone to the basement. They took quite a lot of bed patients there too, before the hospital was struck. Oh, a *chest* patient . . .' She consulted her list, then turned to the nurse sitting beside her. 'Where did chest patients go, Morrison? Weren't they going through the hallway on their way to the shelter?'

The other nurse nodded. 'They'd just gone through. Nobody was hurt,' she added quickly, seeing Cissie's face, 'but some were affected by the dust. The worst patients it could happen to,' she murmured to the first nurse, and then looked up at Cissie again. 'Go down that corridor and through the double doors at the end. Someone there will help you.'

Cissie thanked them both and set off, walking as quickly as she could and wishing she dared break into a run. Affected by dust – the worst patients it could happen to . . . Oh Dick, she thought, please don't get pneumonia all over again. Please don't suffer any more.

Through the double doors, things were quieter. The hubbub of the crowd's anxious questions and the noise of people working outside was shut out, and Cissie's footsteps sounded suddenly loud. A Sister put her head out of a door and looked at her, frowning. Cissie stopped.

'I've come to find out about my husband. He's been in with pneumonia. I was worried after the raid.'

'Name?' the Sister asked briskly.

'Dick Taylor. *Richard* Taylor. He was a chest patient.'

The woman gave her a look as if to say she knew that a man with pneumonia was likely to be a chest patient, and Cissie felt herself blush. But when the Sister spoke again her voice was kind. 'He'll be in there. It was unfortunate that they were rather close to the area affected by the bomb, but nobody was hurt. You can slip in and see him, but please don't stay long. It isn't visiting time, you know.'

'I know. But I just had to find out if he was all right.'

Cissie's voice wobbled. 'I've got to try to find my sister too, she was driving an ambulance last night – and my daughter. She didn't come home either.' A sob caught in her throat and she turned away hastily. 'I won't stay long, just to see he's all right.'

The Sister touched her shoulder. 'Don't worry too much. It was such a bad raid, they're probably still helping somewhere. There must be hundreds of people who haven't managed to get home yet.' She gave Cissie a brief smile and then turned away as a man pushing a trolley thrust his way through the doors and hastened towards them. There was a small girl on the trolley, her face covered in blood and her legs bent at an unnatural angle.

Cissie pushed through the ward door, tears running down her cheeks. So many people hurt and killed, so many almost out of their minds with worry. Just inside the ward, she stood for a moment looking this way and that, trying to make sense of the turmoil of beds hastily squashed in together, the hurrying nurses and the paraphernalia of drips, bedpans and trolleys.

A nurse came up to her, obviously about to order her out, but Cissie forestalled her. 'I've come to see my husband. The Sister outside said I could, just for a few minutes, just to make sure he's all right.'

The nurse looked as if this was highly irregular but for once Cissie stood her ground. She hadn't come this far to be balked now. The woman obviously read this in her face, for she shrugged and said, 'Well, just for a minute or two, then. What's his name?'

'Taylor. Richard Taylor.'

'Oh yes, he's over there.' She pointed to a corner. 'He's rather poorly, I'm afraid. Only a minute, mind,' she added as Cissie started forwards. 'We're very busy.'

Rather poorly! Cissie barely heard the nurse's last words. She almost ran across to the bed in the corner and stared down at her husband. 'Dick! Dick, whatever's happened to you?'

The figure in the bed stared up at her. 'Cis? Is that you?' His voice was as rough as sandpaper.

'Yes, of course it is.' She fell on her knees, gripping his thin hands. 'What's wrong? What's the matter with you? They said no one was hurt.'

'I wasn't.' He could manage only a few words at a time. 'Got a faceful of dust and muck. Breathed it in. Felt like sandpaper, it did. Been coughing all night.' He coughed again, painfully, as if to demonstrate. 'Reckon I've still got some in me lungs. It could turn to pneumonia again, Cis.' He clung to her hand. 'I was coming home tomorrow. Coming *home*.'

'I know.' She gazed at him in distress. 'Oh *Dick*.'

'Want to come home,' he wheezed. 'Take me home, Cis. I don't want to be here any more.'

'Dick, I can't. If you discharge yourself, they won't take you back again. And if you do get pneumonia . . .'

He fixed his eyes on her pleadingly and she stared back in despair. The ward was full of noise. It smelt of urine and faeces and blood, of disinfectant and medicines – the 'hospital' smell that all the wards seemed to share. Nurses were hurrying to and fro, their shoes clattering on the linoleum floor. Voices called out, some demanding, some filled with pain, some in obvious delirium. I wouldn't want to be here either, Cissie thought.

'I'll take you home the first minute I can,' she promised. 'But you'll have to wait for the doctor to say so. I'm sorry, love.'

He looked at her and then turned his head away and stared at the wall. Cissie stroked his hand desperately. 'Dick. Dick, don't look like that. I *can't* take you home now. You might be ill again – you could *die*.' Her voice rose in anguish. 'Dick, I'd take you this minute if I could, but—'

'I'm afraid you'll have to go.' An authoritative voice broke in and she turned quickly to find a tall, weary-looking man standing beside her. Hastily, Cissie let go of Dick's hand and scrambled to her feet. The man looked at her severely. 'I don't know who let you in now, but you'll have to come back at visiting time. That's three o'clock this afternoon.'

'I know, thank you. I've been coming in for the past three weeks.' Cissie looked back towards the bed. 'My husband – is he . . .'

'I haven't examined him yet,' the doctor stated. 'Sister will give you any information this afternoon. Now, if you'd please go.'

'Yes,' Cissie muttered, defeated. She turned back to Dick and felt for his hand once more. 'Bye now, love. I'll be back this afternoon. You'll be all right – I'm sure you'll be all right.' She caught the doctor's eye again, dropped his hand and moved away, walking uncertainly out of the ward. At the door she stopped again. The doctor was bent over Dick, his stethoscope placed on the thin chest. Blinded by tears, Cissie turned away.

Three o'clock this afternoon. *I'll be back*, she promised Dick silently.

But before then, she had to find out what had happened to Judy and Polly.

Chapter Thirteen

The noise as the front of the building fell into the courtyard had been the worst explosion Judy had ever heard. It had reverberated around the tall, narrow space between the other buildings, blasting her eardrums and filling her head with a roar that she thought would never stop. A great cloud of thick, choking dust rose into the air and she buried her face in her sleeve, trying not to breathe in too deeply, the foul, gritty powder coating her tongue and teeth and making her gag and retch to get rid of it. I can't stand this, she thought, I can't stand it any more. Make it go away. *Make it go away.*

Someone pulled her sleeve and she lifted her face away cautiously and saw the young doctor mouthing something at her. Panic gripped her as she realised that she could hear nothing. She tried to yell back, but even inside her head her words sounded distorted and meaningless. She shook her head, terrified, but there was nothing but a strange, roaring silence.

She looked around. Dust was swirling around the narrow space and even the crimson light of the flames outside could only just penetrate the darkness. With another leap of fear, she wondered if the buildings here had caught fire, but could see no fresh flames. It could surely be no more than a matter of time, though. All this wood and plaster needed only a spark to set it off, and even as the thought entered her head she saw a gobbet of flame drift past high above. We've got to get out of here, she thought, and turned to see if the entrance had been blocked.

Polly! For a few seconds, she had forgotten her aunt and the old woman and her son, still trapped in the collapsed building. She whirled back, to find her arm grasped again by the doctor.

Judy shook her off angrily, and tried to shout again, but her voice seemed to have no power. I can't even hear myself, she thought in despair, but there was no time to think about that now. She jabbed her finger urgently at the fallen masonry and made her mouth shape the words, 'My aunt – my aunt –' Whether the other woman understood, she didn't know, but she evidently remembered that they had come here to help someone who was trapped, and nodded quickly before turning herself to follow Judy's pointing finger.

The two men were getting to their feet as well, shaking their heads and rubbing their ears. We've all gone deaf, she thought, and grabbed their arms to drag them in the direction of the fallen house. Even now there were still bricks and slates and slabs of mortar tumbling down from the splintered edges of the roof that was still left, hanging drunkenly from the adjoining buildings. It only wants one of them falling on your head to kill you, Judy thought, but she couldn't give up now. Polly was in there somewhere, and if she left her she would never forgive herself.

Together, the four of them went cautiously forwards, each keeping an eye on the wreckage above. To her amazement, Judy saw that even though almost the entire front of the building had fallen, the doorway itself was still standing. The architrave must have been especially strong – perhaps old oak from an ancient sailing ship, strengthened from years of immersion in salt water. Tentatively, she pushed at the splintered door and it swung open a foot or so, then stopped, blocked by rubble. Judy began to wriggle through the narrow space.

A touch on her arm made her turn. The doctor was shaking her head, obviously warning her of the danger, but

Judy shook her own head in reply. *I'm going in there, whatever happens.* She eased herself very carefully round the edge of the door and picked her way over a pile of bricks.

It hadn't been far to the room where the old woman had lain, but it was now almost pitch dark in there, with only the faintest red glow from the flame-lit sky. Judy tried to remember which way she had gone, and moved very slowly, feeling her way. If only she had a torch . . .

As if in answer to a prayer, a thin beam of light flickered in one corner and her heart jumped. Polly had had a torch! Was she still there, still miraculously alive, perhaps calling out unheard by her deafened rescuers, shining the torch to show them the way? Judy tried again to shout, without any idea as to whether her voice could be heard. Behind her, she was aware of someone following, one of the men or perhaps the doctor. The light had disappeared, but she pointed and felt, rather than saw, the nod of the head, then groped for her companion's arm. The warmth and solidity reassured her, and they went on side by side, taking slow, careful steps and scrabbling with their hands at the mounds of bricks and plaster.

Something soft met Judy's questing fingers. She froze, half afraid of what it might be, then moved her hands cautiously, feeling the softness of fabric coated with gritty dust. It was a garment of some kind, but was it something that had been taken off and flung down, or was it still wrapped around a body? A *body*, she thought in panic, and almost tore her hands away. At the same moment, the fabric shifted under her hands and the light shone again.

'*Polly!*' The name was a thought rather than a cry, but Judy hardly cared now whether she was deaf or not, for there at her feet, half-buried in rubble, lay her aunt, her small torch gripped in one hand and shining towards her grime-coated face. There was blood on her forehead and in her hair, but her eyes were open, and as Judy bent towards her a faint smile curved her lips.

Judy almost fell on her, half laughing, half crying. Beside her, the doctor bent swiftly to press her fingers against Polly's neck and then looked up at Judy and indicated the rubble. Her mouth moved and Judy read the silent message: '*She's alive! We've got to get this off her.*'

Judy began to pull away bricks and slivers of wood. To her immense relief they were all small, or at least within her ability to lift, but she was so thankful to find Polly alive that she felt she could have moved a mountain to get her out. By now, the two men were also in the small space, and together they worked feverishly to free the trapped woman. Oh, let her be all right, Judy prayed. Let her not be hurt too badly. It was uncanny, working in the silence, uncannier still to know that the air must be filled with sound, with the cacophony of aircraft overhead, the roar of exploding bombs, the rattle of ack-ack guns. The raid was still going on – at any moment they might all be blasted to oblivion or burned to death in a firestorm – yet the most important thing in the world now was to get Polly out of her prison, to bring her out alive.

They had shifted all the small stuff now and by the flickering light of Polly's torch, Judy saw with dismay that there was a large beam of wood across her body. Oh God, if she's been crushed . . . she thought in horror, but almost before the thought had formed in her mind she saw that it was balanced on two other lumps of broken masonry, and didn't touch Polly at all. In fact, it had probably saved her life, making a cage around her over which the rubble had fallen, while inside she was barely scratched.

As soon as she was able, Polly began to struggle out from underneath the beam. She was filthy and bedraggled, one leg was dragging and there was still blood trickling down her face, but her eyes were bright and she hugged Judy fervently. Her mouth moved in some question, but Judy shook her head and pointed to her ears. '*I can't hear,*' she mouthed. And then, hoping that Polly could hear her, *'What about the others? The man and his mother?'*

Either Polly heard her or read her lips, for she glanced round the devastated room and shook her head slightly, the movement obviously paining her. The others had already begun to try to dig through the rubble and the two women joined them, but it was clear that there was little chance of finding any other survivors. Eventually, one of the men straightened up and wiped his forehead. *'We can't move any more. We'll have to get help. It's all big stuff, too heavy . . . I don't reckon there's anyone alive in here now anyway.'*

Reluctantly, they turned and battled their way out through the cluttered courtyard. Outside, the raid was still going on, although it seemed to have lessened. We must have shot down some of their planes, surely, Judy thought, and rubbed her ears, suddenly afraid that she was never going to be able to hear again. I'm deaf, she thought in panic.

The young doctor saw the gesture and looked at her in concern. *'Are you still deafened?'* she mouthed, and Judy nodded. The doctor glanced at Polly, parted her hair gently with her fingers to look at the wound in her head, and bent to give her dragging leg a swift examination. Then she straightened up and looked around.

The street was still full of people trying to fight the fires that had broken out. Soldiers, sailors and civilians alike were rushing to and fro with stirrup pumps, buckets, anything that could hold a few drops of water. At least the mains didn't seem to have been fractured this time. Judy moved to go and help, but the doctor gripped her arm.

'Hospital,' she mouthed. *'You both need to go to hospital. We need an ambulance.'* She glanced around again and then pointed to a vehicle which had apparently been abandoned at the side of the road, and a sob of hysteria rose in Judy's throat as she recognised their own old van.

One of the men who had helped her came forwards and

spoke in the doctor's ear. She nodded briskly. *'This man will take you.'* She helped Polly, who was beginning to sway, into the back of the van. Judy, more anxious for her aunt than for herself, followed, and they crouched together on the makeshift bunk fitted inside.

The journey seemed to take hours. Swaying, jerking and bumping through the bombed streets, they had no idea where they were going. Polly was looking dazed and sick, and Judy was unable to communicate with the driver. Exhaustion overtook her, her ears hurt almost unbearably, and she sagged against the cold metal walls of the van. She was unaware of their arrival at the Royal Hospital and the devastation that caused them to be turned away and sent to St James's, and when they finally stumbled out of the van she had no idea where they were.

Once in the foyer, she and Polly stood leaning against one another, almost too bewildered and exhausted to care what happened to them now. The place was in chaos, crowded with nurses, doctors and injured people. Stretchers and trolleys cluttered every space. Judy and Polly found themselves being hustled into a corner where a harassed young nurse began to question them.

'I can't hear.' Judy pointed to her ears and then held her hands over them to show that they were painful. The nurse turned at once to Polly and evidently asked about her injuries. Polly pointed to her head and then her leg, and the nurse pushed her gently on to a bed and began to examine her.

Judy watched anxiously. The head wound seemed to have stopped bleeding and was soon washed and bandaged. The leg seemed to be no worse than a superficial cut on the skin, but it was unpleasantly jagged and might have got germs in it. Having attended to these, the nurse turned her attention to Judy, but all Judy could do was mouth at her, *'I'm not hurt. It's just my ears – the blast – I've gone deaf.'* Tears came to her eyes and she shook her head angrily, furious with herself, but once started they could not be stopped and she crumpled, her hands to her face, her shoulders shaking. *I've gone deaf. I've gone deaf. I'm never going to be able to hear anything again . . .*

'Thank God I've found you.' Cissie collapsed on to a wooden chair beside Polly's bed and stared at her sister. 'Oh, thank God. I thought you and our Judy were both . . .' She couldn't say the word. Tears brimmed out of her eyes and she wiped them away and sniffed, her mouth both smiling and trembling.

'I don't know why they're keeping me in here,' Polly said grumpily. She was sitting up in bed, swathed in a huge white gown. 'I'm all right, it's just a bit of a cut on my leg and a graze on the head. But they want to keep an eye on me in case of concussion, the doctor said. I'm coming out tomorrow though, thank goodness.' She glanced around the overcrowded ward. 'They're doing their best, I know, but it's horrible in here.' She looked at her sister. 'Have you seen Judy yet?'

Cissie nodded. 'She's in a poor way. Oh, not hurt as such, but it's her ears; she can't hear a thing and she thinks she's gone deaf permanent. She's really cut up about it. I had a word with the Sister and she says they'll keep her in for a day or two to make sure there's no other damage, but she thinks the hearing'll come back pretty soon. She says it's a common effect of the blast. They get any amount of people in here just the same way, she said.'

'Oh, I hope she'll be all right. It'd be awful if she was permanently deaf, a young girl like that.' Polly lay back on her pillows. She was white and exhausted still and her voice trembled as she went on, 'She saved my life, you know, Cis. I wouldn't be here now if Judy hadn't come in and dug me out, and got those men and that young doctor to help. I'd have died in there, in all that filth and dust and –' Her voice broke and she began to cry helplessly. 'Oh Cis.'

'Polly. Polly.' Cis slipped her arms about her sister's body and held her like a baby. She always was my baby too, she thought tenderly, remembering her delight when Alice had told her she had a new sister. At twelve years old, Cissie had been of an age to be of real help, cuddling Polly and helping to wash and dress her – although she'd drawn the line at changing nappies, she remembered with a smile. She remembered too her pride as she'd pushed the pram up the street, attracting envious attention from all her friends, and her pleasure in watching the baby grow to a toddler and then a little girl, always looking up to her sister, always ready to be a companion.

Later, when Cissie had married, Polly was her brides-maid, and when Cissie's own children had been born Polly was more like a big sister than an aunt to them. She and Judy had always been special friends, and had formed an additional link between Polly and Cissie herself. The thought that Judy had saved her aunt's life brought a lump to Cissie's throat.

'I'm sorry, Cis,' Polly wept. 'I can't seem to stop crying. I'm so ashamed – but the doctor says it's natural, it's shock. But whenever I think of being buried like that – oh, I can't tell you what it was like, it was so horrible.'

'There, there,' Cissie said soothingly. 'It's all right, Polly. You're all right now. You have a good cry. The doctor's right, it's a natural reaction. Anyone would cry after a thing like that – anyone. You just let it all out and you'll feel better.' She rocked her sister's body in her arms and went on murmuring to her, though her heart was heavy. Polly, her bright, laughing sister, reduced to this sobbing wreck. Her daughter Judy, frantic with the terror of being deaf. Her husband Dick, only just over pneumonia, choking with the dust of yet another bombing and reliving the nightmare of his experiences in the First World War. What are we coming to, she wondered, and what's going to become of us all before this is over?

'I'll have to go soon,' she whispered as Polly's sobs eased. 'I want to pop in on Judy again, and I must be back at the Royal in time to see Dick, and Mum doesn't even know where I am. By the way, you know you've got company in here from April Grove, don't you? I saw Peggy Shaw and Gladys up the other end of the ward. They were at the Royal when it got bombed last night. Peggy was thrown into some rose bushes, and Gladys has got a broken arm.' She hesitated, then decided not to tell her sister that young Graham Philpotts, the sailor who used to go out with Betty Chapman and had been calling round for Gladys just lately, had been killed. He'd been helping with the ambulance, so Peggy had told her quietly when she stopped to have a word with them, and Gladys was blaming herself. But Polly didn't need to know that – not just yet.

This awful war, she thought, making her way slowly out of the ward, sadly aware of the people around her – injured, bereaved, homeless and bewildered. This *awful* war.

Chapter Fourteen

By the beginning of May, Dick, Judy and Polly were all home again, each still somewhat shaken by their experiences. To Cissie's relief, Dick's chest hadn't been as badly affected by the dust as they had feared, but his nerves were a different matter. The violence of the raid and the close proximity of the mine that had hit the hospital had brought back all the old terrors, and his nights, and therefore Cissie's too, were broken by nightmares. In fact, she told Alice privately, that was one of the reasons they'd sent him home from the hospital – his cries and screams were keeping other patients awake. He was nervous and on edge during the day, too, likely to flare up over the least little thing, and although Cissie did her best to remember that this was all part of his illness, she couldn't help getting upset sometimes.

'Where's my glasses gone?' he demanded. 'You've been tidying up again, Cis – I can't find nothing. You've hid them deliberately.'

'Dick, of course I haven't! I wouldn't do a thing like that. I expect you've put them down somewhere and forgotten them.'

'Oh yes, it's bound to be *my* fault, isn't it! Everything that happens in this house has got to be *my* fault. Neither use nor ornament, that's me. I dare say you got on a lot better when I was in that hospital. Better send me back.' He sat down, staring angrily into space. Cissie took a deep breath and put her arms around his shoulders.

'Dick. Please don't talk like that. You know it's not true. All I want is to have you at home and feeling well again.' He had covered his face with his hands and she tried to prise them away. 'Dick, look at me. Please. Let me give you a kiss. Come on, now,' she coaxed him, talking softly, stroking his thin cheek with her fingers. 'Come on. You know you don't mean those things. And look,' she laughed suddenly, 'there are your glasses – on top of your head! They've been there all the time!'

For a moment, he looked even angrier and she was afraid that she'd upset him even more by laughing at him. Then the sense of humour that had always saved them came to the rescue again and his lips pulled into a grin. He pulled her close.

'Sorry, Cis. I'm a twerp. I dunno how you put up with me.'

'Nor do I,' she said, hugging him in relief. 'But just you thank your lucky stars I do, because I don't think you'll find another woman at your age!'

'Don't you be too sure,' he warned her, his temper over as quickly as it had arisen. 'That Ethel Glaister's been giving me some funny looks just lately!' And they both dissolved into laughter.

Polly too was plagued by nightmares. Half a dozen times a night she woke, convinced she was buried under a pile of bricks and rubble, and threw off her blankets, coughing and choking in distress. As soon as she was awake, she realised that it had been a dream, but it took several minutes to regain control of her breathing, and she lay staring into the darkness, almost afraid to go to sleep again.

Judy, who shared the small back bedroom, couldn't help her for she had still not regained her hearing. The few sounds she could hear seemed to come to her through a thick fog of distorted mush, and it was almost worse than not being able to hear at all. The normal family chatter with the wireless on in the background almost drove her demented, and she couldn't understand what anyone said unless they spoke very slowly and exaggerated their lip movements so that she could try to read them.

Even that wasn't very successful.

'Time for tea,' Cissie mouthed, and Judy stared at her blankly.

'By the sea? What's by the sea?'

Sometimes she could see the funny side of it, and laughed, but too often she became upset and angry. 'I'm fed up with this!' she cried, beating her fists together. 'I'm never going to be able to hear again, never – you don't know how awful it is! I'm going to be like this for the rest of my life, and it's like being in prison. I'm caged in all the time – it's *horrible*!'

The doorbell rang and Polly went to answer it. She came back and said to Judy, 'It's someone for you. Chris Barrett, from the Observers.' Judy stared at her uncomprehendingly, and she wrote it down on the little blackboard they'd found in Sylvie's toybox.

'I don't want to see him.'

'But he's come all this way specially.'

'Then he can go back,' Judy said abruptly. 'I don't want to see him – I don't want to see *anyone*, not while I'm like this. What d'you think he's going to say when he realises what I'm like – deaf, half out of my mind? He'll never come again anyway, so there's no point. Tell him to go away.' Her lips trembled and Polly gazed at her anxiously. Judy turned her face aside, but not before the others had seen the tears on her cheeks. 'Tell him to just go away!'

'Perhaps she'll feel a bit more up to it in a week or two,' Polly said gently to the disappointed young man. 'She's had a terrible shock, and she's really not feeling well.'

Chris shrugged. 'All right, Mrs Dunn. Shall I come back, then?'

Polly hesitated. She had no idea what the situation was between him and her niece. 'Better leave it perhaps,' she said, hoping she was doing the right thing. 'I see you out at the Beach, anyway. I can always let you know when she's feeling better.'

Shame, she thought, watching him walk off up the street. He was a nice young man and it would have done Judy good. But Judy didn't seem interested in him. Her deafness seemed to be taking over her life. Time and again she dissolved into tears of frustration and despair, and Cissie began to be seriously worried about her.

'I think she's going to have a nervous breakdown if something can't be done soon,' she told Polly as they ate a hasty breakfast of cornflakes. 'She says it makes her feel so useless. She can't go to work because she can't hear what anyone says to her or use the phone or anything, and when people talk to each other they leave her out, and that's hurtful. She feels as if she's being treated as if she's stupid.'

'I know. And she seems to be shutting herself away from everything. I mean, take that Chris Barrett – nice young feller, he is, and he's obviously a bit struck with our Judy. I was hoping they'd get together, but no. He's asked after her a few times, wanted to come round again and see her but she won't have it. Says nobody'd be interested in a deaf girl. Says it's no use him coming, she won't even go to the door to say hello. And it's not just the deafness, you know,' Polly went on. 'It's Sean as well. She's never grieved properly over him, just pushed it away. You can't do that. I should know. I tried it myself when Johnny died, but you can't put it off for ever.'

'I don't know what we ought to do about her,' Cissie said. 'She needs to get away from all this bombing. Well, we all do. Raids night after night – you know last Tuesday's was the fiftieth, don't you? It was in the *Evening News*. I mean, how are we supposed to stand it?'

'We're not,' Polly said wryly. 'But you're right, Judy needs some peace and quiet. I wonder if the people Sylvie's staying with could put her up for a few days?'

Cissie stared at her in surprise. 'Surely not! They've got those other two kiddies there too, haven't they? I don't suppose they've got room.'

'Well, she could sleep in with Sylvie. Or maybe that nice vicar where I took the Simmons girls could take her, there seemed to be plenty of rooms there. Honestly, Cis, it would do her so much good to be out in the country for a few days, and it'd be lovely there now it's May. Look, I'll talk to the Mayoress. She's really kind and helpful, and she might know of somewhere.' Polly glanced at the clock on the mantelpiece. 'Talking of the Mayoress, I'd better get a move on or I shall be late. I'm going into the main Clothing Store today, we're moving some of the stock to a church hall near Elm Grove. Apparently the Queen wrote to the Mayoress after they came here that time and said we ought to have a few more stores in case the main one got bombed. The Mayoress was already seeing to it, of course, but it just shows the Queen really thinks about these things, doesn't it?'

She gathered up her jacket, bag and gas mask, and hurried out, still limping a little. As soon as she had gone, Judy came down the stairs and Cissie heard her take the lid off the teapot to see if there was any tea left. She put her head round the scullery door.

'Has Polly gone to work?' She had accepted the fact that her voice could be heard by others, although she didn't seem able to get the level right and either whispered or shouted. It was one of the reasons why others found her so hard to talk to, Cissie thought, and felt a fresh wave of sympathy.

'Yes, she's going to the Clothing Store.' She bit her lip, aware that she'd spoken too quickly and without turning her face to Judy's. She tried again, mouthing the words with some exaggeration. '*Clothing – Store.*'

Judy flushed and Cissie knew that the exaggeration itself had upset her. She left the room quickly and then returned with a cup of tea. She put it on the table, sat down, stared at it for a few moments, then leaned her head on her hands and burst into tears.

Cissie moved swiftly round the table and took her in her arms. 'Oh you poor, poor love.' She patted her daughter's shoulders helplessly, brushed her fair hair out of her eyes, wiped her face with her hanky. 'Oh, I know you can't hear me. If only I could help you. Oh my poor, poor love – what are we going to do? What are we going to do?'

'Sorry,' Judy choked. 'Sorry, Mum. Didn't mean to start again.' She dragged in a long, sobbing breath, and leaned her head wearily on one hand while she felt for her own hanky with the other. 'I'm so *useless*. No good to anyone. I wanted to do so much.'

'Don't talk rubbish!' Cissie twisted her round so that she could see her face. Even though her daughter couldn't hear her words, she went on, knowing that she could read the expression on her face. 'That's silly and you know it! You're not useless!' She exaggerated the words. '*Not – useless*. You saved Polly's life, and you're alive too. That's what matters. And your hearing *will* come back. You're not going to be deaf for ever. The doctor said so.' She held Judy by the shoulders, looking intently into her grey eyes. Judy stared back, almost frozen, and Cissie went on more quietly, 'It's not just that, though, is it? It's not just your ears. It's Sean, isn't it?'

'Sean,' Judy whispered, showing that she had understood, and the wide grey eyes flooded with fresh tears. 'Sean – oh, *Sean*.' Once again, she bent her head and began to sob. 'Oh Mum, he's dead! Sean's dead. He's never coming back. We're never going to be married, or have babies, or *anything*. We never had any time together.' She looked down at the ring, now back on her left hand, its tiny diamond winking in the morning light, and twisted it round so that the diamond was hidden and it looked like a wedding band. 'Oh, Mum.'

'I know.' Cissie cradled her head again. Her own eyes

were wet. She and Dick hadn't been keen on the hasty engagement, so soon after the young couple had met, but it was obvious they were head over heels in love, and it was wartime. And now it was over, so swiftly it was easy to forget it had ever happened. But Judy had not forgotten.

'You'll get over it,' she whispered. 'You'll get over it, in time.'

But she knew that Judy could not hear her, and wouldn't believe her if she could.

The Lady Mayoress agreed that Judy must have some time off to recover from the shock of the raid and give her hearing a chance to return. 'She needs some peace and quiet away from these incessant raids.' She gave a small, wry smile and echoed Cissie's words: 'We all do, don't we! But Judy's had a sad time lately. You say her fiancé was lost at sea?'

'Yes. They hadn't known each other long. They wanted to get married before he went away, but there just wasn't time and my sister and her husband weren't keen. Not that they could have stopped her, of course, because she's over twenty-one, but Judy wouldn't have wanted to go against their wishes. Now she blames herself because she didn't just go ahead. She says she feels she let Sean down, and what difference would it have made, as things turned out?'

'Poor girl,' the Mayoress said. 'She must certainly have a few days off, and I agree that it would be ideal for her to get away from Portsmouth for a while. You say you think your own little girl's foster parents might take her in?'

'Yes, they might. And it would be nice for Sylvie to have her there. I'll write and ask them.' Polly went back to sorting clothes, feeling more optimistic. A week or two in the country – it sounded like bliss and would surely be just what Judy needed to set her back on her feet. She's been through too much too quickly, Polly thought. And just because the rest of us have suffered, too, doesn't mean she shouldn't be given the chance to get over it.

The main Clothing Store had been split into several different sections, each situated in a different part of the city so that even if there were another major raid, at least some of them should survive. Polly was working this morning in the Children's Swap Store, where mothers could come with the clothes their own children had grown out of and exchange them for larger sizes.

'My Johnny's right out of these flannel shorts and he can hardly get into this jacket. He's growing so fast these days.'

'Have you got a pretty party frock for my Joan? It's her twelfth birthday next week and I want to give her a nice party, with jelly and everything.'

'Look, I got this skirt and jumper here last week for my Dottie and it's all holes already. I'd have thought you'd have better quality than this, what with it being the Lady Mayoress's pigeon and all.'

Polly was constantly amazed by the requests, and even more so by the quality of some of the clothes brought for 'swapping'. 'This pullover looks as if it's been in a cupboard for years,' she said indignantly to one woman who had tipped a pillowcase full of clothes on to the long trestle table. 'And a damp cupboard, at that. Look, that's green mould, that is.'

'So what?' the woman demanded belligerently. She was a big woman, with a bosom like a shelf and a dark, mannish face. 'It's clothes, innit? You got a notice outside saying you'll swap clothes, aincher? Well, I brought some clothes to swap.'

'Yes, but,' Polly hesitated. 'They're supposed to be swapped for children. I mean,' she corrected herself, aware of a tittering amongst the queue, 'for children's clothes. This is a man's pullover. You can't just come with old clothes that nobody's used for years and take away better ones. How old are your children?'

The woman looked at her and Polly knew at once that she had no children but had simply cleared out a cupboard. Probably she would sell the clothes and then boast about having 'done the Council'. A little worm of anger stirred in Polly's stomach.

'I got six,' the woman declared. 'Six, from a six-month-old baby up to a boy of twelve, and they all needs clothes.' She waved a muscular arm to indicate the festering heap of rags on the table. 'You can see what they've had to put up with ever since this bloody war started. Running about in rags, they are, running about in rags.'

'I'm surprised they're still in Portsmouth,' Polly said boldly, determined to call the woman's bluff. 'Haven't they been evacuated?'

The woman hesitated. 'No. Yes. Well, they *was* – but they come back, see, when there wasn't no raids. Anyway, the baby couldn't go without me, now could she, and what with my hubby being away at sea since the war broke out I got lonely on me own, and—'

'Didn't stay lonely for long then, did you?' someone in the queue butted in. 'Not if the baby's only six months old! Come on, Madge Perkins, you know you never got no kids, so why don't you take your rubbish and get out? Runs a rag-and-bone shop down Rudmore, she does,' the speaker continued indignantly, as the woman turned with a fearsome expression on her face and bunched a massive fist. 'And her hubby died years ago – it was the only way he could get away from her. And you needn't wave your fists at me, neither,' she added, squaring up as the queue joined in with resentful muttering. 'I can fight me corner as well as anyone.'

'Not in here though, please,' Polly intervened hastily. She scooped the rags back into the pillowcase and thrust it at Madge Perkins. 'Take this with you and go, please. If you have clothes to donate – decent clothes, in reasonable condition – one of the other Clothing Stores will be pleased to receive them.'

'And give me nothing for 'em!' The big woman snatched up the bag and glared at her. 'I can't afford to go giving stuff away. I'm not rolling in money. Call this a charity? You Council people, you're all the same, take it all off us in rates and then wants the clothes off our backs as well. I tell you, I'm doing good work with my trade, work for the war effort. And as for you, Jean Barstow,' she turned on the woman who had challenged her, 'I'll have something to say to your Billy next time he comes round wanting to sell me rags and bones. I give him too much for the last lot, out of the goodness of me heart, and look how you repays me!'

She stalked out furiously and the queue made way for her, glowering and muttering. Mrs Barstow poked her tongue out at her departing back and then turned to Polly.

'You don't want to take no notice of Madge Perkins, missus. She'd try it on with anyone. She'll be round all the stores with that lot, trying to get something for it, and it's all stuff that other people have chucked out. Trying to get summat better and then sell it on, that's what she was doing. Talk about working for the war effort!'

'That's right,' someone else chimed in. 'Trying to make money out of the war. Unpatriotic, I call it.'

The queue murmured in agreement and Polly inspected the clothes that Mrs Barstow had brought in. There were two pairs of boys' flannel shorts, a jacket and a girl's skirt and cardigan, both home made. They had all seen better days and she wasn't at all sure that she'd be able to pass them on to anyone else, but she was grateful to the woman for sending Mrs Perkins packing and wanted to help her.

'How many children d'you have?'

'Boy and girl, both ten. They're twins,' she added unnecessarily. 'They're not identical though, see, 'cause they're a boy and girl.'

'Well, I can let you have one pair of shorts and a jacket

for the boy, and there are some skirts over there that might suit your little girl, and some jumpers and cardigans. I'm afraid you can only have one of each garment,' she added apologetically. 'Not everything we get brought in is suitable to be passed on.'

'Not as bad as Madge's stuff, though,' Mrs Barstow said cheerfully. 'OK, missus, I'll have a look through and pick summat out. The boy's things'll be easy enough, but my Susie's getting a bit fussy about what she wears now. I tell her there's a war on and she'll have to be grateful for what she can get, but you know what kiddies are, they don't really understand, do they?' She moved along the table, turning over the neatly folded garments while Polly turned her attention to the next customer.

As soon as she had finished, she went home to write to Mrs Sutton to ask if she could put Judy up for a few days. *I know it's asking a lot*, she wrote, *but my niece really does need some peace and quiet, and I don't know where else to try. We'd pay for her keep of course, and I know she'd give a hand wherever she could*. She chewed the end of her pen, wondering how to end the letter. Whatever else she thought of sounded as if she were trying to make it difficult for Mrs Sutton to refuse, and she didn't want to do that. In the end, she just wrote, *Yours sincerely, P.M. Dunn* and left it at that.

The reply came two days later. It was waiting for Polly when she came home from the hairdresser's, where she was now working for just two or three hours each day after her stint at the Clothing Store. Worn out with standing all day, she dropped into a chair and opened the letter while Cissie brought her a cup of tea.

'Well, isn't that lovely!' She raised a smiling face as Cissie came in from the scullery. 'Mrs Sutton says Judy will be welcome to go and stay with them, so long as she doesn't mind sleeping in the same room as the two girls. She won't mind that, will she?'

'I'm sure she won't,' Cissie was beginning, when Judy herself interrupted them. Her face was flushed and angry.

'You're talking about me – I know you are! What are you saying? What's that letter about?' She jumped up from her chair, trembling. 'You're sending me away. You think I'm mental as well as deaf, and you're sending me away! Aren't you? *Aren't* you?'

'Judy, *no!*' Polly and Cissie spoke together, gazing at her in distress. 'It's not that at all,' Cissie went on, speaking far too quickly for Judy to follow, but Polly brushed her aside and held out the letter. 'Here, read it for yourself. It's from Mrs Sutton,' she said, speaking slowly and clearly so that Judy could read her lips. 'Mrs Sutton. Where Sylvie is. Read it, Judy.'

Judy took the letter, still gazing at her face, a slight, puzzled frown creasing her forehead. She looked down at the sheet of paper and then sat down slowly. Polly heaved a sigh of relief and sank back into her own chair, taking the cup of tea Cissie was still holding out.

'Mrs Sutton,' Judy said in her odd, painful voice. 'Mrs Sutton – she says I can go and stay there?' She looked at Polly. 'You wrote to her.'

'Yes, I wrote the day before yesterday and she's answered straight away.' Polly forgot to speak slowly. 'Isn't that kind of her? You'll like her, Judy, and Sylvie will be so pleased to have her auntie there. And it'll be lovely there now, all the spring flowers will be out and there'll be lambs and—'

'You wrote to her,' Judy said, ignoring her. 'You wrote and told her about me.'

'Well – yes.' Polly began to feel uncomfortable. Judy didn't seem pleased at all. 'I was worried about you, Judy. We all are. We think you need a few days away, out in the country where you can—' She recalled that Judy could barely follow one word in three of this. 'We want you to have a holiday,' she enunciated. 'Some peace and quiet. To help you get better.'

She stopped uncertainly. Judy seemed to understand, but she didn't look any more pleased. She stared from Polly to her mother, then back at the letter in her hand. 'Why didn't you ask me?' she said. 'Why didn't you tell me you were writing?'

Polly glanced helplessly at her sister and Cissie said, 'We only wanted to do what was best for you, love.'

'But why didn't you *ask* me? I've been here all the time. I've still got a brain, you know – I can still decide what I want to do! What if I don't want to go? What if I'd rather stay here?' Her voice trembled. 'I want to go back to work. I want to be *useful*. I don't want to be sent away to the country like a – like a little child. And don't you understand? Don't *any* of you understand what it'll be like for me? Not being able to hear what people say? Being with strangers, and not being able to hear what they say?'

Cissie and Polly looked at each other. Polly put her teacup back on the table and spoke again, very slowly, looking directly into Judy's eyes.

'Judy. Nobody is treating you like a child. We want to help you get better. You need to be away from Portsmouth – away from the bombs. Away from noise. Please go. Just for a few days. That's all we want you to do. *Please.* And the Suttons will understand – I know they will. They're kind people, Judy.'

There was a long silence. Judy looked down at the letter again. Her face was pale. Then she said, 'Just for a few days?'

'Yes. That's all, really. Just to see if it helps.'

'And I'd see Sylvie. It seems so long since I saw Sylvie.'

'She'd love to see you,' Polly said quietly, thinking how long it was since she herself had seen her daughter. Not since that brief hour when she'd taken Stella and Muriel to Bridge End. When the children had first been evacuated, all the parents had expected to be able to visit them regularly – you could even get the fare paid for two or three visits – but once the raids had started there just hadn't been the chance. Railways stations were full of posters – *Is Your Journey Really Necessary?* – and there was so much to do at home. 'I'd feel happier about her if I knew you'd had a chance to spend a few days there,' she said to Judy.

Judy seemed to understand the gist of what she was saying. She nodded and her mouth twisted into a wry smile. 'Well, I suppose I'd better go, then. But only for a few days,' she added warningly. 'I'm not being sent away for ever.'

'Of course not!' Cissie threw her arms around her and kissed her. 'Oh Judy, I'm so glad! It'll do you good, I know it will. And they have much better food out in the country too – lots of milk, and butter and proper eggs. You need a bit of building up. You've been looking so peaky and washed-out lately. Now, we'd better sort out what you're going to take with you. There's that blue skirt you got from the Clothing Store after we were bombed, and you can take my best blouse, and—'

'Wait a minute!' Judy cried, only half understanding what her mother was saying. 'Can't you wait to get rid of me? I didn't say I'd go this minute.'

'No, but there's no point in waiting, is there? Mrs Sutton says she's expecting you any day. And we're just having a spell of nice weather too, so you may as well make the most of it.' Cissie was not to be deflected. She ran upstairs and began pulling open cupboards and drawers. Judy glanced at Polly and smiled ruefully.

'You're determined to make me go, aren't you? But what about Dad? He's the one who's been ill – he could do with a few days in the country. Where is he, anyway?'

'He's gone for a walk,' Polly said. 'You might not have noticed it, but he's really improving with this nice sunny spell. He's gone over to Langstone Harbour – said he just wants to rest his eyes on some water. It's months since he was on the shore.' She saw Judy's face and repeated the main words more slowly, until Judy understood. Then she said, 'You won't feel too awkward, will you, Judy, when you're at the Suttons'? They know about what's happened. And your hearing is getting better, isn't it? You can hear some things now.'

Judy shrugged. 'No, not really. I'm just getting a bit better at lip-reading.'

'Well, I still think this is what you need.' Polly looked into her cup and then stood up. 'This tea's gone cold. I'll make some more, and then help Cissie with supper.' She bent and gave Judy an awkward kiss. 'I'm glad you're going. It'll do you so much good.'

Judy shrugged. 'Perhaps. But it's not going to bring Sean back, is it?' She looked at her aunt. 'I may get my hearing back, but I'll never have my sweetheart again.'

Chapter Fifteen

The whole family walked down to the tiny station next morning to wave Judy off. With a small suitcase from the store, her gas mask in its cardboard box, and two brown paper carrier bags, she looked like a waif as she climbed aboard the train, and there were tears in all the women's eyes. Even Dick cleared his throat rather often, and hugged his daughter tightly before letting her go.

'It's only for a week or so,' she said, leaning out of the window. 'You don't have to look as if you're never going to see me again.'

'Don't talk like that,' Cissie begged her, but what with her deafness and the noise the engine was making, there was no chance of Judy's hearing her. However, she had learned to lip-read surprisingly well and grinned impudently at her mother.

'I might not want to come back. I might decide to stay.'

'Don't you dare! Not but what it wouldn't be good to know you were safe.' The whistle of the engine drowned her words and the train began to pull away. Suddenly crying in earnest, Cissie waved frantically and turned to her husband to bury her face against his shoulder. 'Oh Dick, she's gone! Oh, I hope she'll be all right, going all by herself. I hope we've done the right thing.'

'Of course we've done the right thing – and she's only going to Ashwood. It's not the other end of the world. You're going on as if she was off to the Front.'

'I know.' She sniffed and laughed a little. 'I'm being silly. It's just that so much has happened, and you never know what's going to happen next, and just saying goodbye, even for only a week, makes you think about all the people who go away and never come back, or perhaps there's no home to come back *to*. Oh, I know I'm being silly, I'm talking a lot of nonsense.'

'It's all right, love,' Dick said quietly. 'You're not talking nonsense. We've been through some terrible times, you're bound to worry. And I know you worry about our Terry too, same as I do. We don't know where he is half the time, and all we can do is hope we don't hear it's his ship that's got sunk. It's worry we never thought we'd have, and more than anyone should have to put up with. And I'm not a lot of help to you,' he added ruefully.

'You mustn't say that.' They had begun to walk away from the station. 'You don't know how empty the house seemed while you were in hospital. I feel like I'm just half a person when you're not there.' Cissie stopped and looked into his eyes. 'You're only ill because of what happened to you in the Great War. That was cruel, and you've been suffering ever since. It's not your fault.' She took hold of both his hands. 'Shall I tell you what I think? You're *still* serving your country. Every time you wheeze or cough, you're serving your country, because you wouldn't be like it if you hadn't gone to serve it then. And I thank God on my knees every day – *every day* – that you came home. So don't ever say you're no use. *Ever.*'

'And so say all of us,' Alice said fervently, and Polly agreed.

'We'll go home and have a cup of tea,' she said, 'and then I'll be off down to the Centre.' She lifted her face to the May sunshine. 'Do you realise, we've had five nights now without a raid? Five nights of peace in our own beds. I can't believe it.'

'Nor can I,' Dick said, 'but it won't last. Mark my words, the Germans haven't finished with us yet.' He, too, looked at the blue, innocent sky with its drifting fleet of silver barrage balloons. 'They'll be back. Sure as God made little chickens, they'll be back.'

Judy sat on the train, feeling a little sick. She had refused both her mother's and her aunt's offers to come with her, insisting that she could manage – 'I've only got to get off the train and walk down the lane to the farm' – but inside she felt apprehensive. Suppose the train broke down, or went the wrong way, or she didn't recognise the station when they arrived there? All the signs had been taken down, and she had only Polly's description to go by, and the stations all looked more or less the same. Because she wouldn't be able to hear any announcements, they'd taken the precaution of asking the guard to make sure she got off there, but suppose he forgot? And suppose someone got into the compartment and tried to talk to her? Suppose she got lost and had to ask for directions? Tears came into her eyes as she reflected that even a simple thing like a train journey seemed almost impossible when you were deaf.

Angrily, she brushed the tears away. She had seen enough injuries, and enough death too, during the air raids and in hospital, to know that she had escaped quite lightly in comparison with others. Awake night after night, she'd told herself over and over again that losing her hearing was nothing – *nothing* – and if it really did get better, as the doctors thought it would, then she had no reason to complain. No reason at all to be sorry for herself. No reason for this incessant weeping that kept overtaking her. No reason to get so angry with her mother and aunt just because they tried to help. No reason to feel so *useless*.

Yet everything seemed to be so difficult. The simplest tasks – going shopping, answering the door – seemed suddenly to be almost impossible. Making herself understood was easier, although she suspected her voice was coming out oddly, either too quiet or too loud, but trying to make out what others were saying drove her into a frenzy of frustration. I'll have to learn sign language, she thought, but that was only any use if everyone else learned it too. And she felt left out of conversations. You couldn't expect people to say everything slowly; you just had to sit by, knowing they were talking and laughing but with no idea what the subject or the joke was. It was even worse when they listened to the wireless and you could see them looking dismayed by the news or laughing at *ITMA* or Arthur Askey. It was like living in a glass cage.

There I go again, she thought impatiently, feeling sorry for myself. I've just got to grow up and get on with it. There are worse things than being deaf. Being blind, for instance. Not being able to see this lovely countryside, the cows and sheep and the lambs, skipping about in the grass. The trees all coming into fresh green leaf. The blossom on the wild cherries and the apple trees that had grown beside the track, from cores people had thrown out years ago.

But other people were different when you were blind. They were helpful, considerate. They still treated you as a human being, they took your arm and guided you along, they *talked* to you.

If you were deaf, they treated you as though you were stupid. They talked to you for a few minutes, making big shapes with their mouths, and then they left you out. After a while, it was as if you weren't there at all. As if you were invisible.

The train trundled through the countryside, stopping at every small station and halt and sometimes in between for unexplained rests. The actual distance to the village where Sylvie lived wasn't very great, but the journey took almost two hours and at every stop someone got on or off. There were servicemen and women, Land Girls, civilians in shabby coats or smart suits, workmen carrying bags of tools, and a vicar. He was a tall, spindly man with long arms and legs, and he smiled kindly at Judy as he sat in the corner opposite her. As she had dreaded someone would, he began to make conversation.

'I'm sorry,' she said, pointing at her ears. 'I can't hear.'

His mouth made an 'oh dear' shape, and he looked concerned. '*Since birth?*' he mouthed. '*Or an accident?*'

'Bomb blast,' Judy said briefly. 'In Portsmouth.'

'Portsmouth?' He said something she couldn't catch, then mouthed again. '*I have evacuees from Portsmouth.*'

Judy nodded. She didn't really want the struggle of conversation with a stranger but the vicar was clearly trying hard not to let her feel ignored. The other passengers had stopped their own conversation and were watching and listening. Feeling self-conscious, she said, 'There are some children in our street evacuated out this way somewhere. A village called Bridge End.'

'Bridge End? But that's where I live!' He leaned forwards and repeated his words more slowly. 'Perhaps you know them. Tim and Keith Budd.'

The names were easy to read. Judy forgot her self-consciousness and nodded eagerly. 'I know them! They live in April Grove. My granny lives there too, and we went to stay with her when we were bombed out.' She remembered her aunt's visit here. 'You've got Stella and Muriel Simmons too.'

'That's right.' He looked enormously pleased to have found this point of contact. 'Such sweet girls, and such a sad story. But they're settling in very well.'

'It was my auntie who brought them to you,' Judy said, not really understanding all his words but able to pick up a few. 'Polly Dunn. Do you remember her?'

'Mrs Dunn! Of course I remember! Such a nice woman. So you're her niece.' He sat back and smiled broadly. 'Well, how very pleasant. Are you coming to Bridge End on a visit?'

Once again, she was able to recognise the important words. Perhaps it was because he was a vicar, and used to talking clearly in church. 'No, I'm going on to Ashwood. My niece Sylvie – Polly's little girl – is evacuated there. I'm going to stay with her foster family for a while. The doctors think it might help me get my hearing back.' She had forgotten her shyness, delighted to find someone so easy to talk to, someone who had met Polly and knew people she knew. 'It's shock, you see, and blast, not actual damage.'

'Then I'm sure a stay at Ashwood will do you the world of good. And why don't you try to bring Sylvie over to Bridge End to see us one day? I'm sure Stella and Muriel would like to see an old friend.'

'I don't think they'd know her,' Judy said, having disentangled this invitation. 'But she'd like to come, I'm sure. I'll see if we can manage it.'

The train arrived at yet another small station and the vicar glanced out of the window and jumped to his feet, knocking his head on the luggage rack as he did so. He rubbed his head ruefully and smiled at Judy. 'I'm always doing that. I can never remember how tall I am. Now, don't forget, bring Sylvie over to see us the first chance you get. I'm very easy to find. The vicarage is right beside the church, and my name's Mr Beckett. Everyone knows me.' The train had stopped and he opened the door, tumbling out on to the platform in a tangle of arms and legs. Judy smiled and waved at him, and the other occupants of the compartment laughed.

'I just bet everyone knows him!' said a woman who happened to be looking Judy's way as she spoke. 'A real character, he is.' The rest of the conversation was lost as she turned away and the other passengers joined in, but for once Judy didn't feel left out. She sat back in her corner and smiled to herself, still feeling the warmth of the vicar's conversation and the attention he'd paid to her. Some people understood, then, she thought. Some people understood what it was to be deaf.

*

Ashwood station was only a few miles further down the line and the guard remembered to walk along the platform and open the compartment door for her. Judy smiled her thanks and scrambled down, lugging her suitcase and carrier bags. She stood for a moment on the platform, gathering her thoughts, and then turned quickly as she felt someone tap her arm.

'Sylvie!' With a cry of delight, she scooped the little girl into her arms. 'Oh Sylvie, how lovely! How did you know I'd be on this train?'

Sylvie hugged her aunt and beamed up at her, her lips moving quickly as she chattered. Judy felt a swift lurch of dismay; she'd known she wouldn't be able to hear Sylvie's voice, of course she'd known, but somehow the realisation seemed to hit her more bitterly than since she'd first found she was deaf. 'I'm sorry, Sylvie,' she said regretfully. 'I don't know what you're saying. You have to speak very slowly, and make sure I can see your mouth move. Like this.' She mouthed a few words and to her surprise Sylvie burst into giggles.

'Auntie Judy! You are funny!'

'Funny?' For a moment, Judy felt indignant. Nobody had dared suggest she was funny – indeed, she was sure nobody had even thought so. But suddenly, looking down at the child's bright face, innocent of either embarrassment or the wish to hurt, she laughed. Maybe she *was* funny! Maybe that was the best way to treat this affliction – laugh at it. She bent again and hugged her niece, lifting her in her arms to whirl her round in the air.

'Whee!' The child's scream of pleasure vibrated against her body and Judy set her down again, trembling a little. It was almost like hearing. Perhaps it would come back after all, she thought with a lift of hope.

Sylvie was urging her to come with her now, picking up one of the carrier bags in one hand and dragging Judy by the other. Together, they hurried out of the station and along the lane. Judy looked around her and felt her heart move.

Born and brought up in Portsmouth, she had never been far into the countryside. Before the war started, the family had gone up on Portsdown Hill sometimes for picnics, or caught a bus out to Denmead or Catisfield. Once or twice they'd gone to Petersfield and wandered by the lake, and they'd found bluebell woods and come home with arms full of scented flowers. But for the past eighteen months such jaunts had been impossible, and it was a long time since they'd had a family picnic. Now, the feeling of space and the sense of peace was like a balm to the soreness of her mind.

The lane leading from the station was wide enough for a horse and cart and roughly metalled. It ran between hedges laced with fresh new green, and mossy banks clothed like a king's robes with the gold and purple of primroses and violets. The hedges were alive with birds, darting in and out of the branches, their beaks stuffed with worms and insects. They must all have nests in there, Judy thought in wonder. And I expect they're singing too. It's lovely!

The sky was a soft blue and the sun warm. Sylvie skipped beside her, one hand still clasped in Judy's. Every now and then she peeped up at her aunt and laughed, and Judy laughed back. Mum and Polly were right, she thought. This is what I need. But then, it's probably what *everyone* needs.

In ten minutes, they were at the farmyard gate. Sylvie stopped to unfasten it, putting down the bag to do so, and Judy went through, looking about her with interest. She had never been in a farmyard before, and her knowledge came mostly from picture-books she had had as a child, showing chickens and ducks scratching about the yard, cows in the fields and maybe a horse looking over a stable door.

To her astonishment, that was exactly what it did look like. There was even a big, swaggering rooster, its head crowned with a scarlet cockscomb, its tail spraying out like an iridescent rainbow behind it. It stared at Judy, tilting its head, and she stopped for a moment, feeling as if she had actually strayed into her own childhood picture-book, and gave a laugh of pure pleasure.

I'm laughing! she thought in amazement. I'm actually *laughing*!

The farmhouse itself was a long, low building with a thatched roof and a row of small windows like eyes set beneath curved arches in the thatch. A wide doorway gave it the appearance of a smiling face, and there were flowers growing along its walls. On the far side of the yard there was a well, with a little roof over it, and a woman who was winding up the handle turned at the click of the latch and her face broke into a smile. Hastily, she brought the bucket up to the top, unhooked it and set it on the ground before hurrying over, wiping wet hands on her flowery pinafore.

'Miss Taylor! So you're here! Sylvie's been down to the station all morning, hoping you'd come soon. It's a pleasure to see you, it really is.' She remembered Judy's deafness and repeated her words more slowly, smiling all the time. Her face was round and rosy, her silver-grey hair scraped back into a bun, her figure as comfortable as a cushion. She took both Judy's hands in hers and clasped them warmly.

'Thank you,' Judy said, liking Mrs Sutton at once. No wonder Polly felt happy about her daughter being here. 'It's so kind of you to let me come and stay. And please, call me Judy. Everyone does.'

'Judy. That's a nice name. Now, come in and I'll make some tea.' Mrs Sutton was still speaking slowly, but when she turned away her words were lost. Judy followed her in, ducking her head to go through the low doorway, and standing for a moment to let her eyes get accustomed to the darkness. Sylvie, beside her, squeezed her hand.

It's like a house in a fairytale, she thought, looking about her. The room was not very big – perhaps a couple of feet all round larger than the rooms in April Grove – but it was different from any room she had ever been in. The walls were almost three feet thick and built of huge, uneven blocks of stone. The fireplace was like a small room in itself, sunk deep into the wall and with two stone shelves like seats at the sides. Above one was a small iron door with a handle, and Judy stared at it, wondering what it could be.

Over the fireplace was a lintel that could have made a respectable tombstone, with another great slab down one side. There was no fire burning, but a pile of logs on a mound of ash indicated that cold nights would be cosy in here. A couple of shabby armchairs, placed in the alcoves on either side and covered with chintz in a faded flower pattern, seemed to throw out an invitation to sink into them and rest.

There were other chairs too, and a couple of stools as well as a squashed and battered pouffe that looked as if it had been used by generations of children. In one corner stood a small grandfather clock, its swinging brass pendulum shining like a beacon, and a shelf ran round the room about a foot below the ceiling, with jugs of all colours and sizes ranged upon it. The floor was of stone flags, warmed by colourful rag rugs; the walls were washed a rich cream, broken by wooden beams, and the ceiling was supported by similar beams.

Mrs Sutton had bustled through another door to a room at the back of the house. Sylvie gave Judy a gentle push and she went obediently after her hostess and found her in a large kitchen, with a kitchen range at one end. Judy sat down at the big kitchen table and looked at the dresser with its rows of blue and white striped crockery, thinking how cheerful it all looked.

Sylvie placed herself in front of Judy and spoke slowly and importantly. 'This is the kitchen. We have our dinner here. This is Bossy.' She lifted a large tabby cat from one of the chairs and held him up for inspection. He hung like a rag doll in her arms, sleepy eyes barely open, and Judy stroked his big striped head. Sylvie dumped him down on the chair again like a pile of washing. 'We've got a dog too.'

She was still remembering to speak slowly and clearly. 'He's called Flash. He's out with Uncle Bob. He collects sheep.'

Judy had a vision of the dog with his collection of sheep, poring over them as her brother Terry used to do with his stamp collection. She laughed and Mrs Sutton, standing at the range and pouring water from a kettle into a big brown teapot, looked round and smiled. She said something Judy couldn't hear, but she looked pleased and Judy thought she could guess what the remark had been. Polly had told her that she was low in her spirits, and the farmer's wife was glad to hear her laugh.

All the same, it was no easier to take part in conversations here than it had been at home. The country accent was difficult for Judy to read, and when Mr Sutton came in for dinner with the collie dog Flash at his heels she found that he talked almost without opening his mouth, so that it was almost impossible to read his words. He was welcoming enough and shook her hand warmly, but he seemed shy and wouldn't look her full in the face, which made it even harder to understand him. When he was followed in by Jenny and Brian, the other two evacuees, the chatter became impossible to follow and Judy's initial optimism faded a little. She sat looking at the table, scarred with many years of use, while the conversation flowed about her unheard.

Dinner was toad-in-the-hole with cabbage and potatoes, followed by rice pudding. Afterwards, she helped wash up and then Sylvie took her upstairs to show her where she was to sleep.

The room was the same size as the one downstairs, its uneven walls distempered in a sunny yellow and with yellow gingham curtains at the low window. There was a cupboard in one corner and a chest of drawers. Against one wall were two bunks, both neatly made with patchwork quilts spread over them.

'This is where me and Jenny sleep. My bed's the bottom one. But you're going to sleep in it now, and I'm going to be on the floor.' A mattress had been laid under the window. It looked comfortable enough, and Sylvie knelt on it to lean on the wide windowsill and gaze down into the garden. She turned after a moment and looked enquiringly at her aunt, and Judy realised she must have said something.

She pointed at her ears. 'I didn't hear you. Say it again.' But Sylvie shrugged and shook her head, as if what she had said wasn't worth repeating.

Judy felt a familiar flash of irritation. This happened time and time again. People made casual remarks but when they were unheard, couldn't be bothered to repeat them. It made her feel even more cut off – as if she had no choice in what she was allowed to hear, as if she didn't matter. It made no difference that on the occasions when someone did repeat their casual remarks she thought herself that they weren't worth repeating – she just wanted to *hear*. She wanted to hear *everything* – like other people. Like she had before. She wanted to be able to make up her own mind about what was worth hearing.

The irritation quickly faded, however. It wasn't Sylvie's fault, and she'd been very good about talking directly to Judy. She was pointing down into the garden now, saying something about an apple tree. Judy knelt beside her and found that she was gazing out into an orchard at the back of the house. She gave a little gasp of delight.

The orchard contained a dozen or so trees, every one smothered in blossom. A foam of pale pink and white seemed to wash like waves on the seashore right up to the walls of the house, reaching just below the window. Their scent drifted in through the open window, filling the room with delicate fragrance. Below them, revealed only in glimpses, the grass was sprinkled with late daffodils and Judy saw the cat, Bossy, who had been ejected from his chair at dinnertime, slumbering in a corner, warmed by sunlight.

Judy felt a warmth steal over her body and into her heart.

I'm going to be happy here, she thought. It was the right thing to do. If I can get better anywhere, it will be here.

She gave her cousin a hug. 'Show me the rest of the farm,' she said. 'Show me *everything*.'

Chapter Sixteen

It was not until she experienced the peace of the countryside that Judy realised just how much she had been affected by the terror of the raids on Portsmouth.

For a few days, she just roamed about in a dream. The weather stayed fine and after she had helped Mrs Sutton to tidy the bedrooms and wash some of the everlasting supply of dirty clothes from the children and Mr Sutton, she was free to go outside and lift her face to the sunshine. Often, she took a bowl of vegetables out into the garden and sat on an old chair, preparing them, but more than that Mrs Sutton refused to allow her to do. 'You're here to get built up, not do housework,' she said, making her meaning plain. 'You go for a nice walk. There might be a few bluebells starting to come out.'

The children were at school in the mornings, and Judy wandered alone down the lanes, drinking in the scent of the flowers that bordered the way, and wishing she could hear the song of the birds. She came to the village and stood for a moment gazing at the green with its pond, alive with tadpoles, but turned away quickly when she saw an old man hobbling her way. She wasn't ready to meet strangers, who wouldn't understand her deafness. On her own, with no need to strain to hear, she felt herself again.

Arriving at a crossroads, she took a different way and found herself close to some woods. As Mrs Sutton had suggested, they were filled with early bluebells just beginning to come out – a sea of misty colour rippling in the green dappled light that filtered down through the leaves above. Judy gave a little gasp of pleasure and dropped down amongst them, stretching herself out and breathing in their fragrance. She turned over and gazed up through the leaves at the sky. I could be happy in a place like this, she thought. I could be happy here for ever.

Back in Portsmouth, on the night after Judy left, there was a raid which was concentrated on the Hilsea area, with several high-explosive bombs being dropped close to the gasworks and on the main railway line. A lot of houses were hit too, and three people killed, one of them a friend of Polly's.

'I knew her at school. We used to sit next to each other when we were in Miss Jenkins's class. She went to work at Lipton's, and then she got married to a chap from Tipnor way – dockyardman, he was till he went in the Army.' Polly wiped her eyes. 'They had two boys, must be about my Sylvie's age. I suppose they were evacuated, poor little souls.'

'It's awful for kiddies, losing their mums and dads,' Cissie said. 'Like those two little Simmons girls. Our Judy's going to try to get across to see them, you know. It's not far.'

'She'll see Jess Budd's boys too, then,' Dick observed. 'Not bad nippers, though the older one's a bit of a scamp. He used to knock about with Micky Baxter, you know, when his mother wasn't looking. I should think she's glad to have him out of the way. That boy's a bad influence.'

'Oh, he's not so bad,' Alice said. 'I saw him down Charlotte Street the other day, working on one of the stalls. He told me he's been given a delivery bike, got a little round of his own. Said he wants to join the Army soon as he's old enough – wants to be a hero.'

'Hero!' Dick snorted. 'Dunno what sort of a hero that boy'd be! Look at the trouble he got those other poor little tykes into – Jimmy Cross with one leg blown off, and that Nash boy killed outright. I'd be glad to have *my* youngster out of his way, I can tell you.'

Now that the weather was better, Dick's health had improved and he was able to get out into the back garden and do some digging. The patch where Alice had grown lupins, sweet williams and bunny-rabbits was now entirely given over to vegetables and a couple of currant bushes. Frank Budd, from number fourteen, had given Dick some cabbage seedlings from his allotment, and he had already harvested several pounds of new potatoes and baby carrots. He had also managed to get some sticks for a row of peas and runner beans.

'Dig for Victory,' he said, going out to the shed to fetch his gardening tools. 'Well, at least I can be a bit of use around the place.'

Polly was working almost full-time now as a WVS volunteer. She still did some hairdressing, but it was mostly during the evenings or on Saturday afternoons. For the rest of the time she found herself carrying out a huge variety of tasks – from organising salvage drives to collecting sauce-pans, jelly moulds and kettles for their aluminium, to sweeping up nuts and bolts from factory floors for re-use. Every time the air-raid warning went, she hurried off to present herself at the Emergency Centre, where she collected her old ambulance van and prepared to dash off to the site of the nearest bomb damage.

Often, the raid came to very little, with the planes droning overhead on their way to London, Bristol or some other city. But you never knew when the siren went whether this would be such a night, or whether it was the beginning of another ferocious attack. And you never knew if they might jettison some leftover bombs on the way back. You could never feel safe. Not until the 'Raiders Passed' – or, as most people now called it, the 'All Clear' – sounded its comforting wail.

Cissie and Alice too were doing their bit for the war effort. Alice went to the Centre on the days after a raid and spent her time making tea and sandwiches. On other days she and Cissie presented themselves at one of the two communal feeding centres, where meals were provided for all those who couldn't cook their own, or were unable to get groceries from the shops. There wasn't much variety – just soup at a penny a cup or a plate of minced beef and potatoes at three or fourpence a time – but customers arrived in droves, and when the tables and chairs were all occupied they sat on the floor, the stairs and even outside in the street to eat. The Centres were invariably sold out by one o'clock.

It did seem, however, as if the raids were easing off. After the one on the night following Judy's departure to Ashwood, there was a lull. People began to look and feel better. It was almost summer, they were getting more sleep and some of the bomb damage was being patched up. You could almost think about smiling again.

Not that there was much else to smile about. The war was looking bad in Europe. Yugoslavia and Greece had both been overrun, with Allied forces having to be evacuated from Greece and Crete – 'just like Dunkirk all over again,' Dick said bitterly – and at home there had been devastating raids on Plymouth, Liverpool, Newcastle and Bristol. At this rate, there wouldn't be a city left in the whole country. It wouldn't be worth invading.

Yet the fear of invasion was still very strong. All around the coasts barbed wire was being put up along the beaches, so you couldn't even go for a swim any more, and the Home Guard was on permanent alert. The signal for an invasion was the ringing of the church bells, so they were silenced on every other occasion and Sunday mornings were quiet. You didn't know how much you'd enjoyed hearing the bells till they weren't there any more, Cissie remarked.

At Ashwood, Judy would have welcomed hearing anything at all. She went for walks every day, wishing she could hear the birds singing or the rustling of leaves and the whisper of grass. She avoided meeting the village people or even the other evacuees, knowing they would be embarrassed by her deafness or even think there was something 'strange' about her. They probably think that anyway, she thought sadly, noticing a small group of children cross to the other side of the lane as she approached. They'll be saying I'm mental, or a witch or something. She wondered how many people in the past had become objects of fear or derision simply because they were deaf, or frail in some other way. Lonely old women, stuck in tumbledown cottages because people were afraid to help them. Grumpy old men, surly because they were hurt by their neighbours' treatment of them.

Is this going to happen to me? she wondered. Suppose I never get my hearing back? Am I going to spend the rest of my life like this, avoiding people just because I'm afraid they'll treat me like a leper?

The thought of Sean haunted her still. She grieved for him, yet she had an uneasy feeling that her grief should have been deeper. I *loved* him, she thought, twisting the little ring on her finger. I ought to be even unhappier . . . yet to her dismay she could barely remember what he looked like. She hadn't even a photograph to remember him by. The only person in the family to own a camera was Dick, who had had a box Brownie, lost in the bombing, and with film so hard to come by he had never taken a picture of Sean. Judy tried to capture Sean's face in her mind but it was elusive, fading away every time she thought she had conjured it up. Perhaps it was because they had known each other such a short time; there were so few memories.

She stopped and leaned on a field gate. Another memory came into her mind – a brief glimpse of a tall, fair-haired young man in RAF uniform with a Spitfire badge on his arm. Chris Barrett. She thought of his ready grin, the flash of white teeth and the crinkling of blue eyes. She thought of the hour or so they had spent together trapped in the lift, the easy conversation, the feeling of comfort he had given her.

She thought of his kiss.

With an angry shrug, she pushed the memory away and stared into the field where lambs were playing tag around their mothers' stolid bodies. One jumped up on top of its mother's back, and stood there for all the world as if it were laughing at its playmates. Half a dozen raced off to a grassy knoll and began to skip up to the top and then down again. Another little gang began running races from one side of the field to the other, and soon all had joined in, breaking off after a few minutes to rush back to their mothers for a drink.

Judy watched them and laughed suddenly. I can't hear them but I can still see them, she thought. There's still plenty of joy to be had, and it doesn't help Sean or anyone else to pretend it isn't there. And, with sudden energy, I *don't* have to be sorry for myself – I can still do things to help. I'm fit and strong, and I shouldn't be drifting about as if I'm on holiday. The WVS works even out here in the country, and I ought to be doing something too. I'll find out who's in charge.

She waved goodbye to the lambs and began to walk rapidly down the lane back to the village. Mrs Sutton would know, she thought, and went back to the farmhouse. The farmer's wife was busy making bread, and looked up with a smile.

'Had a nice walk?' She had learned quickly to shape the words so that Judy could read them, and Judy nodded and sat down at the table, watching her hostess's hands knead the floury dough.

'I want to do something to help.'

Mrs Sutton shook her head. 'No, love, you go out and enjoy the sunshine. You've done all the jobs that need doing here. You go and get some roses in your cheeks.'

'No, I mean I want to do something more. In Portsmouth, I was in the WVS. I helped in the raids. I want to do something like that here.'

'But we don't have the raids here, love. Only the odd bomb dropped by mistake, and that usually goes into a field. Old Walter Hart had a couple of cows killed a while back, but that's all.'

'But there must be something,' Judy persisted. 'I thought of offering to help on the farm, but I really ought to see the local WVS organiser. Do you know who she is?'

The floury hands paused. 'Well now, who would that be? It was a Mrs Tupper who brought the evacuee children out at the beginning of the war. She was WVS, or I suppose she was, so she'd know. But I don't know where she lives, so that's not much use to you.' She gazed at Judy, her forehead creased, and then her expression cleared. 'I know who could help you! The vicar – he'd be bound to know. Come to think of it, I do believe Mrs Hazelwood herself's in the WVS. There now!' She beamed. 'That's the answer. She's bound to be high up. Why didn't I think of it before? I'll just set this bread to rise and we'll go round to the vicarage straight away.' She repeated her last words slowly and then began to pound the dough again with vigour.

'No, I'll go by myself.' Judy stood up. 'I've got to start being more independent – I won't be any use if I can't do things for myself. And you're busy, anyway.' She touched Mrs Sutton's arm. 'Thank you. I'll be back at dinnertime.'

The vicarage was a large Victorian house close to the church. Its garden had been given over entirely to the cultivation of vegetables, of which there were neat rows already beginning to flourish. A large man, dressed in rough working clothes, was working with a hoe, and as Judy approached he straightened up and turned round. He was well over six feet tall with a large, black, bushy beard and moustache and to her surprise, she saw that he was wearing a dog-collar.

Judy looked at him and her heart sank. I can't even *see* his lips, she thought, let alone read them. But his eyes looked kind and she plunged into her explanation.

'I'm sorry to bother you. I'm Judy Taylor, I'm staying at the Suttons' farm for a while. I'm in the WVS and wondered if there's anything I can do to help while I'm here. Mrs Sutton says your wife is the local organiser.' Belatedly, she added, 'I'm afraid I can't hear what you say – I'm deaf. Bomb blast.'

The beard moved and she guessed he was speaking. 'I can't read your lips either,' she added apologetically, and was surprised to see that he was laughing. He reached out a big hand and ushered her inside the house. Judy, slightly disconcerted, found herself in a wide hallway, its floor patterned with black and white tiles. An old coat-stand stood near the door and there was a long settle that looked suspiciously like a church pew against the wall. The vicar led her through the door to her right, and she found herself in a big room with a bay window overlooking the garden, shabbily but comfortably furnished with a battered three-piece suite, a large cluttered desk and sundry other mismatched chairs and small tables. The walls were lined with bookshelves.

Mr Hazelwood spoke again and then pushed her gently into a chair. He pulled a sheet of paper across the desk and began to write on it.

You do the talking. I'll do the writing!

Judy laughed and nodded, feeling suddenly at ease with this big man who looked more like a farmhand than a vicar. She said, 'Well, it's just as I said. I work for the WVS in Portsmouth, helping the Lady Mayoress. I was out on an ambulance during the raid a fortnight ago, and we got caught in the bombs. We were all deafened, but the others got their hearing back. The doctor thought I needed a rest. He says it should come back, but no one knows for certain. Anyway, I just thought I ought to be doing something while

I'm here, and Mrs Sutton said that your wife runs the WVS in this area.'

She does, he wrote, *but is that quite what the doctor meant by 'having a rest'?*

'But I'm perfectly well,' Judy protested. 'I feel as if I'm shirking. There must be something I could do.'

I'm sure there is. He paused and looked at her thoughtfully, then seemed to make up his mind. *She's out at the moment, but she'll be back soon. Why don't you go and sit in the garden until she comes back? I'll make you a cup of coffee.*

Judy didn't much like the liquid Camp coffee mixture that most people used. 'Water would be fine,' she said, and he nodded and led her through to a big kitchen where he poured her a cup of water. Carrying this, he opened the back door and she found herself in a tiny garden that had not been taken over for vegetables. There was a patch of lawn with a pond filled with squiggling tadpoles which were being attentively watched by a large black cat with huge yellow eyes. The garden was bounded by a warm brick wall with a flower border that seemed to sweep up to it like a tide of colour, and in the middle was an gnarled apple tree covered with deep pink blossom. It was a tiny patch of tranquillity; a haven from the world outside.

The vicar indicated an old wooden seat under the tree and Judy sat down and accepted the water. He smiled at her and vanished round the corner of the house, and she leaned back her head, closed her eyes and felt the warmth of the sun on her face. After a moment or two, a furry paw touched her knee and the cat jumped on to her lap. She laid her hand on its sun-warmed back and smiled.

When she opened her eyes, a young man was sitting on the grass watching her. Judy started and spilled some water over the cat, which leaped off her lap and sat down a few yards away, shaking its head indignantly.

The man spoke. He looked about the same age as Judy, with dark hair brushed back from his forehead and very blue, eyes under heavy black brows. He was frowning slightly and Judy realised that he must have been speaking for some moments.

'I'm sorry,' she said. 'I can't hear you. I'm deaf.'

'Oh,' he said, and looked nonplussed. Judy held out the sheet of paper the vicar had given her, and he looked at it and smiled. He took the pencil and wrote, *I'm Ben Hazelwood. You must be waiting for my mother.*

Judy nodded. 'My name's Judy Taylor. I'm from Portsmouth.'

He held out his hand and she shook it. His grasp was firm and cool. They looked at each other for a moment, neither quite knowing what to do next. His smile was rather wicked and very attractive, Judy thought. It seemed to light up his rather dark face, which she suspected might be forbidding when he frowned and lowered those heavy brows over the bright blue eyes. But his mouth was wide and curled up at the corners, so that he looked as if he were about to break into a chuckle.

'Are you in the Services?' she asked and he twisted his mouth wryly and shook his head.

I'm not old enough. I'm thinking about lying about my age and volunteering!

'Not old enough?' Judy said in surprise, reading this. 'I thought . . .' She stopped and blushed, and he grinned and held up both hands, fingers stretched, then one hand and only two fingers of the other. 'Seventeen? You look older.'

Eighteen in September. But I want to go before then. I want to fly.

'Fly?' She glanced up at the cloudless sky, remembering the dogfights of last summer and the Battle of Britain that had raged across the South of England. Pilots, many of them barely more than boys, had been dying every day, yet there seemed to be a never-ending supply of young men willing to take their place. She looked at the youthful face, noting now the signs of immaturity – the softness of his

224

cheeks and lips, the eager innocence of his eyes – and thought of him fighting in the skies, perhaps being hit, his plane in flames, spiralling out of control . . .

The sudden vision shook her and she closed her eyes, trying to push it away. When she opened them he was watching her with some concern. She spoke quickly, at random, 'What do your parents think about it?'

He grimaced. *Haven't told them yet. Know I want to join the RAF – don't know I'm thinking of volunteering.* He looked suddenly anxious and started scribbling again. *You won't tell them, will you?*

Judy smiled and shook her head. 'No. I won't tell them.'

Ben looked up suddenly as if he had heard something, and quickly screwed up the piece of paper and stuffed it into his pocket. A moment or two later a tall, rather thin woman came round the corner of the house. She was evidently expecting to see Judy there and smiled and held out her hand, saying something. Ben spoke to her and she nodded.

'Miss Taylor. I'm very pleased to meet you, my dear.' She spoke carefully and Judy guessed that she would have a clear, rather pleasant voice. 'I see you've met my son.'

Judy nodded. Mrs Hazelwood sat down beside her and Ben went into the house, returning a few moments later with a fresh sheet of paper. He smiled at Judy and went away again.

Ben's home from school at the moment, Mrs Hazelwood wrote. *He has a week for Whitsun. Tell me what I can do for you.*

Judy nodded. One of the things you missed when you were deaf, she thought, was the more casual part of conversation – the little asides that didn't really matter, the humorous comments and quips, the remarks that made chatting a pleasurable experience. When you were deaf, it was so difficult for people to get across to you the information they wanted you to have – either by slowly mouthing the words or by writing them down – that they kept it to the bare minimum. It was like receiving a series of telegrams.

'I'm in the WVS in Portsmouth,' she said. 'I work for the Lady Mayoress. I thought perhaps there was something I could do while I'm at Ashwood.'

Mrs Hazelwood's eyes rested on her for a moment. They were a cool grey, set wide apart in a face that was made to look more narrow by pulling back the silver hair into a French pleat. She had a wide mouth too, rather like her son's, with a humorous curve to the lips, and her expression was compassionate.

'Are you here for a rest?' she said carefully.

'Well – yes,' Judy said. 'But there's nothing wrong with me. Apart from my ears, I mean. I'm not ill or anything. Just tired and – and things have been a bit difficult lately.' She felt her eyes fill with tears. 'I'm sorry.'

'There's no need to apologise.' The curved lips were easy to read. 'I know just how difficult things have been in Portsmouth. Was your home bombed?'

Judy nodded and bit her lip, trying to hold back the tears. 'In the first Blitz,' she whispered. 'We were in the shelter – Mum and Dad and Polly – she's my aunt, she's lived with us since her husband was killed. We went to live with my grandmother, and then Sean – *Sean* . . .' To her horror, the tears spilled over and a huge sob forced its way up from her throat. She put her head into her hands, appalled but unable to control the weeping any more, and the sobs tore themselves from her body; hard, painful sobs that wrenched at her chest and shoulders and made her throat feel raw and scraped.

'I'm sorry,' she choked.

She felt Mrs Hazelwood's hand laid gently on her shoulders. It was firm and soothing, and a strength seemed to flow from it into Judy's body. She found a large handkerchief pressed into her hand and after a while the sobs eased and she was able to blow her nose and sit up. She gave her hostess a faint, wobbly smile.

'I'm sorry. I didn't mean to do that.'

'I've told you, there's no need to apologise. You're not the first person to have wept in this garden.' The vicar's wife glanced around the tranquil little haven. 'It's meant for peace, but there are some griefs that have to be expressed in order to find peace. Was Sean your sweetheart?'

Judy nodded, understanding only the last part of this little speech. 'We only knew each other for a short while. We wanted to get married, but there wasn't time.' She looked down at the ring he had given her, with its tiny scrap of diamond. 'I can't seem to believe he's gone. I keep thinking about it, trying to imagine . . .' Her voice shook again. 'He was at sea, like Polly's husband. It must have been so awful.'

'Yes, it must.' Mrs Hazelwood's hand gave her shoulder a final squeeze, then dropped gently away. 'It must be so awful for so many people. For you as well.'

Judy shook her head at once. 'No – *I've* hardly suffered at all. I wasn't hurt in the bombing, I've got somewhere to live and my family are still there. I've been helping, until this happened.' She touched one of her ears. 'I want to help again. I need to *do* something – I can't just spend my time going for country walks and being looked after by other people. It feels wrong. It feels wrong *not* to have suffered.'

Mrs Hazelwood looked at her thoughtfully. 'But perhaps you need to be looked after for a while. There are more kinds of illness than the physical ones, you know.' This was a difficult sentence to read, and she wrote it down. Judy flushed and she shook her head vehemently.

'I'm not mad! Just because I can't hear—'

'No, no, my dear, I didn't mean that at all.' She wrote again. *You've had terrible shocks. You need rest to get over them. You mustn't feel guilty about that.*

'I don't know if I feel guilty or not,' Judy said, 'but I do know I want to do something to help. Please, isn't there anything? I don't mind what it is.'

Mrs Hazelwood looked at her steadily, and then smiled. It was a warm, friendly smile and Judy felt comforted by it. In fact, she thought, she felt comforted simply by being here, in this small, peaceful garden with its flowers and its sheltering walls. 'I hope the vicar never grows vegetables in here,' she said.

'I won't let him. It's a healing place, and that's just as important as cabbages. Food for the soul,' the vicar's wife said, and smiled again. 'Now, let's think what you could do. Have you ever made scrim?' She laughed at Judy's blank expression and wrote it down.

'Scrim?' The word still meant nothing. Judy shook her head. 'I've never heard of it.'

'I don't suppose you have! Nor had we until the war started. Come with me – I'll show you.'

Judy got up and followed her. Scrim! she thought. Whatever can it be? But it didn't really matter. Whatever it was, she was going to be doing something to help the war effort. She was going to be able to feel useful again.

Chapter Seventeen

'Scrim' turned out to be strips of dull green, khaki and grey fabric which had to be woven into huge nets to make camouflage material for the Army. The work was being carried out in a large barn, where a number of women were standing at wide wooden frames on which the net was stretched. The fabric was laid out on the earthen floor and they were painstakingly threading the strips through the netting. They looked up and smiled as the two newcomers arrived, and spoke to the vicar's wife, but in the dim shadows of the barn it was impossible for Judy to read what they were saying.

'It's not quite as easy as it looks,' Mrs Hazelwood said. 'You see, it has to look as real as possible so you have to fade out the edges and make the corners turn so that there are no sudden sharp lines. It's called "breaking shadow". Think of the dappled light of sun falling through trees, and you'll understand. It's rather dirty, tedious work, I'm afraid,' she added apologetically, 'but we all take a turn at it. There are other jobs to do as well, in between.'

Judy found that while she didn't catch all of Mrs Hazelwood's words, she could read enough to understand the gist. She stood beside an elderly woman wearing a pinafore, with a strip of the fabric wound round her head in a turban, watching to see how the work was done.

Mrs Hazelwood spoke to the other women and then smiled at Judy and left the barn. She had evidently explained Judy's problem and they didn't attempt to talk to her, but gave her friendly looks and showed her what to do.

One of them wound some fabric round her fair hair to keep it clean, and in a little while she felt confident enough to join in on her own section of netting.

As Mrs Hazelwood had said, it was dirty work. The air was full of dust and fluff from the fabric, so that she found herself sneezing every few minutes and soon understood why they all wore turbans. It was also hard on the fingers, which were soon sore from twisting the fabric through the stiff, oily netting. Yet even so, the work itself was strangely soothing. And you could take pride in weaving in the subdued colours, making dappled patterns and shadows here, a pool of light there. It's almost like painting, she thought. We're making a picture. And we might be saving soldiers' lives as well.

The other women were mostly elderly, one or two of them sitting on chairs as they worked. There was one enormously plump woman with swollen legs who could have done few other tasks, and another who could only work with one arm. It's a job for the weak and feeble – like me, Judy thought, and she smiled. Anyone and everyone could help the war effort in some way.

It was also a very sociable job. There was no machinery to make a noise and she could see that the other women were enjoying a good gossip and plenty of laughter. She sighed, wishing she could join in, but she was beginning to get accustomed to this sense of isolation now. Accustomed to being deaf, she thought in dismay. And I'm only twenty-two. Am I going to be like this for the rest of my life?

For a moment, she was swept with the sense of desolation that had also become painfully familiar – and then she took a grip on herself. I am *not* going to give way to self-pity, she told herself firmly. I'm fit and well and I'm working again. Plenty of people are far worse off than me.

She picked up another strip of fabric and wove it into the netting. This is a wood, she thought. It's a wood somewhere in Europe, and there are British soldiers creeping through the undergrowth. They're making dugouts to sleep in and they need this camouflage netting to hide them and keep them safe. Or they want to cover a tank or a lorry with it, so that the enemy doesn't know they're advancing. They're depending on me to make a really good camouflage. Someone out in Germany or France is depending on me – Judy Taylor. They're depending on me to keep them alive – and it doesn't matter a scrap to them whether I'm deaf or not.

By the time Mrs Hazelwood returned she had completed a whole frame. Pleased with her work, she stood back to admire it, just as an artist might stand back to assess a painting, and Mrs Hazelwood smiled her approval.

'You've done well, my dear. Now it's time for a break. I dare say Mrs Sutton will be expecting you back for dinner.'

'Goodness, is it that time already?' They came out into the sunlight and Judy glanced up at the church clock. 'I'll come back this afternoon and do some more.'

Mrs Hazelwood shook her head. 'No, I've got something else for you to do, outside in the sunshine. Most people only pop in for an hour or so, or even less, in between their other jobs. Come back at two o'clock and you can help collect sphagnum moss.'

Judy looked at her in bewilderment, totally unable to make out the last two words, Mrs Hazelwood just smiled and said, 'I'll explain when you come back,' so she smiled back a little uncertainly and went off down the lane in the direction of the farm.

'So you've been making scrim?' Mrs Sutton said, serving her a helping of cottage pie. 'I've done a bit of that too. Filthy work, but it's got to be done. And are you going back this afternoon?'

'Not to make scrim,' Judy said, watching her face carefully to read the words. 'I don't know what I'll be doing. I couldn't understand.'

The three children were back from morning school and

sitting up at the table, watching the big dish of cottage pie eagerly and squabbling about who would have the crispy bits round the edges. Sylvie nudged Judy and said, 'Perhaps you'll be digging up acorns. They did that last year, for pigs.'

'Acorns?' Judy said in surprise. 'Why? Can't the pigs dig up their own acorns?'

Mr Sutton, who was washing at the sink, laughed and said, 'That's what the women said, but they were just told to get on with it,' and Brian said scornfully, 'You don't collect acorns in May, silly. Anyway, they got them all last year. There won't be any more till after the summer. I expect it's rosehips for making juice for babies.'

'Well, that just shows who's silly, then!' Sylvie retorted. 'There aren't any rosehips either, so yah boo!'

'That's quite enough of that,' Mrs Sutton said severely. 'We'll have none of that kind of language at the table, Sylvie, if you don't mind.' To Judy, who had missed most of this exchange, she said, 'Perhaps you're going to be collecting moss. I've heard they use it for injuries. Put it on cuts and bruises,' she added, demonstrating.

This time, Judy understood. 'It might have been moss that Mrs Hazelwood said,' she said doubtfully, 'but they don't really put it on people, do they? What good would that do?'

'Don't ask me. It's a wonder what they can do, these days. Why, the vicar himself told me they use spiders' webs in telescopes and submarine periscopes and such, to give them sightings. Spiders' webs! I wouldn't have believed it if anyone else had told me. But he'd know, because he was in the Army. Chaplain, he was.'

Judy gave up on all these complicated words, and fastened instead on the mention of the vicar. 'I met their son in the garden. Ben.'

'Oh, Ben!' Mrs Sutton face broke into a smile. 'Their youngest, he is. Late baby – the others are all quite a few years older. In the Services, all of them – Ian in the Army, chaplain like his father, Alexandra gone for a nurse, Peter in the Navy. It must be a worry for the vicar and his poor wife, but at least they know Ben's safe at school.'

Judy followed this carefully and decided to say nothing about Ben's intentions. Brian, who had been concentrating on his cottage pie, looked up and said, 'Is it true they use spiders' webs for telescopes? Do they pay people to collect them? I could get lots.'

'Yeugh!' Sylvie said. 'Don't you bring them indoors. I hate spiders.'

'That's because you're a girl,' he said dismissively. 'All girls are scared of spiders.' He grinned evilly and made a spidery shape with his fingers, and Sylvie gave a little scream and cowered away.

'That's enough, now,' Mrs Sutton said, and held out the cottage pie dish. 'Does anyone want more of this? It's macaroni pudding for afters.'

'Bags the skin!' the three children shouted in unison, and she handed the dish to Mr Sutton, who scraped his fork round the edges and cleaned out every last scrap.

Judy walked back to the vicarage feeling well-fed and warmed by the cheerful company. The children were certainly better off in the country, she thought. Milk straight from the cow, home-made butter, home-baked bread and fresh eggs such as were rarely seen in the shops in Portsmouth. And peace. Freedom from the raids. Freedom from the wail of the siren, the roar of aircraft, the thunder of exploding bombs. Freedom from fear.

She took a deep breath of clean, country air, and wondered if she really was going to spend the afternoon collecting moss to put on soldiers' wounds.

It turned out to be true. With half a dozen other women, some of them the same age as herself, Judy was directed to a wood a mile or so from the village. The little group strolled along the lane, laughing and joking, and although Judy couldn't hear them she felt less left out than usual. They smiled at her and one, a lanky, red-haired girl with freckles and a ready grin, linked arms with her as they swung along. She smiled back, feeling a little as if she were a foreigner who didn't understand the language, but aware that they were friendly.

After a while they left the lane and crossed two or three fields. In the distance, Judy could see a church tower which she thought must be at Bridge End. She wondered how Stella and Muriel were getting along. She would have liked to go and see them, but her deafness made it too difficult. She still shrank from new situations and encounters.

The wood lay in a hollow, and in the centre of it was a swampy area, with tussocks of tough grass and reeds growing in shallow water. Judy could see the moss growing in thick, soft cushions of bright green everywhere. She looked at it with interest, wondering just why it was so valuable.

'The moss has healing properties,' Mrs Hazelwood had told them as they set off. 'It stops wounds from going septic. We send it out to the troops.'

Everyone was wearing Wellington boots and they set down their baskets on tussocks and began to work. It was quite pleasant, Judy discovered, once you'd got used to plunging your hands into the cool, damp cushions and pulling them up to pack into your basket. It didn't take long to fill them, and within an hour or so they were on their way back, each swinging two tightly packed baskets. As they crossed the fields, they paused to gather wool left on the fences by sheep and crammed it in with the moss. Mrs Hazelwood received them with approval.

'That's excellent. We'll have another moss-gathering party tomorrow.' Most of the women had meals to prepare for menfolk and children, the evacuees as well as their own, so could only spare an hour or two each day. But it was

234

surprising how much could be achieved in a short time, Mrs Hazelwood told Judy, inviting her in for a cup of tea before returning to the farm. An hour or so making scrim in the mornings, another hour spent gathering moss or wool in the afternoon, and it all added up to a substantial contribution towards the war effort.

She took Judy into the garden again. The sun was warm and they took their tea to the seat under the apple tree. Mrs Hazelwood talked carefully, facing Judy so that she could read her words. She talked about her children – Ian, who had taken Orders and followed his father into the Army as a chaplain, Peter who was a Lieutenant in the Navy, and Alexandra who had volunteered as a VAD nurse and was at present working at Haslar Naval Hospital in Gosport.

'It's good to have her so close. She comes home when she can manage it, for her day off. But they've been so busy during the last few months, with all the bombing . . .' She fell silent and sat gazing at the black cat, who was stretched out on his back in the sun, soaking up the warmth. 'I'm glad to know they're all being useful, though,' she said at last.

Judy sipped her tea and thought how difficult it must be for mothers like Mrs Hazelwood, knowing that their children were in danger and unable to do anything to keep them safe. She thought about Ben, who was as safe as anyone could be at his school in Winchester, yet wanted to leave that safety and take to one of the most dangerous of occupations as an RAF pilot. How would the Hazelwoods feel when he took that step, without even consulting them? They'll be upset about it, she thought, but they'll be proud too. And we all have to put our worries away in this war, because it's got to be fought, to save the whole of Europe, maybe the whole world, from tyranny, and none of us is really safe.

A shadow fell across the lawn and Ben himself appeared, tall and loose-limbed in grey flannel trousers and white, open-necked shirt. He grinned at his mother, winked at

Judy, and flung himself down on the grass beside the cat. There were some extra cups on the tray and he poured himself some tea.

Mrs Hazelwood stood up. 'I'll leave you to finish your tea,' she said to Judy. 'And please come back tomorrow if you'd like to do some more – but don't feel you have to. You're here for a rest, remember.'

She walked away across the lawn, her skirt swaying around her lean figure, and Judy watched her, thinking how kind she was, how kind everyone was in this village. She glanced at Ben uncertainly and he reached out a hand and pulled her to her feet.

'Come for a walk. Or are you worn out from all your moss-gathering?'

Judy shook her head. 'I feel I ought to be doing more.'

'Well, we'll take some baskets,' he declared, 'in case we find something useful.' He led her across the garden to the shed where the baskets were kept and handed her one, taking another for himself. Side by side, they strolled off between the green hedges.

A little way along the lane, Ben turned off to the left down a track Judy hadn't noticed before. It was roughly metalled and ran between hawthorn hedges frothed with white blossom. The grassy banks beneath them were misted with bluebells and here and there were patches of starry white wild garlic flowers. Now and then the lane was shaded by a spreading oak, ginger with new leaves just about to burst, or a stand of tall elms crowded with rooks. There were a couple of farm cottages, with small children playing in the dust, and then the lane wound down a hill and forded a river before climbing up out of the valley through woods on the other side.

There was a narrow wooden bridge over the river, and Ben crossed halfway and then sat down, swinging his legs over the side. Judy joined him and they sat quietly for a while, watching the brown water ripple beneath them.

'I suppose there are birds singing,' she said thoughtfully after a moment or two. 'Wish I could hear them.'

'You will,' he said, and she could tell by his expression that his voice was firm, as if he knew that what he said was true. Judy shrugged.

'I hope so. But nobody knows for sure. I might be deaf always.'

He shook his head. 'You won't. You'll hear again. I know you will.' He smiled, full of confidence. 'You've just got to want it badly enough – you've got to believe it.'

Startled, she stared at him, and then, suddenly angry, began to get to her feet. 'Don't say that. Don't you realise, I *do* want to hear again – I want it more than anything in the world! But it's my *ears* – there's something wrong with them, something damaged. Just *believing* isn't going to make any difference.' She scrambled up, but Ben caught her hand and drew her back down beside him.

'I'm sorry. Please don't go, Judy. I didn't mean to upset you.' She looked into his face, reading only some of the words but understanding his expression, and suddenly he looked so young, so pleading, that she burst out laughing.

'All right. But please don't talk like that. It's silly.' She sat down and looked at him again. 'You *don't* know, Ben. You can't. Even the doctors don't know for sure. I could be deaf for the rest of my life. And even if I am,' she paused, 'it can't possibly matter to you.'

Ben opened his mouth and then shut it again. He looked away from her, down into the brown, rippling water, and she saw his mouth move, but he didn't look back at her to repeat his words. She felt a sudden sense of frustration, wanting to be able to talk to him, freely and naturally. I *do* want to be able to hear him, she thought with despair. I want to be able to hear everyone. But wanting isn't enough.

Ben suddenly gripped her hand more tightly, indicating something with his head. Judy followed his gaze and stifled a little cry of delight. A bird was sitting on a branch a few yards further up the river – a bird with brilliant, electric-blue wings and a flame-red breast. As Judy watched, it dived into the water and reappeared a moment later with a small fish struggling in its beak. It flew back to its branch, gave a few quick glances around, and then disappeared into a hole in the bank.

'A kingfisher!' Judy exclaimed. 'I've never seen one before. It was beautiful. But why did it go into that hole? Is it hiding?'

Ben shook his head. 'That's its nest. It must have young in there.' He smiled his wicked, curving smile at her. 'Now are you glad we came?'

Judy nodded, and felt the easy rapport between them return. The moment of uncertainty had disappeared in their shared pleasure. 'Yes, I'm glad. It's a lovely spot. Thank you for bringing me. But I ought to be going back to the farm now. I promised to help Mrs Sutton with the supper.'

He nodded and got to his feet, helping Judy up. They stood facing each other on the narrow bridge for a moment, then Judy turned away and walked back to the bank. Ben caught her up as she bent to pick up the baskets they had left on the grass. He laid his hand on her shoulder. 'You're not cross with me, are you, Judy?'

'No. I'm not cross.' Their eyes met again and she relaxed and smiled. 'I'm not cross at all,' she said softly, and began to walk back up the track.

Ben fell into step beside her. They did not speak again until he left her at the gate to the Suttons' farm.

Chapter Eighteen

It really did seem as if the raids over Portsmouth were easing. There were only four during May, spaced several days or even a week or two apart, and they were light in comparison to the savagery of the three Blitzes. Some houses at Tipnor were damaged and the main railway line put out of action, but many of the bombs fell into the sea and there were only three people killed and just a handful injured.

The Luftwaffe had not given up, however. Liverpool had been cut off by seven nights of continuous bombing, with fires raging uncontrollably throughout, the worst of all being at the Bryant & May match factory. The city centre had been reduced to rubble, and a ship loaded with bombs and ammunition had been set on fire by a barrage balloon which fell blazing from the sky; the explosion sank six other ships and destroyed the dock area. A hospital had received a direct hit, killing sixty staff and patients, and a hundred and sixty children had died when their school shelter was bombed. By the end of the week, almost fifteen hundred people had been killed and seventy thousand were without homes.

London was attacked again. Under a cruelly bright 'Bomber's Moon', the heaviest raid yet left the House of Commons, Westminster Abbey, the Tower of London and the Royal Mint in flames. Every main railway terminus was out of action, over three thousand people were killed or injured and a hundred and fifty thousand homes had no gas, water or electricity.

'They're having a terrible time coping with the homeless,'

the Mayoress told Polly as they walked out of the Royal Beach into the sunshine a few days after the raid. She had been asked to go to London for a meeting at WVS Head Office in Tothill Street. The main railway line had been put out of action and, since the trains weren't running, she had decided to use the official car and asked Polly to drive it.

Polly was rather excited at the prospect. Driving a nice car in daylight would make a welcome change from dashing through blacked-out streets in a converted van. She was looking forward to seeing London, too – she'd only been there three or four times, long before the war had begun, when Alice had taken her and Cissie to visit a cousin. Johnny had talked about taking her to see the sights, but somehow, what with Sylvie's birth and the miscarriages later, it had never happened. Now some of those sights were gone for ever, she thought, and others might not last much longer.

The Lady Mayoress was still talking about the problem of the homeless in London. 'They don't seem to have foreseen such a situation, you see. They expected far more people to be killed – over six hundred thousand were estimated, I believe – and in the event there have been only twenty thousand in London and forty thousand in the entire country. Well,' she caught herself up and gave Polly a wry look, 'one can hardly say *only*, but still it's nothing like as many as were expected. Whereas they did nothing to plan for the homeless, and they already number over two million. It's a terrible problem.'

'And not all of them as lucky as us, with relatives to go to,' Polly said. 'Whatever will happen to them all?' She opened the passenger door of the car and the Mayoress got in. Polly cranked the engine and as it hiccuped and then purred into life she slid into the driver's seat.

The Mayoress sighed. 'I really don't know where they'll all go. That's partly what this meeting is about. It seems a strange time to go to London, with all the devastation there,

240

but it's at this time they need us most. Now, do we have enough petrol? I've got some vouchers so that we can get more if we need it, but of course I'd rather not use them.'

'I think there's enough.' Polly put the car into gear and nosed it carefully out on to the road. South Parade Pier shone as if it had been iced, and the sun was glinting on the sea, turning the waves to white-flecked blue. The fenced-off common was crowded with servicemen and girls, walking arm-in-arm or sitting on the grass. Because it was May, the sailors were all wearing their white cap-covers – one of the first signs of spring, Polly had always thought it. The sight reminded her of Johnny and brought an ache to her heart.

She had looked up the route to London and laid a set of directions on the seat beside her. It was the first time she had driven so far; she had never been further than the Queen Alexandra Hospital before, and driving over Portsdown Hill was like entering new territory. She knew the road to Petersfield from having been on charabanc outings out that way before the war, but from there it became a real adventure.

'You drive very well, Polly,' the Mayoress commented, and Polly blushed and thanked her.

'I like it. My husband could drive and he let me go very slowly in bottom gear in a field once or twice – but I never thought we'd have a car of our own. And even if we had, I don't suppose I'd have driven it. Women don't, do they? Or didn't, before the war,' she added.

'No, and I dare say they'll go back to being passengers once the war's over,' the Lady Mayoress said thoughtfully. 'The men will want their own places back then. And they'll need help to find them, I think. It will be very strange for them to come home to wives who've learned to manage without them. Women will have to take a back seat, even if they don't want to, just to help their men feel at home again.'

'I suppose so. I know I'd be so glad to have my Johnny

241

back that I wouldn't care if I never touched a car again. I'd just want to look after him, like a wife should.' Polly stopped, aware that if she continued to think and talk about Johnny the tears would come, and she couldn't drive with tears in her eyes. 'It's a lovely morning, madam.'

'It is.' The Mayoress gazed out of the window and sighed. 'You know, on a day like this, driving through the countryside with the sun shining and the birds singing, it's hard to believe we're at war. And then you remember the raids and all those poor souls without a home – well, *you* must feel for them especially, Polly, having been in just the same position. You've dealt with it all so well, I'm afraid I tend to forget.'

'Not all that well, madam,' Polly said, thinking of the nightmares and the tears that soaked her pillow. 'But you can't let it get you down, can you? You just have to carry on.'

'And how's Judy? Is the countryside helping her?'

'I think it is. We had a letter this morning – she still can't hear much, but she seems to be more settled in herself. She's found the local WVS organiser and she's doing some work – says she's making scrim!'

'Scrim? Whatever's that?'

'It's camouflage netting, madam,' Polly grinned. 'Apparently the nets are stretched over big frames and you have to weave in strips of fabric. She says it's the filthiest job she's ever done, but she quite likes it because she's making pictures to send to the troops! I'm not sure what she means by that, to tell you the truth. And she's been out collecting some kind of moss; she says they use it like a sort of bandage.'

'Oh yes, I've heard of that. Sphagnum moss, I think it's called. Well, that's excellent news, but I hope she won't overdo it. She's supposed to be having a rest.'

'Oh, Judy's like our Gran,' Polly said. 'She doesn't agree

with resting. What I'm afraid of is that she'll get to like being out there and not want to come home!'

'It's more likely that they won't want to lose her,' the Lady Mayoress said. 'Judy's an excellent worker, and no WVS organiser is going to let someone like that slip through their fingers. I wonder now if I was wise to let her go!'

Polly laughed. 'Well, so long as she's helping the war effort one way or another, it doesn't really matter, does it? It's like our Gran says, cream always rises to the top.'

They drove on. Polly's confidence was increasing and she found herself enjoying the drive along country roads and through small towns and villages. After a while, she said, 'It looks as if the weather's changing, madam. There's a big black cloud ahead, see?'

The Mayoress stared at it. 'I don't think it's an ordinary cloud, Polly,' she said quietly. 'It's smoke. We've seen just the same over Portsmouth after a raid. There must be fires still burning. You'll have to go carefully – we may not be able to get all the way in by car.'

Sobered, they drove on. There was damage in the outskirts of London and, as they approached the city itself, they began to see the devastation of the raids beneath the pall of smoke and dust that darkened the sky.

Buildings on all sides were destroyed or damaged, their roofs splintered and caving in, their walls torn down like a child's sandcastle. Some were smouldering, some still in flames, and although there were firemen and engines everywhere it was clear that it was impossible to deal with them all. Some houses had been just left to burn, with their occupants watching in despair. In one street, Polly saw a housewife in pinny and curlers, hurling buckets of water at the walls of her house. Others seemed to be reasoning with her, trying to get her to leave it, but her face was twisted with anguish and it was as if she barely knew they were there. She shook them off and ran back to the standpipe for more water, crying and screaming in her blind distress. The sight caught at Polly's heart and she remembered her own pain as she and the rest of the family had crept out of their shelter to find their own house in ruins. It isn't fair, she thought helplessly. What had we done to deserve that? What did this poor soul do to deserve it? What in the world is it all for?

'It's dreadful,' the Mayoress said as, having been diverted down street after street, they drove at last through Westminster. 'Worse even than Portsmouth. Row after row of houses, completely demolished. These poor people!'

Polly was almost in tears. 'It gets worse the further in you get,' she said. 'Isn't there anywhere left standing? Oh look – isn't that Westminster Abbey, with its tower all smashed down? And Parliament too! I never realised how bad it was.'

'The House of Commons, yes,' the Mayoress said as they drove slowly past, negotiating the fire engines and hoses. 'They're still burning. Dreadful. Polly, *look*! Surely that's Mr Churchill himself!'

Polly, who had been keeping her eyes on the cluttered road, risked a glance and saw the stumpy figure making his way through the firemen towards the devastated building. He was unmistakable, from the many times she had seen him in newspaper pictures or on film newsreels, and of course from the time he had visited the Royal Beach. He looked just the same, dressed in an overcoat and trilby and with the inevitable cigar gripped between his teeth, and somehow just the sight of his determined, pugnacious figure seemed to instil a little of the defiant hope that his words so often brought to the country. What did he feel like inside? she wondered. Surely even he, at a moment like this, must feel some despair. 'He must be so upset. What will they do now? They'll have to find somewhere else to have Parliament.' A thought struck her. 'They're homeless – same as the rest of us.'

'So they are.' The Mayoress looked out of the window. 'Turn left here, Polly. Tothill Street is the next on the right

– that's it. And there's number forty-one. Thank goodness that seems to have escaped the bombing.' She smiled at Polly. 'Well done. Now, I'm sure if you come in there'll be a cup of coffee for you, and then if you like you can walk through to St James's Park. It used to be very pleasant there – the lake was always full of ducks. I expect they're still there.'

Polly drew the car to a halt beside the kerb. There were a few other cars there, mostly official ones like her own; with petrol so severely rationed, most people who had their own cars had put them on blocks in garages 'for the duration'. She supposed that the other cars had brought people like the Mayoress for the meeting, and there might be some other drivers like herself who would be at a loose end for a few hours. At any other time, the prospect of some free time in London would have been an exciting one. Now, looking at the devastation around her, it was heart-breaking.

Number forty-one Tothill Street was a large house, turned into offices and meeting rooms. They were welcomed into a hall that had probably once seen debutantes setting off to be presented to the King, and top-hatted men and women in evening dress departing for the opera. A graceful stairway rose on one side, and there were tall, heavy doors leading into what had no doubt once been drawing rooms.

The hallway and drawing rooms were now full of bustling women in WVS uniform, or smart tweed or city suits. Polly glimpsed an office very like the one at the Royal Beach, with filing cabinets and girls seated at desks, typing or going through papers. Before she could see more, she was led through to the back regions and found herself in a dining room with a long table and about a dozen chairs, some of them occupied by women drinking coffee and eating toast; and beyond that a large kitchen where someone was busy preparing food and someone else was washing up.

'I might as well help,' Polly said, but the Mayoress shook her head.

'You're to have a cup of coffee and some fresh air. You've had quite a difficult drive. I'll just see how long my meeting's likely to take.' She strode briskly from the room and Polly found herself seated at the table, a cup of steaming coffee in front of her and a plate of toast pushed under her nose.

'It's all right,' said a woman of about her own age with a grin. 'Breakfast goes on until lunchtime here. We're coming and going all the time, you see, and after a bad night people just dash in whenever they've got the chance. My name's Daphne, by the way – Daphne Mallow. Have you driven up from somewhere?'

'Portsmouth.' Polly took a slice of toast and spread it with margarine and marmalade. 'I'm Polly Dunn. I'm with the Lady Mayoress. I'm a driver mostly, but of course I help out wherever I can.'

The other woman nodded. 'That's what's so good about the WVS. We'll turn our hands to anything, we never say no, and we're not bogged down by silly rules and red tape. I hope I'll be able to stay in it for the duration, not get called up into one of the Forces.'

'Why, d'you think we're likely to, at our age? They'll only take the younger ones, surely, in their twenties?'

Daphne shrugged. 'Who knows? The longer it goes on, the more help they'll need. Of course, if it came to it I'd go – that goes without saying – but I'd much rather do my bit with the WVS. All that marching and drilling – seems a waste of time to me.'

Polly nodded. She'd never thought about it before, but it now seemed to her that Daphne might be right. After all, if you were spending your time learning to march in step, you weren't spending it in helping people, and surely that was what doing your bit for the war effort was really all about. 'It's because of discipline, though, isn't it?' she said, trying to remember what Johnny had told her about being in the Navy. 'If you get used to obeying orders without question – even if it's just orders about marching – you'll do it when you're in an emergency and it's really important. I mean, my hubby was at sea, and he told me that if an officer shouted an order it wouldn't be any good if half the men started to argue about it. It could mean the ship being sunk.'

'Well, of course everyone must be sensible about it,' Daphne said. 'But then women are, on the whole. We don't need to have it drilled into us like that. And in the WVS we can think for ourselves. You're not always allowed to do that in the Services.' She glanced at the clock on the wall and jumped up. 'I must go! I've got to deliver a message to an office in Whitehall. See you later, perhaps.' She grinned again at Polly, crammed her green beret on her head, and was gone.

Polly finished her toast and coffee thoughtfully and took the empty plate and cup through to the kitchen. There was a plump woman of around fifty washing up and Polly offered her help. The woman smiled her thanks and Polly collected the rest of the crockery and picked up a tea-towel.

'So you're from Portsmouth?' the woman, who had introduced herself as Mrs Cousins, observed after they had chatted for a few moments. 'I've got an auntie near there. Gosport, she lives in – I dare say you know it.' She had a pleasant face, with warm brown eyes and greying hair.

Polly nodded. 'It's across the harbour. You can get there by ferry – I've been a couple of times, but there's not much there. It's not like Pompey. We've got all the best shops.' She paused, then added, 'At least, we *did* have, before the Germans decided to change things.'

Mrs Cousins gave her a wry look. 'I know, you've had some terrible raids. But it's the same story everywhere – raids and Blitzes, people killed or made homeless. And there don't seem to be no end in sight, neither.' She scrubbed at a large pan that seemed to have been used for making porridge. 'What it is, we've never had this kind of thing in Britain. We've always sent our armies off to fight in other countries, and then gone on much the same as usual at home. But now, with all these air raids, we're all mixed up in it together, and it's children and old people as much as soldiers and sailors.' She regarded the pan and then turned it upside down on the draining board. 'That's what sticks in my craw — seeing little nippers hurt and killed and frightened. Not that there ought to be any here by now,' she added grimly. 'Ought to be out in the country, where they'd be safe.'

Polly began to wipe the pan with her teacloth. 'I know. I don't understand why their parents keep them in towns. My little girl went straight away, right at the beginning. I know a lot of people brought their kiddies back when nothing much seemed to be happening, but surely with the way things are . . .'

'Oh, there are still people who think they know best. And there are plenty who don't really care all that much, to tell you the truth.' Mrs Cousins swished water round in the enamel washbasin and then tipped it down the sink. 'Some of the slums up the East End are a real eye-opener — youngsters in rags who don't see soap and water from one week's end to another, scavenging for food while their parents are in the pub drowning their sorrows in gin or beer and don't know where they are half the time. Mind you, I don't say they're all like that,' she added fairly. 'There are some who try to keep decent no matter how poor they are, but there are plenty who just have no idea. No idea at all. We do our best to help them, of course, but it's an uphill struggle.' She ran water over a dishcloth, squeezed it out and began to wipe down the scrubbed wooden draining boards. 'Well, that's breakfast done and dusted, time to start the dinner things.' She opened the door of a larder and began to heave out a bag of potatoes.

'I'll help you,' Polly offered, but Mrs Cousins shook her head.

'No, I heard the Mayoress tell you to go out and get some fresh air. That meeting's going on till about three – you can either come back and have a bite here, or have something while you're out. There's a Lyons' Corner House not far away – try that. You can always get a decent meal there at a reasonable price, and it's the sort of place a woman can go on her own and not feel conspicuous.'

Polly nodded and found her beret and shoulder bag. At the last minute, she remembered her gas-mask in its cardboard box, and slipped that over her shoulder too. She had still never really got used to taking it with her everywhere she went and often forgot, but here in London with the evidence of the Blitz wherever you looked, it seemed unlucky to go without it. The Germans hadn't used gas so far, but that didn't mean they wouldn't – and she knew from Dick's experiences in the 1914–1918 war just how terrible it could be. He'd had only a whiff and was still suffering; those who had been badly gassed had died in agony.

She walked out of the front door and stood for a moment looking about her. The sun was shining and she had a sudden, unexpected feeling of holiday. For a few hours, she had nothing to do and no one to please save herself. She was in London – a bombstruck, half-ruined London, it was true, but London nevertheless – and there were still sights to see. She decided to do as the Mayoress had suggested and go first to St James's Park.

Really, she thought a few minutes later, having crossed Birdcage Walk and gone through the park gates, you'd hardly know there was a war on. Well, provided you ignored the gun emplacements and trenches, and didn't look up at the fleet of drifting barrage balloons that had been supposed to prevent the enemy aircraft from getting through . . . But apart from those things, the grass was green, the cherry trees a foam of pink blossom, and the ducks on the lake were quacking about their business apparently without a care in the world. I wonder what they make of the bombing, she thought, leaning over the bridge and wishing she'd brought some stale bread. I wonder if it frightens them or if they just accept it as part of everyday life. I wonder how many have been killed . . .

'Hello.' The voice made her jump. 'Aren't you the young lady I met on the train for Ashwood? Whatever are you doing here?'

Polly turned, startled. Beside her, leaning on the railing of the bridge, stood a man – a long-legged man with wavy, iron-grey hair brushed back from a broad forehead, wearing a tweed jacket and grey flannel trousers. His voice was deep and warm, and she remembered it at once and smiled up at him.

'I've come up to WVS Headquarters with my boss – she's at a meeting. I drove her up and now I've been sent out to get some fresh air and exercise.' She laughed self-consciously. 'I feel a bit like a little girl who's been sent out to play!'

He raised his eyebrows, so that his forehead creased into the three crinkly lines that she remembered. Not frown lines, she thought, but humour lines. And there were other little ones too, splayed out from the corners of his dark brown eyes. It was a cheerful, crumpled face, a face that looked as if it had been lived in, and had found something to enjoy in much of what it had seen.

'What a bit of luck,' he said. 'Is this your first time in the Smoke?'

'Mum brought me and my sister a few times when we were children. She had a cousin in St John's Wood.' Polly laughed. 'I was so disappointed the first time I came – I was expecting a real wood! But she showed us St Paul's and the Tower, things like that. It's a long time ago now.' She sighed a little. 'I was going to come with my hubby, but we never got round to it.'

He looked at her for a moment, then said, 'Well, why don't you let me show you a few of the sights now – those that the Germans have left us, anyway. Buckingham Palace ain't far. And then we could walk up Piccadilly and back down Regent Street. What time d'you have to be back?'

'I think they expect the meeting to end at three. But I really ought to go and help. There's a lady there cooking dinner all by herself.'

'She won't be for long,' he said, grinning so that his face crinkled into a million tiny lines. 'My sister will make sure that everyone who walks through the door will lend a hand! I told you she works there, didn't I? She's in charge of the kitchen. In fact, it was probably her you saw – Edna Cousins, her name is.'

'That's right! She told me her name was Mrs Cousins.' Polly gazed at him. 'I can see the likeness now, too.' She put out her hand. 'My name's Polly Dunn.'

'And I'm Joe Turner.' His hand was big and warm, with stubby fingers. 'Pleased to meet you, Polly Dunn.'

They shook hands and then stood looking a little uncertainly at each other. After a minute or two, he said, 'Well, how about it? Going to let me show you the sights?'

'Well, if you think it will be all right,' Polly said, a little doubtfully. 'I still feel a bit guilty, as if I'm taking time off when I ought to be working.'

'You've driven up from Portsmouth,' he said. 'You're going to drive back. You've had some bad raids recently and I'll bet my bottom dollar you've been out night and day, helping and probably risking your life. If your boss has told you to get some fresh air, I think that's what you ought to do!' His face crinkled.

Polly laughed. 'Well, if you put it like that! And I *would* like to see Buckingham Palace – that's if you've got time. You've got other things to do, surely?'

'Not for an hour or two,' he said. 'I'm like you – snatching a bit of time to try to forget the war. We've all got to do that sometimes,' he added, looking down at her as they began to walk slowly through the park, alongside the lake with its crowds of colourful ducks. 'Keeps us from going round the bend.'

They strolled along quietly for a while. Polly wondered what he did. Despite his greying hair and crinkly face, he didn't seem too old to be in the Forces; in fact, when she had met him before, she had put him down as a soldier – a Sergeant, perhaps. Now she noticed that he walked with a stick, favouring his right leg, and wondered if he'd been injured and was on recuperation leave.

'Sorry to be a bit slow,' he said, as if reading her mind, 'but I've got a bit of a gammy leg. Copped it on the beach at Dunkirk. I've applied to go back to my regiment but they seem to think I'd be a liability.' He looked at Polly. 'You've got a kiddy, haven't you, a little girl? You were going to see her at Ashwood. I bet she was tickled pink to see you, wasn't she? Is she OK where she is?'

'Yes, she's with some really nice people. We're lucky, not all the evacuees are in such good billets. Actually, my niece is out there at the moment, too. We thought she needed a break, like you were saying just now.'

'Your niece? Wasn't she evacuated at the same time as your kiddy, then?'

Polly shook her head. 'No, Judy's in her twenties now.'

'Go on! You're not old enough to have a niece in her twenties!'

'I am,' Polly said with dignity, and then grinned. 'I'm quite a bit younger than my sister, Judy's mum, Cissie. There's the same difference between me and Judy as there is between me and Cissie.'

'Don't tell me any more,' he said, 'or I'll start working out your age, and that ain't the way to behave with a lady. And what about your hubby – serving, is he?'

'No. He's dead,' Polly said quietly. 'He was in the Navy, and his ship was sunk right at the beginning of the war.'

'Oh, blimey!' Joe stopped again and took her hand. 'That's me all over – open me big mouth and put me blooming foot straight in it. Sorry, love. Just tell me to shut up.'

'It's all right,' Polly said. She looked down at their hands. Hers, small and slim, was almost lost in his big hand. She saw that, like herself, he wore a plain gold wedding ring. That was unusual, she thought. Not many men did that. She drew in a shaky breath and said, 'I think I'm getting over it a bit now. I mean, so many things have happened and so many people have been killed. You just have to get on with life, don't you?'

'Yes,' he said. 'You do.' There was a moment's silence and then he tucked her hand into the crook of his arm and they walked on. Polly took a deep breath, and then another. Mentioning Johnny always brought an ache to her throat, but she could feel a comfort in the warmth of this big man, with her hand tucked so securely against his body. She had a sudden longing to be held close, to be hugged. No more than that – just to be hugged. To feel the closeness of another human being. To feel the warmth of a living body close to hers.

Oh Johnny, she thought, where are you? What happened to you? And did you think of me, during your last few moments? Did you know how much I loved you – and did it help at all? Or did you forget everything and everyone in those last desperate efforts to stay alive?

The tears came to her eyes and, without knowing it, she tightened her grip on Joe Turner's arm. He glanced down at her but said nothing, and if she had looked up at him then she would have seen that his eyes were wet too.

Chapter Nineteen

Polly and Joe walked right through St James's Park to Buckingham Palace. They stood by the Queen Victoria Memorial, gazing at the iron railings and the rows of windows. The sentries were not dressed in red jackets and tall busbies, as Polly recalled having seen them years ago, but in tin hats and combat uniform. They looked grimly prepared to fight to protect their King and Queen.

'They were bombed too, weren't they?' she said, looking at the big courtyard, and Joe Turner nodded.

'Copped it two or three times, back in March. There was craters there you could've dropped a house into, and there was some damage round the back of the building, too. You gotta hand it to Their Majesties, they didn't let it scare 'em off. Been out round the bombed areas every day, they have, talking to people and shaking their hands. Not just London, neither – Liverpool, Plymouth, anywhere that's been hit.'

'They came to Portsmouth,' Polly said. 'We saw them in our offices and then all the WVS workers went out to one of the hospitals and met the Queen there. She's lovely. She told us that sunshine would come again.'

'Well, she was right. It's come today, for a start,' Joe Turner said, looking at her, and Polly felt her cheeks blush slightly. 'Let's cut across Green Park now and go down Pall Mall.'

'You seem to know London very well,' Polly said as they crossed the park and made their way through a maze of streets. 'Is it where you grew up?'

''S right. Whitechapel, that's my old stamping ground.'

'Does that make you a Cockney? I don't know much about London,' Polly confessed.

'Well, not far off. I reckon you can hear Bow Bells on a good day, with the wind in the right direction. I don't live there now, though.' He closed his mouth, as if he didn't want to say any more, and Polly fell silent. After a few minutes they came to Pall Mall. 'This is where all the posh people hang out. Or used to – most of 'em have gone now, got places out in the country.' He fished an old chain watch from his pocket. 'Tell you what, I'm getting a bit peckish – how about a bite to eat at the Corner House? They do a decent dinner there.'

Polly nodded. 'Mrs Cousins told me that. She said it was the sort of place a woman could go to on her own.'

'Well, so it is, but I hope you ain't going to do that.' He kept her hand pressed firmly between his arm and his body. 'It ain't every day I gets a nice young woman to step out with. And I'll get you back to Tothill Street afterwards in good time to pick up your boss.' They continued along the wide road and then through to Trafalgar Square and Charing Cross. Joe Turner was walking more slowly now, and Polly wondered if his leg pained him. Perhaps we shouldn't have come so far, she thought, but didn't like to say so. She knew from Dick that men could be very funny about admitting to a weakness.

Charing Cross railway station was closed as, it seemed, was every other big station in London, and all the way around Polly could see signs of the massive Blitz. Fires were still smouldering, buildings destroyed, rubble blocking the roads, cars crushed beneath a weight of fallen masonry, and yet amongst it all life was struggling to continue as normal. People were coming out of offices and shops, dressed in their working clothes, as if it were any other lunchtime. And many of them were heading for the imposing white building of the Lyons Corner House.

'It's enormous!' she said, staring up at it. 'Is it all one restaurant?'

''S right. You've heard of Corner Houses, haven't you? And the Nippies – the waitresses there? They're famous, they are.' They joined the queue and moved slowly towards the big doors. 'I'm surprised your mum never brought you here when you come up to see the sights.'

'We couldn't afford restaurants. We always took a few sandwiches.' They were at the doors now, and as they passed through they were met by a smiling young girl who showed them to a table. Polly sat down, feeling rather awed. She had seldom been to a restaurant and thought that Mrs Cousins was wrong. She would never have had the nerve to come in here on her own.

'Mind, they used to be really grand before the war started,' Joe Turner told her. 'Big glass chandeliers, they had, and a gipsy band playing – almost as good as the Café de Paris, they were. And they always had a decent menu, see, not too pricey. So that ordinary people like you and me could come in.' He gazed around for a moment. 'Had to take all that away, of course, in case of bomb damage. You couldn't have glass flying all over the place, getting in the soup.'

Polly stared at him, then caught the twinkle in his eye and laughed. 'I never know whether you're being serious or not,' she said, picking up the menu.

'Oh, you'll know when I am.' He glanced at her for a moment. 'But it ain't very often, so don't look so worried. Now, what're you going to have? You're only allowed one protein per meal, if I remember rightly.'

They both chose shepherd's pie and peas. The peas might even be fresh instead of tinned, he said without much hope, but in any case it would be good. They might not be able to get all the best ingredients now, like they used to, but whatever it was it would be well cooked and the Nippy who served it would have a smile on her face and wouldn't keep them hanging about.

'That's why they're called Nippies,' Joe said. 'But I dunno how much longer they'll last. A lot of them are going into the Wrens and ATS and that now. If the war goes on much longer, we'll all have to queue up and help ourselves, like in a blooming canteen!'

Polly laughed. 'Oh, I'm sure there'll still be plenty of women who'll want waitressing jobs. It won't seem like going out if you have to carry your own tray.' Their own Nippy arrived at that moment and set their plates down before them. As Joe had expected, the peas were tinned but the mashed potato was good and the gravy rich and tasty. Joe had asked for a glass of beer as well, while Polly stuck to water, and they settled hungrily to their food.

This is the first time I've been out with a man since Johnny died, Polly thought – the first time I've been out with *anyone* except Johnny. Yet somehow there seemed to be nothing awkward about it, nothing to make her feel uncomfortable. Of course, it hadn't been arranged, it wasn't a proper date or anything like that, and she didn't suppose she'd ever see him again. To her surprise, the thought of never seeing him again seemed disappointing. He's a nice man, she thought, the sort of man I could be friends with. But of course, she couldn't be – he was a married man. And she still felt herself to be a married woman.

'D'you reckon you'll be coming up to London again with your boss?' he asked, once again seeming to read her thoughts. 'I mean, if she's going to come to meetings regular, she might want you to drive her, same as today. Only, I was thinking, if you could let me know, we might do this again. Have a bit of a walk together, and a bite to eat. If you felt like it, I mean,' he added quickly.

'Well . . .' Polly felt flustered. 'I don't know. I mean, I don't know if the Mayoress – she's never said anything about it before, she usually comes on the train. And anyway, won't you be back with your regiment?'

He shook his head. 'No chance of that.' He glanced down at his leg, stuck awkwardly out from the table. 'Told you I'd got a gammy leg, didn't I? Well, to tell you the truth, it ain't my leg at all. Well, it *is* mine – they give it me, see? At the hospital.' He caught her glance and nodded. 'Wooden one. The other one got shot off just below the knee. They won't want me back on service, that's the truth of it. Pensioning me off.'

'Oh,' Polly said blankly. 'Oh Mr Turner, I'm so sorry. That's awful.'

'Well, it weren't much fun,' he admitted. 'And the name's Joe. I'd take it kindly if you'd call me that.' He looked at her and his face crinkled. 'And I'd like to call you Polly, if you wouldn't mind.'

'No,' she said, 'I wouldn't mind at all.' He reached his hand across the table and she took it. They shook hands formally, as if they'd only just met, and then both laughed a little. 'But what will happen now? I mean, what will you do?'

'Oh, they'll find me things to do,' he said. 'Polish up the knocker on the big front door, that sorta thing. Just for the minute I'm still with my old boss, doing for him, but when he goes overseas again he'll get a new batman. I'm training up a new young chap now. Can't let the Colonel go back with no one to shine his buttons up for him.'

'I'm really sorry,' Polly said inadequately. 'You must be very disappointed. Were you in the Army before the war started?'

He nodded. 'Enlisted as a boy, went through the ranks, finished up as Sergeant. I was in the regimental band – trumpeter. Give you a tune one day, if you like.' He winked. 'Thought I might get a place in a dance band, bit of the old Glenn Miller stuff – "Moonlight Serenade", that sorta thing.'

'Oh, I love Glenn Miller,' Polly exclaimed. 'I like Ambrose, Joe Loss – all those sort of bands. We have the wireless on at home whenever they're on. I live with my sister and her husband,' she added, 'and my niece, Judy. And when we were bombed out we went to live with Mum. It's a bit of a squash but it's better to be all together.'

'Yes,' he said, 'it must be.'

There was an odd note in his voice and Polly gave him a curious glance. For once, he didn't meet her eyes but stared down at his empty plate, scraped almost clean of gravy and potato. Before either of them could speak again, the Nippy was at their side, swiftly removing the plates and asking if they'd like pudding. 'There's tapioca or plums and custard.'

'I'll have the plums,' Polly said, and Joe nodded in agreement. He looked up at last and grinned at her.

'We seem to have the same tastes. Music, food . . .'

'Same tastes as a lot of other people, then,' Polly said, a flicker of panic making her voice come out a little sharply. 'I dare say nearly everyone in the country likes Glenn Miller – and Lyons wouldn't put shepherd's pie and plums on the menu if they didn't think a lot of people would like them.'

'Ouch,' he said. 'Sorry – talking out of turn.'

'No, *I'm* sorry,' Polly told him, feeling ashamed of her sharpness. She gave him a smile. 'You're right, it is nice to meet someone who seems to like the same sort of things as you do. But . . .' she hesitated.

'But don't expect anything to come of it,' he said quietly. 'No, I don't. I don't think we can expect anything at all these days. You've only got to look around you and see all the bomb damage to know that. Here today, gone tomorrow, that's what they say, ain't it – and they never said a truer word. Never.' Once again there was that strained note in his voice. He looked at her, his face suddenly grave, the crinkles no longer of laughter, and said, 'Look, Polly, there's summat I want to tell you. I know I might be talking out of turn again, and I want you to know I wouldn't do this in the ordinary way – let out all my business to someone I've only just met. But somehow – well, it's as if we've known each other a long time. That day we met on the train – I felt it then, a bit. I was sorry you got off so soon. And then, bumping into you again today – well, it seemed to me as if it was meant. I don't feel as if I want to let this chance go by me.'

He stopped as the Nippy appeared again and set two bowls of plums and custard in front of them. Polly stared at him. Her heart was beating fast and she cast a panic-stricken glance around the restaurant. 'Mr Turner—' she began. 'Joe . . .' But he raised one hand to stop her.

'Let me have me say out, Polly. If you don't like it, you can get up and walk out, and I swear I'll never bother you again – but just let me say it. Please.'

His dark brown eyes were fixed on her face, like those of a big, anxious dog. Polly couldn't help smiling at him, and he grinned back, but the grin faded quickly and his eyes were serious again. When he spoke, his voice was husky.

'Maybe I oughter told you before, only it ain't summat I talks about a lot.'

'We've only really known each other a couple of hours,' Polly pointed out, thinking how strange that seemed. 'You've hardly had time.'

'Well, I know, but you told me about your old man, didn't you? I could've told you then.' He paused. 'It's the same for me, see. I lost my missus. Early on in the war – November thirty-nine. So – so I know what it's like.'

Polly gazed at him. The crinkles were all of pain now, a pain she understood all too well. She put out her hand and covered his. 'Joe, I'm so sorry,' she said softly. 'I'm ever so sorry. What happened?'

'It was in the blackout,' he said heavily. 'When it first started. There wasn't no lights allowed at all. Cars and buses were going about in the pitch dark, and you know what London's like for fogs – it was a real pea-souper. Couldn't see your hand in front of your face. Anyway, my Rosie, she had to go out one night, round to her mum's; the old girl'd been poorly for a week or two and took a turn for the worse. Rosie told the woman next door she was worried about her and made up her mind to go round and see if she was all right, settle her down for the night. Only she never got there. Knocked down by a car, she was, two streets away. Banged her head, never knew nothing about it – that was the only comfort.' He stared at their hands, still clasped together on the table. 'Never knew nothing about it.'

'Oh Joe,' Polly whispered. There was a long pause. Then she said, 'Where were you when it happened? Were you away?'

He nodded. 'In France. Couldn't come back, neither, not straight off. They got me back first chance they could, but it was all over by then. Her sister had done everything, the funeral and that, and the nippers were out in the country.'

'*Nippers*? You mean you've got children, too?'

'Two boys,' he said. 'That's where I was going the day we met on that train. They're down in Devon, smashing place, right on the edge of Dartmoor, think they're on a flipping holiday. Well, it hit 'em hard, losing their ma like that, I won't say it didn't, but you know what kids are, they get over it better than we do. Nine and seven, they are,' he said with a touch of pride in his voice. 'Billy and George. Couple of scallywags, too.'

'And what about your wife's mother?' Polly asked, trying to take all this in. 'What happened to her? Did she get better?'

He shook his head. 'Rosie was right. She was poorly. She'd had a bit of a stroke a day or two before, only they didn't realise it, see, and she wouldn't hear of getting the doctor. But when she heard what had happened to Rosie, she had another one and they had to take her into hospital. She died a couple of days later. So that was *two* funerals poor Annie had to sort out. She had 'em both buried in the same plot,' he added. 'It was all over by the time I come home.'

'It must have been dreadful,' Polly said, shaking her head. 'Dreadful.'

'Well, it wasn't a bundle of laughs,' he said. 'But I had the boys home for Christmas – that was when I got leave – and Annie and her hubby had us round there for the day, and it wasn't too bad. They didn't really want to go back to Devon after that – a lot of nippers didn't go back, there was nothing much happening over here then – but Annie couldn't have them and I wanted them out of the way if London did get bombed. And I had to give up me quarters, too. So they went back to Meavy, down in Devon, and I went back to France, and the next time I come home to Blighty it was on a stretcher with half me leg blown away.'

The Nippy appeared beside them again and looked down at their pudding bowls. 'Is there something the matter with the plums?'

Polly jumped and looked guilty. 'I'm sorry, I'd forgotten all about them.' She picked up her spoon, not feeling in the least like eating but guiltily aware that good food mustn't be wasted. The Nippy looked anxious.

'Only there's a lot of people waiting for tables.'

'We'll be finished in a minute or two.' They spooned plums rapidly into their mouths, scarcely tasting their sharpness, and it was not until they were out in the street again that they resumed their conversation. By now, Polly had regained some of her composure. She turned to her companion and tucked her hand into his arm again.

'It's a terribly sad story, Joe. I'm really sorry. But I'm glad you told me, all the same.'

'I just wanted you to know.' He looked down at her and seemed about to add more, then changed his mind. 'I'd like us to be pals, Polly, and pals ought to know the big things about each other.'

'Yes.' They walked in silence for a moment or two. They

were going down Whitehall now, past the great offices of the Government. Soon they would be back in Tothill Street; it was nearly time for the meeting to end. They would have to say goodbye.

'I dunno about you,' he said, 'but I ain't got so many pals I can pass up the chance of another one. So what d'you say? Keep in touch, shall we? Meet up now and then? Write to each other?' His fingers were big and warm about hers and she found herself wondering again what it would be like to be hugged by him. 'Will you say yes to that, Poll?'

Poll. It was as if she had always known him, as if he had always called her that. She nodded, smiling, and his face broke into a big, crinkly grin, his eyes almost disappearing amongst the wrinkles. He flung his arms around her and hugged her tightly.

It was just as she had known it would be. Warm and comforting. Strong. It was all that she had been missing, ever since Johnny went away.

But he was not Johnny. He never would be. And she would never be Rose.

Polly and Joe walked in silence for the rest of the way, past Downing Street where Mr Churchill lived and worked, past the Cenotaph with its list of men killed during the Great War of 1914–1918, and back to Parliament Square where the tower of Big Ben still rose proudly over the bombed House of Commons. They were sobered by both the devastation they could see on every side, and by the story Joe had told, which seemed to bring that wider devastation down to ordinary human terms – the anguish that had been suffered by so many people since this war had begun. It didn't matter whether you were killed by a bomb or by simply walking down the street in the blackout, Polly thought, it was the war that had done it. And her heart went out to the big man beside her, with his crinkly, humorous face and his stoical acceptance of the tragedies he had suffered.

Yet she knew that however stalwart he seemed, deep down he was lonely and bewildered. Her hand was still tucked through his arm, as if he were the stronger, but she could sense that deep need for comfort. I understand it because I feel it too, she thought. We're two lonely people who have met and think we could be friends – and so we could be. But neither of us is ready for any more than that. Perhaps we never will be.

They came to the WVS Headquarters and rang the doorbell. It was Edna Cousins herself who came to answer it, and she stared at them in surprise, her eyebrows lifted.

'Well, you don't need to look so flummoxed, our Edna,' her brother admonished her. 'Me and Mrs Dunn are old acquaintances. Bumped into each other in the park, we did, and been up to the Lyons' Corner House for a bite of dinner, and me being a gentleman I've walked her back here.'

'Where you were coming anyway,' Mrs Cousins told him, unimpressed by his claim. 'Well, trust you to find yourself some nice company. Don't you take no notice of him, love,' she said to Polly. 'He's full of blarney, that one. Our mum had an uncle who came from Ireland, that's where we reckon he got it from.'

'Don't be daft, Uncle Pat wasn't no relation to us, he was only our uncle by marriage to Auntie Margie and she had no more Irish blood in her than this door. Speaking of which, are you going to let us in or ain't you? This foot of mine's had enough, if you want to know the truth.'

'Come on, then.' They walked into the hallway and Polly glanced about a little anxiously, afraid that she might have kept the Mayoress waiting. But the door to the meeting room was still closed and she could hear the murmur of voices within. Joe disappeared into the cloakroom and she followed Mrs Cousins through to the kitchen, where she had evidently just finished washing up after the midday meal. Polly felt a pang of guilt.

'Look at that mountain of crocks! I ought to have stayed and helped you.'

'I told you, you've done your job and you've still got to drive back to Portsmouth. Now, how d'you fancy a cup of tea? I've got the kettle on for them in there and I dare say you're ready for one after your walk. Specially if you've had to put up with *him* nattering on,' she added, with a humorous glance.

Polly hesitated, then said quietly, 'He told me about his wife. It must have been dreadful.'

'He never did! Well!' The cook sat down suddenly, looking upset. 'He don't talk about it much,' she said. 'I wish he would, sometimes, it'd do him good to let it out, but he was always one for keeping cheerful – well, we were brought up that way, all of us. I'm surprised he'd tell someone he's only just met.' A small frown creased her brow and she looked very like her brother. 'But didn't he say you already knew each other?'

'Well, not really. We met on a train a few months ago.' Quickly, Polly recounted the story of their meeting. 'I wouldn't say we *knew* each other.'

Edna Cousins's eyes rested on her thoughtfully. 'Well, there must be something, to make him come out with it like that.' The kettle started to whistle and she got up and began to make the tea. 'You don't want to take no notice of what I says about him,' she said over her shoulder. 'That's just the way we go on. If you've got any brothers, you'll know what I mean.'

'I haven't,' Polly said. 'But I've got a sister, and she's got a son and daughter, so I know what you mean. And I know how he feels too,' she added in a rush. 'I lost my hubby, early in the war. It knocks you sideways, but you've got to carry on. You've got to do your best for the war, for their sake.'

'That's right,' Edna said. 'The hard thing for our Joe is that there don't seem to be nothing he can do, not with his foot. He says he's no use to the Army any more. It's daft – a man who can walk the distance he's walked today could do any amount of jobs – but he's a soldier, see; he wants to go and fight – that's what a soldier *does*, he says – and that's what they won't let him do.'

'But other jobs are as important,' Polly said. 'There must be hundreds of things he can do.'

'Try telling him that,' the cook said, and began to pour milk into a row of cups already set on a big tray.

They heard Joe's footsteps coming along the hall then and the conversation ceased. Polly took the tray into the meeting room and found the Mayoress at the head of a long table with a dozen other women around it. They thanked her for the tea and the Mayoress told her that the meeting would be over soon and she would be ready to go back to Portsmouth. Polly went back to the kitchen, where she found Joe and his sister drinking tea and talking about his boys in Devon.

'Bit different to Blighty, where they are,' he said. 'Little village, it is, proper picture postcard place – church, pub, village green with a big old oak tree, and a lot of little cottages all round. You go up the lane a bit and you're out on Dartmoor.' He pulled a face. 'Don't fancy it meself, big wide open spaces like that with hardly so much as a tree in sight, and all them rocks, but the nippers think they're in paradise. Do what they like, see – roam about making dens and playing cowboys and indians, and nobody to tell 'em to bu— shove off and play somewhere else. Don't reckon as they'll ever want to come home, once it's all over.'

'Don't be silly, Joe,' Edna said. 'You know they wanted to stay with you after Christmas.'

'Yeah, but they went back and had all that snow, didn't they, and since then there's been all the lambs getting born, and I don't know what else, and I reckon they've got their feet well under the table with that woman what's looking

266

after them. She's a widow,' he explained to Polly. 'Never had no nippers, so she treats 'em like they're her own. Stands to reason they'd rather stop with someone like that than come back to their dad with his foot blowed off and no proper job to do, nor even a decent home for them.'

Polly looked at him in dismay. It was the nearest he had come to appearing sorry for himself. Before she could speak, however, his sister said sharply, 'Now you know it's no use talking like that, Joe. It doesn't matter how good Mrs Ellacombe is, she isn't their mum, nor ever will be. Blood's thicker than water and they'll want to come back to their dad once it's safe. It's like you always say – this evacuation's like holiday for them, and nobody wants to be on holiday for ever.'

There was a small silence. Polly glanced at Joe and wondered if the widow Ellacombe had ideas of becoming the boys' stepmother. No doubt she knew of the tragedy of their mother's death, and if she found Joe a congenial companion when he went to visit them she might well have allowed the thought to cross her mind.

The kitchen door opened and the Mayoress appeared. She smiled round at the little gathering and said to Polly, 'We've finished the meeting and I'll be ready to leave in about ten minutes. I just want a word in the office first.' She disappeared and they heard her go into the room where all the typewriters were still clattering away. Polly got up and pushed her chair under the table.

'I'll get my coat. Thanks for the tea, Mrs Cousins.' She hesitated, not knowing quite how to say goodbye to Joe. He stood up too and held out his hand.

'Good luck, Polly. And mind you remember what we said, eh? Keep in touch.' He fished in his pocket and drew out an envelope. 'Look, here's my address. Or you could send a letter here, care of Edna. And tell me your address – I'll write it down.' He tore the back off the envelope and found a stub of pencil.

'It's number nine, April Grove,' Polly said, feeling a little embarrassed under Edna Cousins's gaze. 'Portsmouth, Hants. And – and if you're ever down that way, mind you call in. There's usually someone in.'

They nodded at each other, smiling a little uncertainly, and then shook hands. Polly thought wistfully of the hug they had shared so spontaneously out in the street, for all the world to see, but in here it seemed different. She saw the same thought in his eyes, and then they heard the Mayoress's footsteps approaching again and the moment passed.

He came out of the front door with them, helped both women into the car and then stood on the steps to wave farewell. His sturdy figure, looking suddenly lonely as he leaned on his stick, was the last thing Polly saw as she turned the corner.

'He seems a very nice man,' the Mayoress remarked as they drove slowly through the streets, still blocked with rubble and smoky from the fires that still burned. 'Have you known him long?'

'No,' Polly said. 'Not very long.' But, somehow, she felt that she had.

Chapter Twenty

It was nearly a fortnight before the next raid on Portsmouth, and then it was almost laughable compared with what had gone before, with just a few bombs being dropped into the sea at Spithead, injuring no one and causing no damage except, perhaps, to the fish. 'Bombing sprats and herrings now!' Tommy Vickers said scornfully when Cissie met him in the street. 'I reckon we've seen 'em off, don't you?'

'I don't know, Tommy.' Cissie shivered, despite the warmth of the sunshine. 'I wouldn't put anything past that Hitler. They say he's developing a secret weapon – something worse than anything he's used before.'

'The only secret weapon Hitler's got is fear,' Tommy told her. 'And it hasn't done much for him so far. All right, we're frightened – every time the air-raid warning goes, my backbone turns to ice – but we don't let it stop us doing what we got to do. And I reckon we're doing the same for the Germans anyway; our lads are bombing them to bits every night, same as he's been doing to us.'

Cissie nodded. She couldn't feel glad about that, though. They were ordinary people, she thought, people with homes and families just like in England. Kiddies in their prams, old folk like her mother, men like Dick who were still suffering from the First War. They didn't deserve to be 'bombed to bits' any more than the people at home.

Jess Budd felt the same. She had invited Cissie down to number fourteen to tea once or twice, and when Cissie went into the cosy little back room, crowded with Jess's piano against one wall, two armchairs beside the fire and a square dining table in the middle, she found several other neighbours there too – Jess's sister Annie Chapman, from the end of March Street, Tommy's wife Freda and, since it was early closing day, white-haired old Mrs Seddon who kept the little shop on the corner of October Street. The women all had some knitting to do – nobody sat down these days without a piece of work in their hands. Maureen Budd, who was nearly two years old, was playing on the rug in front of the fireplace with some coloured bricks that had belonged to her brothers.

'Your boys getting on all right out at Bridge End?' Freda asked, and Jess nodded.

'Seem to be. I didn't think they'd take to it, mind, living with a vicar – our Tim's never been one for church, couldn't ever keep still long enough – but Mr Beckett seems to have a way with boys. Girls too,' she added. 'Stella and Muriel have settled down well, in spite of everything.'

'Didn't your Polly take them out there?' Annie asked Cissie, passing her a plate of broken biscuits that Mrs Seddon had brought over.

'Yes. She liked the old man, and his housekeeper – she's the one that looks after them really. Treats the vicar like another boy, so Polly said.'

Jess smiled. 'That's what he is, I reckon. I knew him a bit when I was there, right at the beginning. Always riding round on that old bike of his, dressed up in his cassock like a great big bat. And sometimes, when he took the early service, you could see he was still in his pyjamas underneath! But he's a really kind man, and sort of *wise* too, if you know what I mean. I always felt he understood a lot more than he let on. And you could tell him anything – he'd never be shocked or think you weren't worth helping. He's a real Christian, I suppose.' She sounded half embarrassed. Most of those present went to church, if not every week, but none of them would have felt easy in discussing their beliefs. It was almost as bad as talking about sex, or cancer.

'And how about your Judy?' Mrs Seddon asked. 'I always remember her popping into the shop as a little girl, when you came round to see your mum. Such a dear, polite little soul, holding out her ha'penny and asking for a cone of lemon drops. Not like some of the children these days,' she added, and they all knew who she was thinking about. Micky Baxter, who lived almost opposite the shop, hardly knew the words 'please' and 'thank you'.

'Well, you know she's out at Ashwood, with little Sylvie, at the moment,' Cissie said. 'We're hoping the change will do her good, and some fresh air and country cooking. They say you can even get butter out there! But of course, that can't help her hearing. I don't know if anything can.'

'It's a crying shame.' Annie Chapman, who had an opinion on everything, spoke forcefully. 'Terrible thing to happen to a young girl. And not long after her young man had died too. I don't know what the world's coming to.'

'Nor do I,' Jess Budd said. She looked down at Maureen, who had built a rather lopsided castle with the bricks. 'Little children being bombed – and it's not just here, it's over there too. I mean, they may be German, but they're still kiddies. It doesn't seem right to me, and even Mr Churchill himself can't tell me it is.'

'It's war,' Annie said a little sharply. She was worrying about her daughter Betty, who was a Land Girl out near Bishop's Waltham, and getting more friendly with a young man than Annie and her husband Ted liked. The young man was called Dennis and there was something funny about him; neither of them could understand why he was working on a farm, when most young men of his age were in the Forces. Ted had wondered once or twice if he was a conscientious objector and told Annie in no uncertain terms that young Betty needn't think she could bring him home if that was the case, because he wouldn't have him in the house. Annie couldn't argue with him, partly because Ted was going through a bad patch at present himself, and partly

271

because she agreed with him. Instead, she lay awake at night, going over it all in her mind and not even telling Jess about her suspicions.

There was a ring on the doorbell and Peggy Shaw's voice called out. A moment later she was in the room, looking flushed and excited. 'You'll never guess what's happened!' She looked round at them all. 'Our Gladys is getting a medal! The British Empire Medal! It's for what she did the night of the big raid, when the Royal Hospital got blown up. Can you credit it – our Gladys with a medal, presented by the King himself!'

The others stared at her. 'Well, that's a turn-up for the book, and no mistake,' Annie said at last. 'Someone in April Grove getting a medal! You must be ever so pleased, Peggy.'

'I am.' Peggy sat down on one of the dining chairs and took the cup of tea Jess had poured out. 'Thanks, Jess. Yes, I am pleased, and proud as Punch. So's Bert. But our Gladys doesn't seem too thrilled about it.'

'Why ever not?' The other women stared at her.

'Well, you know she got a bit knocked about – broken arm and that – and I suppose she's still a bit shocked. But she says she doesn't deserve it. Says there were plenty of others did things just as brave – your Polly for one, and Judy,' she said to Cissie. 'And she says it's Graham Philpotts that ought to be given it, because he didn't even need to be there, he was just helping her, and he got killed. She's really upset about that.'

'Well, *I* think she deserves it,' Annie said staunchly, 'and so do our Olive and Betty. They were talking about Gladys yesterday, when Betty came down from Bishop's Waltham for her day off. And look at it this way – they can't give *everyone* medals, so those that do get them are getting them on behalf of all those others that deserve them. It's Graham's and Polly's and Judy's medal, just as much as it's Gladys's, but she happens to be the one that's been picked out. That's all it is.'

Peggy nodded. The flush had faded a little and now she looked worried. 'The other thing is, she's made up her mind to volunteer. Wants to go into the Wrens. She says it'll make up a bit for getting Graham killed. My Bert's none too pleased, but what can you do? They've all had to sign on anyway but they don't actually have to go into the Services till they're called up. But Gladys wants to go now. And on top of that, young Diane's gone and got herself a job at Airspeed – says she wants to learn to fly, of all things!'

'Fly?' Jess echoed. 'I shouldn't think she's got much hope of that – why, she's barely sixteen, surely. They're not going to take young girls as pilots.'

'I dunno,' Peggy said with a sigh. 'I dunno what they'll do. Everything seems turned upside down now.' She looked down at the toddler on the rug. 'Sometimes I wish mine were all this age again. At least you could have a bit of a say in what happens to them and what they do. What with Gladys and Diane, and our Bob away in the Army, I just wonder what it's all about. It's not the life we wanted for them, Jess. It's not at all.'

'I wonder if anyone ever does have the life their parents want for them,' Jess commented sadly. 'Look at us. We had to go through the First War and now, just when we're getting on our feet, along comes this one to mess it all up again. And there's not a thing we can do about it. It's out of our hands.'

Mrs Seddon looked at the little group of women with their sad faces. She too had been through the Great War, and could remember even further back, to the Boer War and other conflicts of the nineteenth and twentieth centuries. 'What we have to realise,' she said in her soft voice, 'is that this *is* life. All these things that go wrong – little things at home and great things overseas, squabbles in the family and quarrels between nations – they're *part* of life, they happen over and over again. They always have and they always will. The important thing, I think, is not what happens to us, but what we do about it.' She paused and the women gazed at her. 'The young people are rising to the occasion, just as we'd want them to,' she said. 'It might not be what we wanted for them – but they're acting in just the ways we would have hoped. I think you can *all* feel proud – of your children and yourselves.' A little pink in the cheeks, she held out her cup. 'Is there any more tea in that pot, Mrs Budd?'

The little tea-party broke up soon after that. The women rolled up their knitting and left to start preparing tea for their husbands. Mrs Seddon, who was a widow, went off saying that she was going to change the window display – not that there was much to display these days, but a new jar of sherbet lemons had come in this morning and she wanted to give it pride of place. She crossed the road to her door, and Cissie, Freda and Annie Chapman walked up the street together.

'That was nice, what Mrs Seddon said, wasn't it?' Cissie said. 'She's a lovely old lady. All the kiddies love her, you know.'

'Well, she's part of April Grove, isn't she,' Annie said. 'I can't remember a time when she wasn't there in that little shop, weighing out biscuits and sweets and dried fruit. I wonder sometimes how she manages to make a living, now that everything's on ration. But I reckon she's right, you know, about all this being a part of life. Wars always have happened and I don't suppose they'll ever stop happening. Look at what they said about the last one – the "war to end all wars", they called it. And here we are again, barely twenty years later, worse than ever. Not that the youngsters seem to mind all that much. Our Betty's having the time of her life out in the country, even though the work's hard. Her dad and me wonder sometimes what she gets up to out there.'

'I think a lot of the young women are getting the sort of freedom they'd never have had otherwise,' Freda agreed.

'Our Eunice is the same, proper let off the leash she is, in the ATS. If it hadn't been for the war they'd have all stopped at home, under their parents' eyes, till they got married. Now you don't know what they're doing.'

'And some of them aren't getting the lives they thought they'd have,' Cissie said quietly. 'Look at our Polly, a widow at thirty-five. And Judy, deaf at twenty-two.' She looked at Annie Chapman. 'And what about your Olive? It must have been ever so hard for her to say goodbye to her husband only a day or two after their wedding.'

The others nodded soberly. There was no making sense of it all, they agreed. They came to Alice Thomas's front door and said goodbye. Cissie went indoors and found Dick sitting in his usual chair, his latest rag rug spread over his knees.

'I dunno as I'll be able to go on with this much more in the hot weather,' he said, looking up. 'It's like having a blanket over me. Have a good natter?'

Cissie nodded and went through to the scullery to start getting tea ready. 'Gladys Shaw's getting a medal,' she called. 'The British Empire Medal, it is, for what she did in the raids. She says she doesn't deserve it, that there's plenty of others did just as much, but she'll have to go and be presented with it all the same. And Peggy says she's going in the Wrens now.'

'Peggy Shaw? She's too old, surely!'

'Not Peggy, Gladys. And Diane, their youngest, she's got a job at Airspeed, wants to learn to fly.'

'They'll never let her. What is she, sixteen? Mind you, she's always been the *flighty* one!' Dick laughed at his joke and rolled up the rug. 'I've had enough of this, Cis, it's making my eyes go funny. What's for tea?'

'I thought we'd have sardines on toast. I got a tin yesterday.' Cissie came in and looked at him a little anxiously. 'You feeling all right, Dick?'

'More or less. I'm just a bit hot. And it's all these

different colours, dazzling me. I dunno who's going to get this one, but they'd better like bright colours.' He grinned again and Cissie laughed too but put her hand on his forehead. 'It's all right, Cis, I haven't got a temperature.'

'No, but all the same … It's not long since that pneumonia, Dick. You've got to be careful.'

'Careful!' he said. 'I don't know how I could be any more careful than I am now. All I do is sit in this chair all day making blinking rugs and listening to the wireless.'

'You go for a walk every day.'

'Yes, up to the end of the street and back. Well, I tell a lie, this morning I walked all the way up to the newsagent's shop. That Alice Brunner, she's looking a bit better these days. Gave me a nice smile, she did. I reckon that girl of hers told her to pull herself together.'

'Joy's a big help to her mum,' Cissie said, 'and Alice has had a lot of worry, with Heinrich being taken away like that. I ask you!' she went on indignantly, coming through the door and waving a bread-knife. 'Interning a man like Heinrich Brunner who's been in England and running his own business all those years! As if he was a spy. It's criminal. And then sending him off on that ship and getting him torpedoed. It's no wonder poor Alice nearly had a nervous breakdown.'

'Well, you needn't stab me to death because of it,' Dick said, pretending to cower in his chair. 'But you're right, Cis, it was a bad do. There must have been hundreds like Heinrich Brunner, been living here for years not doing no harm to nobody, and all put in prison like common criminals. It was like a sort of panic.'

'They've let a lot of them out now,' Cissie said, going back to the scullery. 'But that doesn't help men like poor Mr Brunner, who got killed on that ship.'

She went on getting the tea ready. Presently, Alice came in from her own afternoon spent helping at the local Clothing Store, and then Polly arrived. She had been

276

working at the salon, cutting and setting hair. With no raids for a fortnight, and then just a few bombs dropped in the sea, it seemed almost as if normal life was beginning to return.

'There's another letter for you, Poll,' Dick said, nodding at the mantelpiece. It had come by second post, not long after Polly had left for the salon, and Cissie and he had indulged in some conjecture about it before placing it behind the photo of Terry in his naval uniform. Letters weren't all that common unless they were from Sylvie out at Ashwood or Terry, somewhere at sea, and this wasn't from either of them. It bore a London postmark, and it wasn't the first to have arrived in the last couple of weeks.

Polly took it and blushed. 'I'll just slip upstairs and change out of this skirt and blouse,' she said, trying to sound casual, and Dick winked at Cissie who had come through from the scullery.

'Reckon she's found herself a fancy man?' he asked in a whisper.

'Well, I don't know. That's the third, isn't it? But I never thought she'd be interested again, not this soon after losing Johnny.'

'It's eighteen months or more,' Dick pointed out. 'And she's not old, Cis.'

Cissie pursed her lips. 'Well, I wouldn't object myself, but you know what Mum is like about second marriages. She wouldn't like it if Polly got serious about another man.'

'Yes, but that's just being old-fashioned. People aren't so strict these days, and with so many men getting killed—'

'Ssh.' Cissie put her finger to her lips. Alice was coming in from the outside lavatory, already beginning to tell them about a woman she'd had in the Clothing Store that afternoon, trying to exchange a tattered old jacket for a good three-piece suit. Cissie gave Dick a warning glance and went back to the scullery where she was spreading margarine on bread and getting out a new pot of jam from the store Alice had made last summer.

When Polly came down in her old skirt and blouse, they all sat down round the table. Cissie set the plates of sardines on toast in front of them and looked at her sister, hoping for some remark about the letter. But Polly didn't mention it. Instead, she said, 'I had that Ethel Glaister from number fifteen in for a perm this afternoon. What a cat she is! Doesn't have a good word to say for a soul. Seems to think she's too good for April Grove or anyone in it.'

'Dunno why she goes on living here then,' Dick remarked. 'If she's so posh, why doesn't she move up to Hilsea or somewhere?'

'Oh, she says they were just going to when the war started, and then of course everything stopped. Her hubby was in the Territorials and he went straight off into the regular Army. Honestly, you'd think he did it just to spite her.' Polly giggled. 'I dare say he was glad of the excuse to get away! It must have seemed like a dream come true to him when war broke out.'

'Polly! That's a terrible thing to say,' Cissie reproved her, but the others were laughing and she had to smile. 'Well, I can't say I'd like to live with Ethel Glaister for long. How did you do her hair, Poll?'

'Oh, the latest fashion of course – Marcel waves. And I'll tell you something else.' Polly leaned over the table and glanced from side to side as if there might be a spy lurking behind a chair. 'That hair of hers isn't really yellow at all! It's practically grey! We have to touch up the roots every six weeks to stop it showing through.'

'*Dyed*! Well, I always suspected it,' Alice said disapprovingly. 'You know, I sometimes wonder about Ethel Glaister and where she goes off to every afternoon in her smart suit and high heels. Now I wonder even more. If you ask me, she's no better than Nancy Baxter.'

'Well, you'd better not say so,' Polly advised her. 'You

could get into trouble. And don't any of you dare tell anyone about her hair. I'd get the sack if Mrs Carson knew I'd let out something like that about one of the ladies.'

'Why?' Dick asked. 'It's not that bad, surely. Plenty of women dye their hair.'

'Not decent women,' Alice retorted, but Polly shook her head.

'It's because they don't want people to know they're going grey. Women like Ethel Glaister who think they're smart and glamorous,' the family hooted with laughter, 'they like people to think it's natural, see? So that everyone thinks they're younger than they really are.'

'As if it mattered,' Alice said in disgust. 'We've all got to get older. It's nothing to be ashamed of. If you ask me, people like Ethel Glaister haven't got enough to do. Ought to come down the Clothing Store of an afternoon with me and do a hand's turn to help. That'd take her mind off being *glamorous*.'

The evening passed quietly with a game of whist, and at nine o'clock they switched on the wireless to hear the news. No matter how quiet it might have been in Portsmouth, there was always news of some terrible event somewhere else. A bombing raid on another city, a battle in Africa or the Mediterranean, a ship sunk by a U-boat in the Atlantic.

'*What was that?*' Cissie gasped, her hand at her throat.

They stared at her, then at each other. Polly opened her mouth but Dick gestured to her to be silent. In horror, they listened again to the newsreader's words, and then the bulletin ended and Dick reached out a slow, trembling hand and turned the knob.

'I can't believe it,' Alice whispered, her face as white as paper. 'HMS *Hood*, blown up and sunk in just four minutes. There can't be anyone left alive, there *can't* be.'

'Our Terry,' Cis whimpered, covering her face with her hands. 'He said it was the best ship in the whole of the Fleet. Dick,' blindly, she reached a hand out to her

279

husband, 'Dick, our Terry's been killed. Our *Terry's* been killed.'

'We don't know that, love.' But his voice was shaking and tears were trickling down his cheeks. 'We don't know it for sure. They haven't said everyone was killed. There might've been survivors.'

'When it was blown up and sunk in *four minutes*?' She shook her head. 'How could anyone have lived through that? Oh Dick.' She began to cry, while the others wept as well. Despite Dick's words, they all knew that Terry's chances were very low. Even if he had survived the explosion, how could he have lived more than a few minutes in the icy waters off Greenland where the battle had taken place? People said you froze to death almost at once. And none of the family had any faith in the Germans having picked up men in the water. That's what they were supposed to do, but would they have done it?

There was little sleep that night in number nine. Cissie could not stop crying. Every time her sobs eased a little, she thought of the news announcement, or some little reminder of her son, and started all over again. She took his photo down from the mantelpiece and wept afresh, stroking his laughing face with her fingertips. 'It's the only one we've got,' she sobbed. 'All those pictures of him at school and that lovely one that photographer took of him out at Southsea, with that parrot on his arm, we lost all those in the Blitz. And all his toys and things, his Meccano and his comics that he wanted saved – they've all gone. We've got nothing left. It's as if he never existed.'

'Of course it's not, Cis.' Polly, her own eyes red and swollen, tried to comfort her sister. 'It'll never be as if he never existed, never. We'll all remember him all our lives, and so will lots of other people. All the neighbours who knew him, and Dick's brother and his family, and Jean Foster.'

'Jean!' Cissie lifted her face and stared at her. 'She'll have heard the news too. Oh, poor Jean – he was talking about asking her to get engaged, last time he was home. I'll have to go round and see her.'

'Tomorrow.' Alice, looking grey and weary, came in with a cup of cocoa for them all. 'Drink this, Cis. It'll make you feel better and help you to sleep. Come on, now, it's no use making yourself ill. And like Dick said, we don't *know* he's dead. Miracles do happen.' She sighed and Polly, glancing at her, knew that in spite of her words, she too had almost given up hope. 'Drink it up and let's go to bed,' she said gently.

Still sobbing, Cissie managed to drink her cocoa and the family gathered up the cards that had been lying forgotten on the table and prepared for bed. One by one, they went outside to the lavatory, washed at the sink, cleaned their teeth, each going through the motions like an automaton. Then Cissie and Dick went slowly up the stairs and Polly and her mother were left alone.

'She's taking this very hard,' Alice said, shaking her head. 'Not that you can blame her. That's three good men we've lost at sea in this family. Three good men! Where's it going to end, Poll?'

Polly shook her head. 'I don't know, Mum. But I tell you what – I think we'd better get our Judy back home, don't you? It's the only thing that'll help Cis through this, having her back. It's a shame, because I think it's doing her good to be out in the country, but I reckon it's the best thing to do.'

'You're right,' Alice said. 'And I wouldn't be surprised if she turns up tomorrow without even being sent for. I bet she's packing her bags at this very minute.'

Chapter Twenty-One

It was not Judy who arrived next day, however. It was somebody else who turned up, quite unexpectedly, on the doorstep of number nine.

After all her crying, Cissie had fallen into a deep sleep and woke late, heavy-eyed and feeling as if she'd been crying even in her dreams. Dick had slept badly, tossing and turning as his mind filled again with the horrific memories of his own war experiences. He was pale and shaky when he stumbled downstairs to find Polly making tea and Alice sitting at the table, looking shrunken and grey in an old dressing-gown.

'Dick, you look like death warmed up,' Polly said, and then closed her eyes. 'Oh, I'm sorry – I could bite my tongue off sometimes. Have a cup of tea, and take one up for Cis. Is she awake yet?'

'Just stirring.' He rested against the door to the staircase. 'Tell you the truth, Poll, I don't feel too good at all. Don't tell Cis, though. She's got enough to upset her.'

'Don't feel too good?' Polly stopped with the teapot raised and looked at him closely. 'What is it? One of your attacks?'

'No, it's not like that. Just sort of tingly, and I've got a sort of ache—' He stopped as they heard movements from above, and opened the staircase door to call up: 'You stop in bed a bit longer, Cis. I'm just bringing you a cuppa.' To Polly, he said, 'I don't suppose it's anything much. Shock, probably, and I didn't sleep too well.'

'I don't suppose any of us did.' Polly handed him a cup

and went through to her mother. 'Here you are, Mum. Drink that down. It's hot, if nothing else. We're nearly out of tea again. I'll go up the street in a minute, see if there's anything in the papers.'

She looked through the cupboards to see what they could have for breakfast. There was half a packet of cornflakes, the end of a loaf that was going stale, some dried egg and some margarine and the pot of jam they'd started yesterday. Normally they wouldn't dream of having jam for breakfast, but this was her mother's own blackberry and apple, made last autumn with blackberries from Hilsea Lines, and Cissie was especially fond of it. It wasn't that a slice of bread and jam would make up for losing Terry, Polly thought, that would be daft, but a little treat at a time like this couldn't do any harm. She lit the grill to make toast and put some cornflakes in a bowl. Cissie could have breakfast in bed.

Dick came treading down the stairs again. He looked as grey as Alice, and was breathing heavily. Polly glanced at him and wondered if he could after all be heading for an asthma attack. It wasn't all that long since his pneumonia, and shock could bring it on. It looks as if I'm going to have to look after the lot of them, she thought, glancing from Dick's ashen face to her mother's. While I'm up the street getting the papers, I'd better ring up and let the office know I won't be able to go in today.

She went to the telephone box first, searching for pennies for the call, and then walked along to the newsagent's. Alice Brunner's daughter Joy was there, sorting the papers. Polly looked at the headlines: SINK THE BISMARCK.

She read the report beneath. It was the *Bismarck* which had presented such a serious threat to Allied shipping that a flotilla of ships had set off from Scapa Flow in pursuit – HMS *Hood*, *Prince of Wales*, *King George V*, *Victorious* and a number of others. It was the *Bismarck* which, with just one shell, had sunk the *Hood*, penetrating the weak armour of its sides and striking the store of ammunition within to cause the huge and devastating explosion that had destroyed the ship and killed almost fifteen hundred men. Few, if any, could have been saved.

Now the hunt was on in earnest for the killer ship. The order had gone out – she was to be sunk at all costs. And that meant more men killed, Polly thought, trudging back down October Street with an armful of newspapers and a heavy heart. More young men like Terry and Johnny and Sean. And it wouldn't bring even one of them back. Not one.

Nobody had been able to eat much breakfast. Cissie had come downstairs, saying she couldn't stop in bed, and after they'd washed up, feeling as if nothing was really worthwhile doing but not knowing what else to do, she and Dick set off to see Jean Foster, who had been Terry's sweetheart since they'd been at school. Jean had worked in the Landport Drapery Bazaar, in Guildhall Square, but since the bombing the shop had re-opened in several different places in town, and now she was in Lake Road. Since they would pass it on the way to her home, they called in there first to see if she had come to work.

Jean was serving a customer. She looked a little plumper than when they had last seen her, during Terry's Christmas leave, but her clear skin was glowing, her brown hair springing with natural curls and her pretty face smiling as she talked to the customer. Cissie and Dick looked at each other in dismay.

'She doesn't know,' Cissie mouthed. 'Oh Dick, we've got to tell her ourselves.' Her lips trembled. 'I don't think I can.'

'I dunno what else we can do, love.' Dick half turned awkwardly, as if to slip out again, but at that moment Jean glanced up and saw them. She hesitated, looking embarrassed, and then finished giving the customer her change and came over.

'Mrs Taylor! Mr Taylor – I didn't expect to see you

here.' She looked flushed and embarrassed and they gazed at her silently, taken aback by her manner. 'I don't know who's told you,' she went on quickly, 'but I haven't done anything wrong. We'd been going steady for a long time, and what with Christmas and Terry going away, and us never knowing when we'd see each other again, well . . .' she tilted her chin a little defiantly '. . . it just happened, that's all, and there's nothing anyone can do about it now, I've written to tell Terry and—'

Dick interrupted her. 'We don't know what you're talking about, Jean. We just came to see if you'd heard the news. It was on last night. Haven't you heard?'

The girl stared at them. She seemed to notice their swollen eyes for the first time and her colour faded. Nervously, she said, 'News? What news? I haven't heard no news.'

'The *Hood*,' Cissie said in a dry, aching voice. 'She's been sunk. D'you mean to say you hadn't heard? It's all over the papers.'

Jean turned white. 'The *Hood*? Sunk? But – oh, *no*.' She reached out a hand and laid it against the wall, swaying a little. 'But – Terry – isn't he all right? Wasn't he saved?'

'We don't know,' Dick said quietly. 'We don't think he could have been. The ship went down in four minutes.'

'Four minutes?' The ashen white turned to a sickly green and Dick stepped forwards quickly to catch the girl as she crumpled. He staggered beneath her weight and the shop supervisor noticed what was happening and came quickly across to help. Between them, they got Jean on to the chair put beside the counter for customers. Cissie pressed her head down to her knees while Dick steadied her and the supervisor hurried off for a cup of water.

'Drink this.' She held the cup beneath Jean's lips. 'Just a sip or two. It'll make you feel better.' They all watched anxiously as Jean sipped and took a couple of shuddering breaths. The supervisor looked at Dick and Cissie. 'Has she had bad news?'

Cissie nodded. 'We all have.' Her eyes filled with tears again. 'The *Hood*,' she said, chokingly. 'On the news last night.'

The woman nodded. 'I heard it. It's in the papers this morning. Terrible.' Her eyes sharpened. 'You mean, someone was on it? Someone Jean knew – was fond of?'

'Our son was one of the crew,' Dick said hoarsely. 'And Jean and him – well, they've been going steady ever since they left school. He was hoping they'd get engaged, the next time he got leave.' He looked down at the girl's bent head. 'We'd have been pleased. We're fond of Jean – we'd have been proud to have her as a daughter-in-law.'

The supervisor's eyes softened. 'Oh, I'm so sorry. That's dreadful. But Jean never said. She's been just the same as usual this morning, a bit quiet, but then she has been just lately. Missing her sweetheart, naturally. I'd no idea.'

'I don't think she knew,' Cissie said. 'That's why it was such a shock to her when we told her just now.'

'The poor girl. And you as well.' The woman hesitated, then glanced down at the bent head. 'Jean,' she said kindly, 'when you feel well enough, I think you'd better go home for the rest of the day. We can manage without you. Take the rest of the week off and come back on Monday, when you've had time to get over the shock. I know just how you must be feeling.' She said quietly, 'I lost my brother a few months ago, so I do understand.'

Jean looked up at last. Her face was like parchment, her eyes like bruises against the yellowish-green tinge of her normally rosy cheeks. She looked at them all with a dull, hopeless stare and said in a flat voice that seemed to have been drained of all feeling, 'You *don't* understand, Miss Browning. Nobody does.' Her eyes went to Dick's face and then to Cissie's. 'It's not just Terry, you see. I'm in trouble anyway. Bad trouble.' She took a deep breath, as if gathering courage, and then said in a rush, 'I'm expecting. I'm in the family way. And now Terry's never coming back, I don't know what to do.' Her voice wavered and cracked, and she broke into a storm of crying. 'I just don't know what I'm going to do!'

Locked behind her wall of silence, Judy had no idea what had happened.

She had gone to bed early the night before, just as the family was sitting down to listen to the nine o'clock news. It was one of the most frustrating times for her, watching their faces and wondering what was going on in the world. They would tell her, of course, Mrs Sutton either mouthing the words carefully or writing them down on a scrap of paper – but she was sure they didn't tell her everything they heard. It was too laborious, too much trouble. She had formed the habit of going outside to sit under the apple tree, watching the sky deepen from soft blue to deep purple, streaked and patterned with glowing crimson as the sun dipped below the wooded hill. Tomorrow, she would read the newspaper to find out what had happened; tonight she would sleep in peace.

On this night, however, it was dull and there was a drizzle in the air. Judy had been making scrim almost all day and had come home tired and dirty. While the family were listening to the wireless, she shut herself in the scullery for a good wash, and then went straight up to bed, calling her goodnight through the half-open door. She tiptoed into the room she shared with Sylvie, checked that her niece was asleep and properly covered, and then slipped into bed.

She had been here for a fortnight now, and it seemed like home. Although she missed her family, the Suttons had been so kind that she felt almost as if she had found a second family, and the cottage and the countryside around were like a balm to her unhappy soul. It was a balm she had needed desperately. The loss of first her brother-in-law and then her fiancé had struck at her heart, the bombing of her home had left her feeling lost and disoriented, and her deafness had been a final cruel blow. Over and over again she told herself how lucky she was – she still had her parents, her sister, her little niece and her grandmother, her brother Terry was serving on one of Britain's greatest ships, she had been able to come to this peaceful village and stay with these kind people – yet she could not rid herself of the deep, searing loneliness of her silent world. If only I could hear again, she thought. If *only* . . .

It was strange that the one person with whom she felt completely at ease was Ben Hazelwood, the boy who seemed so much older than seventeen, who had taken her down to the river and shown her a kingfisher and told her she would hear again. She had seen him again several times over the next few days. He had come to the farm and sat with her under the apple tree in the orchard, looking intently into her eyes as he talked. With him, she had felt her pain begin to ease and the scars in her mind begin to heal.

He had gone back to school in Winchester now, but he had written to her and she had written back. It was strange to strike up so close a friendship with a boy still at school, yet he didn't seem so young, and in any case there were boys not much older serving at this moment in the Armed Forces. If Ben got his way – and she felt sure he would – he would soon be one of them.

Her mind drifted to another young man whose eyes had looked into hers as he talked, who had held her for a while with his magnetism. Chris Barrett, the Observer who spent his time on the roof of the Royal Beach searching for enemy aircraft, and who had sat with her on the floor of the lift, his arms around her in comfort; who had kissed her to the sound of cheers as the lift arrived at the eighth floor. She thought of the way she had treated him after that – hiding in a cupboard when she saw him coming, pushing past him in the corridors, snapping his head off when she'd met him on the steps. I wasn't very nice to him, she thought. And I really think all he wanted to do was say sorry. Polly said in her letter that he's asked after me two or three times and wanted her to send his good wishes to me. I really ought to send mine back, just to show no hard feelings. It wasn't his fault the lift arrived when it did. He was a nice chap. And it was a lovely kiss . . .

She lay in bed, thinking of Chris and thinking of Ben until, smiling a little, she fell asleep.

There was no time to read a newspaper next morning. It was always busy then, because of the milking, but today one of the cows was having difficulty calving and Judy was sent down to a neighbouring farm to get help. She came back to find that Sylvie had been sick and was back in bed, looking pale and miserable, so she ate a hasty breakfast and went up to look after her. The newspaper, brought from the station by a neighbouring farmer, was tossed into a corner where Mrs Sutton dropped a bundle of washing on top of it, and if the wireless was on at all Judy didn't hear it. She didn't even wonder what the news might have been. It was always the same anyway, she thought, sponging Sylvie's face gently. Bombing, and more bombing. Deaths, and more deaths.

There were believed to have been just three survivors from the *Hood*.

'Three mothers will be happy, at least,' Alice said as Polly switched off the wireless after listening to the one o'clock news. 'But I don't think our Cis'll be one of them. I mean, I know one of those boys *could* have been our Terry – but you know what they say. Things go in threes. First your Johnny, then Sean and now Terry. It seems like fate, somehow.'

Polly nodded. She didn't really believe in superstition and refused to throw spilled salt over her shoulder, or avoid the cracks in pavements, but now she had the same feeling as her mother, that it wasn't likely that Terry was one of the three who had survived that terrible blast. For one thing, he worked in the engine rooms so he would almost certainly have been below decks when it happened. Terry wouldn't have had a chance.

'At least it must have been quick,' she said, trying to find a crumb of comfort. 'He wouldn't have known anything about it. He wouldn't have been floating about in the sea for hours.' Like Johnny, she thought. Like Johnny and, probably, Sean.

Alice nodded, but the comfort wasn't enough to stop her face crumpling again and the tears welling up in her eyes. 'Our Terry,' she said, choking on his name. 'It don't seem possible, Poll. He was always so full of life, so bright and breezy all the time. I can't believe all that's gone. I can't believe we'll never see him again.'

'Oh Mum.' Polly moved to put her arm round her mother's shoulders. She was as thin as a bird, she thought, feeling the tiny bones beneath her hands. She's getting smaller, I'm sure. 'There's still a chance,' she murmured. 'He could have been one of those saved.'

'No,' Alice wept, shaking her head so that the grey hair, not yet properly brushed and pinned up that morning, straggled across her brow. 'No, he's not. We'd have heard, you know that. If they know there's three saved, they must know their names and they'd have sent someone round. He's gone, Polly, and we've got to face up to it. But it's so hard.' She broke down in a storm of sobs. 'Oh Poll, it's so *hard*, losing all our men like this. It's so *cruel*.'

Polly could not speak. The tears were pouring down her cheeks and she was holding her mother now as much to gain comfort as to give it. For some time they clung to each other, weeping as if their hearts were broken, and then at last Alice gave a sniff and felt for a hanky. She blew her nose hard, drew a deep, shuddering breath and looked at her daughter with wet but determined eyes.

'Well, we can't sit here piping our eyes all day, Poll. We've still got to do our jobs, same as usual. Cis and Dick'll be home any minute for their dinner, and we haven't even done the potatoes.' She glanced at the clock. 'Look at the time! Wherever can they be?'

'They were going to see Jean.' Polly frowned anxiously. 'I hope Dick hasn't had an attack. He hasn't been looking at all well lately, and what with the shock and upset and everything . . .'

'That would just about put the tin lid on things.' Alice wiped her eyes again and then looked up in relief as the doorbell shrilled. 'Oh, that'll be them now. Go and let them in, Poll.'

'But they'd have a key.' Her heart thumping with anxiety, Polly hurried to the front door. Something had happened, she was sure of it. Then a new thought occurred to her. Judy – it must be Judy, rushing home as soon as she had heard the news. She opened the door, a smile of welcome battling with the grief still pulling at her face.

For a moment, she did not recognise the man who stood there. She stared at him as if at a stranger, half-recognised, dimly remembered. It seemed a lifetime since he had played any part in her thoughts. Blankly, she shook her head.

'Well, Poll,' Joe Turner said, his crinkly face spread all over with delight, 'don't you know me no more?'

Chapter Twenty-Two

Joe's first reaction, on hearing the news, was to leave immediately. Polly had asked him in, embarrassed because the house was in a 'state' – nothing yet done, breakfast things still piled by the sink, Alice's bed in the front room not yet made – and he'd realised at once there was something wrong. It had needed only a few words to tell him what it was.

'Blimey, that's a facer and no mistake,' he said, staring from one to the other. 'No wonder you looked at me as if I'd just fell down from the moon. Here,' he turned towards the door. 'You won't want me around. I'll get out of your way.'

'No!' Polly reached out a hand involuntarily. 'No, don't rush off, not after you've taken the trouble to come all this way. Stop and have a cup of tea at least.'

'Well . . .' He hesitated. 'Maybe I could do something to help. Not that there's much anyone can do at a time like this, but – you know, I could take a message somewhere, do a bit of shopping, whatever you like. Go and get you some fish and chips for your dinner. Anything. Just say the word.'

Polly looked at him. 'Well, there is something you can do. It's Cis and Dick. They went to see Terry's girlfriend, Jean – she works at the Landport.' She realised that this meant nothing to him. 'In a shop. Only they've been gone hours and we're getting, worried. Dick's a bit of an invalid, you see; he gets asthma and he's only just got over pneumonia and we're afraid he might have had an attack. I was thinking of going to look for him, but I don't like leaving Mum.' She gestured at the old woman, who seemed to have lost all her sprightliness and sunk into a small, crumpled heap of misery. 'She's taking it very hard,' Polly whispered.

'I'll go,' he offered. 'Just tell me where. Only, I don't know Portsmouth at all, see, never been here in me life. Where do I start looking?' Then he grimaced. 'Come to that, who do I look for?'

'Oh dear, you don't even know what they look like, do you? So that's no good.' Polly went out to the scullery and filled the kettle. 'You'd better have a cup of tea anyway – we all will. And I was just going to start doing some potatoes for dinner. You'd better stop and have a bite with us.' He had followed her and stood leaning against the door-jamb. She looked at him regretfully. 'I'm sorry you had to find us all at sixes and sevens like this. It's just been such a shock, you see, and now with Cis and Dick not coming home I hardly know what I'm doing.'

'That's all right,' he said quietly. His crinkly face was soft with compassion. He hesitated for a moment, then stepped forwards and held out his arms. Polly stared at him. Her mouth drew itself down at the corners, her lips trembled and her eyes filled once again with hot, stinging tears. Without being aware that she had moved, she found herself leaning against his chest, her face against his shoulder, weeping as he held her close, weeping as she had not wept since Johnny had died. 'Oh Joe,' she sobbed, holding him tightly.

'There,' he murmured, stroking her back with a big, warm hand. 'There, there. You have a good cry, Poll, you just have a good cry. Let it all out – that's right. It'll do you good. And now you sit yourself down by your mum and I'll make that tea. I'll peel the spuds as well, and get you a bit of dinner, and then if your sis hasn't come back we'll think what to do next. You need someone to look after you. You all do.'

He led her back into the other room and pushed her gently into Dick's armchair. Polly sniffed, and blew her nose and wiped her eyes, and looked at him gratefully as he placed a cup of tea beside her. 'You don't have to do all that, Joe.'

'Don't see why not,' he said. 'I come all this way to see you, I ain't going to turn round and go without making meself a bit useful. Unless you wants me to, of course,' he added quickly. 'You've only got to say the word, if that's what you'd rather.'

'No. No, I don't want you to go.' She gave him a watery smile and he grinned at her and went back to the scullery.

Polly looked at her mother. Alice had recovered a little and was sipping her tea. She gave her daughter a quizzical look, almost like her old self.

'I must say, he seems a nice feller, Poll – but who is he? You never mentioned no Joe Turner before.'

Polly blushed, aware that Joe could hear everything they said. 'I met him that day I went to London with the Mayoress, Mum. His sister's the cook at WVS Headquarters. I said if he ever came down to Pompey he ought to come and see us, and I suppose that's what he's done.'

'Hm. Come down special, just for a cup of tea?' Alice gave her a sideways glance. 'And I dare say that's where those letters have been coming from too, is it? The ones you don't say nothing about?' Then she seemed to remember the trouble they were in and her face crumpled again. 'Not that it seems to matter much now,' she said despondently. 'Nothing seems to matter now.'

'Oh Mum . . .' But whatever Polly had been about to say was lost in the sound of the front door being opened, and voices as Cissie and Dick came into the passage. The two women looked at each other with relief, and Polly jumped to her feet.

'Cissie! Dick!' she cried as they came through to the back room. 'Wherever have you been? We've been so worried.' She caught the expression on their faces and stopped.

'What's happened now? What's the matter? Is it Jean? Is she ill?'

Cissie sat down on the nearest chair, as if her legs refused to hold her up any longer. She leaned her elbow on the table and supported her head in her palm. She heaved a huge sigh and Dick stood beside her, resting his hand on her shoulder, although he too looked grey and shocked. Polly stared at them in alarm. 'What's happened? Tell me what's happened!'

'Not ill, as such,' Cissie said, shaking her head. 'We had to take her home from the shop – she fainted when we told her the news. But it wasn't just that that made her faint,' she added bitterly, as Polly gave a little exclamation of pity. 'And I don't reckon it was the first time she done it, neither.' She raised her eyes and looked at her sister. 'The silly girl – the silly, *silly* girl – she's gone and got herself into trouble. She's *expecting*, Poll. She's expecting our Terry's baby – and what's she going to do now, I ask you! What in heaven's *name* does she think she's going to do now?'

In the first few moments after Cissie's announcement, Polly forgot all about Joe, still out in the scullery. It was only when a sound of swishing water made them all look round that she remembered he was there, presumably peeling potatoes. Her hand to her mouth, she went swiftly out and brought him through.

'This is Joe Turner,' she announced to her bewildered sister and brother-in-law. 'He – he popped down to see me. From London.' She could feel her face flooding with scarlet. 'We ran into each other when I went up with the Mayoress that time.'

'Popped in?' Dick echoed, his glance taking in Joe's rolled-up sleeves and the potato peeler in his hand. 'From *London*? But what the flipping heck is he doing in our scullery?'

'I was just helping with the dinner,' Joe explained. 'Poll

told me about your lad – I thought I'd give a bit of a hand. But you don't want me now, I can see that. Right, I'll be off.' He looked at Polly. 'Some other time, eh?'

She stared at him, distressed, and then turned to Cissie. 'I asked him to stop for a bite to eat, him having come all that way. But now . . .'

'It don't matter,' Joe said, shrugging into the jacket he'd slipped off when he began work. 'I can see you're in trouble. I just wanted to help, but if there's nothing else I can do . . .'

'No,' Dick said, his eyes hard and suspicious. 'There isn't.'

The women looked at him in surprise. Polly flushed again, and began, 'There's no need—' but Cissie interrupted her.

'Wait a mo.' She looked at Joe. 'It's a lot to ask, but if you really wouldn't mind . . . It's our Judy – my daughter. She's out in the country, and we don't know if she's heard about the ship. You see, she's deaf.'

He nodded. 'I know. Polly told me.'

'Well, we ought to let her know. I meant to send a telegram while we were out, but we went to see Jean first and then when she told us about her trouble –' Cissie coloured, embarrassed first by the trouble itself and then by the realisation that Joe must have heard her blurt it out, 'well, it went right out of my mind. But if you wouldn't mind doing that for us, I'd be really grateful. I'll give you the money,' she added, reaching for her purse.

'Don't you worry about that,' Joe said. 'And I tell you what, I won't send a telegram – I'll go out there meself, on the train. I dare say she'll want to come home, and she'll need someone with her, 'specially with her being deaf and all.' He looked at Polly. 'Ashwood, isn't it? Give me her address and I'll go straight away.'

'Oh, but you can't,' Polly began, glancing from him to Dick, who was still looking unfriendly.

'Don't see why not. You write out a note for her, so she knows I'm kosher. Look, I got nothing else to do. And don't worry about the fare, we'll sort all that out after. The main thing is to let her know what's happened and see what she wants to do.' He buttoned his jacket and found the cap he'd been wearing, while Polly scribbled a hasty note. She handed it to him and he held her hand for a brief second, his eyes meeting hers. 'Don't you worry, Poll,' he said quietly. 'She'll be all right with me.'

The door closed behind him and they all stared at each other. Dick sat down heavily beside his wife and Polly sank back into the armchair.

'Well!' he said. 'And who was that, might I ask? Coming in here, taking over, saying what's to be done and all. Well, Polly?'

'You needn't look at me as if I'd done something wrong, Dick Taylor,' she said with asperity. 'Joe's a decent man. His sister's Cook at the WVS Headquarters in London—'

'I don't care if his sister's the Queen of England,' Dick broke in. 'What I want to know is, who is he, and what's he doing here in my house?'

'My *mother's* house,' Polly reminded him sharply, getting to her feet. 'Just because you're Cissie's husband . . .'

'Look, I may not be much cop as far as you're concerned, but I'm the man around here and I'm head of the family!' Dick's voice rose. 'And I don't much like coming home and finding some other bloke what I've never seen before nor heard of, making free with my kitchen – all right, your *mother's* kitchen. I don't say there's anything wrong with the bloke, I don't say that, I just don't like it, that's all. 'Specially when we got our own private family business to talk about. You don't know what he might have heard before we knew he was out there. And now he's gone off to fetch our Judy from the country, for all the world as if he's one of the family himself. It's all too quick, that's what it is, and *I don't like it.*'

'Dick,' Cissie begged, 'don't upset yourself.' She cast an anxious glance towards Polly. 'You know what he's like when he gets upset.'

Polly bit her lip and sat down again. She knew very well what happened when Dick got upset. He didn't lose his temper often, but he could blow up quite unpredictably, and then he would be quite unreasonable, keeping a row going for hours and only ending it with an asthma attack. Over the years, they had all grown accustomed to fending off any situation which might cause an outbreak, but the present troubles were too great to be ignored.

'Let's forget about Joe,' she said quietly. 'He's a decent man and he just wants to help. I'll tell you about him later, but we've got other things to worry about now. Tell me about Jean. Is it true what you said? Is she really expecting?'

Cissie nodded miserably. 'She said it happened the last night he was on leave at Christmas. You know he stopped over at their house because they were out late. She said they just couldn't help it. He was going away, and they didn't know when they might see each other again, and they wanted to get engaged – they wanted to get married but there wasn't time. And they were there in her mum's front room, saying goodnight, and everyone else had gone to bed and – and . . .' She started to cry and Dick's hand moved on her shoulder. 'Oh Polly, it was just the once, she swears it was just the once.'

'But once is enough,' Dick said grimly. 'And you can guess who did the leading on.'

'Dick, we don't know that.'

'Don't we? Look, our Terry was a decent boy. We always brought him up to know right from wrong same as we did our Judy, and when he went off to join the Army I had a talk with him. Keep yourself decent, I told him, and you'll never have no trouble. I know what it's like when these young chaps get off in a gang in foreign parts. There's a lot of temptation and—'

'But Terry wasn't in foreign parts,' Polly said. 'He was home with Jean.'

Dick glared at her and she remembered suddenly that he was fifteen years older than she, and had known her as a little girl. Perhaps he still thought of her that way. 'There's no need to get clever, Polly,' he said heavily. 'The facts speak for themselves. Our Terry's dead, and young Jean Foster's carrying his baby, and it don't matter which way round you look at it, they been daft and done wrong, both of them. But I know what it's like to be a young bloke going off to war, and I know it don't take much to—' He closed his mouth abruptly. 'Well, never you mind. I just know it wasn't all our Terry's fault, that's all.'

'I don't see as it matters whose fault it was,' Alice said suddenly, speaking for the first time. 'What we've got to think about now is what we're going to do about it.'

There was a short silence. They looked at her, and then at each other. Cissie was the first to find her voice.

'Do about it, Mum? Why, what can we do about it? It's for Jean to make up her mind about that. It's her baby. Not but what we won't do what we can to help, of course,' she added. 'I mean, we'll make it a few clothes and that sort of thing, we can't let it go naked. But I dare say she'll get it adopted, won't she? There's not much else she can do.'

'Get it adopted?' Alice stared at them. 'Your grandchild? My great-grandchild? The first I'll have – maybe the only one I'll ever have? Get it *adopted*?'

They were silent again, astonished by her outburst. Then Polly said in a reasonable tone, 'But what else can she do, Mum? I mean, she can't keep it, can she, not without a man to stand by her. How could she afford to? And what would everyone say? You know what it's like for a girl in her position.'

'I know what people would say,' the old lady said grimly. 'I know it wouldn't be easy for her. But she's not the first one to have a baby born the wrong side of the blanket and she won't be the last, neither. And I reckon there'll be a lot more kiddies like this before this lot's over. Children who won't ever know their daddies, but still need their mothers – *and* their grandparents and great-grandparents too,' she added forcefully. 'Why should they have to go to strangers when they've got a family already? Why shouldn't they be with their own family, with the people who'll love them just because they're their own flesh and blood? Don't they have no say in the matter – don't they have no rights? And don't the rest of the family have no rights neither? This is *our Terry's* baby,' she said, fixing them all with a brilliant stare. 'Our Terry's. It might look like him. It might be him all over again. We've found out about it only a few hours after we've heard about Terry. Doesn't it seem to you as if it's meant? How can you talk about giving it away?'

The silence this time was longer. They glanced at each other uneasily. Dick was staring at the table, his lips tight, his jaw clenched. Cissie was crying again, silently, the tears running down her face. Polly felt a huge lump in her throat, a lump that wouldn't go away.

'But Mum,' she said, trying to talk past it, 'it's going to be so hard for Jean. You know what people are like. They won't talk to her. They won't have anything to do with her. How's she going to manage?' She glanced at Cissie. 'What do her own mum and dad think about it? What do they say?'

'People forget,' Alice said before Cissie could answer. 'They might cross the street when they see her coming at first, but they'll get used to it. And babies bring their love with them. Once it's born and she's pushing a pram, people will want to stop and look at it. They might be funny at first, but they'll come round.'

'Not all of them,' Cissie said. 'Some people will stay funny all their lives.'

'Well,' Alice said, 'they're not worth bothering about then. They'll only be people like Ethel Glaister down the road and who takes any notice of her?'

They had to smile at this. Nobody liked Ethel Glaister, who had a sharp word to say about everything and made no bones about letting folk see that she thought herself better than they. But Cissie's smile faded quickly and she frowned.

'I still don't see what we can do about it, Mum. It's for Jean and her mum and dad to work out. It's not really our business, is it?'

Alice thumped her wrinkled hand on the arm of her chair and spoke forcefully. 'Of *course* it's our business! Isn't that just what I've been trying to say? It's *our* baby too – *our* flesh and blood. We can't just stand by and let it be given away to strangers. It's our Terry's little boy or girl. *Think* about it!'

They stared at her. Polly thought about the baby, still a tiny being curled up in its mother's womb. She thought of how it would look after it was born – streaked with blood and mucus, screaming its way into life and, later, bathed and wrapped in soft white clothes, sleeping peacefully in its mother's arms. She thought of it as a toddler, running about with its fingers into everything. Looking like Terry had looked. Laughing like Terry had laughed, crying as he had cried.

'Mum's right,' she said, feeling the ache of loss in her breast even though just an hour ago she hadn't even known of the baby's existence. 'If it's Terry's baby, it's ours too.' She hesitated. 'What I don't understand is why nobody knew. I mean – it was Christmas, wasn't it? And now it's May. That's five months. Isn't she showing?'

'Well, she's just started to,' Cissie admitted. 'But you know Jean, she's a plump little thing and if you don't have any reason to suspect anything, you'd just think she was putting on a bit more weight. Her mum was beginning to wonder, I think, but it would've been another couple of weeks before she could be sure.'

'And how did she take it?' Alice asked. 'Her dad wasn't there, I suppose, so they'll need to talk it over when he comes home from work, but how did her mum seem?'

'Well, what d'you think? She was proper upset. I thought she was going to hit Jean for a minute. Then she started to cry, and Jean started again, and –'

'And you joined in,' Dick said. 'I had to go and make them all a cup of tea,' he told Alice. 'Me! In someone else's kitchen and all. Couldn't get no sense out of any of 'em, so I said to Cis we ought to come away and leave 'em to it. Say what you will, Ma, it's their business more than it's ours. It's Jean who's in the family way, and it's them who'll have to decide what to do about it.' He set his jaw grimly.

Alice took no notice. 'We can still put our point of view. We'd better go round there one evening and talk it over. And we'd better make it soon, in case they turn her out.'

'They wouldn't do that,' Cissie said. 'Not Mrs Foster.'

'Mr Foster might,' Alice said with a glance at Dick. 'Men are harder about these things. And Mrs Foster always struck me as one who'd set a lot of store on what the neighbours say. They might not turn her out as such, but they might send her to one of them homes for unmarried mothers, where they can stop until the baby's born. And you know what happens then. They give the babies up and never see them again.' She drew in a ragged breath and her eyes filled with tears. 'I don't want that to happen, Cis, I really don't. It's as if it's *meant* – finding out about it the very day we lose our Terry. I can't bear to think of losing his baby without even setting eyes on its dear little face.'

Cissie and Polly began to cry again in sympathy. They moved to sit together, their arms about each other as they wept for Terry and for the baby he had left behind, the baby he had not even known existed.

Dick stared at them. There was a lump in his throat too, and an uncomfortable feeling that he was the outsider, the one who didn't fit in, the one who had let himself down in some way. I've only said what any other bloke with a sense of decency would say, he told himself rebelliously. The girl probably *did* lead Terry on. It was in her house it happened.

302

And it *is* for her and her mum and dad to sort out. They probably won't thank us for interfering if we do go round there.

And yet, he couldn't ignore the pictures conjured up by Alice's words. Like Polly, he had seen the baby in its cot, the laughing toddler staggering about the room. He had also seen the boy that Terry had been, that his baby might become. The schoolboy, his socks down round his ankles, kicking a ball along the street, the twelve-year-old riding an old bike, the sixteen-year-old out at work, on a Dockyard apprenticeship perhaps, turning into a young man . . .

'Blimey,' he said in disgust, surveying the women. 'It'll be like a blooming swimming pool in here in a minute. I suppose I'd better go and make another cup of tea.'

Judy was out in the orchard with Sylvie when Joe Turner arrived. The little girl was feeling better and had managed to eat a piece of dry toast for her dinner, and was now lying on an old blanket in the shade of the apple tree. Its new leaves whispered above her, and she had fallen asleep while Judy sat beside her on a cushion, darning socks.

She looked up at the click of the gate, wondering who the stranger was who was standing there with Mrs Sutton. He was stocky, with a face that looked as if someone had screwed it up in a ball and then tried to iron out the creases. But she could see that it was a friendly, good-humoured face, even though just at present it looked grave. The farmer's wife too was looking upset, and Judy felt a sudden pang of dread.

'What is it?' she asked, and started to scramble to her feet. 'What's happened?'

'This is Mr Turner,' Mrs Sutton said. 'He's come to see you, Judy.'

'To see me? But why?' Judy stared from one to the other. Joe Turner produced a letter and she looked at it uneasily. 'What is it? What's happened? Have they had another raid in Portsmouth?' She felt herself shrink away from the note as if by not reading it she could push away whatever dreadful news he had brought. 'Has Grandma's house been bombed? Has – has anyone been hurt?'

'No!' She could see just how forceful the word was, and felt her body sag with relief. But his face was still solemn. 'Not anyone at home, anyway.' He nodded at the letter. 'You'd better read it. I'm sorry.'

'That's right, love,' Mrs Sutton said. 'Read the letter.'

Slowly, Judy reached out to take it. It was addressed in her aunt's writing and began by introducing Joe Turner as a friend. You can trust him, Polly had said. And then, as if she found the words difficult to write, came the news that had brought Joe to Ashwood. The news of HMS *Hood*.

Judy stared at the words. They blurred and danced in front of her eyes, and the orchard and the grass and the sunshine seemed to fall away into darkness. She shook her head, feeling sick and frightened, and found a cup of water pressed to her lips. Mrs Sutton must have brought it with her, knowing she would need it. She sank down again on the cushion and reached a hand out to Sylvie, who was still fast asleep. Her tears beginning to fall, she whispered, 'Let's go somewhere else. I don't want Sylvie to see. She'll be frightened.'

The others nodded and Joe Turner helped Judy to her feet. She found her legs shaking, and leaned upon him as they went softly from the orchard. Sylvie would probably sleep for an hour or two yet, and would not be alarmed to find herself alone when she woke. They went into the cool, dim kitchen and Mrs Sutton shifted the kettle on to the hot plate.

'I can't believe it,' Judy said in bewilderment, staring at the letter. 'Our Terry. It's awful.' She shook her head and looked at Mrs Sutton. 'I went to bed early last night, before the news. Did you hear it? Did you know the *Hood* had been sunk?'

'Well, yes, I did,' the farmer's wife confessed. 'We both heard it. But we didn't know your brother was on board. All we knew was that he was in the Navy.' She spoke slowly and clearly, so that Judy could follow her, and wrote it down to make sure. 'I'm so sorry,' she added in shaky handwriting, and tears fell on to the paper.

'Our Terry,' Judy said. 'Oh, I don't think I can bear it!' She bent her head and burst into tears, sobbing wildly. 'It's not fair! First Johnny, and then Sean – and now Terry! It's just not *fair*!'

'Judy, Judy.' She felt Mrs Sutton's arms around her and her head was drawn down on to the warm cushion of her bosom. A comforting hand stroked her hair and another, harder and hornier but just as comforting, patted her hand. She could feel the vibrations in the woman's body that meant she was speaking, and although she couldn't hear the words, she knew what they must be. 'Poor love. You poor, poor love. There, there. Cry it out, now, cry it out. Poor, poor love.'

At length, with no more tears in her for the time being, Judy hiccuped into silence. She screwed up the third of the hankies Mrs Sutton had pressed into her hand, and gazed at it through swollen eyes. Then she looked up at the two who watched her so sympathetically.

'I'll have to go home. They'll want me there.'

Mrs Sutton nodded. 'I thought you'd say that. Mr Turner here says he'll take you back as soon as you like.' She glanced at the clock. 'There's a train in an hour – you can pack your things while I get some tea ready for you. And you can take some fresh eggs and butter back for your family. I dare say they'll be glad of them. I'll put in a few slices of bacon as well.'

Judy barely followed this, but understood that she was to go and pack and that Joe Turner would take her back to Portsmouth. She looked at him doubtfully and he gave her his crinkly grin. 'Go on, love. I'll wait for you here.' He seemed to realise why she was doubtful and added, 'I'm a friend of your Aunt Polly's. Met her in London when she come up to WVS Headquarters a couple of weeks back. My sister's the cook there.' He followed Mrs Sutton's example and wrote the words down and Judy read them, nodding.

'Are you sure you want to bother? I could manage on my own.'

He laughed. 'Well, I can't stop out here, can I! I've got to go back to Pompey, so I might as well see you safe back home. Anyway, I don't reckon me and Polly would be friends any more if I didn't.' He saw that she hadn't followed this and said gently and more slowly, 'You go and get yourself ready, love. We'll go back to Portsmouth together.'

Judy gave in and went upstairs. She stood at the door of the room she had shared with Sylvie, the room that had become so familiar and so dear. The walls were distempered a sunny yellow, there were yellow curtains flowered with blue at the window and yellow cushions on the low, deep windowsill. It was a room that seemed filled with sunshine on even the dullest of days, and here, as she had sat on that windowsill gazing down into the orchard, she had found comfort and healing. Now she was to leave it and go back to the grey, ruined streets of Portsmouth, and she felt torn between a desire to see her family again and a longing to stay here for ever.

She crossed the room and looked down into the orchard. Sylvie was still asleep on her blanket under the apple tree. How many times have I sat under that tree in the past two weeks? Judy thought. By myself, with Sylvie – and with Ben. She thought of the tall, dark-haired boy with his bright blue eyes beneath the heavy brows. They had shared an easy understanding, a ready friendship, and she had found it difficult to believe that he was only seventeen. He seemed so much older, so much more mature. He felt it himself too, with his restless desire to leave school and join the RAF. He was ready for manhood.

She turned her mind away from that disturbing thought and lifted her suitcase down from the top of the wardrobe. Then she took her few clothes from the cupboard and drawers and began to fold them on the bed.

Chapter Twenty-Three

During their light meal of sliced ham, early lettuce and beetroot, Judy noticed that Joe Turner seemed uneasy, as if there were something else on his mind. He said nothing, however, until Judy had made her tearful farewells and Sylvie, who had come in yawning and hungry after her sleep, had accompanied them to the station where they could catch the train back to Portsmouth. The little girl clung to her aunt, begging to be allowed to go back to Portsmouth with her, and Judy had been in tears yet again as she gently unwound the small arms from around her neck.

'You're better off here. We're still getting raids – it's not safe. And you know you're happy here with the Suttons and the other children.'

'I'd rather be home with you and Mummy,' Sylvie said mutinously.

'You will be,' Judy promised, hoping it was true. 'Once all this bombing's over you'll come back straight away, I promise.' Her words were lost as the train arrived, huffing to a stop beside the platform. 'I'll have to go now, Sylvie. Be good for me, won't you? And look after Cavalier.' Cavalier was the farmyard rooster, so named for his spectacular feathers. She gave Sylvie a final hug and then turned away quickly, dashing the tears from her eyes. I don't know where they all come from, she thought, but I wish I could smile as much as I cry.

Joe opened the carriage door and helped her up into an empty compartment, following with her case. He pulled down the window so that she could lean out and wave goodbye to Sylvie, then the train gathered speed and surged out of the station. In another moment the platform was out of sight and Judy sat down and heaved a trembling sigh.

Joe Turner looked at her. 'You all right, love?'

Judy nodded. He had such an expressive face, she found him easy to understand. 'I suppose so. It's just a bit much to take in. A couple of hours ago I was sitting under the apple tree darning socks without a care in the world – well, not too many anyway,' she amended, thinking ruefully of Sean and her deafness. 'I suppose I was used to the ones I had! And now, here I am on my way back home, and – and I've lost my brother.' Her voice trembled. 'Oh dear, I'm going to start crying again. I'm sorry.'

'It's all right, love.' He handed her a large khaki handkerchief. 'You cry all you want. You've been through a lot.'

'So have other people,' Judy wept. 'It's no worse for me than it is for Mum and Dad – or Polly, or Grandma. We've all been through the same.'

'And you've all had a good cry,' he said. 'It's natural.'

Judy gathered control of herself, glad that there was no one else in the compartment. She gazed out of the window at the fields and woods, thinking how strange it was that war was being waged less than a hundred miles away – not much further than it was from Portsmouth to London – yet here it seemed so peaceful, and so lovely. 'Why do people have to hate each other?' she asked. 'Why do they have to fight? Why can't people just live peacefully together, like we used to?'

Joe shrugged. 'Not for us to ask that, love,' he said. 'It's up to them that lead us.' He hesitated and then said carefully, 'You'll need to prepare yourself for another bit of news when you get home.'

Judy stared at him. 'Another bit of news? Why, what else

has happened?' Her eyes sharpened. 'You said everyone was all right.'

'They are, love. They're all fine – well, as fine as can be expected, in the circs. But there's summat else – look, it ain't for me to tell you. I just thought you ought to be prepared, that's all.'

'I can't follow all this,' Judy said despairingly. 'You'll have to write it down. Oh, I *hate* being deaf!'

He looked at her sympathetically and felt in his pockets for paper and a pencil. But all he had was the train tickets, and neither of them had anything to write with. They gave up and sat helplessly gazing at each other. Something else? Judy thought. What can it be? Oh, I wish he hadn't said it! And yet, she knew that it was better for her to be prepared. It would make it easier for the family to tell her.

The train rumbled on through Botley and Fareham, and then along the top of the harbour. Judy stared out at the expanse of water stretching away to the south, and thought of Terry's last leave. She had seen the great ship he was on, and stood on the Sallyport to watch it sail away through the narrow neck of the harbour. Now it was at the bottom of the sea, somewhere off Greenland, and only three of its great crew of almost fifteen hundred men would ever return.

Judy stared at her mother in disbelief. 'Jean Foster's having a *baby*?'

Now, more than ever, she hated her deafness. To have to stare at people's mouths as they spoke, unable to understand any but the most obvious words, or wait while they wrote things down, pausing as they wondered how to spell the words – all that was bad enough. But now, with everyone talking at once about these new events, so important to them all, turning to each other and speaking too quickly for her to follow, was nothing short of agonising. I wish I'd never gone back to that building, she thought bitterly. It didn't do any good, and we nearly lost Polly as well.

'What are you saying?' she asked loudly, so that they all stopped talking and turned to her. 'What's the use of me coming back if you won't even tell me what's going on?' Her shock and distress over Terry, the hurried return home and now the news of the baby had left her shaken and on edge, ready either to burst into tears all over again or to lose her temper completely. 'Don't I matter any more?' she went on, aware that she was shouting. 'Can't anyone even be bothered to *look* at me when they're talking? I feel as if I'm in a glass jar – I can see your mouths moving, but all I can hear is a sort of *woolly* sound. I can't make out any words, and I feel so left out, and it's awful. *Awful!*' Temper and tears came together then, and she buried her face in her hands, sobbing wildly. 'You don't know what it's like! None of you knows what it's like!'

'Oh, Judy!' Arms came around her and hands patted her back. Over her head, Cissie and Polly looked at each other. 'She's right,' Polly said in a low voice, although there was no danger of Judy's overhearing her. 'We do leave her out, and it's not fair. Terry was her brother and she's just as upset about it all as we are. We've got to do our best to help her.'

'It's not that I don't want to,' Cissie said in distress. 'I'd do anything I can to help her. But I can't help just saying what comes into my head, and I forget to look at her all the time.' She tightened her arms around Judy's bent shoulders. 'To be honest, I wonder if it was a bit selfish to ask her to come home. I want her here, I really do, but maybe it was better for her to be out in the country. She seemed to be settling down so well out there.'

'I think she'd have come whatever we said,' Polly said. 'Joe told me it was the first thing she said, that she'd come home. She said we'd need her.'

She sighed. Joe had refused even to stop for a cup of tea after delivering Judy at the door. 'You've got your own troubles,' he'd told her on the doorstep of number nine.

'You don't want strangers around. I'll be in touch.' And then he'd gone, limping away up the street and turning at the corner to wave a cheery hand, and she realised that she didn't even know what he was going to do next. Would he get a train back to London, or was he staying somewhere in Portsmouth? She had followed Judy indoors feeling frustrated.

'And so we do need her,' Cissie said. 'I need her, and so does Dick. We all need her.' She put her hand under Judy's chin and lifted the wet, swollen face, speaking slowly and clearly. 'Judy, we're all glad you've come home. We need you here. Do you understand that? We *need* you.'

Judy drew in a ragged breath and nodded, trying to smile. 'OK, Mum. Sorry. It's just – well, it's all been such a shock.' She twisted her lips ruefully. 'It must have been an awful shock for you too, hearing that from Jean. What's she going to do?'

'We don't know yet. We only found out this morning.' Cissie shook her head wonderingly. It seemed as if an age had passed since they had spoken to Jean in the shop. 'Your grandma thinks we ought to help her to keep the baby.'

'Keep it?' It was a moment or two before Judy fully understood what she was saying. 'But how could she, all on her own? What about her parents?'

Alice had been writing on an old envelope, and passed it to Judy. She read the words aloud. '*It's Terry's baby, and there'll never be another one. It's my great-grandchild. I don't want it to go to strangers.* Oh Gran,' she said. 'Oh Gran, of course you don't.'

Dick spoke up from his corner. He had been silent during the halting conversation, retreating there after first greeting Judy with a brief kiss. 'That's all very well. But it's not easy for a young woman on her own with a little 'un.'

'You don't have to tell *me* that!' Alice's voice was sharp. She had not yet forgiven him for his assumption that, in *her* house and *her* kitchen, he was the master. 'I brought up two on my own after my hubby died. Of course it's not easy!'

'Yes, but they were the right side of the blanket,' Dick retorted. 'Not by-blows, like Jean's is going to be!'

For a moment, it looked as if the quarrel would break out again. Alice and Dick glared at each other, while Judy stared at them in uncomprehending astonishment. Then Cissie put both hands on their shoulders and spoke with unusual firmness.

'Now, you needn't start that all over again! We had all that out before our Judy got here and she didn't come all this way to watch you two squabbling. Just you calm down, Dick, you'll make yourself ill getting your rag out like that, and we've got enough on our plates without having you back in hospital. And while I'm thinking about it, you might say sorry to Polly for the way you behaved to Mr Turner. I'm sure he never wanted to intrude on family problems, and he's been a real help, going out to fetch our Judy and all, but from the way you acted, anyone would have thought he'd come to pinch all the family silver. Supposing we'd got any to pinch,' she added, and Dick, who had been staring at her in astonishment, suddenly laughed. 'There,' she said, smiling, 'that's better.'

'Well, I suppose you're right, Cis,' he said, and looked over at Polly. 'Sorry, Poll, but I didn't know what to think when I found him here, and what with the shock over Terry and then Jean, I was knocked all of a heap . . . And I'm sorry to you too, Ma,' he went on, turning to Alice. 'You're right, we ought to give the girl a hand. It's not the time to start argufying over things that can't be altered.' He glanced at Judy, who was once again watching them in bewilderment. 'And here we are, leaving our Judy out again. Don't worry, gal, we haven't forgot you. We're glad to have you home again.'

'I've been thinking,' Polly said. 'Judy and Jean are pretty good friends. Why don't we ask her to go round and have a talk? Tell her what we've been thinking, see if we can do anything.'

'That's a good idea,' Alice said at once, and when they conveyed this idea to Judy she nodded.

'I will, if she wants to see me. She might feel awkward, though.'

'Not with you. You've known each other all your lives. You were in the same class at school.'

'I mean, because of me not being able to hear,' Judy said, but they shook their heads and Polly said she would let Judy use the writing-pad she'd been saving for writing to Sylvie. 'All right, I'll go round tomorrow. It's too late now.'

'You're right,' Alice said, looking at the clock. 'It's almost nine o'clock. Time for the news.'

They looked at each other. It was on last night's news that they'd heard of the sinking of HMS *Hood*. Only twenty-four hours ago!

'It seems like a lifetime,' Polly said soberly, and the others nodded. This time last night, they'd been more or less happy, thinking that Terry was still alive. Now, knowing not only that he must be dead but that he'd left his sweetheart pregnant, everything had changed.

Nobody had the heart to switch the wireless on for tonight's news. They'd had enough of news for a while, Polly thought as she went out to the scullery to make cocoa. Enough for a long time. In fact, if she had her way she'd never listen to the news again.

You couldn't just ignore it, though. You had to know what was going on. You had to care about other people as well as yourself, or why should they care about you? And even if you'd never wanted the war in the first place, even though nobody had asked your opinion nor listened if you gave it, you were still a part of it all. You had to stand by what was right.

And that went for what was happening in the family too. You had to stand by what was right – and Gran was right about this. Jean Foster's baby – Terry's baby – was a part of their family, a part that would be all they had left of Terry himself. What was done was done, and they would all do their best by the girl Terry had loved, and the baby she bore.

What's done is done, Polly repeated to herself. Who knows? Maybe in the end we'll be glad of it.

Judy went round to see Jean Foster the next evening, thinking that she would probably have gone to work as usual in the morning. She found her friend looking wan and red-eyed, picking listlessly at a plate of boiled fish and mashed potatoes.

'Perhaps you can talk some sense into her,' Mrs Foster said, leading Judy past a door leading to a front room that looked like a furniture shop showroom, with a three-piece suite daintily attired in lace antimacassars and a small occasional table with china figurines arranged upon it. She took her into an almost equally tidy back room. 'Done nothing but cry her eyes out, she has, ever since she heard, but I've told her, it's no use letting it all get on top of you. You've made your bed, my girl, and now you've got to lay in it,' she said to her daughter in a sharp, exasperated voice. 'And it's no good piping your eye all day over what can't be mended.'

Judy heard none of this but could tell from Mrs Foster's expression and gestures what sort of thing she was saying. She gave Jean a sympathetic smile and touched her ears. 'I've brought some paper for you to write on. It makes things easier. Could we go up to your bedroom or somewhere, so we don't disturb everyone else?'

'Oh, don't mind me,' Mrs Foster cried. 'Jean doesn't tell *me* what she's doing. Nor her dad, neither. Well, go on then,' she snapped, seeing that Judy had not understood. '*I* don't mind doing the washing-up, I'm sure, seeing as you've got company.'

Judy followed the other girl up the stairs. Mr Foster was a foreman in the Dockyard on a good wage and the Fosters' house was larger than Alice's, with three bedrooms and an indoor lavatory (which Mrs Foster called the WC) and bathroom. It had nice front rooms too, with rounded bay windows, and a little patch of front garden. Jean's room was at the back, overlooking a larger garden with a patch of lawn, and a small, neat vegetable plot, together with the inevitable Anderson shelter. *I bet they've got proper chairs and a table down there,* Judy thought, *with a fresh white tablecloth every Sunday!*

The girls sat down on Jean's bed, rumpling the bright green satin bedspread, and Jean drew in a deep breath and burst into tears. Judy put her arm around her shoulders, but her own grief overtook her and they wept together for several minutes, mourning the brother and the sweetheart who had been taken from them. *I seem to have been here before,* Judy thought, remembering the pain of losing Sean, and she held Jean tightly against her, scarcely knowing whether she did so to give comfort or to receive it.

'I *did* love him,' Jean sobbed. 'I really did. I still do! It wasn't just being wicked, like Mum says. We couldn't help it – we *loved* each other. He was going away, and we just couldn't bear it. We had to do what we did.'

'Jean, I'm sorry, I can't hear you,' Judy said gently. She rummaged in her bag for the writing-pad. 'Write it down. It doesn't matter what it is – just write it down. I get so fed up with people only putting down *bits* of what they're saying,' she added with feeling.

Jean wrote down what she had said, and then added, *It was only once. But I wish now it had been lots of times – so there!* and looked at Judy with an expression that was half-apologetic, half-defiant.

Judy grinned despite her unhappiness. 'I'll tell you something, Jean – I wish me and Sean had done it, too! He wanted to, I know, though he wouldn't ask me. We'd only known each other a little while, and Mum and Dad nearly hit the roof about our getting engaged. But now – well, I wish we had. Just so that he could have had that to remember.' And me, too, she thought. I'd like to have it to remember as well.

'You wouldn't,' Jean said tonelessly. 'Not if you'd found yourself in the mess I'm in now.' She scribbled the words quickly and handed the pad to Judy again.

'No, maybe not. But that's why I've come to see you. Mum and Dad and Gran – and me and Polly too, come to that – we've been wondering what you're going to do. Have you thought about it yet?' She made a face. 'That's a daft thing to say – you can't have been thinking about anything else since you realised.' Involuntarily, her glance drifted to Jean's stomach, beginning to show a swelling beneath her loose dress.

'I haven't, actually,' Jean confessed, and wrote down her next words. *I tried to push it out of my mind. I suppose I hoped it would go away! Stupid, but that's how it was.*

'But now your parents know, what do they think you should do?'

Mum was all for turning me out straight away! Dad wouldn't let her, though. He said if I went, he'd go too. Jean looked apprehensive, as though she thought it might really come to that, and Judy remembered that Jean Foster had always been the apple of her father's eye. *So Mum stopped saying it, but she's hardly spoken to me since. I don't know what I'm going to do.*

'That's why I've come round. We want you to know that you can always live with us, if it comes to it. I don't know where we'd put you, mind,' she added with a grin. 'You might have to sleep in the Anderson! But Gran said we'll do whatever we can, for Terry's sake, and because the baby's her great-grandchild and she doesn't want it going to strangers.'

Once again, Jean dissolved into tears. 'Oh Judy, I don't

know what to say. I didn't think anyone would want anything to do with me. I thought I'd be sent away, and have to give my baby up.' Unconsciously, her hand moved protectively to her stomach. 'I mean, I knew if Terry could come home it would be all right because he'd stand by me, but I didn't know how long he'd be away. This horrible war's going on and on and it doesn't look as if it's *ever* going to end, and I was so scared. I thought, What'll happen to me if he doesn't come home? And then yesterday, when I found out he *wasn't* going to – well, I just didn't know what I was going to do. And Mum's been so awful – we had such a terrible row last night over it – and I've been missing Terry so much, and now I'm never going to see him again, and – and . . .' The storm of weeping overtook her again and she sobbed uncontrollably.

Judy held her tightly, not needing to hear the words, her tears once more mingling with the frightened girl's. As the weeping eased again, she said, 'Look, Jean, you don't have to worry any more. We'll stand by you, since Terry can't. We're your family now too. It's your baby, and you've got to decide what you want to do, but whatever you decide, we'll help you.' She hesitated. 'If you want to give it up for adoption, we won't stand in your way, but we don't want you to do that. It's our Terry's baby as well as yours, and we want it to be part of our family.'

Jean wiped her face and blew her nose. She looked at Judy gratefully and attempted a smile. 'Thanks, Judy. It's really helped, having you come round. And I don't want to give my baby away either. It's just that, I don't really know how I'll manage. How am I going to be able to keep it? How can I *afford* to? There's so much a baby needs – a pram and a cot, and lots of clothes and nappies – and how could I go to work with a baby to look after? How can I earn a living for us both?' The tears were falling again as she picked up the pencil. *How am I going to manage, Judy?*

'We'll work it out,' Judy promised, managing to follow

the gist of Jean's tearful questions. 'We'll all put our heads together, and we'll work it out. I'm sure Mum and Gran will help, and I expect your mum'll come round, once she gets used to the idea. Anyway, just remember this, Jean – you're not on your own. We're all going to help you.' She wondered if she ought to say it, then added quietly, 'I almost wish it *had* happened to me, in some ways. I'd like to have something of Sean to remember him by – his baby, a part of him. As it is, all I've got is a ring and a few memories, and even those are starting to fade.'

It's better to have loved and lost than never to have loved at all, Jean wrote with shaking fingers. *I just wish it didn't hurt so much, Judy – having loved and lost. I wish everything didn't seem so hopeless.*

'It's not,' Judy said, wondering if she believed it. 'There's always hope, Jean. That's what Gran says. While there's life, there's hope.' She touched her friend's stomach wonderingly. 'That's where our hope is – in there. Your baby. Terry's baby. *Our* baby.'

'Hope,' Jean said, also touching her stomach. 'That's what I'll call it – if it's a girl. Hope.'

Judy looked at the name, written on a single sheet in the writing-pad. *Hope*. It was an unusual name but a good one. Perhaps this baby would be a turning point for them all. A new life, to make up for the one that had been lost.

'I'll tell them at home,' she said. 'They'll like that. It's what we all need, Jean. Hope.'

Chapter Twenty-Four

'I might have known you'd come home with some fancy ideas,' Dick said disgustedly as they sat round the supper-table that evening. 'Hope! Trouble, more like. It isn't going to be as easy as you all seem to think, not for young Jean anyway. A baby costs money, and it goes *on* costing money. How's a girl like Jean, working in a shop for – what? Fifteen bob a week? – how's she going to be able to afford to bring up a nipper? I mean, if they'd been married she'd have had a pension, but as it is she can't expect nothing from the Army, nothing at all. And we haven't got the means to help her out.'

The women looked at each other. They knew Dick was right: his own income was a war pension, and Cissie had had to take in dressmaking for years to make ends meet. It was easier once Terry and Judy were old enough to leave school and go out to work, and Terry had been sending money home regularly since he joined the Army, but now that would stop. Alice too had only her small pension. There wasn't anything left over for a baby.

'Well, we're going to have to do something,' Polly said with determination. 'Like Gran says, the baby is part of our family, and if Jean wants to keep it, we've got to help her. I don't mind chipping in a bit. There's always something I can go without.'

'Well, I dunno what it is, then,' Dick said. 'We're going without just about everything already.' He sighed. 'If you're all so set on it there's nothing more I can say, is there? I never had much chance with three women lined up against me, anyway. You'd better tell young Jean to come round here for tea on Sundays.' A thought struck him. 'I bet her mum doesn't go much on all this, does she? I remember her as a girl at the dances down the Oddfellows – stuck-up piece, she was. What did she have to say about all this?'

He looked interrogatively at Judy and she stared back blankly. Polly mouthed at her, 'Mrs Foster. What did she say?'

'Oh, Jean's mum,' Judy said, and made a face. 'Jean says she's been awful. They've had a really bad row over it, and Jean thought she was going to turn her out, but her dad wouldn't let her. I don't know what she'll say about Jean keeping the baby, though. I can't see her letting them stay there.'

'No, nor can I,' Cissie said. 'And she won't have the same feeling about it that we have. After all, Jean could have other children, in wedlock. But if she does keep the baby, it might spoil her chances of getting married at all.'

Polly sighed. 'What a problem. I don't know what to suggest. We really haven't got room for her here, we're like sardines as it is.' She stood up and started to gather the plates together. 'Let's clear this away and listen to the news. Perhaps they'll have caught the *Bismarck* by now. That might cheer us up a bit.'

The pursuit of the German ship was the topic on everyone's lips. It had become an ogre in everyone's minds, a symbol of the terror that stalked the world. It was as if nothing more could be achieved until it had been hunted down and destroyed. To the family in number nine, as to so many other families in the country, it seemed a personal retribution – a just reprisal for the terrible loss they had suffered – yet the need was almost as great to those who had not known any of the crew. The *Hood* represented something vital to the national sense of strength, and its loss must be balanced by an equal loss to the Germans.

'An eye for an eye, a tooth for a tooth,' Dick said grimly. 'That's what it is. And a ship for a ship.'

'And a thousand mothers' sons for a thousand mothers' sons,' Cissie said sadly. 'I don't know, it seems wrong to me, looking at it that way. The whole thing about war – leaders like Hitler sending ordinary young men to do his dirty work for him and the rest of us having to join in and send ours to stop them – well, it doesn't seem Christian to me.'

'But there've always been wars,' Polly said. 'The Bible's full of them. It's full of talk about God smiting people down.'

'Well, I can't understand it,' Cissie said. 'But there, I suppose it's not for folk like us to understand, we haven't got the education. We just have to do as we're told. And send our lads to be killed,' she added bitterly.

The wireless began its burbling warm-up and a moment or two later the announcer's voice came through. 'This is the nine o'clock news, and this is Alvar Liddell reading it. The hunt for the German battleship *Bismarck* goes on as she evades the British Force sent to engage her. There has been more heavy fighting on the island of Crete which was invaded three days ago by almost five hundred Junker transport planes bringing thousands of paratroopers. Lord Louis Mountbatten's ship HMS *Kelly* has been reported sunk, together with her sister ship HMS *Kashmir*. Many of the survivors, including Lord Mountbatten, were rescued by HMS *Kipling*, after being machine-gunned in the water. More fighter aircraft have been delivered to the besieged island of Malta, which has been under heavy attack from the Luftwaffe. HMS *Ark Royal* and HMS *Furious* between them brought a total forty-eight Hurricanes. German High Command is believed to be building up a massive attack force on the Russian Front. There were no reports of air raids over Britain over the past twenty-four hours . . .'

'That's one bit of good news anyway,' Alice said as they switched off the wireless and stared at each other. 'I shouldn't think they had enough planes to raid us anyway. They seem to be everywhere!'

'It's terrible,' Cissie said, 'Lord Mountbatten being machine-gunned in the water! And all those poor souls on Malta. I heard yesterday that they're just living in holes in the ground, frightened to come out. And Crete – they can't leave our boys there, surely? They'll have to go and get them out.'

'It's another Dunkirk,' Dick said. He shook his head. 'I can't see how we can beat them this time. They've been getting ready for it for years, while we've been shutting our eyes to what's been going on.'

'Well, I believe in Mr Churchill,' Alice said staunchly, 'and if *he* says we'll win, I reckon we will.'

Dick looked at her gravely. 'I'm not sure that's what he has said, Ma,' he said in a quiet voice. 'He's said we'll fight them. He's said we'll fight them on the beaches and in the streets and in the hills. He's said we'll never surrender. But I don't think he's ever said we're going to *win*.'

The *Bismarck* was sunk two days later, after a desperate chase across the Atlantic, pursued by over a hundred ships. She was finally caught a few hundred miles off the coast of Brittany and hit, first by torpedoes from the *Ark Royal*, which destroyed her steering gear, and then by shells fired from the numerous ships which were closing in upon her. In the end, defiant to the last, the German Commander ordered that she be scuttled, and the great ship turned over and sank, with the loss of over two thousand men.

Britain breathed a sigh of relief. The seas were a little less dangerous now, even though there were still plenty of enemy ships patrolling them, but it was mainly a sense of justice that caused them to celebrate. An eye for an eye. A tooth for a tooth. A ship for a ship . . .

'It's just like children squabbling in a playground,' Cissie said privately to Polly, but they didn't repeat these sentiments to others. April Grove was full of people stopping to congratulate each other on the victory, and you didn't want to be thought either a 'conchie' or a Fifth Columnist. It only needed some busybody like Ethel Glaister to hear you saying something like that, and you could find yourself in prison!

All the same, Cissie couldn't help feeling glad that the men who had killed her Terry were now themselves dead, even though she knew that in Germany there were a lot of mothers suffering the same grief as herself. It doesn't make sense, she thought. How can I be glad and sorry both at the same time? But then, nothing about war really made sense.

Jean Foster came round to see them the day after the *Bismarck* had been sunk. She was pale, red-eyed and nervous, obviously both grieving for Terry and in a panic over her own situation. She looked a different girl from the pleasant, smiling shop assistant Dick and Cissie had seen the day before. She also looked plumper, as if her figure were blossoming by the day, and she told them she was sure some of the neighbours were beginning to look at her a bit funny.

'Mum says I've got to go away before they notice,' she said, 'but where can I go? And what shall I do for money? I don't know what I'm going to do, I don't really.' She sat on one of the dining chairs and stared at them all fearfully. 'I'm ever so sorry, Mrs Taylor, for bringing all this trouble on you. I never meant – me and Terry, we just – well, we never thought that just *once* . . .'

'It only takes once,' Dick said grimly. 'And we brought our Terry up to know right from wrong.'

'Well, *I* know right from wrong too, Mr Taylor.' Jean's cheeks flushed. 'We both did. But he was going away the next day, and we loved each other so much. We just couldn't help ourselves.' She began to cry again. 'I know what you think of me – I know what everyone'll say, that I'm a hussy and a trollop and all the rest of it – but we couldn't help it, we *couldn't*, and I tell you what, I'm glad we did it. I never meant it to be like this and nor did Terry, but I'm glad all the same. At least he was happy when he went away, and *I made him happy*.' She lifted her chin and gave Dick a challenging stare. 'He said so. And I'm *glad*.'

There was a short silence. Dick flushed too but he let his eyes drop. He glanced down sideways into the empty fireplace and his jaw clenched. Cissie watched him, biting her lip, afraid that he was going to give way to a burst of temper, and Alice seemed to square her shoulders as if she too were ready to join in the fray. Judy, unable to follow their words, glanced anxiously at Polly, who gave her a small smile, as if to say that she thought Jean had got the better of the angry man.

Dick took a breath. He turned his eyes back to Jean's defiant face.

'All right, young lady,' he said stonily. 'So you're glad. You're going to look after yourself then, are you? You won't come looking for help from no one else?'

Jean's defiance faded a little. 'I'm not saying that, Mr Taylor,' she said. 'I'd do that if I could. And maybe I will, if I can find a way. Maybe I can get a job somewhere, where I can have my baby with me. I thought it was only right to come and see you, but I'm not asking for help from anyone who doesn't want to give it,' she added with a flash of spirit. 'If you don't want me round here, just say so and I'll go. It was only that Judy said you and her mum would like to see me.' She began to get up. 'If you don't, I'll be off.'

'No! No, don't go.' Cissie looked at her husband. 'Dick'll be the one to go if he doesn't want you here, won't you, Dick? You can take yourself out for a walk if you don't want anything to do with young Jean, but just remember what Mum said – this is our Terry's baby, come what may, and our grandchild, and there's never going to be another, not from Terry. All right, they did wrong, but it's Jean who's got to carry the can, and with our Terry not here to stand by her – and he *would* have done, you know he would – then we've got to do it in his place. So you'd better make up your mind: are you going to stop here and give the girl some support with the rest of us, or are you going to make yourself scarce?'

Their eyes met. The others watched them, knowing that Cissie rarely opposed Dick like this. Partly because she held to the view that a wife must love, honour and *obey*, just as it said in the marriage service, and partly because she had always been extra careful with Dick owing to his illness, she always tried to steer clear of arguments. But this time she was standing firm, and they could all see that there would be no moving her.

Dick saw it too. A look of wary admiration came into his eyes and he seemed to settle back in his chair. He wasn't giving in too readily, though.

'All right,' he said with a shrug. 'Have it your own way. You always do, anyway. Bloke doesn't have a chance in a house full of women.' It was an old war cry, spoken usually in jest, and they looked at each other a little uncertainly and then decided to ignore the touch of bitterness in his tone and take it as one now. They smiled and Cissie leaned across and patted his knee.

'That's better,' she said, and gave him her loving smile. 'Now we can start to think what to do next.' She turned to Jean and asked tentatively, 'How about your mum, Jean? How's she taking it now?'

Jean lifted her shoulders hopelessly. 'She's either going on and on at me or she's not speaking to me at all, and I don't know which is worse. All the usual things: always brought me up to be decent, what will the neighbours say, never be able to hold up her head again in public . . . And then she starts to cry, and she won't let me say anything, or even touch her, and after that she goes out to the kitchen and won't speak to me. She won't even let me help get dinner ready. It's as if she's pretending I'm not there – don't even exist.'

There was a note of real pain in her last words and Polly experienced a moment of insight into the girl's frightened mind. Poor little mite, she thought compassionately. She's lost the man she loves – and Judy and me both know what *that* feels like – and on top of that she's in the worst trouble a girl can be in, without any chance of her chap standing by her, and her own mother's trying to make out she doesn't exist. She doesn't know where to turn.

She went swiftly across to Jean and put her arms around her. 'Well, you exist here,' she said firmly, 'and we'll help you all we can. Now, what we've got to do first is think what you want to do, and then see how you can do it. That's the best way, isn't it?'

'Trust you, Polly,' her mother said admiringly. 'You could always see right to the nub of things.'

'Well, being in the WVS helps,' Polly admitted. 'You get used to solving problems. Now, what do you want most, Jean – apart from what we all know you can't have,' she added hastily as Jean's eyes filled with tears. 'We've all got to face up to not having our Terry back again.'

'I want to keep my baby,' the girl whispered. 'Terry and me were going to get married the next time he came home. It would have been all right then, and we'd have been a family.' She raised anguished eyes to Polly's face. 'I can't lose our baby as well as Terry. I *can't*.'

'No, you can't,' Polly said. She looked around at the others. 'You can all see that, can't you? She can't give the baby away. And we don't want her to. It's Terry's.'

Nobody spoke for a moment, and then Judy said a little plaintively, 'I wish somebody'd tell me what you're all saying.'

As if it were a relief, they all began to talk at once, and Judy shook her head helplessly. 'It's no use! You *know* I can't hear you. Write it down, someone – please. Oh,' she clapped her hands over her ears, 'it's awful not being able to

327

hear. You just get left out of *everything*, and I'm *fed up* with it!'

'Judy, I'm sorry,' Polly said, and found some paper. Hastily, she wrote a brief account of what was happening, finishing with the words, *and we're going to help Jean all we can*. Judy read them and nodded.

'That's all right, then. So what are we going to do?'

'That's what we've got to decide,' Polly said, remembering to look at her and speak clearly. Judy could still not lip-read a great deal, but could usually manage to pick up the gist, as much from the speaker's expression as from the carefully articulated words. Polly looked at Jean, who was controlling her sobs and wiping her eyes on an already sodden handkerchief. 'Now then, Jean. You want to keep your baby. What we've got to do is work out how you can do that.'

Jean nodded. 'But I don't see how,' she whispered. 'If Mum says I've got to go, and you can't have me here, what am I going to do? There's nowhere else I can think of.'

'Are you sure your mum won't come round? It's early days yet, and it must have been a shock for her.' Cissie spoke kindly, but with some feeling for the other mother. It had been a shock for her, to know that Terry had gone against his upbringing, and it was all the worse when it was a daughter, who would carry the evidence of her wrong-doing. 'What about your dad?'

'Oh, Dad's all right. He's upset, I know he is, but,' she glanced at them apologetically, 'he's more angry with Terry than he is with me. He hasn't said too much about that because of Terry being killed, but I know he is. I've told him it was just as much me as him,' she added.

Dick cleared his throat. 'Well, I can understand that. I know how I'd feel if some bloke had taken advantage of one of my girls and then left her in the lurch.' There was an immediate outcry from all except Judy and he raised one hand. 'All right, all right, I'm not saying that's what our

Terry did, but I can understand Mr Foster thinking that way. Any father would.'

'So you agree we've got to do what Terry would do if he was here?' Cissie challenged him. 'You're ready to stand by and help Jean?'

Dick glowered for a moment, then said, 'I've already said so, haven't I? Course I will!' He glanced at the girl. 'I won't say I'm pleased about what you've done,' he said heavily, 'and if our Terry was here I'd give him the rough edge of my tongue. But there's no doubt he'd have stood by you and married you if he was here, and since he isn't nor ever will be,' a flicker of pain twisted his lips but he went on with determination, 'then we'll look after you and the baby as best we can. Only it's like Polly says, we've got to work out how to do it. I don't see how we can have you here, not without someone having to sleep out in the shed!'

The little flash of humour made them all smile and eased the tension. Cissie went out to the scullery to make some tea, and Polly said, 'How are you feeling in yourself, Jean? Have you been to a doctor yet?'

Jean shook her head. 'I've felt really well. To tell you the truth, I never even realised what had happened till I'd,' she glanced at Dick and blushed, 'till I'd missed twice. Then I started to wonder, but I still didn't think it could be true. I was never sick, or anything like that. I did feel a bit tired for a while, but that passed off and I felt better than ever. And then when I missed again – well, I felt too scared to go to a doctor. I suppose I didn't want to know it was true.' She looked round at their faces. 'It is true, though. I know it is, and soon everyone else will know as well.'

'Well, there's nothing we can do about that.' Polly spoke briskly. If there was one thing she'd learned during her service with the WVS it was that problems were best solved by looking at them straight in the face, without emotion. 'If you're going to keep this baby, everyone's going to know anyway, and the sooner the better if you ask me. They won't have so much time to wonder and gossip, and they can start getting used to the idea. I tell you what, Jean, you're not the first girl to be caught like this and you won't be the last. I reckon there'll be plenty more in the position you're in, with a baby whose father's never coming home. As for those folk who look down their noses and cross the street when they see you coming, well, all I can say is, good luck to 'em and it makes more room on the pavements for the rest of us!'

Everyone else laughed. Judy looked at them and opened her mouth in exasperation, but Polly cut in swiftly. 'I'm sorry, Judy, I can't write it all down. We're just saying we'll do all we can to help Jeanie, that's all.'

'But you *laughed*,' Judy said. 'You all did. You made a joke and everyone else laughed, and I don't know what it was. It's the worst thing of all,' she added, 'not knowing what jokes are. I never get anything to laugh at now.'

There was a brief silence. Then Polly wrote down some words quickly and Judy read them and flushed with anger. She bit her lip, and then sighed and nodded.

'Sorry, Poll. You're right, I'm getting sorry for myself. And it's Jean we've got to be thinking about.' She turned to Jean. 'Look, I was wondering – if you want to go away, maybe we could ask Mrs Sutton to have you for a while. She's our Sylvie's foster-mother, out at Ashwood. I've just come back from there and she's ever so nice.' She looked at Polly. 'What d'you think?'

'Well, it's an idea,' Polly said. Cissie came in with the tea and passed cups round. 'Judy just suggested Jean might go out to the Suttons'.'

'I know, I heard her.' Cissie sat down again. 'But would Mrs Sutton want her? Not that she'd be nasty at all,' she added quickly. 'I mean, I haven't met her myself but Judy and Polly both say what a nice woman she is. But she's already taken our Judy in, and I don't know that we could ask her to take Jean. She's not running a convalescent home, after all. And she couldn't do it for nothing. Where would the money come from to pay her?'

'And Jean would have to sleep in with Sylvie,' Polly added dubiously. 'She hasn't got another spare room.'

Jean sipped her tea. She was looking better now, the colour back in her cheeks, although her eyes were still swollen. It would be a day or two before that went down, Polly thought, even if she didn't cry any more, and she probably would. 'What about your job?' she asked suddenly. 'Do they know why you haven't gone in to work today?'

Jean nodded. 'Well, they know about Terry, of course, because that's where I was when Mr and Mrs Taylor came to tell me. And I think Miss Anstruther must have realised, when I fainted. She's passed one or two remarks lately about my figure. I needed a new black frock for working in the shop, and I had to have a bigger size. She's been putting two and two together for a week or two now, I think.'

'What will she do? Will she let you go on working there?'

'I don't know,' Jean said miserably. 'She might if I was in the office or the stores, but I don't know about serving the public. It gives the shop a bad name, see.'

'Perhaps she'll let you change over to something else.'

'But I couldn't work in the stores because of lifting things,' Jean pointed out. 'And I don't know anything about office work. I can't type, and I don't understand invoices – and they're not going to teach me, are they, not when they know I'll have to leave soon anyway.'

'But you're going to need a job afterwards,' Polly said. 'Will she take you back then?'

'I don't know,' Jean said again. 'And anyway, I'll have the baby then, won't I? I don't know what I'll be able to do.'

They gazed at her, beginning to realise the difficulties of her situation. Then Judy was struck by an idea.

'But you'll be eligible for evacuation! If you've got a baby, you can go out to the country. You can go to Ashwood, if there's anyone who can take you in, and Mrs Sutton will help look after you, and you can see Sylvie too. I know you've still got to pay the billeting money,' she added doubtfully, 'but can't you get National Assistance or something?' She looked at Polly. 'They'll know at the office, won't they?'

'Of course they will. And even if there isn't anything official, the WVS will help. It's what we're for. One of the things we're for, anyway. Look, I'm going in tomorrow, I'll find out whatever I can and come straight round to your house to tell you, Jean. That's if it'll be all right to do that,' she added, remembering Mrs Foster's attitude.

'It'll be all right,' Jean said. 'I still live there, after all. At least, I suppose I do.' Her mouth creased. 'I don't think Dad will let Mum turn me out that easy.'

'Poor Jean,' Cissie said after she had gone. 'It's only when you start to think about it that you realise what a terrible position she's in. In a lot of ways, it'd be easier for her to give the baby away and start afresh.'

'And could you have done that?' Polly demanded. 'Given Judy or Terry away, just because it wasn't convenient to have them? I know I wouldn't ever have parted with my Sylvie, no matter what it cost to keep her. And now I've had to part with her anyway,' she added sadly, thinking of the months it had been since Sylvie had lived at home and wondering how many more months, perhaps even years, it would be before she could return. 'But at least she's still mine.'

Cissie glanced at Judy and her eyes filled with tears. 'You're right, Polly. I know it would have torn me to bits to let my babies go. But this is different, isn't it? We didn't have the problems Jeanie's got.'

'It'd still hurt her just as much,' Polly said. 'Maybe even more.'

They were silent for a while. Cissie gathered up the cups and took them out to the scullery. Judy joined her there and said, 'I'll do these, Mum, and then get the supper ready.

You go in with the others. You've got a lot to talk about and I'm not much use at that, the way I am.'

'Judy, don't talk like that! Of course you're useful. Why, it was you who suggested Jean could be evacuated.' But Cissie knew that Judy was right. It was too difficult to include her in discussions between several people, and you couldn't write down everything. She laid her hand on her daughter's arm. 'I know how hard this is for you, love,' she said, speaking slowly. 'It's horrible for you. I just wish there was something we could do about it.'

Judy gave her a wry smile. 'Well, the doctor said it might come back all of a sudden, so perhaps it will. She said a sudden loud noise might do it – or a shock – or just nothing at all. I might wake up one morning and be able to hear all the rude things you're saying about me!'

Cissie laughed, even though she felt more like crying – a sensation that was becoming all too familiar these days – and went back to the others. Polly and Alice were discussing the possibility of Jean's being evacuated, while Dick listened. He was looking grey again, Cissie noticed, and breathing as if it hurt.

'Are you all right?' she asked, and he nodded impatiently. She folded her lips and made up her mind to keep an eye on him. The last thing they wanted now was for Dick to be ill again. They had quite enough on their plates, without that.

'Well then,' she said, sitting on one of the straight-backed dining chairs and looking around the room. 'Let's start making plans. We're going to have a new baby in the family, and I for one want to make sure we're ready to welcome the poor little mite as we should!'

Chapter Twenty-Five

When Polly arrived at the Royal Beach next morning, she went straight to the Lady Mayoress's office and asked to speak to her. The Mayoress was busy with a list of all the personnel of HMS *Hood*, trying to arrange visits to all the families who lived in Portsmouth, but she stopped what she was doing to listen to Polly's story.

'Jean knows they did wrong,' Polly finished. 'But I think it's understandable, madam, and I don't suppose they're the only ones, not by a long chalk. It was just Jean's bad luck to get caught.'

The Mayoress nodded. 'Poor child. She must be in a terrible state, hardly able to grieve properly over losing her sweetheart because of the trouble she's in. Well, it won't help anyone to be judgemental over it, Polly. What we have to do now is think how best to help her. You say she's determined to keep the baby?'

'Yes, madam, and we want to help her. It's our Terry's baby, you see – none of us wants it to go to strangers.'

'You realise that the baby itself will face difficulties as it grows up? There's a terrible stigma to being illegitimate.'

'I know, madam.' Polly flushed at the use of the word they had all avoided. 'But there's going to be such a lot of kiddies without fathers, we thought perhaps after a while nobody will think too much of it. I mean, they'll just think he was lost in the war. As he *was*. And Jeanie could call herself Mrs, couldn't she? It's not against the law, is it?'

'No, although she couldn't use it on legal documents. Well, those are problems for the future. So long as you're all aware of them.' The Mayoress tapped her teeth thoughtfully with her pencil. 'Now, you've suggested the idea of evacuation. I think that would be a good idea, if only for the girl's own safety and that of her child. And she'll certainly be eligible.'

'It's money that's the problem,' Polly ventured. 'She doesn't think she'll be able to keep her job at the Landport, you see, and we haven't got much to spare. I don't know about her own family, but if Mrs Foster isn't willing to help . . .'

'I expect she'll come round,' the Mayoress said. 'Mothers usually do, especially once the baby's born. It's fathers who are usually the problem. But I think we can find some help for her in one of our funds, and I'm sure she'll be entitled to National Assistance. The people to ask about that are the Citizens' Advice Bureau. The Misses Kelly will know, although I believe they're snowed under with requests for help.' She sighed. 'One Bureau in a city that needs at least five! If only we could have a little respite – just time to get ourselves properly organised. We seem to lurch from one crisis to another.'

Polly had heard a great many complaints about this. The townspeople of Portsmouth were forever grumbling about the Council offices being 'all the way out at Southsea' and the Citizens' Advice Bureau practically unfindable. They seemed to have no idea how difficult it was to run a city in wartime, especially one that had been bombed as heavily as Portsmouth. You never knew what was going to happen next, what new situation would face you, what needs there would be. She thought of the plans the authorities had made to treat the injured and bury the dead – hundreds of thousands of them – when what they should have been planning was how to help the homeless. But how could they have known that? There had never been a war like this in the entire history of the world. No country had been subjected to these massive and sustained air raids. Nobody had known what the effects would be.

'Nobody knew there was going to be a war,' she said, trying to comfort the other woman. 'Nobody knew we were going to have to do all this.'

'But we *should* have done! We were warned enough. Mr Churchill himself tried to warn us, and what happened? He was laughed at. Treated with scorn. Now he's leading us, and we all realise at last what a great leader he is – but we could have lost him, you know, Polly. We could have thrown away the only man who seems able to reach the people, to touch our hearts and to give us strength to carry on.'

She sighed again, her face creased with worry, and then seemed to pull herself physically together. With a brisk lift of her head, she looked up at Polly and said, 'Well, we must get on. We'll do whatever we can to help your brother's fiancée. And we have a lot of other tasks this morning too, but before you go, tell me about Judy. How is she now?'

'I'm not sure really,' Polly said, pausing in the doorway. 'She came home as soon as we told her about Terry, of course. I think it did her good, being in the country – she looks a lot better – but she still can't hear anything much, and it's making her so miserable. She feels left out of everything. She's been working out there though, making camouflage, and collecting moss for soldiers. It heals their wounds, apparently. I'm not sure *I'd* want a lump of dirty moss slapped on a cut, mind you, but they say it really helps to heal them.'

'Well, I'm sure it will be good for her, working out in the fresh air. When is she going back?'

'Oh, she's not. She wants to stay at home now. She says she'd like to come back to work if you'll have her.'

'Have her? I'll be delighted. Tell her to come in as soon as she feels ready and we'll find work for her to do. And now,' the Mayoress drew a pile of papers towards her 'I really must attend to these. Thank you for coming in, Polly.'

'Thank *you*, madam.' Polly withdrew. Evidently there was going to be no driving for her to do that day, so she began to collect tasks from the other women in the office and then went to her desk.

Judy was planning to fetch Jean and bring her out to Southsea that afternoon. Before beginning on any of her tasks, Polly started to investigate the help that Jean could ask for, and the possibilities of evacuation.

If she could go out to Ashwood, or Bridge End, where there were already people they knew, Polly was sure she would find kindness and warmth. Country people, in her experience, were more likely to accept you for what you were and not what they might think you ought to be. There, with people like the Suttons, she would be able to grieve properly for Terry and look forward to the birth of her baby – the baby called Hope.

Crete had fallen and, as Dick had predicted, there was an evacuation not very different from that of Dunkirk. Fighting on the island had been bitter, but the German invaders had been too powerful and the Royal Navy had been sent in to bring out as many men as possible. This time, many of the Allied soldiers who were killed or rescued were from New Zealand and Australia. Once again, there were stories of heroism and suffering and, once again, there was grieving over men who had been lost.

'I can't bear to think about it,' Cissie said. 'Mothers in Australia and New Zealand feeling just as bad as me and all the rest of us who've lost their boys. Wives like you, Polly, and girls like our Judy. Kiddies like Sylvie.'

'Don't,' Polly begged. 'It's no good going on like that, Cis. It just makes you feel worse. You've got to try and think about other things.'

'Other things?' Cissie was pale and drawn. Her eyes were

337

dull and her hair lank and straggly, with signs of grey. 'How can I think of other things? I've lost my boy. The boy I carried for nine months inside me, and fed with my own milk, and loved and looked after – he's *gone*, Polly. I'm never going to see him again. He's never going to come through that door again and say, "Hello, Mum," and sit down at that table and eat the food I've cooked for him. He's never going to ask to scrape out the bowl when I've made a cake, or take the last roast potato, or bring in the coal or—'

'*Cissie*! You've got to stop this or you'll make yourself ill.' Polly cut in across the rising voice and put her hands on her sister's shoulders. 'Look, I *know* what you're going through – I've already lost my man, remember? And I've had to send my little girl away to strangers, not knowing when I'll be able to have her with me again. I'm upset about Terry too – we all are. But we've got to carry on. Going over it all, over and over again, won't do any of us any good. It won't bring him back. What we've got to think about now is the living. The rest of us here – the things we can do to help. And Jean and her baby,' she added in a low voice.

Cissie stared at her and then seemed to sag. She turned away and sank into a chair.

'I know, Poll. I know all that, but it just comes over me. I've *got* to cry for him. I've got a *right* to cry for him – he was my boy. I never expected him to die before me. I thought he'd still be alive when I went myself. I thought he'd always be here – a part of my life, a part of me. It's not what you have children for,' she said, looking up at her sister. 'Seeing them go off to war, knowing they've died, hundreds of miles away, not even able to be with them at the end. It's not what you ever think of. Not when they never meant it themselves. It's different if they went into the Forces beforehand, but when they've been conscripted . . .'

'I know,' Polly said. 'I know you've got to grieve for him, Cis. You always will – that's never going to stop. It's the

338

worst thing in the world, losing a child, but you can't let it get on top of you.'

'But I feel I want to. Just for a little while, Poll. I feel I want to let go and let it all wash over me.' Cissie put her head into her hands and rocked to and fro. 'I just want to cry and cry and cry, and there doesn't seem to be *time*. There's always so much to do, so much to worry about, and I can't even have time to grieve properly over my own boy. It doesn't seem fair.'

'Well, I think we've got to stop thinking about what's fair,' Polly said ruefully. 'Nothing's fair, these days. In fact, I wonder whether it ever was. There's always been unfair things happening, Cis.'

On the last day of May, there was another raid on Portsmouth. Two houses in Tipnor were completely destroyed and a number of others badly damaged. Once again the fire engines were out and the bomb disposal squad called in, but the residents had reached safety in their shelters and nobody was hurt. Instead, the WVS found themselves back at their old task of handing out food and hot drinks to people who were homeless, giving them clothes from the Lady Mayoress's Clothing Store, and searching for places for them to live.

The newspapers were full of the scandal of the Jewish internees who had fled from Hitler's regime and been taken to Australia almost a year earlier. Polly read it and thought of her words to Cissie, that nothing seemed to be fair. But it doesn't have to be this unfair, she thought angrily. People don't have to be this cruel to each other.

'Those poor souls!' she said indignantly. 'Kept down below decks like slaves in a slave ship, and when they got to Australia all their luggage was taken away from them and they were treated like criminals. And these are the people we're supposed to be fighting for! I don't understand it, I really don't.'

'What it boils down to,' Dick said, 'is that there's good

and bad in most countries. And I don't know what it is, but nobody seems to like refugees. It doesn't matter how bad they've been treated in their own countries, nor how much we say they ought to be helped, nobody seems to want them. It's not even as if Australia was crowded with people, like we are here – there's space enough for all.'

'I don't think it was the Australians that did this, though. It's the British soldiers who were in charge of them who've been court-martialled.' Polly sighed and folded the newspaper. 'I've had enough of reading this. It's all misery, wherever you look. Who wants to go to the pictures?'

The cinema was only partially an escape, though, for between the two films – the 'big' picture that everyone went to see and the 'little' picture that you saw whether you wanted to or not – they sandwiched the *Pathé Pictorial News*. This showed a resumé of the week's events with, inevitably, most of it about the war. The news you had heard on the wireless over the past few days came dramatically to life as you watched shots of soldiers marching in the desert, ships at sea and bomb damage. Sometimes you saw the bombs actually falling and exploding, and people clambering over the wreckage afterwards as they searched for their family, friends and belongings. The scenes were all too familiar to Portsmouth folk.

All the same, it was good to go and be entertained for a few hours and the whole family went to see George Formby when he came to the Odeon to put on a fund-raising show for air-raid victims one afternoon. He sprang on to the stage with his ukelele, singing his cheeky songs 'When I'm Cleaning Windows' and 'Sitting in the Maginot Line', and had them all laughing within seconds. They were still laughing as they came out into the sunlight after the show had ended, and returned home feeling better than they had since before Terry's death. Even Judy had enjoyed it.

Polly had received another letter from Joe Turner. He was still working in the offices at Whitehall, although he was vague about what he was actually doing. She thought of his rueful words – 'polishing up the knocker on the big front door' – and wondered what a man with only one foot could do, apart from such menial tasks. He had been down to Devon again to see his boys and said they were well and happy, spending all their spare time either helping around the farm or out on the moors playing cowboys and Indians. *They'll forget they were ever Cockneys*, he wrote wryly.

Polly thought about Joe as she went about her tasks. She could hardly believe that another man could be important to her after Johnny's death, and she reminded herself that he had offered her nothing but friendship – a shoulder to cry on, a helping hand when she'd needed it. Yet how many friends, especially ones so newly made, would have done all that Joe Turner had done? He'd come all the way from London to see her, and he'd been a real help in their time of trouble, making cups of tea, doing the veg and going out to fetch Judy home. And when he'd held out his arms to her and hugged her against him, she'd felt a deep, warm closeness between them that she hadn't known since Johnny had gone away. For a moment, it had been like coming home.

But since then, he seemed to have cooled off. His letter was no more than a letter that any casual friend or acquaintance might have written – pleasant, friendly, chatty. No more than that. No mention of another visit.

Perhaps seeing me at home made some sort of difference, she thought. Perhaps I was different from what he'd thought. Perhaps since he's been down to Devon again and seen that Mrs Ellacombe who's looking after his boys, he's got more interested in her.

It didn't matter. He was a man she'd met briefly a couple of times, had a pleasant day with and who'd been helpful to her family when they were in trouble. That was all there was to it. Probably he wouldn't bother to write again. She decided to put him out of her mind.

Judy had had a letter too. Hers was from Ben, still at school in Winchester. He wrote of school activities – lessons, exams, sports – with impatience. *Only a few more weeks to go*, he wrote, *and I can leave for ever*. He had already applied to join the RAF and expected to be called up almost as soon as the school holidays began. Judy wondered what the Hazelwoods would say about that. She was sure that Ben hadn't mentioned his plans to his parents.

It was strange, she thought, that a boy of eighteen could go to fight in a war without asking his parents' permission, whereas he couldn't get married, vote or even stay out late without it until he was twenty-one.

Chapter Twenty-Six

Life was still a lonely, silent affair for Judy. She spent her days working in the Clothing Store, keeping a check on what garments they had. It was even more important now, for on the first day of June, clothing rationing was announced and people weren't so ready to give away unwanted items. Instead, they would have to take old winter coats to bits to make new ones for children, cut down frocks that had got too tight round the bodice to make skirts, and unpick jumpers that had gone at the elbows to make pullovers or gloves. There were complaints, of course – Ethel Glaister was especially bitter about the new rules against pleats and frills – but it was just one more thing to put up with. In fact, Alice remarked, it probably didn't hit the people of April Grove as hard as the smarter ones who lived in better streets and had bigger houses. They weren't used to make do and mend, while for April Grove folk it had always been a way of life.

However, apart from the clothes rationing and a series of raids, including one night when it was announced that there had been more alarms than on any other since the beginning of the war, June did bring a few items of good news. The first was when the news ran round the Clothing Store that the Lord Mayor had been knighted in the King's Birthday Honours list.

'You mean he'll be a Sir?' Judy asked when this had been explained to her by Laura, who was also working in the store. 'Instead of Lord Mayor?'

'No, he'll still be Lord Mayor, but he'll be "Sir" as well.

And the Lady Mayoress will be "Lady", even after she stops being Lady Mayoress. Isn't it smashing!' Laura finished sorting a pile of children's jumpers and set them aside. 'It just shows that the King thinks a lot of him. It's for services to Civil Defence.'

'I've never known a knight before.' Judy's ideas of knights of the realm were mostly gained from a hotchpotch of children's stories, and legends from St George to King Arthur. She tried to imagine the Lord Mayor in armour and failed. 'Will he have to wear special clothes and go to Buckingham Palace and all that?'

'Well, to be knighted, I suppose he will.' Laura didn't know much about it herself. 'I don't suppose he'll be all that different the rest of the time.'

The *Evening News* was full of the new appointment and recounted messages of congratulation from all over England as well as running an article on all the many things the Mayor and his wife had done to help the city and its people during the hardships of the past two years. But even this news couldn't compete for long with the war itself, and it seemed almost like a deliberate insult when the Luftwaffe came again that very night and dropped high explosive and oil bombs on several of the city's military establishments, including the RAOC camp in Copnor Road where a number of soldiers were killed. The families in April Grove huddled in their shelters, hearing the bombs explode frighteningly close, and dreading the thought of being made homeless again. I couldn't bear it, Cissie thought, not a second time, and reached for her husband's hand. Alice, too, looked fearful by the flickering light of the hurricane lamp, and all three were thinking of Polly and Judy, out together in the ambulance. I don't know how our Judy stands it, Cissie thought, nor our Polly, not after what's already happened to them. They're brave as lions, the pair of them. They ought to be knighted too, only they don't knight women, but they

344

ought to get medals at least. All those girls and women ought to get medals.

However, despite the damage and the tragedy of the RAOC camp, there was not much more damage in the area and April Grove lived – as Granny Kinch put it, standing at her door as usual in her steel hair curlers – to fight another day.

'We're bound to get some good news soon,' she said staunchly. 'Bound to. Old Hitler can't have things all his own way.'

And her words were proved true only two days later, when Jess Budd came down the street in a state of high excitement, almost dragging little Maureen along by one hand, and reported that Heinrich Brunner had come home.

'I saw him out in the street first,' she told Cissie, who was scrubbing the front doorstep. 'I never even recognised him! He's gone ever so thin, and his hair's grey and he's got these shaggy whiskers, and he looks as if he's been sleeping rough. I did think he looked a bit familiar but then I thought he was some old tramp that I might have seen before. And then he came into the shop. Alice and Joy were both there, marking up the papers, the trains were late and half the paper boys hadn't turned up and Alice was saying how they'd all be late and people would be complaining – and they looked at him for a minute as if they didn't recognise him either! And he looked as if he hardly knew where he was. And then he said, "Alice, don't you know me?" and we all realised who he was. Well, you should have seen Alice Brunner's face! She looked as if the sun had come out just behind her eyes. And then he sort of swayed a bit and she came round the counter like a flash of lightning and caught him, and he said, "It's me, Alice, it's Heinrich, I've come home," and they all started crying . . .' Jess wiped her own eyes and her voice broke a little '. . . and I came away. I don't think people will be getting their papers till teatime today, if they get them at all!'

'Well, isn't that wonderful.' Cissie stood up with her scrubbing brush in her hand, gazing at Jess. 'That's really good news. It was never right, putting people like Heinrich Brunner in prison. I mean, what harm would he do? He'd been in England for years. And poor Alice has had a hard time running that shop by herself.'

'I know. Mind, I'm not sure as he's going to be much help to her, not to start with anyway. He looks as if he's going to need a bit of looking after himself. But I don't suppose she'll mind that. Just having him back is going to make all the difference.' She pulled Maureen away from Cissie's bucket of water. 'Leave that alone, Maureen. We're going to see Auntie Annie now and tell her. D'you know, Cissie, it's really done me good, seeing something nice happen for a change!'

It's done me good, too, Cissie thought, picking up her bucket and going back indoors. I just wish it could have been my Terry. It was three weeks now since the *Hood* had been sunk, and her secret hope that he might have been one of the three men saved had been dashed. Yet she still couldn't rid herself of the feeling that he might yet come back. A mistake might have been made. There could have been four survivors. One might have been taken prisoner by one of the German ships. Or he might somehow have managed to reach Greenland or Iceland and been saved by Eskimos who were even now taking care of him in some isolated igloo . . . During the daytime, she knew that none of these miracles had happened, but as she lay awake at night or sat in the Anderson listening to the drone of aircraft or the *'crump'* of an exploding bomb, anything seemed possible. Miracles *did* happen. Look at Heinrich Brunner. Everyone had thought him lost in the torpedoing of the ship that had been transporting him and other internees to Canada. Now here he was, returned from the dead. If it could happen to him, couldn't it happen to Terry?

'Heinrich Brunner's come back,' she said to her mother

and Dick as she went into the back room. 'He came down September Street looking like a tramp, Jess Budd said, and nobody knew him at first. Alice Brunner's over the moon, she's shut the shop for the day and left the papers in a pile outside for people to collect for themselves, and Jess Budd says she's sent up a tin of salmon she's had put by, for their tea.'

'I don't suppose poor Mr Brunner's seen tinned salmon for months and months,' Alice said, beaming. 'Well, what lovely news. It's like an answer to all our prayers. He never ought to have been taken away in the first place. I thought he was gone for good.'

'So did Mrs Brunner. She's been looking terrible just lately, letting herself go and leaving the shop to young Joy to manage. She'll buck up now.'

'Well, I don't know as it's something to get all that fussed about,' Dick said from his corner. He had started on a new rag rug but the canvas had slipped off his knees and was lying on the floor. 'Whether he was a spy or not, they had to intern all the aliens just in case, it stands to reason. You can't trust foreigners, not at a time like this.'

'But Mr Brunner wasn't a foreigner! He's been in England for twenty years.'

'He's a foreigner,' Dick stated. 'He's a German. He's got a German name and he speaks with a German accent. You can't get round that.'

Cissie opened her mouth to argue, then glanced at her mother and folded her lips. When Dick was in this mood, there was no reasoning with him. He knew Heinrich Brunner as well as they did, he'd been in and out of the newsagent's shop ever since he'd first come to April Grove to court Cissie, he'd laughed and joked with the man and watched young Joy grow up from a baby. She knew that deep down he agreed with them, but his mood lately had been growing more and more morose. It was as if no matter what you said, he had to take the opposite view.

It's all been too much for him, she thought, going out to the scullery to empty her bucket and start on the next chore. It's getting him down, all of it, the air raids, the shortages, and then his illness. He couldn't even get any rest from the bombing in hospital. It was enough to send anybody crackers.

Not that Dick was crackers! He was just miserable. Depressed and miserable – and who could blame him?

Jean was six months pregnant now and beginning to show. Nobody could be in any doubt about her condition and the supervisor at the shop had told her that she'd have to leave.

'It's not decent, not with mothers bringing their children in, and you getting more and more obvious, without even a ring on your finger. You'd better take a week's wages and go now.'

Jean had stared at her, shocked and hurt. 'You mean straight away? Without even time to say goodbye?'

'I don't suppose anyone wants to say goodbye to you anyway,' the supervisor said brusquely. 'You're an embarrassment, the way you are. A lot of people would have given you your cards before this.'

Jean turned and ran out of the shop. She saw some of the other assistants staring as she hurried past, and one girl put out her hand to stop her. But Jean shook her head and pushed past, the tears streaming down her face. I'll never go there again, she thought, never. I'll never buy anything in that horrible place again, not as long as I live.

On the pavement, well away from the door, she stopped, wondering what to do next. The thought of going home and admitting she'd been sacked was unbearable. She'd have to do it eventually, of course, but not now, at only half past nine in the morning. Her mother would have enough to say as it was, when she found out, and Jean didn't want to spend the entire day listening to her recriminations.

She wandered through the streets, wiping away her tears,

and after a while found herself outside the church hall that was being used for one of the Lady Mayoress's Clothing Stores. Glancing through the open door, she caught sight of Judy sorting a pile of clothes, and as she hesitated Judy looked up and saw her.

'Jean! Whatever are you doing here?' She hurried out into the sunshine, gazing at her friend in concern. 'What's the matter? You look awful. Come in and sit down – I'll get you a glass of water.' She guided Jean to a chair and pushed her into it, then disappeared for a moment, returning with a cup which she held to Jean's lips. 'Here. Sip this. It's – it's not the baby, is it?'

Jean shook her head. 'No, she's all right.' She was quite certain it would be a girl. 'Kicking me to death as usual!' She laid her hand on her stomach. 'Judy, I've been given the sack.'

'What?' Judy stared at her and Jean bit her lip. For a few minutes she had forgotten that Judy couldn't hear. She repeated her words more carefully and saw by Judy's face that she understood. 'The *sack*? But why? Because of the baby?'

Jean nodded. 'I'm too embarrassing to have in the shop any more. I knew it would happen, of course, but I didn't think it would be like this.' Her voice shook and tears brimmed over again. 'She was so horrible to me, Judy. Said I wasn't decent and that nobody would want to talk to me. She wouldn't even let me say goodbye to the others. And now they'll all know, and nobody *will* want to speak to me and – and I don't know how I'm going to tell Mum, she'll start going on at me all over again, and Dad will be upset, and – and I just don't think I can bear it, Judy. I don't know what I'm going to do.' She put down her cup and leaned forwards, sinking her face into her hands.

Judy didn't need to hear to know what Jean was saying and feeling. She knelt beside the distraught girl, putting her arms around the shaking shoulders and drawing her close.

'It's all right, Jean. It's all right. Everything's going to be all right. We'll stand by you – all of us. We'll look after you. Don't worry. Don't be frightened. You've still got us. We're your family now, too, and we won't let you down.'

'Oh, Judy.' The weeping girl turned and buried her face against Judy's shoulder. 'It's so awful. I never thought it would be like this. I never thought it would lead to all this trouble, and people hating me and not wanting to know me. And Terry would never have wanted me to do it if he'd known. We just didn't think, we wanted to love each other so much, it seemed so right and natural at the time – and now he's gone and he's never coming back.' Her words were lost in a series of hiccuping sobs.

'Sssh, sssh, it'll be all right.' Judy held her close, murmuring comforting words. One of the other volunteers came over and looked questioningly at her, and she shook her head. 'It's all right, thanks. I can manage. I know her. It's all right, Jean, we'll look after you. Don't worry, it's going to be all right, I promise.'

Gradually, the sobs eased. Judy found a hanky and pressed it into Jean's hand. Jean wiped her face and blew her nose, then drew in a shaky breath. She looked at Judy.

'I'm sorry. I shouldn't have come here, making a scene.'

'Don't be silly.' Once again, Judy could guess at what she was saying. 'Look, you just sit here and rest for a bit. I've got to finish this job and then I'll take you home. *My* home,' she added firmly as Jean began to protest. 'You know Mum and Gran and Polly are all on your side as well as me. Dad too,' she added with slightly less conviction. Dick seemed to veer from one point of view to another these days, for no apparent reason. 'And you know we've written to Mrs Sutton to see if there's anywhere in the village you can stay. Why, there might be a letter there now, for all we know. Anyway, you've got to stop worrying. Everything's going to be all right.'

She went back to her work, hoping that what she had said

was true. However much the family rallied round to help, Jean's path was not going to be an easy one to tread. Being an unmarried mother, even in wartime when quite a few young women were finding themselves in the same position, was no picnic. There were plenty of people all too ready to criticise, plenty who would turn the other way or cross the street to avoid speaking to the girl whose sin was so obvious. And having to manage on your own, with no breadwinner to support the family, was so difficult that not many girls even tried. They gave their babies up for adoption, hoping that the new family would be able to give the child all that they couldn't provide, and then got on with their lives and tried to forget.

I don't know how you could forget though, Judy thought as she went back to sorting children's clothes. I don't know how you could *ever* forget having a baby.

When Polly came home from the Royal Beach that day she found the whole family waiting for her, with Jean ensconced in Dick's armchair, looking pale and red-eyed. She stopped in the doorway.

'What's up? What's happened?'

'It's all right, Poll,' Alice said quickly. 'Nothing's wrong. Well,' she glanced at Jean, 'nothing too serious, anyway. Jean's been put out of her job, that's what it is. It's not as if it wasn't expected.'

'Put out? Oh Jean!' Polly crossed the room quickly and took the girl's hands. 'Didn't they even give you proper notice?'

Jean shook her head. 'Miss Browning told me I was getting embarrassing and I'd better go. She said she'd give me a week's wages, but I was so upset, I just rushed out. I suppose I'll have to go back for my cards.'

'One of us will do that,' Polly said firmly. 'You don't have to go anywhere near the place again. Spiteful old cat!'

'I don't know why she was so nasty,' Jean said woefully.

'She seemed to understand at first, when we first heard about Terry. She was so nice. But since she found out about the baby . . .'

The others glanced at each other. 'Well, you're going to have to put up with a lot of that,' Alice said reasonably. 'You've got to get used to it. It's the baby I'm sorry for.' She stopped and bit her lip, and Jean looked up at her in dismay.

'You mean people will be nasty to her as well? My baby? But it's not her fault.'

'Some people will be,' Polly said. 'There's always some people who take every chance of being spiteful. But you don't have to worry about them. Remember what we used to say as kiddies? "Sticks and stones may break my bones, but names will never hurt me!" That's what you've got to remember. And I think there's going to be more than one girl in your position before this war's over, so we're all going to have to be a bit more understanding. Anyway, that doesn't matter now. What we've got to do now is decide what's going to happen next.'

'We've been talking about that,' Cissie said. 'We think she ought to go out to Ashdown straight away. You said she could be evacuated, didn't you, Polly? And there's a letter for you here, look, with an Ashdown postmark. Maybe it's from Mrs Sutton herself with some news.'

'You mean you've been sitting here all day and never opened it?' Polly snatched the envelope. 'Honestly, I wouldn't have minded.' She tore it open and scanned the sheet of paper inside. 'Yes, it is! She says she's been talking to the vicar's wife – Mrs Hazelwood – about Jean, and Mrs Hazelwood says she can go there.' She lifted her head and looked at them with sparkling eyes. 'To the vicarage itself. Isn't that kind of them!'

'The vicarage?' Jean repeated doubtfully. 'Oh, I don't think – I mean, I hardly ever go to church. Do they know about me?' She touched her stomach. 'Do they know about the baby?'

'Of course they know about you. That's why she's offered to have you.' Polly glanced round and caught sight of Judy, sitting in the corner trying to follow the excited chatter. She passed the letter across. 'Read this, Judy. Isn't it lovely?'

'Yes,' Judy said, but there was a tinge of uncertainty in her voice. 'Yes, it is. But – I don't understand. They've already got a houseful, with Mr Hazelwood's old parents and two Army officers billeted there. The only other room is Ben's. What's he going to do when he comes home from school?'

Jean stared at her. 'You mean they haven't got room? I can't stay there?'

'Of course you can,' Polly said. 'Mrs Hazelwood says so, doesn't she?' She looked at Judy. 'Didn't you say he wanted to go into the RAF?'

'Yes, but he hadn't even discussed it with his parents. And he's not old enough. I don't understand.' She looked at the letter again. 'Mrs Hazelwood says Jean can go out as soon as she likes.'

'Then that's all right,' Polly said, and turned back to Jean. 'Is that what you want to do? Go out to Ashwood straight away?'

Jean nodded. 'Yes, but it would help if someone could go with me. I mean, I don't know anyone there and—'

'I'll go with you,' Judy said, before anyone else could speak. They weren't even sure whether she had understood Jean's plea, or whether she was still speaking her own thoughts. She looked at the letter in her hand and then at Jean. 'I'll go with you. I can introduce you to everyone. I'm not much use here, after all.' And as they all looked at her, opening their mouths to deny it, she added, 'It'll be nice to see them all again anyway.'

Then, to herself she added, *And I can find out what's happening to Ben.*

Chapter Twenty-Seven

Jean and Judy travelled out to Ashwood the next day. The Fosters had been taken aback and not very pleased to find that the whole thing had been discussed and decided without their presence, but as Jean had said, they'd made it clear that they didn't approve anyway, so what was the point? 'You'd rather I gave my baby away,' she said, wrapping her arms across her stomach. 'You'd rather I went away and had it and then came back and pretended it had never happened. Well, I *am* going away and you can pretend that if you want to, but I won't be coming back. Not until I can bring my baby with me.'

Mrs Foster had looked angry and told Jean that she wasn't going to be told what to do in her own house, and if that was the way she felt she'd better pack her things and go. And when Mr Foster tried to reason with her she had turned on him asking how Jean could possibly keep the baby, what would they live on and what, oh *what* would the neighbours say when they saw her walking down the street pushing a pram?

'That was what finished it for me,' Jean said, her face white. 'My own mother putting more store on what spiteful cats like Mrs Barrow next door and Mrs Parry over the road think than on what happens to her own daughter.' She looked at Cissie. 'You're my mum now, Mrs Taylor. You're my family.'

Cissie looked as if she might begin to cry, and Dick cleared his throat and said gruffly, 'You didn't ought to talk like that, Jean. They're your mum and dad and nothing can change that. But we'll do what we can for you, all the same. And I reckon it'll be better for you when you get out to Ashwood. There's no need for folk there to know what's happened. No need to know you're not married, I mean,' he added, glancing away from Jean's plump figure.

'No, there's not,' Alice said. 'And if you've got a ring on your finger, they won't even wonder. Here.' She pulled the gold ring from her own finger and held it out. 'Wear that. That'll put paid to any gossip. You can just tell them the truth about what happened to Terry, and nobody will ask any more questions.'

'*Mum!*' Cissie exclaimed, and Alice looked at her defiantly.

'All right, our Cis, you needn't look like that. It's not your dad's ring. It's your gran's – my mum's. I've had it on me finger since the day she died, but now I reckon it'll do more good passed down the family to Jean. I was going to offer it to Terry anyway, so she'd have had it if he'd lived.'

Jean took the ring and stared at it. It was thin, its edges soft with many years of wear, but it was still bright. Her eyes filled with tears. 'I can't take this, Mrs Thomas.'

'I've told you, I'd have given it to Terry anyway.' Nobody knew if this were really true, but Alice's look dared them to question it. 'Now, put it on – never mind if it feels like a lie. You and Terry were married in the sight of God, that's how I look at it, and you're one of the family now. And no more calling me Mrs Thomas, neither. I'm Gran to young Judy here and I'll be Gran to you as well, all right?'

'Yes, Mrs – Gran,' Jean said, and her voice broke. 'Thank you. Thank you very much.'

Jean spent the night in Judy's bed, while Judy slept on cushions on the floor, and next morning they all walked down to the little halt, carrying the two suitcases that held all Jean's belongings, with a few clothes pushed in for Judy. She was going to stay a few days, just to see Jean settled in, she said, but after the train had pulled away Polly remarked to Cissie that she wouldn't be surprised if the girl didn't stay on. 'She's never properly settled back home, you know. She seems to feel left out of things so much. It was different out in the country, where there's not so many people anyway. I reckon she felt easier there, somehow.'

'I thought she might have got her hearing back by now,' Cissie said. 'The last doctor she saw said there was nothing really wrong with her ears. It was to do with the blast – a sort of shock.'

'I can tell you what it is,' Dick said. 'It's nerves. It's like she doesn't *want* to hear any more.'

'Dick!' Cissie said. 'How can you say that? Of *course* she wants to hear! It's awful for her, being deaf. Anyone can see that.'

'I don't mean it's deliberate. She can't help it. But it's like we had in the First War – shell-shock. That night it happened,' he looked at Polly, 'there was a lot of noise, wasn't there? Explosions and ack-ack and planes going over, all that sort of thing.'

'Of course there was. And buildings crashing down, and flames crackling and roaring – no end of din. But—'

'And then you were buried and she thought you were dead. Well, I think she *was* deafened to begin with, same as a lot of people are when bombs drop, but it didn't wear off like it usually does because she found out that if she was deaf she didn't have to hear all those things that reminded her of when she thought you'd been killed.' He stopped. 'You don't have to stare at me like that. I just think that's what it is, that's all. I've thought so all along, to tell you the truth. And you know what she's always been like about being shut in small spaces. Well, I reckon that was what it felt like to her then. Shut in, and all that din going on round her.'

'Dick!' Cissie said again. 'Wherever did you get all them ideas?'

'I heard a talk about it on the wireless. This what d'you

call 'em, psychologist, he was talking about nerves and what we used to call shell-shock, and the way he explained it, I thought, That's what's happened to our Judy. Only it was just after that I got pneumonia so I never got a chance to say nothing, and I didn't think you'd believe me anyway. But I think that's what it is, all the same.'

'I suppose it might be,' Polly said thoughtfully. 'But if it is, will she ever get better? I mean, if there's nothing actually wrong, and she doesn't know she's doing it, how can she ever stop? I can't see her believing it, Dick. She'd be ever so upset if you told her she could hear if she wanted to. She'd think you were saying she was putting it on.'

'That's why I've never said nothing,' he said. 'And I don't know what would make her better. Maybe another shock, but I don't know what sort. Bombs'd only make it worse.'

'Rest and peace and quiet, that's what'll help her,' Alice said firmly. 'I don't know if Dick's right or not, but I do know they're what our Judy needs most. I hope she does decide to stay out in the country. It's the best thing for her, whichever way you look at it.'

Judy thought so too, as the train chuffed to a halt at Ashdown station. She stood up and got Jean's suitcases down from the rack, then helped her drag them out on to the platform. They stood for a moment breathing in the fresh, warm air, and Jean smiled.

'It's lovely,' she said, turning to face Judy so that her lips could be read. 'I can hear birds singing – oh, Judy, I'm sorry!' She put her hand to her mouth. 'I never meant—'

'It's all right.' Judy wasn't sure what she'd said anyway, only that it was clearly something to do with hearing. She picked up the cases. 'Come on. It's not far to walk.'

'Well, you can let me carry one of the cases then.' Jean took the lighter one and they strolled along between the leafy hedges. There had been primroses and violets here a few weeks ago, Judy reflected, and bright, sunshiny celandines. Now the grass had grown and a froth of wild parsley on both banks almost met across the narrow way, so that it was almost like walking through a shower of foam. Small birds were dustbathing in shallow potholes, and a rabbit scuttled into a hole as the two girls rounded a corner. Above them, the sky was a deeper blue than it had been in the spring, and the sun hotter. You don't notice the seasons half as much in a town, Judy thought, yet here everything seems to have changed in just a few weeks.

The vicarage garden had changed too. The big vegetable patch was flourishing, with rows of lettuces already big enough to pick, and runner beans climbing vigorously up a row of tall poles. A shorter row was bushing out with peas and there were several furrows of potatoes which had already been dug over, and a line of feathery carrots. Judy looked at them enviously. Some of the men in April Grove had allotments and grew vegetables like these but Dick had never been strong enough to do heavy gardening, and in any case until they'd moved to Alice's house they'd lived too far away. Except for a few things Alice and Cissie had planted in the small garden at the back of the house, the Taylors were dependent upon vegetables from Atkinson's, the greengrocer's in September Street.

'You're going to eat well here,' she said to Jean. 'It'll be good for you and good for the baby.'

She opened the small wicket gate into the patch of garden that the Hazelwoods had kept for relaxation. Here too the flowers had grown and the apple trees had lost their blossom and now bore small green fruits. Beneath the one where she had been sitting on the day that she had first met Ben, there was a deckchair and at the sight of it, Judy stopped short.

'Ben!'

The lanky figure stretched in the chair stirred. A pair of dark, rather heavy brows lifted enquiringly and bright blue eyes met hers. The wide mouth spread into a curling grin and Ben unfolded himself and came to his feet.

'Judy! I thought you were never coming.' He pulled her into his long arms and hugged her tightly.

Judy, laughing, expostulated, 'Ben, don't be silly. What are you doing here? Shouldn't you be at school? Oh, it *is* good to see you.'

He let her go, making a rueful face. 'Well, that puts me in my place. *Shouldn't you be at school*, indeed! Just when I was hoping to impress this lovely lady you've brought with you.'

'I don't know what you're saying but I'm sure it's ridiculous,' Judy said firmly. 'Ben, this is Jean Foster. She's come to stay here for a while. But we thought – well, *I* thought you'd be away at school. I thought she'd be having your bedroom.' She stopped, feeling her face turn pink, and Ben laughed.

'Well, so she can.' He spoke clearly so that she could understand. 'I'm leaving today – that's why I was hoping you'd arrive this afternoon. I didn't want to miss you.'

'Leaving?' Judy stared at him. 'Going back to school, you mean?'

He sighed. 'There you go again. No, I've left school. I've joined the RAF.' Excitement broke out over his face. 'I'm going to train to be a pilot, Judy! A *pilot*!' He spread his arms and tilted from side to side, like a small boy playing Spitfires, then flung his hands skywards. 'I'm going to be up there, flying my own aeroplane and doing my bit for the war at last!'

Judy stared at him. Even when the words escaped her, it was easy to understand what Ben was saying, and how pleased he was to be saying it. But Judy couldn't feel pleased for him. A cold fear settled round her heart. Not another one going off to be killed, she thought. Not another boy like Sean and Terry and Johnny, setting off full of hope and courage, to die in some horrible way without ever having really had his chance at life . . .

Ben had turned to Jean and was shaking her hand, obviously welcoming her to the vicarage and Jean, who had been standing shyly by, was flushed and smiling as she responded. Judy wondered how much he knew about her condition. Had his mother and father discussed it in front of him? Did he know enough to notice that she was pregnant? She watched them a little sadly, the boy who was about to risk his life and the girl who had lost her sweetheart. It all seemed so peaceful and innocent, standing in the sunshine in this tranquil garden, yet the shadow of death was reaching out to them both.

'What am I doing, keeping you standing out here?' Ben exclaimed, picking up both suitcases. 'Come in and we'll find Mother. She'll want to make you a cup of tea or a glass of lemonade or something. It won't be real lemonade, of course,' he went on, striding off towards the French windows. 'We can't get lemons now, although I did hear a consignment of oranges has arrived in Southampton. But the stuff we make with those crystals isn't too bad.' He went on talking as he led them through the cool house, but for once Judy didn't feel left out. She looked about her, glad to be back here, glad to be at Ashdown, glad to be with Ben.

I've missed them all while I've been back in Portsmouth, she thought with some surprise. I've missed the peace and quiet. And then she caught herself up in surprise.

How could a deaf person say that she missed the peace and quiet?

Back at the Royal Beach, Polly was kept busy with a variety of jobs. Sometimes she found herself driving round the city all day, delivering messages or packages, at others she was in one of the Clothing Stores, or on another day she might be driving the Lady Mayoress or some important visitor. There were no more trips to London, however, and Joe Turner didn't seem to be likely to visit Portsmouth again.

Polly had tried to put him out of her mind, but without

success. There was nothing special about him, she told herself – he was no oil painting, he was several years older than she, and he was a widower with two sons to bring up. Yet his face was friendly, his eyes warm and his presence comforting. She could not forget how he had taken her into his arms to comfort her, and how she had felt as if she had come home. Oh Johnny, she thought, would you mind very much? Would you be very hurt if I found someone else to love? It wouldn't make any difference to you and me – I could never forget how we loved each other. But there are so many years ahead, so many years to spend alone, and if I could just have the sort of comfort Joe Turner gave me, it would make the years so much easier to bear.

And then she shook herself. Joe Turner had never given her any reason to suppose that he wanted or would offer anything more than friendship. And look at the last time he came here – flung headlong into a family crisis, sent off into the countryside to fetch home an unknown girl, and one who couldn't even hear him when he talked to her? He wasn't likely to risk that again!

Deep in thought, she mounted the steps to the Royal Beach and jumped, startled, as someone touched her on the arm. She looked up and recognised the young Observer who had been stuck in the lift with Judy.

'Hello, you're Chris Barrett, aren't you?'

'That's right,' he said, 'and you're Mrs Dunn – Judy Taylor's aunt.'

'Polly,' she said, smiling at him. 'I feel we're almost family after what happened to you and Judy.'

He looked rueful. 'I'm never going to hear the last of that. It would start at just that moment! I never meant to embarrass her, you know, Mrs Dunn. I didn't even mean to make a pass – it just happened. We were talking, and then—'

'It's *Polly*. Please.' She hesitated. 'I think you should forget about that. It wasn't really that important, after all.'

'I know.' He lifted his shoulders. 'I suppose I ought to put Judy out of my mind – I know she's engaged – but somehow, I can't. How is she, Mrs Dunn? Is she all right? Will she get better?'

Polly stared at him. 'Better? You mean her ears? Well, we hope so, but nobody really knows. But – what was that you said about her being engaged?'

'Well, she is, isn't she? She was wearing a ring anyway, that day in the lift.' He stared at her, a small frown creasing his brows. 'She said she was going to tell me about it – we were going to go out together, but it was the Sunday of the big raid and I had to stay on duty. And after that – well, she wouldn't see me again. And I've been away for a while, on a training course. When I came back, I didn't know what to do next.'

Polly remembered Judy coming home a few days before the raid, different somehow, her eyes brighter and her face more alive than it had looked for weeks. Was that because she had made a date with Chris Barrett? Was it then that she had moved Sean's ring over to her right hand? Had she been going to tell Chris about the young Irish sailor?

But if so, they had never had their date and she had never told him. Polly remembered the young man's attempts to come and see Judy in April Grove, and her refusal even to go to the door. Perhaps she had regretted agreeing to see him. Or perhaps she really did believe he would no longer be interested in her. And then she'd moved the ring back again.

'Judy was engaged,' she said, making up her mind. 'But her fiancé died – he was lost at sea around the time of the first Blitz. I expect that was what she was going to tell you.'

He gazed at her. 'So we could have gone out together. She wasn't being disloyal or anything. But why won't she see me again? What happened to make her decide not to have anything more to do with me?'

'It's not just you,' Polly said gently. 'She's had a bad

time. That's why we got her to go out to the country – for some peace and rest. You see, she's not as strong as she likes to think. She has this terrible fear of being shut in.'

'I know,' he said. 'She was scared stiff in the lift, but she tried hard not to show it. I thought she was really brave.'

'She is, but in the Blitz that night we were trapped in a building with high walls all around. It was terrible – there was a woman dying, we were trying to get her out and then the building was bombed again – we thought we weren't going to get out at all. Judy was a heroine, she saved me. I wouldn't be here now if it weren't for her, but afterwards she seemed to go right down. The doctors say there's nothing wrong with her ears, nothing physical. And my brother-in-law thinks it's like shell-shock. It's as if she doesn't want to hear, as if she's shut everything out – the noise and the fear, everything.'

'But that's terrible,' he said. 'She's shut herself into a worse space than ever.'

'I know,' Polly said. 'That's why we're so worried about her. But out in the country – well, she seems more able to manage. She seems stronger.'

Chris nodded. Then he said, 'D'you think she'd see me if I went out there? D'you think she'd send me away?'

Polly looked at him. His fair, open face was troubled. She said carefully, 'I think you ought to leave her for a while, Chris. She needs time to get over Sean. She needs the peace and quiet of the countryside, with no more complications. Perhaps in a few weeks, if you still feel the same . . .'

'I'll still feel the same,' he said. He met her eyes candidly. 'I think a lot of Judy, Mrs Dunn – Polly. The first time I saw her, I thought, That's the girl for me. That's the girl I want to marry.' He paused. 'I don't know if she could ever come to feel anything for me, but when we were in the lift it was as if there was something between us, something special. So, I'd like to try again. I'd like to see if there is a chance. And I'm ready to wait.'

'And suppose she's deaf for the rest of her life?' Polly asked. 'It isn't easy, you know, for anybody.'

'She'll still be Judy,' he said simply. 'She'll still be the girl for me.'

Chapter Twenty-Eight

Jean settled into the vicarage more quickly than anyone had thought possible. The arrangement was that she would have her board and lodging in return for whatever household duties she could manage, and Mrs Hazelwood found herself continually remonstrating with her for doing too much. 'You're not supposed to slave from morning till night, my dear. You're expecting a baby – you ought to be putting your feet up.'

'I did.' Jean was cleaning the French windows with a screwed-up newspaper. 'I was out there in the deckchair for nearly an hour. Then I noticed the glass was all smeary where the cat was trying to get out to chase the birds, and once I'd started—'

'Once you'd started you decided to clean every window in the house.' Mrs Hazelwood took away the newspaper and spoke firmly. 'Jean, I do not expect you to work all day long. If you'll just help out a bit in the mornings with some cleaning – *light* cleaning – and doing the vegetables for lunch, that will be quite enough. I mean it.'

'But it's not enough! I know it isn't. A great big house like this,' Jean waved her hand at the sprawling Victorian house, built in an age when vicars were expected to have large families. 'It needs a lot of looking after. And I'm supposed to be working for my keep. Just doing a bit of sweeping and peeling a few potatoes isn't enough for that.'

'Well,' Mrs Hazelwood hesitated. 'If you really want to do more, you could take over the ironing. The vicar needs a clean shirt every day, and there's his dog-collars and his surplices – there always seems to be a mountain of ironing waiting to be done. But I don't want you to stand for long periods. You can sit on a high stool to do it, and you must promise me that you'll stop at once if you feel tired or your back starts to ache.'

'I'll do that,' Jean promised. 'I quite like ironing anyway. And I thought I might look after the ornaments in the morning room as well. All those lovely pieces of china – I'd really enjoy dusting them. That's if you'll trust me not to drop them,' she added hastily.

Mrs Hazelwood smiled. 'Of course I trust you, my dear. And I'd just like to say how much the vicar and I enjoy having you with us. You seem to have fitted in so well – it's hard to believe you've only been here a week. And with Ben gone, the house would seem so empty.'

Ben had written already from his RAF training camp, and seemed to be enjoying it very much. He had written to Judy as well, telling her rather more than he told his parents, and she read his letter two or three times and then put it in a drawer beside her bed. He seemed so young, she thought, so young to be a pilot and risk his life. She thought of her brother Terry, only a few years older and dead already. Ben was a bit like a younger brother; she hoped he would survive. Surely some of them must. Or would the war just go on and on until there was nobody left to fight?

There had been more raids on Portsmouth and Polly wrote to tell her that a huge bomb had fallen in Torrington Road, not far from September Street, and buried itself beneath a house. The bomb disposal squad had come to defuse it and announced that, although it was now safe, it couldn't be moved. There just wasn't time, when there were so many other bombs all over the city. It wasn't a danger to anyone so could be left where it was for the time being.

I wouldn't like it, though, Polly had written. *Imagine knowing there was a bomb under your floor! I mean, how do they know for certain it's safe?*

Towards the end of the month Hitler invaded Russia. He sent in three million troops – three *million*! Judy thought in astonishment – and kept only six hundred thousand to cover Europe and North Africa. Even that sounded a lot. Mr Churchill immediately proposed an alliance with Russia and Stalin accepted. It seemed very strange, when you remembered that Russia had once been on Germany's side, but this war seemed to grow stranger and stranger as time went on. Friends one day, enemies the next, and then the whole lot ganging up on someone else. Like children in a playground, Judy thought, only these games were much more dangerous.

Now that she was out in the country, she felt her anxiety begin to diminish again. The peace she had known when she was here before stole over her heart again, and the panic that never seemed far away when she was in Portsmouth receded. She felt ashamed, thinking of all those she had left behind to face the bombing and the dangers, and threw herself even more whole-heartedly into her voluntary work.

'You could help with the pie scheme,' Mrs Hazelwood suggested when Judy went to ask what she could do. 'We always seem to need volunteers for that.'

'The pie scheme?'

'Yes. It's called the Hampshire County Pie Scheme and it's approved by the Ministry of Food. A baker in Romsey makes the pies and we pay him threepence-ha'penny each. The public pays fourpence, so we make a ha'penny profit, which we pay into our bank account and then send on to Winchester. We're allowed to deduct our expenses – postage, telephone calls and so on. We can order up to three hundred pies a week, but if we need more we have to apply for the baker to be permitted extra fat and meat.'

'But what happens to the pies?' Judy asked when she had digested this information, conveyed by a mixture of clear speaking and written notes. 'Who has them all?'

'Oh, all sorts of people. Land Girls, farmers, villagers, old people who can't manage to cook a meal any more. The pies are very much appreciated, I can tell you. We collect them in the mornings when they're baked and take them all around the village and quite a long way into the outlying countryside. It helps the rations along and saves people cooking at lunchtime.'

'Lunchtime' to Judy had always been 'dinnertime', when she was used to having the main meal of the day. She could see that it would be helpful to farmers' wives not to have to cook a large midday meal for all the farmworkers, and would save their having to return to the house from distant fields. 'So would you want me to take pies round?' she asked a little doubtfully. 'I mean, I don't really know the area that well. I might get lost and wouldn't be able to find my way back, what with all the signposts being taken down and not being able to ask the way. And I'm not sure how many pies I could carry on my bike.'

'No, we wouldn't expect you to do that. We use one of the vans in the car pool. But if you could just take over the paperwork?'

A few hours later, Judy found herself poring over a large box filled with forms and letters. 'I can see why you always need volunteers for this,' she said ruefully, and Mrs Hazelwood looked a little apologetic.

'I know. It's dreadful, isn't it, all that paperwork just for a few pies. But the Ministry insists, and I suppose they know best.' She glanced at the heap of letters. 'You wouldn't think there was a paper shortage, would you!'

'I should think this is the reason *why* there's a paper shortage,' Judy said grimly, beginning to sort through. 'It's worse than Portsmouth Corporation!'

The pie scheme was meticulously recorded. First, there was a letter telling Mrs Hazelwood that approval had been given for Ashwood to be a part of it, and explaining the prices. Enclosed with this had been the forms for making out monthly returns which must be sent in together with the bakers' receipts and paying-in slips (in duplicate). Then

368

there was a paying-in book (in triplicate) which must be used every time money was paid into the bank. There was a licence for the baker to make meat pies, listing the ingredients he was permitted to use and a large number (including such items as syrup, table jellies and crystallised fruits) which could not by any stretch of the imagination be found in meat pies. Some of them Judy had not seen since before the war; some, like soya flour, she had never even heard of.

Well, it was probably meant to cover all contingencies, not just meat pies. She turned to the next letter, which appeared to be a stern reproof to someone for not enclosing the baker's receipt with the previous return. This was followed by an equally severe reminder that *on no account* must the baker be asked for pies beyond the number for which he was licensed, and then a request that another form be completed to show the number of pies distributed each week during the eight weeks of April and May. The weeks were numbered one to eight (that's clever! Judy thought sarcastically) and the pies should be entered in the column headed *subs. meals* (what did that mean when it was at home?) and no other entry was required, other than a signature. Judy tried hard but could not think of any other entry that the unfortunate filler-in might be tempted to make. On the other hand, she thought, maybe I can.

The correspondence went on. Someone had noticed that some months had five weeks and there was a letter about this. A form had been sent out to ask for an overdue return – there must have been quite a few, Judy thought, for them to make a special form about them – and a somewhat plaintive note that not so many pies had been distributed during the previous month. Were the people who received them less keen on the pies? Was there something wrong with the pies? Perhaps it would be better to have pies only twice a week instead of three times, or even just on Fridays. Returns would, of course, still have to be made and the money paid in as usual. Oh, and a shilling too much had been paid in last week and could the sender please deduct this amount next time. By the time Mrs Hazelwood came in again with a cup of coffee Judy's head was spinning and she felt that she never wanted to see a meat pie again in the whole of her life.

'Listen to this!' she said, barely acknowledging the coffee and biscuit that had been placed beside her. 'Just listen! *You have entered 1/- as Petty Cash and instead of deducting it from the ha'penny levy of £1.5.6d you have added it on and paid in £1.6.6d, which of course is 2/- too much, and there is also the 1/- paid in excess last month, so that altogether you appear to have paid in 3/- too much. Perhaps you will be good enough to adjust this when you next pay money in to the Pie Account.* Someone,' she said, looking indignantly at Mrs Hazelwood, 'has spent time – precious, valuable *time* – working out what's been paid in and what hasn't and where it should have been instead. It must cost more to do that than they ever get back in profit. Why do they bother? And look – just *look* at this return. It's worse than an exam. It'll take half the afternoon just to fill it in, let alone add this and deduct that, and get it all right! And it doesn't matter how often they write,' she went on, scrabbling amongst the papers, 'or what the letter's about, it always ends up with *I enclose a few monthly returns.* What do they think we do with them all, *eat* them? Or maybe they think we put them into the pies. Honestly, I can see why nobody sticks this job for long.'

Mrs Hazelwood was almost helpless with laughter. She sank into a chair and wiped her streaming eyes while Judy continued to stare at her indignantly. Then Judy's lips began to twitch and she began to giggle. She turned the box upside down and tipped the papers out on to the floor.

'There! That's what I think of that! Still, I suppose it'll have to be done, or the poor people who buy these pies will have to go without. But honestly, Mrs Hazelwood, is it really doing any good?'

'Well, it isn't as successful as it was expected to be,' the vicar's wife admitted. 'But even if only one person who needs pies gets them it will be worthwhile. And who knows what the poor woman who writes these letters feels about it all? If she believes she's doing useful work towards the war effort, then it's good for her, isn't it?'

Judy managed to get the gist of this and bent to scoop up the papers. 'I suppose so. But if they make all this fuss and write all these letters about a few pies, how on earth do they manage to run a war? Anyway, I'm sure we don't need all these letters now, Mrs Hazelwood. Is it all right if I throw the old ones away?'

'I should think so. But don't just put them in the bin, will you? They are official correspondence and we ought to dispose of them carefully. You'd better put the important ones into a box and store it in a cupboard somewhere, and then take the rest down to the end of the garden. Mr Honey's having a bonfire.'

Judy drank her coffee and sorted through the papers again, setting aside those she considered worth keeping (including the monthly returns) and piling the others on her desk. Then she set off to the end of the garden, where the ancient man who came in three days a week to tend the vegetables was stoking up a bonfire of prunings and spring clippings.

'Ah,' he said when Judy approached. 'Come to have a bit of a warm, have 'ee?' He laughed uproariously while Judy smiled politely, having no idea what he had said. He saw the papers in her arms. 'Want to put them papers on the fire?'

'Yes, please. Shall I throw them on now?'

He shook his head decisively. 'No, that'll do no good, they'll just scorch round the edges if you puts 'em on in a pile, see, and then drift about all over the village in the wind.' He tapped the side of his nose. 'Secret papers, be they?'

'Not really; no,' Judy said, catching on to the last phrase.

'But they've got to be disposed of.' She made to throw them on but the old man caught her arm.

'I told 'ee, not all in a heap. Put 'em on one be one, look, like this here.' He took a letter and crumpled it in his fist, throwing it into the heart of the fire where it caught and quickly burned away. 'See? That's the way you wants to do it.'

'All right.' Judy began to follow his example, screwing up each letter separately and throwing them into the flames. Well, that should keep the country's secrets safe, she thought, dusting her hands off and watching the last paper shrivel to nothing. I wonder what vital task I'll be asked to do next.

She stood for a moment watching the fire revert to its normal fare of twigs and dried grass clippings. To her surprise, she was feeling better than she had for some time. It's being out in the country again, she thought. The war's still on and we're all still as anxious about it, but it isn't the only thing there is. In the towns and cities, where you live in fear of bombing all the time, where you can't put your head out of doors without seeing the damage, it seems to be the only thing that matters. But out here, where you can see trees coming into leaf and vegetables growing and where an old man can spend his afternoon with a bonfire – out here, you remember what life is all about. And it isn't about war at all, not really. It's about peace.

Mr Honey was leaning on a gnarled stick, watching the flames. He feels it too, she thought. He's seen war himself – he must have been through the Great War – and he knows that it's peace which is important. He knows the truth.

He turned suddenly and looked into her eyes. For a moment, as their eyes met, they were in perfect accord. Then Judy smiled at him and turned, going back to the house to see what she might do next to help, in however small a way, so that England might once again be at peace.

Chapter Twenty-Nine

As the summer continued, Jean and Judy became closer than ever. Always friends, they were now more like sisters. And so we would have been, Judy thought, if Terry had lived.

She was now working on several different tasks for the local WVS. As well as the pie scheme, which seemed to have settled down since she had sorted out the paperwork, she had gone back to making scrim and going out on the sphagnum moss parties. Jean came too, although her figure was now making it difficult for her to bend easily, and they took bottles of lemonade and a few sandwiches and made a picnic of it.

'I never thought I'd like it in the country,' Jean said, sitting on a fallen tree and unwrapping the sandwiches. 'I always thought it was just trees and fields, with nothing to do.' She lowered her voice and glanced around to make sure that nobody was listening. 'And I thought country people were all a bit stupid. But they're not. They're nice.'

Judy's lip-reading skills had increased, particularly with people she knew well, and she understood most of what Jean was saying. 'They're just different,' she agreed. 'They've got more time, that's why they seem slow. But they're not stupid. They just know different things.'

Jean nodded. 'The children like it here, too – most of them. They've settled in really well.'

There were a number of evacuees in Ashdown. Judy's cousin Sylvie and many of her schoolmates were scattered around the village and attended classes in the local school, sharing it turn and turn about with the local children. There

had been some difficulties with this arrangement to begin
with – the local children resented the newcomers coming
into their classrooms and using their desks – but when they
realised that the new timetables meant they only had to
attend for half the day, they soon saw the advantages. Over
the months, the two factions had become warily friendly,
although the evacuees still tended to band together. It was
only natural, Mrs Sutton observed, for kiddies to stick with
their own.

The children from the April Grove area, being from a
different school, were at Bridge End. Judy went over to see
Stella and Muriel Simmons so that she could report back to
Polly and Mrs Budd. Tim and Keith Budd were there as
well, and the four children were busy picking strawberries in
the vicarage garden when Judy arrived. They looked happy
and occupied, and Judy was able to write a cheerful report
to her aunt. She saw some of the other children from the
April Grove area too – Brian Collins, living on a farm,
Sammy Hodges who was staying with a young widow, and a
cluster of others. They were wary of Judy at first, finding
her deafness difficult to cope with, but once Tim had told
them she had been in a bombing raid they looked at her with
more respect.

'Wish I could've been in Pompey in the raids,' one boy
said enviously. ''S not fair, being sent out here where there's
nothing happening. I could help, I could. I could watch out
for Jerries and put out incendiaries.'

Judy also went to visit some refugee families who were
staying in the village. The invasion of the Low Countries a
year before had brought thousands over to England, and
they too had to be billeted. There were a number in a large
country house nearby, and Judy spent one or two afternoons
a week there, helping in the kitchens. It was just another job
she could do without having to talk to people.

I wonder if I'll ever be able to hear again, she thought
wistfully. Here in the country, people seemed to have more

time to listen to her and try to communicate their own thoughts. Yet she was still miserably aware of how isolated she was, especially in a crowd. Apart from her work, she spent almost all her time alone, or with Jean or Sylvie.

Much of this time, she spent thinking of Sean. He seemed very far away now, as if he were slowly receding into the distance. She tried to recapture the sound of his voice or the look of his face, but her memory was patchy and the harder she concentrated the more difficult it became to picture him. We didn't know each other long enough, she thought sadly. There aren't enough memories. Oh Sean . . .

Another face came more readily to her mind – a fair, open face with glinting blue eyes and a laughing mouth. Irritated, she tried to push it away, but the memory of the two hours she had spent in the lift with Chris Barrett were sharper than any of those she had tried to recapture of Sean. She could recall every word of their conversation, hear every laugh as he tried to cheer her up and feel again the comfort he had given her as he slipped his arm around her to drive away her fears. And she could remember the kiss. The only kiss they had ever shared. The only kiss, she thought sadly, they ever would share, for she had refused to see him when he came to the door after that terrible raid, and by now he would have forgotten all about her.

By now, he would be kissing some other girl.

As it happened, Judy was wrong about Chris. He was not kissing some other girl. As he stood in his wooden turret on top of the Royal Beach peering incessantly over the Solent through his binoculars to watch for enemy aircraft, his thoughts were not of other girls, but of Judy herself, and he was growing more and more impatient.

'How long's it going to be before she gets better?' he demanded. 'I saw her aunt again this morning and asked her, and she says there's been no change. It doesn't seem right, a lovely girl like that deaf for the rest of her life. Can't they do anything for her?'

Spud Murphy shrugged. 'No good asking me, mate. I dunno nothing about it.'

'Well, I'm getting fed up with it,' Chris said. He stared moodily out across the glittering sea towards the Island. 'We were going to go out together. I reckon there was a good chance for us – we got on all right when we were stuck in that lift.'

'So we all noticed!' Spud said with a grin.

'I thought there was something really special about her,' Chris went on, ignoring him. He had come in for so much ribbing over that episode that he barely noticed it now. 'You know how you do, sometimes? I thought she was a real smasher.'

'Yeah, but that's months ago now. If she'd wanted to see you she'd have let you know. If you ask me,' Spud advised from a store of experience which comprised a different girlfriend every week, 'you oughter forget her and find yourself some other little popsie. There's plenty around. Come to the dance over on the Pier on Saturday, why don't you? I'll fix you up with someone.'

'No thanks. I don't want to be fixed up with someone. I want to see Judy again.'

Spud eyed him. 'Well, if it's that bad, why don't you do that? Go out and see her. Talk to her. Tell her how you feel. And if she can't hear you, tell her some other way.' He winked. 'I'm sure you can think of something!'

Chris put down the binoculars and stared at him. Then he took Spud's pencil to take his turn at writing the log and said, 'You're right, Spud! It's not very often you're right, but you're right this time. That's what I'll do. I'll go out to wherever it is she's staying, in the country, and this time I won't take no for an answer. I'll *make* her see me. If she's not interested after that, I'll leave her alone – but at least I'll have tried.'

'Atta boy!' Spud said, grinning. He picked up the binoculars and trained them on the view. 'Hey, look! What's that coming in over the Island? Is it a Dornier or a Heinkel?'

Chris grabbed the glasses back. He stared for a minute, then punched his friend on the arm.

'You twerp! It's a bloody *seagull*!'

The summer was hot and long, as if to make up for the bitter winter. In July, it was declared that London had just had the sunnicst day of the century – almost sixteen hours of it. If there hadn't been a war on, it would have meant long, lazy afternoons on the beach at Southsea or walks on Portsdown Hill. The harbour would have been filled with sailing dinghies and yachts, and the Solent would have been a mass of white sails, especially during Cowes Week when the big yacht races were held and you felt you could almost walk across to Cowes on their decks, without getting your feet wet. But all that was just a memory. The last time the Solent had been filled with little boats was during the Dunkirk evacuation, and it was now grey warships that forged their way through the Channel.

But the war was still very much on. The air-raid sirens were still sounding, although the raids weren't as heavy as before. The end of June and beginning of July saw thousands of incendiaries showered on the city and on Portsdown Hill, starting a blaze of gorse fires, and a number of high-explosive bombs were dropped into the sea off Stamshaw. In August it was announced that tunnels had been driven deep into Portsdown Hill, beneath the chalk pits, and three thousand people would be given tickets. Mothers with children, and people without their own bunked shelters would get first choice. Jess Budd, who had her baby Maureen at home, was entitled to go, and so was Nancy Baxter, who had Micky and Vera, but Jess said she was happy with the Anderson, and Nancy had her own reasons for not wanting to be stuck in a tunnel all night.

Everyone was wondering if America would come into the war. Already their aircraft were patrolling the North Atlantic, searching for U-boats, and their forces had joined British and Canadian troops in Iceland to help its defence. All young American men of twenty-one and over were compelled to register for the 'draft' and it seemed as if they might be preparing to join the Allies. Yet still they held off. The Japanese threat was one they didn't want to confront, and it was feared that if they declared war on Germany it would open the way for fighting in the Far East.

'It's all so complicated,' Cissie complained. 'The Japanese are attacking China now. I mean, what do *they* have to do with it all? Why make it all worse?'

'That's just what they want to do, isn't it?' Dick said, blowing his nose. The summer weather helped his chest but now he had hay fever and hardly dared venture outdoors to enjoy the sunshine. 'They reckon if they go into China now, while we're all busy in Europe and Africa, nobody will be able to stop them. And they don't like the Yanks having all those bases in the South Pacific, either. It's a bit too close to home for them.'

Cissie was reading the local paper. 'The *Evening News* says we've got to register for new ration books, by the end of this week, or we won't get them. What would someone do who didn't know, or forgot? Would they just starve to death?'

'Nobody'll be able to forget, with notices up everywhere and the paper putting in these big adverts,' Polly said. 'And the WVS and Citizens' Advice Bureau are helping people who can't manage on their own.' She lay back in her chair and closed her eyes. It had been an exhausting day, filled with irritating tasks that never seemed to get done properly. She had been sent on several errands, delivering messages to people who weren't there, meeting others who didn't arrive, searching for documents that had mysteriously disappeared and answering innumerable questions from Portsmouth residents who had trekked complainingly out to the Royal Beach only to find that the Council office they needed was in a different building, as often as not one that they'd passed on their way. Polly could understand their frustration but wished they could in turn understand the difficulties the Corporation had faced in finding and setting up new premises after the bombing of the Guildhall. We had to start from scratch, she thought, and we still haven't got it all organised, but they just won't accept that.

'There's a letter here for you,' Cissie said, handing her an envelope. 'Looks like it's from your friend Mr Turner.'

Polly took it and turned it over. Joe had written a few times and she'd written back, but their letters had been no more than the letters of friends – brief descriptions of their lives, mention of more important events, a joke or two. They were pleasant to receive, but didn't seem to be going anywhere and once or twice lately Polly had wondered if they were worth going on with. Yet she knew that she would miss having him in her life, however tenuously. So long as he was there, she had a small hope that one day things might change.

She opened the letter and gave an exclamation. Cissie and Dick both looked at her, and Alice popped her head round the scullery door. 'What's going on? What's our Poll squeaking about?'

'It's that Joe Turner,' Dick said. He still harboured a strange disapproval of the man his sister-in-law had met, and there was a grumbling note in his voice whenever he mentioned him. 'Been writing to her again.'

'Oh.' Alice came right into the room, wiping her hands on her pinny, and they all gazed expectantly at Polly. She looked up and met their eyes

'Well, I don't know what you lot think you're staring at! I've had letters from Joe before.'

'Yes, but you haven't looked like that before,' Alice said shrewdly. 'Come on, what's he say?'

'Like what? I don't know what you mean,' Polly said, blushing.

'Like a young girl who's just come in from her first date,' Cissie laughed. 'Come on, Polly, out with it!'

She gave them a look of exasperation. 'There's no privacy in this family, none at all. Everyone wants to know everyone else's business. Well, if you must know, he's coming down to Pompey again and wants to take me out to tea, and *that's all*. Nothing out of the ordinary in that, is there? Nothing to make a song and dance about?'

'Well, I wouldn't have said so,' Alice said, 'but it's not me who's looking ten years younger all of a sudden. More's the pity,' she added, touching her grey hair.

Polly laughed and shook her head. 'You're awful, all of you. Look, Joe and me, we're just friends, that's all. I can be pleased a friend's coming to see me, can't I, without you turning it into something more than what it is?'

'Well, maybe we are and maybe we're not,' Cissie said. 'Time will tell. So when's he coming, Poll?'

'Next Tuesday,' she said, looking at the letter again. 'He's coming down on the afternoon train and staying overnight.'

'Where?' Dick broke in. 'I hope he's not expecting us to put him up here. I hope you've told him we haven't got room, Poll.'

'Of course he's not expecting to stay here. He's been here, hasn't he? He knows what the house is like. I don't know where he's staying, he doesn't say. He just says he'd like to take me out to tea and maybe to the pictures or for a walk or something.' She raised her eyes again. 'There's no harm in that, is there? You don't think you ought to come too, Dick, just to make sure he doesn't take advantage of me?'

'There's no need to talk like that,' he began, his colour rising, and Cissie intervened hastily.

'Now, don't you two start getting all aeriated. Dick's just concerned about you, Polly, you know that. He doesn't mean anything by it.'

'Well, he doesn't have to be concerned,' Polly said resentfully. 'I'm not a young girl and he's not my father. I've been a married woman—'

'And now you're a widow,' Dick said. 'And I've got a responsibility towards you, Polly. You're living in my house –' he caught Alice's sharp movement and amended his words hastily '– all right, it's not my house now, but you were living in my house till we got bombed out, and that gives me a responsibility. I took it on when Johnny died and I'm not taking it lightly.'

There was a silence. Then Polly said in a tight voice, 'You don't have to remind me I'm a widow, Dick. I remember it every day of my life. And you don't have to take responsibility for me, either. I'm not a child, I'm thirty-six years old, I'm doing responsible work and I can take responsibility for myself, thank you very much. And if you don't like it,' she rose to her feet and looked down at him with a glint of challenge in her eye, 'maybe it's time for me to find somewhere else to live!'

She marched out of the room and they heard her feet going up the stairs. For a moment or two there was complete silence and then Cissie turned on Dick, her eyes filled with angry tears.

'There!' she said furiously. '*Now* see what you've done! And you needn't start coughing and sneezing neither, because you've brought it on yourself and just for once I'm not sorry for you. Not a *bit* sorry!'

Judy was walking home from the big house where the refugee families were living, having spent the afternoon preparing vegetables and making pastry for their evening meal of meat and vegetable pie (more vegetable than meat), when she paused on the hill above the railway cutting, and sat down in the shade of an oak tree.

The sky was cloudless and the air stirred by only the faintest of breezes. Below, deep in the cutting, the railway lines shimmered in the heat. The grass had grown long and in the fields the corn was a deep gold, almost ready to harvest. Bees hovered over the mauve and cream globes of clover, and Judy watched them wistfully, knowing that the air must be filled with their humming. I *wish* I could hear them, she thought. I wish so much that I could hear them . . .

A movement caught her eye and she saw a train pull in at the station. The ancient station master came out of his office and someone in the guard's van threw a few parcels on to the platform. Two or three passengers alighted: a man in a suit, a woman with several shopping bags, and a tall young man in RAF uniform.

Judy watched. She saw the woman drop one of the parcels and the young airman stoop to pick it up. He handed it back to her, then took two of the bags to carry. They walked out of the station and along the lane, talking animatedly.

I wonder who he is, Judy thought. For a moment, as he had first alighted, he had reminded her sharply of Chris Barrett, and her heart had skipped a beat. Surely not . . . But as she saw him walking along with the woman, carrying her bags, she dismissed the thought. It must be someone from the village, come home on leave. Her heart sank a little and she shrugged away the brief disappointment. I don't want it to be him anyway, she told herself sharply. I don't want it to be anyone I know.

The two had disappeared between the hedges that bordered the lane. Now they appeared again, directly below her, and she could see their faces clearly. The woman was a spinster who lived at the other end of the village with her elderly mother. And the young man –

'Chris!' she breathed, and her whole body turned cold and then flushed with warmth. 'Chris . . .'

'I didn't know if you'd want to see me,' he said. He'd looked

382

up and seen Judy at the same moment, almost thrusting the bags back at the spinster in his haste to come racing up the hill. He saw the incomprehension in her face and repeated slowly, enunciating his words. 'I – didn't – know – if – you'd – want – to see – me.'

'So why did you come?' He'd caught her hands, his whole face glowing with delight, and she withdrew them quickly. She felt a turmoil of strange emotions – pleasure at seeing him, wonder that he should have bothered to come, dismay and embarrassment at her own condition. I didn't want him to see me like this, she thought, and then came anger that he had caught her unawares and she hadn't had time to hide. 'Why didn't you let me know?'

'And what would you have done?' he asked simply, and then said more slowly. 'You would not have seen me. You would have hidden away. Like you did before. Wouldn't you?' He looked at her accusingly.

Judy understood. She met his eyes and said, 'Yes.'

'But why?' His frustration showed in the crease of his brows, the brightness of his eyes. 'Why don't you want to see me, Judy? What have I done?'

'It's not you. It's me. I'm *deaf*, Chris. I can't hear you. I can't hear anyone – or anything.' She waved her hand at the trees, the hedges, the railway. 'There could be all sorts of sounds – trains coming, birds singing, cows and sheep, people in the lane – but I can't hear a thing. It's just a sort of mushy sound all the time. It's horrible.' She paused and stared at him. 'It's horrible for everyone else too. Having to speak slowly, having to make sure I can see them. Even then, most of the time I can't understand them. Some people don't open their lips much, they don't make any shape at all with their words – I shall *never* understand people like that. And they have to write it down for me, and then I can't read their writing or they can't spell the words and then they're even more embarrassed. You don't know what it's like, Chris. *Nobody* knows what it's like.'

'Isn't there a sort of sign language?' he asked doubtfully. 'I'm sure I've heard of something.' Once again, forgetting already, he had spoken too quickly and Judy looked at him in exasperation.

'You see? You see how difficult it is?'

Chris bit his lip and repeated his words, determined to be understood, and Judy shrugged.

'Yes, I think so. But I don't see what use it is. It's no use just me learning it, is it? Everyone else would have to know it too.'

'I'd learn it,' he said quickly, and Judy shook her head.

'It's no use, Chris. I don't know why you bothered to come. You'd better go back.'

'No!' He was angry now. 'I came because I wanted to see you. We had a date, remember? We were going to go out together – have a walk, talk to each other, get to know each other.' Once again, he saw her look of incomprehension, and was forced to speak more slowly. 'We had a *date*, Judy. I've come for my *date*.'

Judy's eyes met his and the penny dropped. 'You said more than that,' she said dully. 'This is another thing that happens. People can't be bothered to talk properly to me. They just talk in a sort of shorthand. It's not like proper talking at all.'

Chris stared at her. Then he caught both her hands in his again and shook them. 'Judy! You've got to stop feeling sorry for yourself!' Her eyes flicked up at him again, shocked by the fierceness of his grip and the anger in his face. '*Stop feeling sorry for yourself*,' he enunciated, watching her eyes to make sure that she understood. 'Deafness isn't the end of the world. You're young – you're pretty – *I* think you're beautiful – and there's nothing else wrong with you. Being deaf isn't the worst thing that can happen to you.' He waved at the countryside about them, then put his hands to his eyes. 'Suppose you were blind. Suppose you couldn't see all this? Suppose you couldn't walk anywhere without someone to guide you?'

Judy understood his meaning. She looked down at their hands, then around at the banks. They were thick with ragged robin and campions, guelder roses and a froth of wild parsley. Queen Anne's Lace, Mrs Sutton called it. She looked at the ash trees just breaking into leaf, later than all the other trees, and caught a glimpse of a thrush sitting on a branch, its beak open and its throat swelling as it sang the song she knew she would never hear again.

'It would be awful,' she agreed quietly, 'but it's *not* as awful as being deaf. People take trouble with a blind person. They look after them and talk to them, and they tell them things they can't see. When you're deaf, people only care for a while, and after that you're left alone. You can't take part in any conversations. You can't listen to the wireless and laugh when they laugh. You can't be part of the family any more, not in the same way. You're just a nuisance.'

There was a long silence. Chris looked at her as if he didn't know what to do next. After a while, he said in a low voice, 'I care, Judy. I care a lot. I'd like to look after you, and I wouldn't leave you out of things.'

'You wouldn't be able to help it,' she said. 'Look at the Suttons – they're really kind, but they can't help leaving me out. They've got things to talk about – the farm, the war, village things – they can't just look at *me* all the time they're talking. It's the same with everyone. I don't mean they don't care,' she added, frowning as she tried to explain. 'I don't mean they're deliberately unkind. But they just can't do it. Nobody can. It's just too difficult.'

Again, they were silent. Then Chris said, 'But won't you let me try, Judy? Won't you at least let me try? May I come and see you sometimes – take you out? We could learn the sign language – we could talk then.'

Judy hesitated. She looked at the fair, open face, the anxious blue eyes, the mouth that could curl so easily into a grin, the lips that had kissed hers. For a moment, she longed to say yes, to see the face light up with joy, the eyes dance, the mouth break into a laugh. She yearned to be in his arms and to be kissed again as he had kissed her in the lift.

She took a deep breath and then shook her head.

'No. Please, Chris, don't ask me. I can't see *anyone*, not in that way. It's too hard. All the repeating and the writing down and the misunderstandings and the worry of it all. I can't do it. I just can't.' She pulled away and began to walk quickly along the lane. 'I'm sorry, Chris. I'm sorry we ever met. I'm sorry we agreed to have a date. I'm sorry you've come all this way. Please – just go away now. Forget me. There are plenty of other girls – girls who can *hear* what you say. Go and ask one of them out.' She was aware that he was close behind her and turned swiftly to face him. 'Go *away*, Chris,' she said, and pointed down the embankment towards the railway line. 'Look. There's a train coming – you can catch it now and go back to Portsmouth and forget you ever saw me. Go on. Go *away*.'

He stood his ground. 'Tell me that's what you *want* me to do,' he said and then shouted at her in his frustration. '*Tell me!* Tell me you *want* me to go away!'

Judy's eyes filled with tears. She looked into his face and said, 'There, you see? That's what it's like. That's what it *would* be like.' And then she turned and walked away from him.

This time, Chris did not follow her. He knew there was nothing more he could say. Burning with shame, his head bowed, he walked back to the station where the train was just pulling in. The station master stared at him.

'Quick visit,' he said. 'Didn't she want you, then?'

Chris gave him a furious glare and climbed aboard the train without answering. He dropped into the seat and gazed morosely out of the window. As the train pulled out of the station, he could just see the lane and there, between the froth of Queen Anne's Lace, the figure of a young woman

386

walking slowly and doggedly up the sloping lane in the opposite direction.

Chris stared at her, willing her to turn. If she does, he thought, I'll get off the train at the next station and come straight back. And this time I won't take no for an answer.

But Judy did not turn. Not until the train was almost out of sight and Chris had given up and slumped back into the seat. At just that moment, as she came to the crest of the slope, she paused and looked back and, as the train disappeared round a bend and into a wood, she lifted her hand and waved, even though her eyes were too full of tears to see.

Chapter Thirty

Joe came straight out to the Royal Beach to meet Polly from work. She walked down the steps to see him standing on the other side of the road, near the entrance to South Parade Pier, and she paused for a moment, her heart skipping a little. He was leaning on the railing, staring out to sea, and she had a moment or two to observe him. She came slowly down to the pavement.

There was nothing special about him, she thought, nothing at all. He was just an ordinary man, a friend, come to see her and take her for a cup of tea. Nothing more than that. He was certainly not in the least like Johnny, the laughing young sailor who had swept her off her feet and married her and promised to spend the rest of his life with her. He wasn't tall or handsome, he probably wasn't all that clever – but then, neither was she. I don't know what I'd do with a man who was clever, she thought.

And yet – there was something about him that quickened her heart. Something that reached out to her, something to which she responded. And when he turned and saw her standing there, the way his face lit up told her that he felt it too. And that what they shared – or could share – was not at all ordinary.

'Polly!' He crossed the road swiftly, limping a little, and she ran towards him. They met in the middle and hesitated, neither knowing quite which way to go next. A trolley-bus coming towards them sounded its horn and Joe gripped her arm and hurried her back to the pavement on the pier side, and then they stood looking into each other's eyes and laughing.

'Blimey, I thought he was going to run us down!' Joe said. 'I bet he felt like it, an' all! How are you, Polly? It's good to see you again, by golly it is.'

'It's good to see you too, Joe.' She smiled at him, and saw the warmth in his dark brown eyes. This is what's special about him, she thought. He's so warm, so good-hearted. You can see it in his face. It wraps itself around you, like a lovely blanket. Impulsively, she put both hands on his shoulders, stood on tiptoe and kissed him.

Joe looked startled and she saw his skin colour. 'Blimey, Poll, I didn't expect that. That's a real welcome, that is. Thanks.' He tucked her hand into his arm and turned to walk her along the promenade. 'Where's a good place for tea?'

'There's a café a bit further on.' They strolled along the top of the beach, arm in arm, lifting their faces to the sunshine. Once again, Polly had that sensation of being at home. 'How long are you down here for, Joe?'

'Just a day or two.' He hesitated. 'I've got summat to tell you, Poll. That's why I came. I wanted to see you – to tell you face to face, like. Then I'm going on down to Devon to see my boys.'

'What?' She stopped and looked at him, pierced by sudden anxiety. 'What is it? What's happened?'

'Don't look like that, love. It's nothing bad – at least, I don't think it is.' He grinned at her. 'But there's summat I want to ask you as well. I meant to leave it till later on, but now I've started I might as well come out with the lot.' They stopped and she felt him take a deep breath. 'D'you reckon you could get a day or two off, Poll? I mean, right now? Day after tomorrow, perhaps?'

'A day or two off?' she repeated in bewilderment. 'I might be able to. Now that all the new ration books have been issued we're not quite so pushed, though there's always a lot of work to do. But why? What do you want me to do? You're not asking me to go to Devon with you, are you?'

'That's right,' he said. 'I want you to meet my nippers. I want them to meet you.' He sighed and rubbed a hand over his face. 'I'm doing this all the wrong way round. Look, what I want to tell you is, I'm being moved. My bloke, the one I've been batman to, is going overseas with the regiment. I can't go – I've asked enough, I've told him a tin foot's as good as any other for polishing up his kit, and better if it comes to being shot again – but it's not on. So I'm coming down to Pompey – well, Gosport really – to St George's Barracks. Looks like I'll be there permanent. And that means we'll be able to see a bit of each other. If that's what you want,' he added anxiously.

'You're coming down to Gosport? You'll be just across the harbour!' A flicker of excitement ran through her. 'Joe, that's lovely! Of course we'll be able to see each other. But—'

'It's more than that,' he interrupted, taking her hands and gripping them tightly. 'See, it's like this. I've never been what they call a ladies' man. Even when I was a youngster, I was never one for clicking with the girls. I met my Rosie and that was it, we both knew straight off we were right for each other, and I never bothered with no one else.' He looked down into her eyes. 'I felt the same when I first saw you, Polly. That first time on the train, I felt it then. I didn't think it would ever come to anything, of course, 'cause I didn't think I'd ever see you again. But I just knew that you were someone I could get along with. I knew you could be special.'

Polly stared at him. Her heart was beating fast. She whispered, 'I think I felt it too, Joe. But I couldn't – it was too soon after Johnny.'

'I know. And I hadn't long lost my Rosie neither. It just seemed too soon, like you say. But when we met again, well,

I reckoned maybe there was summat in it. Summat meant. And then, when I come down and you were in all that trouble, I thought, Better back off a bit, Joe Turner, she don't want you muddling things up. So that's what I did. I just wrote to you like a pal, just to try to keep the door open. But now, seeing you again, I don't reckon I want to back off any more. And if I'm going to be down here permanent, I want to know if you feel the same. If there's any hope. 'Cause I don't think I could manage to see you regular just as a friend. I know I'd want more than that, and if it's never going to be, well, we'd be better not to start. Sorry,' he finished, 'I haven't put any of that the way I wanted to, and if you want to tell me to go to hell you'd better say so. I know I'm not the bloke your hubby was, nor ever will be.'

'No, you won't,' Polly said quietly, looking down at his hands. 'But you don't have to be, Joe. You're *you* – and that's all that matters now.' She lifted her eyes. 'I can't say for sure what's going to happen to us, but I'm willing to give it a try. Can you take it like that, Joe? No promises – just hope?'

'Hope,' he said, smiling at her. 'I like that, Polly. Hope. And will you come down with me to see the boys? It's important, see. They're mine, and if I'm going to be seeing someone regular . . .'

'You might be putting someone else into their mother's place,' Polly nodded. 'It's a test, isn't it? If they don't like me, or I don't like them . . .'

'I didn't think of it like that,' he said. 'I just wanted you to see them, and I wanted them to see you. It's not a test.'

'But you'll feel better about it if we all like each other,' Polly said. She thought for a moment, and then nodded. 'All right. I'll ask the Mayoress tomorrow if I can have time off. I'm sure it will be all right. And now,' she looked at him with a teasing smile, 'what about that cup of tea you promised me?'

'Tea?' he exclaimed, and she saw with a little leap of

delight that his face had suddenly lost its creases, the lines of worry had gone from his brow and he looked almost like a boy again, the boy he had been when he first met his Rosie, and as laughing and merry as Johnny had been when she first knew him. 'Tea? It's not tea we oughter be having now – it's bloody champagne! Pardon my French,' he added with a guilty look, and Polly laughed and took his arm again, leading him across the road.

'Tea will do for now, Joe. And the way I'm feeling, I think it will taste like champagne anyway. Oh Joe,' she drew him to a stop, right in the middle of the road, 'I *am* glad we met that day on the train!'

A honking noise made them both jump and they looked round to see a trolley-bus approaching, its driver glaring down at them. Joe pulled her quickly out of its way and they scurried across to the pavement, almost convulsed with giggles.

'It was the same flipping driver!' he panted as they reached the kerb. 'Blimey, he must think we're a couple of lunatics!'

'I feel like one,' Polly said, laughing up at him. 'I don't know what it is about you, Joe, but when I'm with you, that's exactly how I feel!'

Jean was growing bigger and heavier by the day. She still did as much as possible in the house, but Mrs Hazelwood insisted that she rest. 'Are you sure this baby's not due until September?' she asked worriedly, looking at Jean's bulging stomach. 'You couldn't have got your dates wrong?'

Jean shook her head. 'It can't be. It was just after Christmas we –' she blushed '– well, it was only the once anyway. I've never – it was the first time I ever . . .'

'All right, Jean, I understand. But I think it would be a good idea to get the midwife in to have a look at you, just the same. She'd be coming in a week or two anyway.'

The midwife was a middle-aged woman, thin as a strand

of wire, with iron-grey hair and a beaky nose. She gave Jean a quick examination, felt her stomach all over and gave a sharp nod. 'Nothing wrong there. Going to be a big lad, though. Might be a week or two early.'

'It's not a lad,' Jean said. 'It's a girl.'

'Oh, and how d'you know that? Done the wedding-ring test, have you?' Her glance strayed to Jean's left hand and Jean felt thankful for the wedding ring Alice Thomas had given her.

'The wedding-ring test?'

'That's right. You tie the ring to a bit of cotton and someone holds it over your belly to see which way it swings. If it goes backwards and forwards it's a boy, if it goes round in a circle, it's a girl. Do it now, if you like.' She took Jean's hand and made to pull off the ring.

Jean snatched her hand away. 'No! I don't want to. I don't want to take my ring off – and anyway, it's a girl.' She stared defiantly at the midwife. 'I don't need to do any tests at all. I *know* it's a girl.'

The midwife shrugged. 'Hoity-toity!' she sniffed. 'Well, have it your own way. But if it's a girl, it's a mighty big one. You'd better get yourself decent again. I'll come back in a fortnight, see how you are.'

Jean watched her go, half-annoyed, half-frightened. Later, telling Judy about it, she said, 'I didn't like her much. I don't really want her there when the baby's born.'

'You'll have to have her though, won't you?' Judy asked. 'I mean, suppose something goes wrong? And if the baby really is going to be big . . .'

'Oh, I know I'll have to have her. And I expect she's all right really. Mrs Hazelwood says she's delivered any amount of babies round the village. I just didn't like her much.'

'Well, never mind,' Judy said comfortably. 'It's weeks away yet, anyway.'

They were sitting on a blanket and some cushions in the

garden, beneath the apple tree where Judy had first met Ben. The small green apples which had followed the blossom were growing fast and some were beginning to redden. By the time Jean's baby was born they would be ready to pick and eat, and Mrs Hazelwood said they were good keepers. A heavy crop would see them right through the winter.

Ben had almost completed his training as a pilot. He wrote to Judy once or twice, his letters enthusiastic, his desire to get into the air throbbing through every line. She read the letters a little sadly, wondering how long he would survive once he did. So many young men were being killed in the air, some of them on their first mission. She prayed that wouldn't happen to Ben. He was so young, so ardent, so full of life. And he had told her once that she would hear again.

I wish I could, she thought. I wish I could, just for him. Just to hear his voice. I've never heard his voice.

There were so many voices she had never heard. And even those she knew well were beginning to fade. Maybe even if I did get my hearing back, she thought, I wouldn't know them. They could come up behind me and speak – Jean, or Mum and Dad, Gran, Polly, Chris – and I wouldn't know who they were. I'd have to learn them all over again.

The thought of Chris brought back the memory of that last meeting, when he had told her not to be sorry for herself. Judy had walked away from the train that day feeling hurt and angry. Why shouldn't I be sorry for myself? she had wondered. I'm entitled to be . . . But slowly she had begun to see the sense of his words. She began to realise that she had changed during the past few months. Locked in her own, silent world, she had forgotten that other people had feelings too, forgotten that they had problems as great as hers. The old man who lived in a tumbledown cottage down the lane and crept about, too crippled with arthritis to be able to draw a bucket of water from the well, his hands too gnarled and stiff to cut a slice of bread. The woman in the broken-down hovel who had four children under seven and whose husband had been killed at Dunkirk. The Hazelwoods, afraid of losing their youngest son. Polly, widowed at thirty-five. Her own parents, losing Terry . . . But I lost him too, she argued, and then reminded herself sharply that this was exactly what she was doing wrong. Always looking for her own griefs and sorrows, dismissing those of other people.

I'm sorry, Chris, she thought sadly. You were right, and I was wrong. And she regretted, bitterly, that she had sent him away. He won't come back now, she thought. Even if I wrote and begged him – he wouldn't come back now.

'Judy!'

Jean grabbed her arm and Judy turned quickly. At the look on her friend's face, she gasped. 'What is it? What's wrong?'

'I don't know. I got this sudden pain.' Jean's face twisted again and she bent and pressed both hands to her back.

'Is it the baby? It can't be, surely.' Judy was on her feet, glancing wildly towards the house. 'It's much too soon.'

'She said it might come early.' The pain seemed to have faded and Jean was breathing quickly. 'But it was in my back, not my stomach. It's gone off a bit now anyway.' She lay back on the cushions. 'I suppose it was just a twinge.'

'It looked as if it was more than a twinge.' Judy sat down again, looking at her doubtfully. 'Do you think I ought to fetch someone?'

'Not yet. It takes hours and hours for a baby to be born. There's no one to fetch, anyway. The vicar's gone to Bridge End and Mrs Hazelwood's at the WI meeting. And everyone else is out in the fields, haymaking.'

Jean understood only the shaking head and the words 'WI' and 'haymaking' but they were enough. Anyway, Jean looked better now. Perhaps it had been no more than a twinge. She'd had a number of aches and pains by now –

her back hurt if she walked too far or tried to do too much work, she had heartburn after meals, and she'd had a fierce stabbing pain down one leg that Mrs Sutton said was sciatica. It was caused by the baby lying on a nerve, apparently. There must be other nerves the baby could lie against, especially now that it was getting so big.

'*Ouch*!' Jean exclaimed, her face contorting again. 'Oh no, no, *no*.'

'What is it?' Judy was on her feet again, thoroughly alarmed. Jean was half sitting, half lying, leaning one elbow on the cushions, the other arm held tightly over her stomach as she rocked with pain. 'Oh Jeanie, what's happening? I'd better get someone.'

'No!' Jean reached out a hand to stop her. 'Don't go away! Don't leave me!' She pulled at her skirt and stared down in horror at the blanket. 'Look!'

Appalled and frightened, Judy looked down and saw a dark stain spreading over the rug. 'What is it? Whatever is it?'

'It's my waters,' Jean said, forgetting to look Judy in the face as she spoke. She remembered and raised her head. 'My *waters*. They've *broken*.'

Judy gazed at her helplessly. 'I don't understand.'

'It means the baby's coming.' The pain seemed to have receded, and Jean lay back again, breathing heavily.

'I'll have to fetch someone.'

'No! Don't go! It's coming now – I can feel it. Oh!' Jean's voice rose to a scream and she fell back and flailed wildly with her arms. 'Oh Judy, Judy, Judy – it hurts so much! Aaaah! *Aaaaaaah*!'

Judy knelt beside her, terrified. She had never seen a baby being born, had no idea what happened. She had been only ten years old when Sylvie was born and had not even known that Polly was expecting a baby until the day it happened. What she knew about 'the facts of life' had been gleaned gradually over the years from other girls, equally ignorant, much of the knowledge distorted, and although she now understood about sex she still had very little idea how the baby that had been conceived would actually be born. Jean herself didn't know very much more.

'What shall we do?' Judy asked when the pain faded again. 'How quickly will it come?'

'I don't know.' Jean's face was white and beaded with sweat. 'Oh Judy, it hurts so much. People say it can go on for hours – even days. I don't think I'll be able to stand it.' Tears came into her eyes. 'I'll die. I'm going to die.'

'No!' Judy's terror pierced her voice. 'No, you're not going to die, Jean, you can't. I'll *have* to get someone—'

'It's starting again!' Jean clutched her arm, digging her fingers in like talons. Her nails bit into Judy's bare flesh. 'Oh God – here it comes – ah – aaah – *aaaaaah*! I can't do it!' she yelled, twisting frantically on the blanket. '*I can't bloody do it! Aaaaaaah! Aaaaaah! Aaaaaaah!*'

Judy put her hands on the writhing body and tried to hold her still. One of Jean's hands was still gripping her arm, the other flailing in the air, beating on the ground, pulling at her own hair. Judy reached across and grabbed it, holding it tightly, trying to calm the desperate girl. She could hear none of Jean's cries but knew from her face that she was making a lot of noise. Perhaps someone will hear, she thought. Perhaps she's shouting loudly enough for someone to hear and come.

'What shall we do?' she asked when the pain subsided. 'What do we have to do?'

'Better get my knickers off. It's got to be able to come out, and they're soaking wet anyway.'

'Out here?' Judy was scandalised. She looked around the garden. It was in full sight of the vicarage, and anyone passing by could look over the wall. She forgot for a moment that she had been praying for someone to do just that.

Jean threw her a scornful glance. 'I don't care if we're in

the Lord Mayor's parlour! I'm having a baby. Judy – quick, it's starting again. Get them off. Oh . . .' The two girls scrabbled frantically and dragged off the sodden garment, tossing it out of the way. They were just in time. The pain came again, a fresh wave even stronger than before, and Jean lay back, crying out again, reaching for Judy's hands. As Judy caught them in hers, she realised that something else was happening. Jean was using all her strength to tense her body, arching her back so that the swollen stomach rose like a whale, her screams now as much groans of effort as cries of pain.

Dimly, Judy remembered hearing the phrase 'bear down'. You had to 'bear down' when you were having a baby. She had had no idea what it meant, but now she thought she understood. 'Bearing down' was pushing, pushing the baby out, and you did it when the pain gripped you, when it was at its fiercest. She knelt beside the twisting, screaming girl and spoke in her ear.

'That's it, Jean. That's it. Bear down. Push. That's right. Keep going, keep trying.' She risked a quick glance beneath the rucked-up skirt and caught a glimpse of a mass of fair pubic hair and something else – something swollen, like a massive growth, protruding from Jean's body. For a moment she stared, horrified, and then Jean relaxed as the pain faded, and the growth drew back inside. In that second, she realised what it was.

'It's the baby! I can see its head! Oh Jean, Jean, I can see the baby's head!' Beside herself with terror and excitement, she gripped Jean's hands. 'Jean, the baby's almost born! *I can see its head*!'

'I don't want it!' Jean yelled. 'I don't want it any more! It hurts too much! It bloody well *hurts*! Take it away! Take it *away*! I don't *want* it! Oh – oh – *ohhhh*!'

'You *do* want it. You *do*. Oh, *please* let someone come, let someone come soon.' Judy was crying now, gripping Jean's hands as the wave of pain rose once more. 'Oh Jean, keep trying, just keep trying. It'll be over soon. It's coming soon, I know it is, and it'll all be over and you'll have a lovely little baby girl – or maybe a boy, you wouldn't really mind if it was a boy, would you – and – and – oh Jean, Jean, that's right, bear down, push hard – it's coming now, I can see it.' She wrenched her hands from Jean's grasp and caught at her thighs, parting them so that the baby's head could push its way out. It was clear now, a round, hard little ball, wet and dark and slimy, and as Jean screamed she saw it surge suddenly forward, thrusting itself out into the world – head, shoulders, body and legs – and Judy reached out and caught it in her hands, a thrill juddering through her whole body as she felt the warm, slippery, squirming flesh. A baby, she thought wonderingly, a *baby*, and I'm the first one ever in the whole world to hold it. But there was no time for wonder. With the baby came a rush of water and blood, and she lifted it clear and saw to her horror that there was something else – a thick, twisted rope that was attached to the baby's stomach and seemed to disappear back into Jean's body. At that moment the baby began to cry, its mouth opening to a square in its tiny red face, and Judy stared at it in wonder.

'Is it all right?' Jean was leaning up on one elbow, panting. She stared down at Judy and reached out one hand. 'My baby? Is it all right? Is it a girl?'

'Yes.' Judy gave a quick look to make sure. 'Yes, it is. Oh, Jean, you've got a little girl. But there's this thing, this sort of rope . . .'

'It's the cord. Let me hold her.' Jean reached out her arms and Judy, a little doubtful as to whether the cord would reach, laid the baby on her mother's breast. She dragged the cushions from where they had been flung and heaped them behind Jean's back, and Jean rested against them, smiling. For a moment they stayed there, recovering their breath, gazing in wonder at the baby, so small and so new, already turning its face into its mother's breast, seeking the nipple.

'She's beautiful,' Jean whispered. 'Oh Judy, she's so beautiful.'

Judy, looking at the crumpled red face, peaceful now, at the hair plastered wetly against the little skull, at the naked body that was grey with slime and flecked with blood, thought that beautiful was perhaps an odd word to use. And yet it was the right word. It was exactly the right word. And then she caught her breath as she realised what else had happened.

'Jean,' she whispered disbelievingly.

Jean turned her head and met her eyes enquiringly. Judy went on, in a voice that trembled, 'Jean, I can *hear*. I heard the baby cry. I can hear what you're saying to me. I can hear birds singing – and the leaves rustling – and people calling to each other in the hayfield. Jean – *I can hear again.*'

Chapter Thirty-One

It was only a few moments after that when help began to arrive. Someone had heard Jean's final scream and was hurrying down the lane. Mrs Hazelwood had come back from the Women's Institute meeting. In seconds it seemed that Jean was surrounded by people, people who knew what to do. The midwife was called. There was a flurry of activity as the afterbirth was expelled, and then the midwife arrived, clucking as she saw what had happened, and the cord was cut and tied. Jean was lifted and carried into the house, where she and the baby were both bathed, and by the time Judy saw her again an hour or two later she was in bed, the baby dressed in a fresh white nightgown and cradled in the crook of one arm.

'Thanks, Judy,' she said, smiling sleepily. 'I don't know what I'd have done without you.'

'I didn't do much. I didn't know what to do.' The miracle of her hearing seemed almost as great to Judy as the miracle of new life before her. 'Oh Jean, I'm glad I was there. I'm so glad. It was awful – but it was wonderful too. She's a lovely baby.' She smiled. 'You were right. It *is* a girl.'

'And I'm calling her Hope, just like I said.' Jean was quiet for a moment, gazing at her baby and stroking her head gently. 'You'll let everyone know, won't you? Mum and Dad, and your family. They'll be surprised she's so early.'

'But she's all right, isn't she? It doesn't matter about her coming so soon?'

'Well, she's very small. I'll have to take a lot of care of her. But the midwife says she'll be all right. And Mrs

Hazelwood is going to get the doctor to come and make sure.' Jean looked at her. 'And you really can hear, Judy?'

Judy nodded. 'I can hear just as well as I ever could. I think Dad was right, you know – it was a shock that stopped me hearing, and it's a shock that's brought it back again. A nice one, though.' She smiled and touched the baby gently with one finger. 'And I wanted to hear again so much – just to hear her cry.'

Jean was almost asleep and Judy tiptoed out of the room. She went into the garden and sat down on the old bench, and began to think of all the people she must telegraph about the new arrival.

The warm late-summer sky was deepening into evening. The sun was going down beyond the wall and the woods, casting an apricot glow on the old stones and lighting the first few golden tints of autumn in the trees. A blackbird was singing at the top of the tree, and Judy tilted her head, listening to it. Next to the baby's cry that had been her first realisation that she could hear again, and she thought it must be the most beautiful sound in the world.

I'll have to go back to the farm soon, she thought. And I'll have to decide what to do next. Everything's different now – the baby's here and Jean's so happy with her, and I can hear again, I can do all the things I did before. But – will there still be a place for me, back in Portsmouth? I've been happy here in the country, as happy as I could be while I was locked away in that silent world. Will I be able to go back?

She listened again to the blackbird's song and decided to put away all her worries until tomorrow. Just for now, she would be content to sit here, watching the sun set and listening to the sounds she had thought never to hear again. Just for now, there was no better place to be than here – under the apple tree, where Hope had been born.

For a few days, all was quiet at Ashdown. Judy had sent off telegrams to both families and her mother had written back at once to both her and Jean. Cissie had never been much of a letter-writer and these must have been awkward letters for her to write, Judy thought, reading the rather stilted congratulations to Jean. However pleased she must be to have a grandchild, you couldn't get around the fact that Hope was illegitimate and that life was never going to be easy for her or her mother. And nobody could forget that Terry, the baby's father, Cissie's only son, was dead, had died even before he knew she was on the way. I expect they hoped the baby would be a boy, she thought, a boy who'd be like Terry, and they haven't even got that.

Polly wrote too, rather more warmly. She had set aside her own feelings about the rights and wrongs of it all, and poured out all her sympathy to Jean, the sympathy that came from having lost her own husband and knowing what it was like to be a woman alone with a child to bring up. *But you have a family who will help you through this*, she wrote, *and we'll always stand by you and your baby*. She added that she would be coming out to see them all as soon as possible – she and Joe.

Joe was at St George's Barracks by now, and he and Polly had been down to Devon to see the boys. They were living in a small cottage with the widow who 'looked after them as if they were her own'. Polly was secretly relieved to find that she was a comfortable woman in her fifties who was friendly with a local farmer – he was there when she and Joe arrived – and that she clearly took the view that the boys had been loaned to her for an indefinite period but would one day be going back to their father. She had set a tea such as Polly had not seen for years – salad with thick slices of real ham, hard-boiled eggs, a mound of potatoes, a loaf of bread fresh from the oven and stewed plums with rich, yellow clotted cream.

It seems awful to think of all those poor people in Leningrad, starving to death, Polly wrote to Judy, *when we had all that put in front of us. But it doesn't do them any good for us not to*

*eat it, does it? And there are people in our own cities who aren't
a lot better off – not starving, but not well-fed either. I feel a bit
guilty about them too.*

Mrs Ellacombe had given her some eggs and a jam jar full
of clotted cream to take back to the family, but it wasn't the
food that interested Polly most about the visit. She'd been
nervous about meeting Joe's sons, she didn't mind admitting
it to Judy, but thank goodness there hadn't been any
problem at all. They'd been out playing on the moor when
she arrived and came in muddy and dirty, carrying baskets
of blackberries, their shirts hanging out of their shorts and
their socks down round their ankles just like any other little
boys, and had flung themselves at their father, obviously
thrilled to bits to see him again.

They'd been a bit shy with Polly at first, but once they'd
found out she drove an ambulance during the raids and had
seen lots of bombs falling, they had pelted her with
questions and obviously thought her a fitting friend for their
father. *I don't suppose they think any further than that*, she
wrote, *and there's no need to for a long time yet. Me and Joe
want to take things slowly. We're not in any hurry.* But it was
clear to Judy that they both knew perfectly well where they
wanted their relationship to go, and she folded her letter
wistfully, thinking sadly of the young Observer she had sent
away and wondering what would have happened, had she let
him stay.

There was a strange feeling of expectation in the air.
Everyone was waiting for America to decide to come into
the war. Japan seemed to be making preparations, and
American patrol ships were being attacked off Iceland.
Britain was bombing major cities such as Hamburg while
German troops were invading Russia. There was a shared
belief that, however bad it was now and however much was
happening, there was worse to come.

Yet nothing could take away the joy that Hope had
brought with her. She was well-named, Mrs Hazelwood said

as she wheeled out the old pram and set it under the apple tree. You could swear she was smiling, even at two weeks old – surely such a lovely, happy expression couldn't be just wind! – and she hardly ever cried. When Jean was allowed out of bed to come and sit with her in the garden, it was like the beginning of the world itself – a woman who had given birth, at peace with her child.

Judy was with her one afternoon at the beginning of September, the month when Hope should have been born. She had been making scrim all morning. She'd scrubbed her hands and face but there were still traces of dark green and brown dye on them and even though she'd been wearing a turban there was still dust in her hair.

'I sometimes think I'll never be clean again,' she said ruefully. 'I'd much rather collect sphagnum moss, or even acorns – it'll be time for them again soon.'

'I ought to be doing something too,' Jean said, stirring restlessly. 'I'm sick of being treated like an invalid. Honestly, I feel better than I ever have in all my life – just getting rid of that huge bump and not getting backache or heartburn any more is wonderful, but the midwife says I mustn't do too much. And of course Hope needs a lot of attention. She's so tiny.' She touched the blanket that had been spread over the baby to keep her warm, even though there wasn't a chill in the air. For the first few days of her life, Hope's smallness and premature birth had caused a little anxiety, but she had made up her birthweight again and was obviously thriving. 'But I don't know what I *should* be doing. I can't put upon the Hazelwoods for ever. And I'm not doing any real war work.'

'You could always make scrim!' Judy joked. The charm of weaving camouflage had quickly worn off and she now loathed the job as much as the other women did. 'But you'll be helping Mrs Hazelwood again, like you did before, won't you? Didn't they say you could stay on after the baby was born?'

'Yes, but it's not fair to expect them to keep me *and* Hope.' Jean sighed. 'I don't know where else I could go, though. Not back to Pompey, that's for sure!'

'You still haven't heard from your mum or dad, then?'

Jean shook her head. 'Nor likely to, I reckon. They've washed their hands of me, just like Mum said they would.' She paused, then said, 'Judy, there's something I want to ask you.'

She sounded a little diffident and Judy looked at her in surprise.

'What is it?' she asked.

'I'd like you to be Hope's godmother. Mr Hazelwood says she ought to be christened in a few weeks. I want it done here at Ashwood and I'd like you and Polly to be godmothers. You can't be related to her in any other way,' she went on sadly, 'and you'd have been her aunts if Terry and me had been married. So – will you?'

'Oh Jean, I'd love to.' Judy's eyes filled with tears. 'But we still *are* her aunts, Jean.' She grinned suddenly. 'And Polly's her great-aunt! I wonder if she's thought of that? It sounds so old, doesn't it! Who will you ask to be godfather?'

'I thought I'd ask Ben.' Jean blushed a little. 'You know he came home last weekend and he seemed to just fall in love with her. And we got on well too,' the blush deepened, 'and as the Hazelwoods have been so kind to me – well, it seemed a good idea . . .' She floundered to a stop and Judy laughed.

'It *is* a good idea! And Ben'll be a good friend to you both.' She eyed Jean, wondering about that blush, but before she could say any more she heard voices and they both looked up to see Mrs Hazelwood coming through the French doors and into the garden. There were two other people with her, and at the sight of them Judy gasped and Jean turned pale; but before either of them could say anything, one of the newcomers came forward, speaking in a quick, high voice as if she were embarrassed and upset and happy all at once.

'Jean!'

'*Mum!*' Jean sprang to her feet. 'Mum, I didn't think you'd come. You didn't write –'

'I didn't know what to say.' Mrs Foster stopped a foot or two away and the two gazed at each other, neither knowing quite what to do next. 'I did try. I tried a few times, but the words just wouldn't come out right. And then your dad said why not just come here and see you, so we got on the train – and here we are.' She moved towards the pram and looked down at the sleeping baby.

'She's called Hope,' Jean said, putting her hand on the baby's blanket.

'I know. Judy told us in the telegram. Oh Jeanie.' Mrs Foster bent closer. She touched the blanket, drawing it away from the baby's face, and stared down at her. Tears began to slip down her cheeks and she whispered in a breaking voice, 'Jeanie, she's so lovely.'

She turned suddenly and caught her daughter in her arms. Jean, who had been standing a little stiffly, crumpled against her and the two held each other close, sobbing. Mr Foster cleared his throat and came forward to look down into the pram, and Judy saw that his eyes too were bright and wet with tears.

'She's been breaking her heart over this,' he murmured. 'Thought we'd lost our Jeanie for good and it was all her fault. I said to her, "You're the girl's mother, she'll want to make it up" – but she was that upset, she made up her mind that Jeanie wouldn't want to know. It took a lot for her to come out here.' He reached out a hand and touched the baby's face with the tip of one finger. 'Hope,' he murmured. 'Our Jean's baby. Our granddaughter. Well, what a little peach you are. What a little beauty.' He turned to his daughter. 'Come here, girl, and give your dad a kiss.'

Judy caught Mrs Hazelwood's eye. The vicar's wife nodded to her and they both tiptoed back into the house.

'They'll need to be alone,' Mrs Hazelwood said. 'I'll take

out some tea in a little while. I think things will be all right now.'

'Yes,' Judy said, and glanced out through the French windows at the little group under the apple tree. 'I think they will.'

Once the Fosters had been to see their daughter and new granddaughter, Judy felt more at a loose end than ever. There was plenty to do, for they were making desert scrim now, the colour of sand, and instead of black and green their hands were stained with pink and brown. The sphagnum collecting was still going on and there were blackberries and mushrooms coming along. Nothing could be wasted; even though in the country fresh food was more plentiful than in town, anything that couldn't be produced locally or had to be imported was just as strictly rationed. And even some of the local foods were under threat. The Suttons were desperately anxious about their cows, many of whom would have to be slaughtered when winter came because no grain was being imported and there would be no feed for them.

'That means a shortage of milk and butter and no cream at all,' Mrs Sutton said. 'And the hens'll have to go too, though they can live on scraps – if there are any.' She sighed. 'I don't know what we're all going do, I'm sure. I don't know what the world's coming to.'

Judy went out into the orchard and looked up at the apple trees. The fruit was swelling and ripening now, little globes of gold and scarlet amongst the leaves. She thought back to the first time she had stood under these trees, when they had been smothered in pink and white blossom, its scent strong enough to waft through her open window at night. So short a time ago, and yet so much had happened. The bombing – that terrible raid in which Polly had been trapped in that collapsed building – her deafness – Terry's death – Jean's pregnancy and now the birth of Hope. All in a few months.

And the war was not yet over. It was clear now that it

would go on for months, maybe years. If America came in, and Japan attacked, what would happen then? Like Mrs Sutton, she didn't know what the world was coming to.

Other things had happened too, she thought. Sean had died, and she'd met Chris Barrett. Chris, who had come out here to Ashdown to find her. Whom she'd sent away because she was deaf and couldn't hear his voice.

What a stupid reason, she thought, suddenly and savagely. What a stupid, *stupid* reason!

A sound made her turn. Mrs Hazelwood was coming into the orchard. She smiled at Judy and came over to her.

'Mrs Sutton told me you were here.' She was carrying a folder and some papers. 'There's something I want to ask you, Judy. Can we sit down for a moment?'

Judy led her to the old seat that stood against the wall where it could catch the last of the evening sun. Mr Sutton, who seldom rested, occasionally sat here with a glass of cider after the day's work was over. 'What is it? What's happened? Is Jean all right – and the baby?'

'Yes, yes, they're both well. And Jean's starting to work again in the house and helping with some of the local war work as well. I've told her she can stay as long as she likes – we're glad to have her – and I think that's what she's going to do,' Mrs Hazelwood said. 'No, the reason I came was to ask what you were going to do now, Judy. I've thought just lately that you seemed a little uncertain – as if you felt that now you had your hearing back, you ought to be doing more.'

'Well, I do.' Judy met her eyes. 'And I should, shouldn't I? I'm fit and healthy – there's nothing wrong with me now. I ought to be doing my bit, same as everyone else my age. I mean, I don't mind making scrim – not more than anyone else does, anyway – but I ought to be doing something more than that.'

'And have you thought what that might be?' the vicar's wife asked quietly. She tapped the folder on her lap. 'I have a few suggestions to make, if you haven't made up your mind. The women's Services – you may well be called up soon anyway, and it's better to volunteer so that you have a choice. But the WVS can always find a place for young women like you, energetic and capable, and if you feel you'd like to stay here with us, I can certainly offer you plenty of work. Perhaps you'd like to think about it.'

Judy gazed at her. She looked around the orchard and up into the rippling leaves of the tree, lit by its gleaming fruits. She thought of the devastation of Portsmouth, the nights of fear and destruction, the terror of thinking Polly dead and the nightmare of her deafness. She thought of Sean and Terry and Johnny, all dead, and then of Chris, who was still alive.

'No,' she said slowly, and then again as certainty grew in her mind, 'no, Mrs Hazelwood. Thank you, but I can't stay in the country. I love it here – I hope I'll come back to see you all, lots of times, when peace comes. But for now, I've got to go back. I've got a job in Portsmouth, with the Lady Mayoress. There's work for me to do there. And – and there's someone I have to see as well.'

There was a small silence. Then, with the thought of Chris filling her mind and warming her heart, she added quietly, 'That's where my life is – in Portsmouth. That's where I belong.'

Chapter One

'No! Don't!' You mustn't!'

The man just about to lower a sack into the choppy waters of Portsmouth Harbour turned in surprise as a girl rushed towards him, her dark curls flying out from under the scarf she wore around her head. With half a dozen others, she had been walking through the Naval Armament Depot of Priddy's Hard, on her way to the shifting room, when through the dim morning mist she had seen Sam Reece stride past, carrying the sack. From the size and shape of it, and the way something inside wriggled, she knew just what he was about to do.

'He's drowning the kittens!' Forgetting all about work, she pushed past the other girls and rushed across to the Camber. Sam was almost at the quayside now, a shadowy figure bending to find a space between the barges where he could drop his burden into the waves that slapped against the wall. Kate screamed at the top of her voice, and several men, at work loading the lighters to take munitions across the harbour, straightened up and stared at her. Sam Reece himself jumped like a naughty boy caught in the act of mischief, and then flushed a dark, angry red. He was a squat, swarthy man with small, permanently bloodshot eyes and a surly scowl, and he'd never approved of bringing women in to work at Priddy's Hard.

'You yelling at me, girl?'

'Yes, I am!' Kate was beside him now, breathless, her

1

eyes spitting blue fire. She snatched at the bag and tried to pull it away from him. 'You're going to drop them in, aren't you? Our Tibby's kittens – you're going to drop them in the water.'

'Yeah. What of it?' He dragged the sack back and a chorus of faint mewing sounds rose from inside. Kate's eyes filled with tears. 'You know we can't keep all the bloody kittens that are born here. Leave go, and get over to the shifting room, or you'll be late clocking on.'

'I don't care if I am!' It would mean a dock in her pay but Kate ignored that. 'You're not drowning these kittens.'

'For cripes' sake—' Sam was beginning, when another voice broke in and they both turned to see the office manager bearing down upon them. Thank goodness, Kate thought, seeing the tall, broad figure. It's Mr Milner – he'll understand. She let go of the sack and stepped towards him.

'What's going on here?' Arthur Milner stopped and stared at them both. 'I could hear the shouting back in the office. Why aren't you getting ready for work, young lady, and what's in that bag?'

'It's the kittens, Mr Milner,' Kate began, but Sam's voice overrode hers, taking on an indignant whine. 'I'm just trying to carry out orders, sir. It's nothing to do with this young woman. She just flew at me, started on about how I mustn't do this, can't do that – if you ask me, it's a pity they ever brought women into the yard. Nothing but trouble, they bin, ever since they first walked in the gates!'

'Well, that's a matter of opinion,' Mr Milner said, cutting in on the flow. 'We'd be in a poor way without them. Anyway, you haven't answered my question. What's in the bag and what were you going to do with it?'

'It's the *kittens*,' Kate began again, but the manager lifted his hand to silence her and looked at Sam.

'Well?'

The workman thrust out his lower lip. 'All right, so it's kittens. I was going to drop 'em over the side – it's what we always do when there's too many. Blooming cats bin popping off all over the place the past few weeks; we can't let 'em all live, now can we?' He appealed to Mr Milner, as man to man. 'I mean, I likes animals as much as the next bloke – got a cat of me own at home, Ginger he's called and soft as butter 'cept when another tom comes sniffing round – but anyone with any sense'd see that we can't just let 'em breed willy-nilly. Wouldn't be able to move for the little perishers, now would we? So when we gets a new litter, we just puts 'em in an old sack with a couple of stones and drops 'em over the side, nice and tidy. It's the best way. They don't know nothing about it.'

'Of course they know about it!' Kate burst out. 'They're *drowning*! It must be horrible for them. It's *cruel*.'

Arthur Milner looked uncomfortable. 'Yes, but Reece has got a point,' he said. 'We'd be overrun with cats if we let them all live. We need a few to keep down rats, and if anyone wants to give a kitten a home they're welcome to take them, but apart from that they've got to be put down. And they don't suffer much, not if it's done almost as soon as they're born.'

Kate stared at him. 'You mean you're going to let him *do* it?' She snatched the bag and Sam, taken unawares, released his grip. Kate untied the bit of string that was knotted around its neck and peered inside. 'I knew it! *These* haven't just been born – they're nearly six weeks old! They're Tibby's kittens, from our hut. We've been helping her look after them.' She cradled the bag against her and looked fiercely at the two men. 'You're not drowning Tibby's kittens.'

There was a moment's silence. Kate was suddenly aware of the clatter going on around her – the noise of the munitions factory at work, the clanging and shouting as the lighters were loaded with crates of shells, the sounds of the great harbour that lay beyond the jetties of the little dock. In a few moments she should be clocking on, and even

3

one minute late would mean the loss of half a day's pay. She stood her ground, meeting the manager's eye, and he sighed.

'These kittens ought to have been dealt with before,' he told Reece. 'Five weeks is too late – they're almost ready to leave their mother. Why wasn't this done sooner?'

'It's them bleeding girls,' the man grumbled. 'You heard what she said. Bin looking after them, they have. Hiding them in a locker, I dare say, bringing in food for 'em, giving the mother milk. You knows what girls are.'

Mr Milner glanced at Kate and she felt her face colour. 'We were going to find homes for them all,' she said defensively. 'And they're so pretty. One of them's a tortoiseshell – look – and one's black with a white bib and paws, just as if he was going to a posh party. And this one's pure white. Look, see how fluffy—'

'Yes, yes, all right,' Mr Milner said hastily as she drew out the tiny creatures, one after another, to display their charms. 'They're pretty little mites, but they still ought to have been dealt with sooner.' He sighed. 'You say you've found homes for them all?'

'Well, I'm having the tortoisehell,' Kate said eagerly, seeing victory within her grasp. 'Maxine Fowler wants the white one, Elsie Philpotts says she'll have the fluffy ginger one, and I'm sure someone will have the black and white one.' She looked up at him, opening her dark blue eyes very wide. '*You* wouldn't like him, would you, Mr Milner? He's got ever such a sweet face. And they're almost ready to go – we were going to take them home on Friday.' She put her head on one side. 'Don't let him drown them, Mr Milner. Please don't let him drown them.'

The office manager hesitated. Sam Reece heaved a loud, heavy sigh. Kate cuddled the tortoiseshell kitten against her breast and kissed the top of its head, then looked up at Mr Milner from under her lashes. He pursued his lips in resignation.

'All right. You can take them back. So long as they're not

in a dangerous place – dangerous to the job and the workers, I mean. They've got to be out on Friday, mind – and if the mother cat gives birth again you must let your supervisor know at once, and leave them to be disposed of. Understood?'

For a moment, Kate struggled with her feelings. Then she nodded. 'Yes, sir.'

Mr Milner glanced at Sam Reece. 'Right. You'd better both get back to work. The whistle will be going at any minute and we've got a big job on. Nobody's going to have time to worry about kittens for the next few weeks, I can tell you that.'

He turned and strode away. Kate and the workman looked at each other.

'Bleedin' kittens!' he said disgustedly. 'Bleedin' *girls*!'

The other girls looked at Kate as she strode towards the shifting room, triumphantly holding up the sack of wriggling, mewing kittens. 'You did it! You stopped him! What did Mr Milner say?'

'He said they were too old to drown. But next time Tibby has kittens, we've got to let someone know, so they can be "disposed of".' She snorted. 'Disposed of! He means drowned, just like these would've been. It's cruel.'

'My dad always drowns our Micky's kittens,' one of the girls said sadly. 'He says they don't feel it when they're so young. He leaves her one though, otherwise she's got nothing to take the milk, see.'

'Well, I don't believe it. Of course they feel it.' Kate carried the sack over to the corner just outside the long shed, where the mother cat had a nest made of old rags in a disused wooden bomb crate. Tibby wasn't there – she'd probably gone hunting – and wouldn't even know that her babies had been missing. Kate opeend the sack and tipped the kittens gently into the crate, watching them as they scrambled about in a heap of fur.

5

'Come on, Kate.' Maxine Fowler, Kate's best friend, was at her elbow. 'The whistle will be going any minute and you're nowhere near ready. They'll be all right now.'

Kate nodded and opened her locker. Each girl had one, a green-painted metal cupboard where she could put her outdoor clothes and valuables while she was at work. Not that anyone had anything of real value, except for wedding or engagement rings, but even these must be put into the locker. Anything made of metal could cause a spark and blow the entire site sky-high. It had happened years ago – her grandfather, who had also worked here, still talked about the men who had been killed then – and again, in 1921, when her father had been here. Four men had been killed then, all Gosport chaps, and it had brought home to everyone on the site the dangers of the materials they worked with.

The shriek of the whistle broke into her thoughts. She closed the locker door and followed the others into the shifting room. They had five minutes now, to take off their jumpers and skirts and hang them up, then step across the painted red line in their underclothes into the 'clean' area and put on their magazine clothing – loose brown overalls and a cloth cap. Some of the caps bore a red spot, denoting that its wearer worked with gunpowder, while those who worked with more modern explosives were marked by a black spot.

'I feel like Blind Pugh,' Kate observed when she was first given her cap, and when the others looked blank she explained, 'You know. The old pirate in *Treasure Island*.' They nodded then. The story had been read to most of them at school and they remembered the sinister tap-tap-tap of the blind man's stick, and the horror of having the 'black spot' laid on you. It had haunted Kate for a week, and she'd been unable to sleep at nights, certain that every little tapping sound was Blind Pugh coming for her. Her brother Ian had discovered this and stood outside her bedroom door when she was in bed, tapping on the stairs and driving her into nightmares from which she woke screaming, but she'd never told her mother what was frightening her so much. She didn't want her complaining to the teacher who read the story to them, in case he stopped.

From the shifting room, the girls trooped through to the laboratory and took their places at the benches where they would spend the next twelve hours inspecting and putting together ammunition. As soon as the chargehand's back was turned, Kate ducked down and lifted a section of floorboard to reveal her tea can. She pushed in the paper bag of sandwiches she had brought with her, replaced the board swiftly and stood up, winking at Maxine. 'That's for tea-break. We'll make a cuppa from the outlet pipe when old Fred goes up to the office.'

'You'll get caught one of these days,' Maxine said, but Kate shrugged.

'Everyone does it – reckon they know, anyway. They never search us for food. A couple of Marmite sandwiches won't set the cordite off – and I haven't noticed you turning your nose up when I offer you one!'

Maxine grinned. 'Matter of fact, I've got a bit of cake this morning. Mum found a packet of sultanas at the back of the cupboard and made one at the weekend.' She didn't add that she'd deliberately refused a piece when it was offered her at Sunday tea-time, just to upset her mother, Clarrie, and only grudgingly accepted it for her lunch-box.

'*Fruit* cake!' Kate rolled her eyes. 'You'll share it around, naturally.'

'Only with my best friend,' Maxine said, and then turned hastily to her work as the chargehand bore down upon them.

They worked steadily through the morning, stopping only for the illicit tea-break when the supervisor was out of the way, and then for their official lunchtime at twelve. By then, Kate's legs were aching from having stood for nearly six hours, and she was glad to push her way out with the rest of the girls and get a bit of fresh air.

Set on a peninsula of land on the western shores of Portsmouth Harbour, the armament depot covered a large area of what had once been waste ground, a 'hard' area of solid mud, its channels washed twice a day by the tide, and covered with tough grass and furze bushes which burst into golden flowers every spring. Until it had been taken over by the government nearly two hundred years ago, the area had been more or less wild, with the grassy ramparts of Gosport Lines – the earthern fortifications once constructed to ward off possible invasion by the French – forming a long low hill across its neck.

Before then, Naval munitions had been made and loaded at the Gunwharf, on the Portsmouth side of the harbour, but that had been considered too dangerous for the fleet of ships coming through the narrow entrance and mooring at the jetties, so the work had been transferred to Gosport. By 1777, the huge Magazine had been built and munitions were being shipped across the harbour by barge, or lighter, just as they were now.

The ramparts were still there, making a good buffer against possible explosions, and other hillocks had been pushed up between the sheds so that each was protected from the others. What with these and the old moats that ran between the Lines, with blackberry bushes growing along their banks, and the groves of walnut trees that had been planted to provide wood for rifle butts and pistol grips, it was almost like being out in the country.

'They say you can't see Piddy's from the air at all, with all the roofs being painted green to match the grass,' Maxine observed. 'That's why we don't get bombed. Makes you wonder why they don't paint everyone's roofs green, doesn't it.' She looked up at the sky and unbuttoned her brown herringbone tweed coat. 'Look – sunshine!'

'Don't blink, it'll be gone in a minute,' Kate advised. 'It's

8

only the first of March, you know, not Midsummer Day.' She grinned as a chilly wind sprang up and Maxine hurriedly pulled her coat around her again. 'Not a bad day really, though: in like a lion, out like a lamb, they say, don't they? Don't really know what today is like, it's just sort of grey and draughty. Like a seagull, perhaps,' she added as half a dozen birds flew over, cackling.

'It'd be quite nice if you pushed away the clouds and switched off the wind,' Hazel Jackman remarked. 'At least it's not raining.' She gazed across the harbour at the warships that lay at the jetties, awaiting their load of ammunition. 'Did you hear Mr Churchill was in Pompey last Monday? My Uncle Joe came round last night for a game of cards, and he said heaps of people saw him walking round looking at the bomb damage. He was smoking a cigar and he gave them the V-sign and everything.'

'Well, *I'm* more interested in all those Canadians who arrived at the weekend,' Maxine declared with a wink. 'Reckon it'll be worth taking a trip over the water on Saturday? I bet there'll be quite a few on the lookout for a nice girl to show them the sights, and they'll have plenty of money to spend as well.'

'Maxine! You're awful.' Kate poked her friend in the ribs. 'You'll get into trouble one of these days, the way you go on.'

'Not me! I may not always be good, but I'm *always* careful.' Maxine tossed her blonde curls and giggled. 'Why don't you come too? It's only a bit of fun – they're decent blokes, most of them.'

'Sad to say,' another girl put in, and they all laughed. 'Let's all go. Safety in numbers and all that. What about it?'

Maxine nodded vigorously. 'I'm on! Hazel? Janice? Val? Kate, you'll come, won't you?'

'I don't know,' Kate said, and the others stared at her in surprise. 'I'll be taking Topsy home on Friday. She'll be lonely – I can't really leave her to Mum.'

9

'For goodness' sake, you can't stay in all weekend for a *kitten*! She'll be all right – probably sleep most of the time anyway. Look, you'll have all Saturday afternoon to play nursemaid, and you can come out with us in the evening – what about that? We'll go over to South Parade Pier, there's bound to be a dance on and they always have a good band. You don't even need to *talk* to a boy if you don't want to.'

'Well, that sounds like a really good night out,' Kate said. 'I can sit on a chair being a wallflower and not open my mouth all evening, while the rest of you get off with rich Canadians. Thanks a lot!'

Maxine laughed. 'I can't really see you doing that! You talk more than all the rest of us put together. Anyway, I thought maybe we could get some of them to take us to the pictures on Sunday. That new Bob Hope and Bing Crosby film's on at the Gaiety – *Road to Zanzibar*. They say it's ever so good. It's got Dorothy Lamour in it as well, she's really glamorous. But if you're not interested . . .'

Kate clutched her arm. 'I didn't mean it! I was only joking. I'll come. Only – I don't want to come home on my own, all right? No malarkey – you'll have to promise to catch the last boat with me.'

'Well, what else d'you think we're going to do? Of course we'll catch the last boat, dope!' The irrepressible blue eyes gleamed. 'There's plenty of time for a bit of malarkey before then.' Maxine grinned. 'Don't worry, Kate, *we'll* be good. Won't we, girls? The question is – will *you*?'

The others giggled and nudged each other. Val said, 'We might find ourselves a nice rich husband, what about that? I wouldn't mind going to live in Canada.'

'Gosh, yes! That'd be nearly as good as America – better, because they're still British. Part of the Empire, anyway.' Maxine stretched her arms above her head. 'Just think of it, no food rationing, plenty of nylons, plenty of *everything*.'

'That's just greed,' Kate protested. 'You wouldn't marry someone just for nylons. You'd have to love him.'

'Well, I would love him,' Maxine said. 'I'd love anyone who could give me a new pair of nylons every day!'

They screamed with laughter, and Kate gave them a reproving look. 'Well, *I'm* not going to look for a rich Canadian to marry. I'm not looking for a steady boy at all. Not till the war's over, and maybe not even then.'

'We'll all be old by the time the war's over,' Hazel told her. 'Nobody will look at us. You've got to take your chances when they come, Kate. There's a Mr Right for all of us. You never know when you might meet him. Anyway, I'm just looking for a bit of fun – a good dance, and a nice kiss and cuddle at the end of it.'

'And that's all?' Janice asked slyly, and they laughed again.

Kate shrugged but joined in their laughter, while privately making up her mind that although she was happy to dance with boys, British *or* Canadian, and even go to the pictures with them, any goodnight kisses would be just that – a kiss and no more. And there would be no question of finding 'Mr Right'.

I wish I *could* be like the others, she thought, eating her sandwiches and gazing out across the grey, choppy waters. I wish I *could* believe that there's a boy out there who's meant for me. But I just can't. I can't forget what happened before, and I can't believe it won't happen again.

It would take one very special man to make her believe in love again. Perhaps there really was one somewhere, and one day she would meet him.

Perhaps.

All Orion/Phoenix titles are available at your local bookshop or from the following address:

Mail Order Department
Littlehampton Book Services
FREEPOST BR535
Worthing, West Sussex, BN13 3BR
telephone 01903 828503, *facsimile* 01903 828802
e-mail MailOrders@lbsltd.co.uk
(Please ensure that you include full postal address details)

Payment can be made either by credit/debit card (Visa, Mastercard, Access and Switch accepted) or by sending a £ Sterling cheque or postal order made payable to *Littlehampton Book Services*.
DO NOT SEND CASH OR CURRENCY

Please add the following to cover postage and packing

UK and BFPO:
£1.50 for the first book, and 50p for each additional book to a maximum of £3.50

Overseas and Eire:
£2.50 for the first book plus £1.00 for the second book and 50p for each additional book ordered

---

BLOCK CAPITALS PLEASE

name of cardholder ....

delivery address
(if different from cardholder)

address of cardholder ....
....
....
....

postcode ....

postcode ....

☐ I enclose my remittance for £ ....

☐ please debit my Mastercard/Visa/Access/Switch (delete as appropriate)

card number ☐☐☐☐ ☐☐☐☐ ☐☐☐☐ ☐☐☐☐

expiry date ☐☐☐☐   Switch issue no. ☐☐

signature ....

prices and availability are subject to change without notice